RELIC HUNTED

TERRY W. ERVIN II

Gryphonwood

Gryphonwood Press

Published by Gryphonwood Press
www.gryphonwoodpress.com

ISBN-10: 1-940095-42-5
ISBN-13: 978-1-940095-42-4

Cover art by Drazenka Kimpel

Printed in the United States of America

RELIC HUNTED

Never underestimate a Relic!

Intelligence picks up Security Specialist Keesay's contract, hoping to direct the Relic's tenacity and skills against his nemesis, the Capital Galactic Investment Group. But the rogue corporation has its own plans concerning Keesay: a bounty on the security specialist's head.

Time is running out for mankind, with the Crax striking deep into human territory, targeting colonies on Pluto and Io. Keesay knows whatever plans others might have, fighting the Crax is more important than blending in, or looking over his shoulder.

Stepping forward, Keesay accompanies Special Agents Guymin and Vingee on their mission to rescue key prisoners taken by Capital Galactic, before they're handed over to the Crax. In doing so, Keesay pits his shotgun and brass knuckles, his daring and mysterious connection to the rat-like Chicher, against anyone that gets in his way.

PRAISE FOR TERRY W. ERVIN II AND THE CRAX WAR CHRONICLES!

"Full of non-stop action and space battles combined with characters you'll grow to love. This is classic style space opera at its best." **–Angie Lofthouse, author of Defenders of the Covenant**

"You won't be able to put this book down as you wade through battles, intrigue, and relationships brought together in a fast-paced sci-fi story." **-Dean Sault, author of The Last Human War**

"The tech level premise is fascinating, but what really makes the novel special is the spirit of Krakista Keesay. Kra is a hero to root for—often underestimated, adept with brass knuckles, bayonet, shotgun, and all sorts of old style weaponry. He proves that, while technology matters, so do courage, intelligence, and daring."**—Tony Daniel, Hugo-finalist, author of Metaplanetary and Guardian of Night**

"One of the most inventive and compelling fantasy sagas I have read in years!"**-Stephen Zimmer, author of the Fires in Eden Series and The Rising Dawn Saga.**

BOOKS BY TERRY W. ERVIN II

Crax War Chronicles
Relic Tech
Relic Hunted

First Civilization's Legacy
Flank Hawk
Blood Sword
Soul Forge

Collections
Genre Shotgun

DEDICATION

This novel is dedicated to my father, Terry W. Ervin, Sr. He saw my first short story in print, but cancer took him before he was able to see my first novel published. Residing in Heaven, however, doesn't preclude Dad from such observations.

ACKNOWLEDGEMENTS

First, I would also like to thank Kathy, my wife, and Genevieve and Mira, my daughters, for their patience and understanding in allowing me the countless hours to imagine, plot, research, write, revise and edit—all things necessary to complete a novel.

Second, I would like to thanks my co-workers, family, friends, and the members of Flankers, all of whom encouraged, questioned, and prodded me along to finish Relic Hunted (the final title after a number of working titles).

As for the character Gerard, the readers can thank Alan C, a fellow Roger Zelazny fan. He was selected from the hundreds who signed up for the chance to name a character in the second installment of the Crax War Chronicles. It was a pleasure to work with him on that creative endeavor.

I can't forget mentioning Drazenka Kimpel, for providing her skills and talent in creating the outstanding art that graces this novel's cover.

Finally, I'd like to thank the folks at Gryphonwood Press, especially K.S. Brooks for editing Relic Hunted, and David Wood for not only believing enough in my first novel to publish it, but for his advice and insight, and continuing to provide an avenue for me to share my tales, including Security Specialist Keesay's second adventure.

That leaves you, the reader. You're the reason I wrote Relic Hunted. Thank you for choosing my SF novel from the hundreds of thousands available. I truly hope you enjoy the story. With that in mind, don't hesitate to send an email or post a review to let me know your thoughts.

.

CHAPTER 1

There are experiences worse than enduring a series of neural function scans. Taking several Crax caustic rounds in the gut is one of them. I'm one of the few who actually survived such an ordeal and can attest to the fact.

I sat on a stool in the sterile examination room and watched the med tech prepare injections for my scan. It'd been five weeks since I regained consciousness. Five weeks since completing a memory transcription procedure in a bid to prove my innocence, having been accused of a litany of horrific crimes. Against all odds, I'd survived the experimental Cranaltar IV's memory probes—survived with my mind intact.

Scratching my neck while taking a deep breath, I didn't realize how anxious I was to learn if the minor seizure I'd suffered three weeks ago would be my last. Sporadic seizures, diminishing in frequency and intensity since disconnection from the Cranaltar, proved to be the only detrimental side effect. At least that I or Dr. Goldsen and her medical team had noticed.

"You're pretty quiet today," I said to Medical Technician Marshner, standing with his back to me. He'd rolled the medical dispensary cart into the examination room, seemingly unaware that I was sitting next to the aesthetically sterile examination bed. When the tech didn't respond to my comment, I added, "Must be even deeper in thought than me, Tech Marshner."

He continued working with his back to me, manipulating equipment and observing data on the cart's flat screen. He pulled something from a pocket inside his white lab coat, sat it on the tray and, from what I could see, put it back in his pocket.

Wasn't I supposed to be the nervous one? After a short laugh, I pressed on. "Although many might mock the notion of an R-Tech deep in thought."

Med Tech Marshner's curly brown hair bounced as he nodded and forced a laugh.

I remembered seeing the dark circles under his eyes when he came in. "Trouble sleeping last night?" I asked.

"No, Security Specialist Keesay." He hesitated before entering data into the computer clip next to the cart's tray holding the syringes. Errant taps forced him to reset the screen twice.

I stepped over to the examination bed and sat on its edge before unbuttoning my cuff and rolling up the sleeve of my gray-green coveralls. He'd performed test procedures on me before, and we'd dispensed with the full titles. I thought back on previous small talk between us. "Any word from home? Still planning to visit your daughter, Regina?"

"Yes," he snapped. Some equipment clattered on the tray. "Sorry, Security Specialist. Just having a bad morning." He shook his head, still keeping his back to me. "Yes, the trip is still on. Actually, I'm packed and scheduled to board a direct Io—to—Earth transport shuttle in less than an hour."

The first three times he prepped me, Tech Marshner had been quite talkative, and prepared the injections while facing me, grinning and razzing me about being a Relic. The last time he'd been quiet and avoided eye contact—just like this time. Except this time he did everything possible to avoid facing me.

"Contract renewal coming up?" I asked, my right hand drifting across my belt to where my duty revolver should've been. Dr. Goldsen frowned upon—actually forbid me—to carry a firearm in her research lab, despite the fact that I was a 4th Class Security Specialist. The last time I brought it up, she glared at me over her wire-rimmed glasses and reminded me of the Colonial Marine posted just down the hall.

It was difficult for me to argue. With Negral Corp in disarray, the fact that I'd divested myself of all corporate sponsors prior to being connected to the Cranaltar, and that I was still waiting for Intelligence to pick up my contract as I'd been led to believe they would, I lacked legal standing to carry a firearm. Despite the fact that I was near the top of Capital Galactic Investment's termination list.

"No," Tech Marshner said, filling the first syringe. "Any changes or concerns I should note for Dr. Goldsen?"

"None. I spoke with her earlier this morning. She predicted this should be my last scan."

"Final scan…I am aware of that, Specialist," he said, pointing to what must've been text on the clip's screen. His left hand shook before clenching into a fist. "Just following protocol…Specialist." After a breath he turned to face me with one of the three hypodermic needles in his right hand and a sterilizing swab in his left. "Actually, the company found room for me on the next shuttle to Earth. Leaves in an hour." Again, his eyes avoided mine, gazing beyond me and then at the floor.

"Really?" I asked. Something was definitely wrong—and troubling Marshner. "Med Tech, that needle." He halted, tensing up as I pointed at the syringe in his right hand. "What would happen if you accidentally stuck yourself?"

"What?" His right hand trembled for a second. He shook his head and forced a smile. "What kind of question is that?"

I shrugged my shoulders and watched sweat form above his brow. Whatever he was preparing to do made him nervous. Administering routine pre-scan injections shouldn't concern any competent med tech.

"Left arm, ahhh…please? Just like last time."

I extended my left arm. When he began to swab my forearm, hand shaking again, I reached across and clamped my right hand onto his right wrist. Surprised, he met my gaze and tried to yank his hand free.

I punched him in the gut. He must've sensed it coming and tightened up so I didn't knock the wind out of him.

After a brief struggle, I managed to twist the arm holding the syringe behind his back. "Drop it, Marshner!"

Instead of complying or struggling to get away, he rotated his wrist and stuck himself in the lower back.

I yanked his arm down. Liquid shot from the needle. Not knowing what the syringe contained, I let go and jumped back to avoid the spray. When he turned to face me, I picked up my stool and smashed its aluminum seat across his jaw.

A security specialist ran into the room as Tech Marshner hit the floor. Dr. Goldsen arrived a fraction of a second later. How did they know there was trouble? Cameras monitoring the room? If so, where was the Marine guard?

The security specialist trained his magnetic pulse pistol on me instead of the unconscious Marshner. "Freeze!" He glanced from me, down to Marshner, and back. "Why did you assault the med tech?"

"Have Dr. Goldsen check that syringe," I answered, raising my hands. "Then ask me that question again."

Two hours later, I strode into the same examination room. A petite, graying woman wearing wire-rimmed bifocals and a white lab coat sat on a padded stool, waiting. "Eventful morning, Mr. Keesay. How are we doing this afternoon?"

"Dr. Goldsen," I said, "you're the only one who refers to me as Mister. I don't think I'll ever get used to it." She was one of the few Intermediate Techs, or I-Techs, I didn't have to look up to, physically. "This will be the last scan?"

"As I indicated previously," she said, looking at my holstered .22 caliber pistol, "it will be the final scan if all goes well."

I ignored Dr. Goldsen's stare. She'd requested I, as all of her patients, should arrive to my examinations unarmed. The small caliber firearm was all I had access too. After the confrontation with Tech Marshner, courtesy was out of the question, including her request. I was in the unfortunate predicament of having enemies and lacking a corporate or governmental sponsor. I rolled up the left sleeve of my gray-green duty coveralls. Their color identified me as a security specialist. The buttons, collar, and loose cut, as a Relic.

Rumor had it that once Dr. Goldsen reported me fit for duty, Intelligence would pick up my contract. If so, I figured they'd issue me a quasi-military gray uniform.

After the three injections, Dr. Goldsen directed me to the examination table. "While we are waiting, I believe obtaining an ultrasound scan of your chest and abdominal region would be advantageous."

I removed my equipment belt, coveralls and undershirt before lying down.

Dr. Goldsen maneuvered a scanner over the pink and white scar tissue. "Your injuries have healed far better than I expected," she said while comparing the results to a computer clip's display. "You report no difficulty breathing. No unusual pain or discomfort?"

"Correct," I said, shuddering as I recalled the caustic Crax rounds eating through my combat coveralls and body armor. And the memory of V'Gun surgeons, an alien species that reminded me of a cross between a Chihuahua-sized spider topped by a squid, working on the wounds. Not to heal me. Just to stabilize me so that Capital Galactic lawyers could interrogate me.

After I took a deep breath, she asked, "No episodes since we last spoke?"

"That is correct, Doctor. No seizures."

She tapped the screen. "The last recorded seizure was minor, with a three-second duration." She reached behind my right ear to place a thumbnail-sized neural transmitting device.

I shifted position and turned my head.

Dr. Goldsen lifted six more neural devices from a sterile tray and placed them on my forehead, scalp, and the base of my skull. "It appears that anti-seizure medication will not be necessary. That *is* positive news, Mr. Keesay."

"Agreed," I said. When the doctor wasn't performing as my physician, she sometimes called me Kra, but I always referred to her as Dr. Goldsen. It just seemed proper.

She continued manipulating the diagnostic equipment. "You are not very talkative today."

"Simply waiting for release to duty. Sitting and thinking has put me in a sour mood."

She shook her head. "The incident with Medical Technician Marshner?"

Out of habit I looked up at the surveillance cameras. Dr. Goldsen had witnessed the entire *Documentary*, as viewers called the downloaded presentation of my memories. With Umbelgarri support, she'd largely reengineered the alien device for experimental use on humans. Without the Cranaltar device's scan and downloading of my memories, I'd have been convicted of aiding and abetting a non-human enemy, desertion, intragalactic espionage, abduction, planetary quarantine violation, sabotage of corporate property, insurrection and first degree treason, among a number of other crimes. Normally, the Cranaltar device scrambles all cognitive functions. In my case Bahklacks, the Umbelgarri's crab-like thralls, directly assisted Dr. Goldsen, so I came out okay, with a few minor modifications.

I'd been stewing for most of my recovery and decided it might help to tell someone. "I'm a little angry, Dr. Goldsen."

She looked over the rims of her glasses. "Oh? Why is that?"

I sat up. "You've seen the *Documentary*. I was recruited by Dr. Maximar Drizdon to ensure the safety of his son. A dangerous assignment and I wasn't informed of the situation."

"That is accurate," she said.

"I don't put much stock in precognition, but that's irrelevant. Dr. Drizdon selected me, and put me in the line of fire. Then, after I accomplished the mission, I was left to pay the price."

"You blame your injuries on Dr. Drizdon?"

"No. We're at war. When the elite Crax took me down, that was legitimate. But Capital Galactic's interrogation and the short circuiting of my memory? The trial that followed?" I shook my head. "I survived saboteurs, an enemy boarding action, a quarantined planet, and the Crax invasion of Tallavaster." I finished by pointing at my head. "You know better than anyone else, I'm *very* lucky to have survived, let alone mentally intact."

Dr. Goldsen sat on the nearby stool. "Is it possible that he knew you would survive and turn the tables on the Capital Galactic Investment Group?"

"No," I said. "No measure was taken on my behalf after his family reached safety."

She smiled. "You think that Dr. Drizdon, renowned military strategist, randomly picked you, Specialist Keesay?" She adjusted her glasses. "A Relic Tech Security Specialist to watch over his wife and son as they traveled on the civil transport *Kalavar*? You simply happened to be newly assigned even as they sought refuge from the enemy aliens *and* their human agents?"

"Incorrect, Doctor. I believe that they were traveling as R-Tech colonists. They recruited me because I'm one of the rare space-faring R-Techs specializing in security. I had a history due to my actions in the Colonization Riots, so I was competent and deemed reliable. Reliable, but expendable."

She nodded and stood. "I appreciate your perspective. However, I do not agree with your assessment."

I smiled. "Thanks for listening anyway."

"Lie back down, Mr. Keesay." She pursed her lips before continuing. "Med Tech Marshner's interrogation is still in progress." She glanced over her shoulder at a wall-mounted screen. "Are you ready?"

"I know the routine." I signaled for her to wait and pulled my pistol from its holster. Actually it was Deputy Director Karlton Simms' antique pistol. I was just keeping track of it for him until we crossed paths again. If he was still alive. A real long shot.

Dr. Goldsen handed me a metal tray on which to place the firearm before covering me with a white sheet. She set the tray next to me.

"Hopefully," I said, still unsure of my future, "if this goes well, I'll get to say good bye to this place."

Dr. Goldsen tapped at the examination table's console. "Seeking better accommodations, Mr. Keesay?"

"Not exactly. If Intel *does* recruit me, Agent Vingee indicated I might be assigned to her team."

Dr. Goldsen walked toward the door. "Bed, follow." The examination table trailed Dr. Goldsen down the hall, and into the scanning room. "Bed, position patient for cranial scan." Dr. Goldsen took the pan, set it on a stool and stood by the wall of computers. "Do you like Agent Vingee?"

"Vingee? She's demonstrated competence and loyalty. What more could someone ask?"

She gave me a quizzical look. "Whichever career path you choose, Mr. Keesay, I am confident you will meet with unmitigated success." She tapped at a screen. "The door is locked. I appreciate your willingness to temporarily part with your weapon."

"Not a problem," I said and winked before closing my eyes.

During the scan, my mind shifted to dealing out payback to Capital Galactic and their pack of traitors. The Crax and their allies warring against the Umbelgarri-Human-Chicher Alliance was one thing. Humans turning on their own kind? That was another.

The scan was over before I knew it. Dr. Goldsen began removing the neural transmitting disks. "You should refrain from clenching your teeth, Mr. Keesay." She then gingerly retrieved the pan holding my firearm.

I checked and reholstered the weapon. I didn't figure Dr. Goldsen was a pacifist, but through the Cranaltar's first-person presentation, she'd witnessed me injure, maim, and kill dozens of humans, and even more aliens. More than I cared to think about, or pray for. I forced a smile. "Thank you for your patience with me and my…paranoia, Doctor."

"It's perfectly understandable, Mr. Keesay. I have seen several Marines with that look when they are disarmed." She stepped closer and patted my hand. As if reading my mind, she said, "You did, and will continue to do what needs to be done. What many are unable to do. And you survived my experimental project."

"The Cranaltar IV? I'm glad you modified it. Made it compatible for humans."

"We all do our part for humanity, Mr. Keesay."

After returning to the examination room I dressed, sat on the stool, and watched Dr. Goldsen at work with the diagnostic computers. She did well treating me as a person and not as a specimen. After voicing and tapping in several commands, she asked, "Any opinions on the war?"

"Your information is better than mine, Doctor. I'm limited to holo-newscasts, and discussions with your staff."

She, I, and everyone else were keenly aware of the situation. We were losing.

CHAPTER 2

Special Agent Vingee stared across the table at me with her pale green eyes. We were in a lounge down the hall from the medical wing. A tan-paneled room, in addition to the table and four metal chairs, held a cushioned couch and chair, and a counter containing a dispensary for flavored drinks and packaged energy bars. Vingee had fixed her brown hair into one long braid, hanging down instead of twirled up into its usual bun. "Okay, Keesay, how'd you know the injection was toxic?"

I smiled in return. "You must've seen the security recording. I'd been around Med Tech Marshner before. He was nervous for no apparent reason." I leaned forward, resting my hands on the table. "Almost like he wanted to get caught."

"Would you care to see the interrogation file?"

I leaned back from the table. "No, thank you. Give me the essentials and we'll go from there." I bet that surprised her.

She crossed her arms and stretched her legs. "Awfully trusting. Not your style, Keesay."

"You may have witnessed the *Documentary*, but that doesn't mean you know me." I shrugged. "Passed my scan. All's clear for Intel to recruit me. I've heard we might be partners if that happens."

"You're taking this rather well considering someone just attempted to kill you."

I feigned disinterest. "Nothing new for me. I heard a while back that the Capital Galactic Investment Group placed a bounty on my head. I'd better get used to it." Trying not to lean forward, I asked, "So, how much did it take to tempt Tech Marshner?"

"It's obvious Tech Marshner's not a professional bounty hunter," she said. "Let alone an assassin. I don't think he has the channels or even knows how to collect." Vingee sat up straight. "It appears that Capital Galactic operatives put pressure on him. Threatened to take action against his family." She shook her head and frowned. "They'll do whatever it takes to get back at you for revealing their treachery."

Treachery. I was sure in some twisted way the true believers, traitors that they were, believed their actions were ensuring the survival of the human race. The Felgans were overrun, the Umbelgarri on the brink. Humanity next. "I thought this place is supposed to be secure," I said, knowing that, with the chaos of the war, resources of every kind were stretched thin. "Capital Galactic's assets are frozen. All of its board members, executives, major investors, and upper management are under primary investigation. If they're not locked up, they're supposed to be under constant monitoring."

"Keesay, you know as well as I do that hundreds of major players at

Capital Galactic are unaccounted for." The Intel agent let out a long breath. "It'll take time for other corporations to find and organize the pieces of the fallen corporate empire."

"Correct," I said. "And innocent or not, many Capital Galactic personnel, at all levels, are less than cooperative." I shook my head. "They must be thinking that if we lose the war, their resistance will count for something."

"Only some of them. People are frightened." Her statement was matter-of-fact rather than sympathetic. "Back to Marshner. Capital Galactic operatives threatened his family, unless he took action against you. Information from Earth indicates his family is missing, recently. My guess is Capital Galactic operatives decided to take control of them as incentive. Sooner or later the operatives will learn of his failure. They might not…dispose of them. Not if they believe it'll encourage Marshner to remain uncooperative."

"Doesn't surprise me," I said. "Any corporation willing to support the Crax invasion wouldn't think twice about breaking an agreement with a Class 2 Med Tech. Maybe his family went into hiding." I slowly shook my head, not really believing the statement. "What'll happen to Marshner?"

"He'll be further interrogated, then put on trial. He's been classified as cooperative."

"Just another reason," I said, trying not to clench my teeth. "They picked the wrong man. Marshner has a conscience." I patted the small .22 caliber pistol holstered on my equipment belt, a blued steel with rosewood grips antique. "And that was the last time I'll heed Dr. Goldsen's or anyone's wishes to refrain from carrying protection." I placed my hands on the table, reaffirming to myself that I'd never move about unarmed.

"Still carrying Deputy Director Simms' archaic firearm?" A hint of sadness lingered in Vingee's question, one to which she knew the answer.

"The only one I have, until I obtain an official sponsor or I can access my new, *secure* account. Besides, small arms shipments to Io aren't a priority."

"Are you so sure?" She dragged the last two words out in a playful lilt.

I stared at Vingee, trying to assess her. "Don't be coy, Agent."

She stood. "Two items of good news, Specialist Keesay. Some of your equipment has arrived from Tallavaster. I don't know how much. And second, Field Director Lidov is here to sign you on with the Agency." She winked. "If you're interested."

Looking up reminded me how tall Agent Vingee was, even for an I-Tech. I stood and pushed in my chair before answering. "No other offers appear to be on the horizon. At least not appealing ones."

For me, signing on as a special agent for the Governmental Intelligence Agency was straight-forward. The Cranaltar's download and presentation provided more reliable data than any battery of psychological tests and background checks ever could. Maybe Representative Vorishnov pulled some strings. Saving him from assassination had to count for something. Maybe the Umbelgarri did. Or maybe Intel wanted me because the Umbelgarri had enabled me to comprehend their language while restoring my cognitive functions.

I considered all this before confirming my acceptance as an Intel agent with a screen signature, followed by an old-fashioned R-Tech thumbprint and blood DNA scan. I missed Negral Corp. My previous employer had been one of the few that still included real paper as part of their paperwork.

Field Director Lidov stood and shook my hand. "Welcome aboard, Special Agent Keesay." He was dark skinned with remnants of kinky, gray hair scattered across his balding scalp. He blinked and nodded. "Your new account is in order. Funds equivalent to your original balance, plus Negral's back-pay, have been deposited." He started to turn, but stopped. "Well, almost. There's a small bonus."

"What for, Director?"

"Let's just say that establishing a new account with the exact amount due could provide a clue for any individual tracking your whereabouts."

He'd almost exited the conference room before turning again. "Special Agent Vingee will have account access information."

"Understood, Director."

"Oh, and should you ever attempt accessing one of your old accounts, a yellow flag will show on the DNA scan. You can thank the deceased Chicher diplomat for that." He uttered the last phrase as the door slid shut.

The mention of the Chicher diplomat caught me off guard. The rat-like alien had taken an acid round while helping me escape a quarantined planet. Seconds before dying, he chattered something and bit me just below my V-ID.

I stood to follow Director Lidov, but didn't. It'd be improper to chase down an Intel director with questions. Besides, his departure demonstrated his unwillingness to explain.

Having been an R-Tech Security Specialist, I was used to being out of the information loop. I waited thirty seconds before seeking Agent Vingee and the whereabouts of my equipment.

"Your cart and its contents were lost or destroyed," Agent Vingee said, after leading me into another of Io's meeting rooms. Like most rooms and halls, the walls were a mottled gray stone, carved out by Umbelgarri technology. "Probably when New Birmingham fell."

I examined what was on the narrow table before taking and strapping on my equipment belt. An emailed file contained an inventory of what had been recovered. "Or when Tallavaster was retaken," I said while inspecting and then loading jacketed hollow point rounds into my .357 magnum single-action revolver. I felt better armed with a more powerful sidearm. While holstering it, I considered upgrading to a double-action revolver. The same caliber and variety of rounds, just faster to reload.

Agent Vingee said, "This portion of your equipment was recovered from the *Pars Griffin*." She stepped back and leaned against a wall, absentmindedly rubbing her chin. "I suspect Capital Galactic intended to use it as supporting evidence against you."

I held up my former duty coveralls. They'd been top-of the-line body armor capable of resisting both projectiles and lasers. But front line combat and an encounter with Crax acid had left them severely damaged. "Below the waist should be salvageable," I said. "Maybe the back, and parts of the sleeves."

Agent Vingee smiled. "You can requisition equivalent quality without having to salvage scraps." She started to say something else, then frowned. After a few breaths, she shrugged. "As to your boots? Leather ones are rare. Some Capital Galactic operative must have helped himself to them."

I shrugged in return. The black ones I wore, made of synthesized leather, were comfortable enough. "Maybe they're gathering dust in a possession locker while their new owner rots in prison." I pulled my shotgun's long bayonet and tested the blade on a frayed sleeve of my damaged uniform. "This cuts it," I said. "It'll be too hard to stitch and look proper. Maybe I'll find an adhesive and patch underneath my new duty coveralls in strategic locations." I examined the blade and read the etched the phrase, recalling Odthe, the exploration pilot who'd made the bayonet from an Umbelgarri alloy. "*Nemo me impune lacessit.*" My voice trailed off, remembering how Pilot Odthe had died. A Crax attack craft, supported by Capital Galactic treachery. So many had died because of that duo.

Agent Vingee brought my mind back to the present, saying, "In ancient Latin: no one injures me with impunity."

"You *do* have a good memory," I said.

"How could I forget your motto? How often have you lived up to it?"

"More times than I care to count." I slid the bayonet into its scabbard hanging on my belt and picked up my 12-gauge pump-action shotgun. It, like my revolver, had been well-maintained. I ran my fingers over the perforated jacket that protected the barrel. It also contained a strengthening Umbelgarri alloy. I loaded my shotgun, alternating slug rounds with 00 buckshot, adjusted the sling, and slid it into place on my shoulder.

Vingee walked over to the table, picked up my watch and handed it to me. "Old-style face with spinning hands and Roman numerals. The attached sound dampener's been calibrated." She then handed me a com-set. "I took the liberty of obtaining a new ocular. Everything's been set. Channels, encryption, voice authorization. We can adjust the ocular later."

I clipped the com-set on my belt and adjusted the headset and microphone-ocular combo. Being an R-Tech, I used older style equipment. Most I-Techs, like Agent Vingee, had chip implants in their ears to receive, and micro-mics, usually in their collars, to send communications. They had eye lenses to pick up visual data. I spoke into my headset's mic, saying, "Agent Vingee, testing."

She automatically moved her right hand to her ear when her implanted chip received—a polite non-verbal cue. Then she spoke into her collar. "Agent Keesay, clear." She went back to leaning against the wall. "You could requisition modern duty equipment."

Suited up and armed, I asked Vingee, "When can I get an upgraded, official Intel uniform?"

"I'm serious, Keesay. An MP pistol. Get a laser carbine to replace the shotgun if you feel the need for firepower. You're trained and competent in their use."

"Agent Vingee, these are what I'm comfortable with." I decided not to mention my notion of a new revolver. "They're effective and I'm more than competent with them. In signing me, Intel knew well what it was getting."

She let out a long breath. "There are times you'll need to blend."

"When the time comes, I'll blend. In some situations, I wager, better than you."

"You've already refused to change your name."

"Look, I am who I am. Capital Galactic has it out for me, sure. But I'm not going to skulk around the rest of my life. I've already endured an isolation assignment on Pluto after the Colonization Riots." A cutting motion with my hand emphasized my next statement. "Not going to happen again."

Agent Vingee shook her head. "Exactly how Agent Guymin said you'd respond." She checked the chronometer above the door. "He should contact us soon, to brief us on our assignment."

"You think they'll issue me popcorn nukes if I ask?"

"You can ask Agent Guymin how the upper echelon'll respond to that request."

"So, what you're saying is that neither you nor Agent Guymin has much pull."

CHAPTER 3

An hour later Agent Vingee led me down one of the series of long, gray stone corridors that interconnected sections of Io's research colony. We passed a few orange-clad engineers and one engineering tech wearing the standard red coveralls. Agent Vingee ignored them as we passed, but I nodded to each. Only the engineering tech acknowledged me with a return nod.

It was difficult to keep up with Vingee's long strides, but I didn't say anything as she seemed anxious. Finally, I asked, "Nervous about our assignment?"

She slowed her pace. "What makes you so confident that we'll be assigned together?"

"It was hinted at," I said. "Plus, I think they'd have assigned you elsewhere by now. Caylar, too."

"A logical assumption. And, you might consider referring to Caylar as Special Agent Guymin. He is superior to you within the agency."

"Understood." I'd known Special Agent Guymin only by his first name when he acted as my stand-in nurse aboard the *Pars Griffin*. That seemed decades ago. For some reason his first name felt like it'd been imprinted on my brain. Standard protocol called for an individual to be addressed by their classification and surname, unless directed to do otherwise. I'd take care to avoid the casual impulse and follow protocol instead.

After a gap in our conversation, I said, "Since the agency assigns rank based upon seniority—for those at the same classification, guess I'll be low man on the totem pole once again."

Agent Vingee gave me a confused glance. "Unlike within the corporate structure, your R-Tech status won't impede rising in seniority."

"Maybe not initially, but not many R-Techs advance to directorships, do they?"

She didn't answer. Instead she stopped in front of one of the many sliding steel doors.

"That's okay," I said. "I don't care for file work much anyway."

She ran the back of her hand across the scanner, allowing the subdermal microchip to be read. "What leads you to believe that special agents don't complete file work?"

I answered as the door slid open. "I'm sure there's routine file work, just as there is with security duty. But computer interface isn't my strong suit and I don't think Intel took me on to gather data, or compile it."

Neither of us stepped through the doorway until I said, "Ladies first." When she frowned I tried, "Superiors first?"

She rolled her eyes and strode through.

Agent Guymin sat in the dimly lit conference room behind a shiny metal table. His hair, which must have been blond in youth but had long since darkened, was cropped short. Other than the intense gaze of his blue eyes, his looks were as unremarkable as his gray uniform. On the rectangular table rested a pitcher of water with three glasses, and a dish of powdery-red synthesized fruit strips. Probably strawberry flavored. A metal box with a handle and latches, like a briefcase but larger, sat on the floor next to the table.

Agent Guymin tapped at a computer screen built into the tabletop and the door closed. He stood and offered us each a chair. "Is there a problem?"

I answered, "She's a little uptight," the same time Agent Vingee said, "None that I'm aware of." I decided not to hold Agent Vingee's chair for her. Instead, I selected the left seat and slung my shotgun across the back before sitting down.

"Ah," said Caylar, while centering his chair across from us. "Time's short, so let's get down to business." He stretched his fingers before tapping away at the table screen for a moment. "I've just sent files on our assignment to your accounts, but here it is in brief. We're to locate and, if possible, recover Deputy Director Karlton Simms. It's believed he is still held by operatives of Capital Galactic, but may be turned over to the Crax. Once with them, it's unlikely we'll be able to recover the director, even if they don't ship him beyond the outer colonies."

"So," I said, "Director Simms didn't die aboard the *Pars Griffin*."

Agent Vingee took in a sharp breath but said nothing. Cay—Agent Guymin had been there with me, on the *Pars Griffin*, when Director Simms went down. I'd been on the luxury transport, slowly dying from my Crax-inflicted wounds. And Agent Vingee had probably read the reports. His capture occurred on the way to Io so I could be hooked up to the experimental Cranaltar IV.

My thoughts shifted back to that moment, me upon the medical bed, aboard the *Pars Griffin*...

We entered the corridor and went left. The Pars Griffin *was a luxury passenger transport mainly utilized for cruises and business travel. Although, like all interstellar vessels, space was allocated for interstellar freight. The corridor was eight-feet wide and equally high. Unlike most interstellar ships, the usual exposed pipes and conduits weren't visible. The passage was clean and empty.*

Private Varney, a dark-skinned and gung-ho Colonial Marine, set a brisk pace down the well-lit corridor. I had difficulty seeing what was going on but Diplomat Silvre and Field Director Simms appeared alert. The sound of footfalls and the rhythmic breathing of my escorts around my self-propelled bed mingled with the faint humming of the transport's engines preparing for departure. I set my hand on the pistol under the sheets. My heartbeat fell into cadence with the pace.

I heard the whirring noise of a supplemental security robot approach. Most are triangular in shape, squat, and maneuver on three wheels. The marine, carbine leveled, blocked my view. To my right, the Intelligence field director, a nondescript man with a square jaw and intense eyes, pulled what looked like a holo-display remote control from an inside pocket. It sported far more buttons and tiny screen icons than standard remotes. With his left-hand thumb he tapped in rapid succession. The whirring stopped.

"Deactivated," the Intelligence man said to the marine. "Check it out."

Keeping his body between the robot and myself, Private Varney advanced. I scanned the walls, wondering if the nurse was watching our rear. I spotted a security camera recessed in a light casing. At the crack of magnetic pulse gunfire I whipped my head to the front. Too fast. The pain rush brought on distorting, gray flashes.

After a few seconds my head cleared. Simms was pressing forward, calling the Iron Armadillo. "...terrorist robot, rally point red one! Yellow pass through!"

He didn't wait for the response that crackled from the remote, "Understood."

Varney was down. The sec-bot had deployed its stun net. Despite the electrical current coursing through the entangling mesh, the marine unsteadily maneuvered his carbine. Simms opened up on the sec-bot with his sidearm. The explosive MP rounds rocked the sec-bot, but only managed to make large pockmarks in what had to be a hardened armor casing. Simms's old .22 caliber pistol at my side wouldn't help.

I didn't know what the nurse was doing but Silvre was making hasty adjustments to a foot-long cylindrical object. In quick succession, two flashing blasts from Varney's laser burned into the armored menace.

I looked back up at the surveillance camera near the ceiling. I knew that lawyer, Falshire Hawks was watching. With effort I raised my pistol and fired two quick shots at it. Both painfully jarred my arm. The semi-auto's fire was considerably louder than the snapping crack of MP gunfire.

Varney's laser blasts must have penetrated as the security robot sat smoking and silent. Simms was lifting the stunned private to his feet when the faltering machine emitted a metallic click followed by an explosion. The flash temporarily blinded me.

Simms was down with Varney laying on him. The marine and my defense screen took most of the blast. Several thumb-sized metal fragments lay harmlessly on my bed sheets.

My nurse didn't wait to evaluate the situation. We rolled up to Simms, who pushed the dead marine aside. Blood flowed from the Intel man's face and forearm. He tossed his remote to the nurse, waving us past. The nurse discarded Varney's wrecked carbine and snatched the dead marine's sidearm. The stench of scorched metal and singed flesh hung in the air. Anger overcame my rising nausea.

Silvre said, "Caylar, you take point. I'll bring Keesay. Simms, follow and watch our back."

We had twenty yards to go before the cross-hall with the turn to the elevator in sight. My nurse, Caylar, picked up the pace. When a door ahead to the left slid open, Caylar dropped to one knee, sending several cracking shots. A gray-clad man fell into the hallway along with a scope mounted MP assault rifle. Another door immediately to my right slid open. Without hesitation I raised my pistol and fired blindly at what should have been chest level. Two quick shots. If he was an innocent passenger, he should've stayed in his room. And if he'd had any type of synthetic armor I wouldn't have lived to confirm it. A brief, gurgling cry and thump said my second shot must've risen, or the target had been short.

"Good shot!" Diplomat Silvre said from behind.

I couldn't respond. I was too busy fighting the pain in my chest those good shots had inflicted.

Caylar stopped near the crossway. Several cracks of MP gunfire sounded from behind followed by a return volley. Then shots from multiple calibers intermingled.

Caylar pulled out an old-fashioned circular mirror used by R-Tech practitioners to examine teeth. He knelt, holding the mirror close to the floor and peered around the corner. He spun back just as parts of the wall buckled and shattered under impacting automatic fire. Caylar signaled Silvre to move up. Holding his hand a yard off the floor, he said, "Two each side, twelve to fifteen meters back. Heavily armed." Caylar produced a palm-grenade, winked at Silvre, and then tossed it around the corner. The fire abated. Nothing else happened.

Three clicks resembling marbles striking wet plexiglas, each followed by instantaneous cracks of MP fire, reverberated just behind my bed. Caylar rushed back and opened fire to my rear while Silvre made more adjustments to several washer-like disks at the base of her gray baton. In less than a second she finished. Only then I realized what she had. "Poor bastards," I whispered.

"The director is down," Caylar said, firing several more shots down the hall. "Good thing your screen's still up or you'd be dead."

"No," Agent Guymin said, snapping me back from mentally reliving that event. "Director Simms was critically injured. An emergency evac-shuttle, Fleet and Intel lost track of it shortly after it departed from the heavy transport. Director Simms is believed to have been on board."

I pushed an image of Deputy Director Simms, his plain face covered in blood, sprawled out on the *Pars Griffin*'s deck from my mind. I didn't see him fall, and figured him to be dead, just like Diplomat Silvre, killed aboard the *Iron Armadillo*. Ambushed by a Crax frigate hidden in the asteroid belt, lying in wait. She, Deputy Director Karlton Simms, Private Varney—the entire crew of the *Armadillo* had died, enabling me to reach Io for my encounter with the experimental Cranaltar IV.

Capital Galactic, at least those in charge of arranging the ambushes, were past due for payback. Some had been captured, but not nearly all. Destroyed records and obscured trails left the company in disarray. They crippled the war effort, threatening humanity's existence—at least as a free people not under the yoke and chains of the Crax.

Agent Guymin poured everyone a glass of water and took a sip before continuing. "Working on a tip, a police cutter intercepted the *Pars Griffin* when she dropped out of condensed space beyond the Kuiper Belt. She was to rendezvous with a number of yachts carrying sought after Capital Galactic personnel. The cutter disabled the heavy transport when she tried to evade. The *Pars Griffin*'s captain refused to answer questions so, after interrogating a number of her officers and crew, we introduced the captain to the Cranaltar IV."

I involuntarily flinched, recalling my experience. The thousands of needle-like probes sinking into my scalp, and dividing like needles on a pine branch, again and again. It was my turn to remain silent.

Agent Vingee asked, "The captain revealed Director Simms's location?"

"Not exactly. He was less than cooperative, resulting in a less than accurate brain mapping. Without access to routing and location of key memories, the download was both jumbled and incomplete." Agent Guymin directed his gaze at me. "The procedure proved fatal."

"Dr. Goldsen went along with it?" I asked. "I know convicted death row criminals ended up as test subjects, but the captain was only a suspect."

"We're at war," Agent Guymin said. "She knows the score."

"Just asking," I replied. "The captain denied a request to allow Marines from the *Iron Armadillo* to board his transport vessel after my pretrial. If they'd been allowed to escort me off, Simms wouldn't have been wounded." I didn't mention Diplomat Silvre's demise. I knew Caylar had sought after her, hoping against hope that she'd survived in one of the escape pods—ones the Crax frigate had targeted, even as it was being converged upon by police cutters, patrol gunboats and the *Red Bison*, a light cruiser.

I shook my head. "The *Pars Griffin*'s captain used a technicality to keep the Colonial Marines off his vessel, and I'll bet a technicality enabled his connection to the Cranaltar."

"I didn't think you'd have any qualms about it," Agent Guymin said after taking a sip of water. "From what we've been able to piece together with the Cranaltar and other collected data, the Celestial Unicorn Palace may be a place to pick up the trail."

"Makes sense," Agent Vingee said. "I read a news brief that stated the Unicorn Palace declared independence shortly after the war started."

Agent Guymin nodded. "It did." He smiled at me. "And due to a *technicality* in its financing and charter as one of the first colonies, it was legally able to withdraw from governmental jurisdiction."

"It's not like Earth has a lot of assets to send out to the 70 Virginis system," I said, "but isn't that like asking the Crax to move in?"

"They've contracted with the Troh-gots," Agent Vingee said. "From the report I read."

"The only direct encounter humanity ever had with the Troh-gots," Agent Guymin added, "was during the botched Treaty Zone Negotiations. From that we gathered they prefer an atmosphere laced with methane. Not much else on them, other than they count in base 8."

I leaned forward. "They weren't much of a factor in the Silicate War. I've never read about them fighting in any major actions. They only scouted and provided intel."

"No, you're right there," Agent Guymin agreed. "But they were a factor. They fought the Shards, but never in conjunction with any of our forces, human forces, at least not that Intel knows of. They hauled and set prefabricated foundation structures which the Umbelgarri, or more accurately the Bahklack—their thralls, completed."

I'd read voraciously about the Silicate War. Not much to do when working warehouse duty on Pluto, especially during the off hours. "Nothing I've read or heard even hinted at that."

"Neither had I," Guymin said. "Not until I was granted access for our assignment. Still, beyond the negotiating diplomats, only two humans have actually seen one. Needless to say, we lack any firm biological data." He wiped his hand across imaginary dust on the computer screen. "Even more secretive than the Umbelgarri."

Agent Vingee asked, "Are the Troh-gots allied with the Crax?"

He shrugged. "No evidence indicates they are."

"Are they A-Tech?" I asked. "Or I-Tech like us?"

"Advanced tech?" He pursed his lips and raised his eyebrows before answering. "Estimates suggest they're probably intermediate tech like us, but closer to the Selgum Crax than we are."

"I interpret your information," Agent Vingee said, wrapping her long fingers around her glass of water, "as an estimate based upon a number of incalculable variables. Is any of the source data Umbelgarri?"

"No reference was indicated. But that doesn't mean anything. The Umbelgarri are less popular than humanity, so it's unlikely they've had much contact with the Troh-gots, at least not since the Silicate War."

"So the Troh-gots may or may not be hostile," I said. "But if nothing else, opportunistic."

"Back to the Celestial Unicorn Palace," Guymin said. "Besides being an exclusive resort for wealthy executives, occasionally it was a layover for tugs hauling equipment to the outer-colony region."

"Are the commercial advertisements accurate?" I asked.

Agent Vingee shot me a disgusted glance before sarcastically stating the Palace's slogan. "Come be a stallion on our ranch."

"Yes, Keesay," Agent Guymin said, eyeing Agent Vingee with apparent curiosity. "To my understanding the seven-foot voluptuous blondes that chant the slogan are there, and then some. But more to the point, it's believed that Capital Galactic executives are fleeing there, or more accurately to the Bonnisbin Space Dock to which the Palace is attached." He paused. "At least as a temporary haven, before moving on. Identity alteration through surgery and DNA manipulation, V-ID manipulation. It makes them far more difficult to track down."

Agent Guymin again looked at me. "That reminds me, Special Agent Keesay, you need to update your inoculations. I was told they'd not only add the inoculation information to your V-ID pattern, but alter it, should anybody gain access to the government files and try to use it to track you."

"Understood," I said, wondering how long it'd take me to get used to being called Special Agent instead of Security Specialist. I nodded once. "The CGIG bounty."

"Special Agent Vingee informed me you refused to undergo cosmetic surgery or DNA modification."

"Correct," I said. "I am who I am, and will always be who I am."

"Until you're killed," Agent Vingee said. "He insists on carrying his old equipment, which will ID him faster than a standard facial scan."

I frowned and said to her, "The billions of humans, the number of colonies, the confusion of the war. Decent odds for me, I'd say."

"All of the steps you're resisting are elementary, Special Agent Keesay. Even if you believe the chances small, those steps would reduce the chances even further."

Agent Vingee seemed a lot different back when I was injured and prepping for the Cranaltar. She'd gotten angry once when she thought I'd back out of undergoing the Cranaltar procedure. She'd acted without hesitation to keep me from being killed just after my recovery. Maybe she'd reflected upon what was revealed through the *Documentary*. I was flawed, like any human, anything but perfect—far, far from it. But most people get to hide their inner self, and project what they hope others will see—at least most of the time. The Cranaltar cut through all that.

"Special Agent Vingee," I said. "Engineer McAllister and I managed, despite our history. You have the advantage, knowing me better than any Intel partner might know another. We can make a decent team."

She started to say something, but settled for nodding once.

I turned to Agent Guymin. "Director Lidov said something about the Chicher and my DNA. Do you know anything about that?"

"No, I don't Special Agent Keesay, but I'd say that you and Special Agent Vingee better work out your differences. If not, it'll be harder on you."

I leaned back in my chair and looked from Guymin to Vingee and back.

"We're to take an upgraded second series exploration shuttle to the Unicorn Palace and pick up the trail." He held up a finger before either Vingee or I could question him. "It's been modified to look like a long range transport shuttle. Superficial scans will ID it as such.

"Agent Vingee's cover is an executive from Mayfair Mining and Industrials, in their newly acquired hydroponics division. They outbid several corporations to obtain this portion of the seized Capital Galactic Investment Group. Vingee will be seeking to contract with the 70 Virginis system's main space dock to upgrade and maintain their hydroponic systems. I'm her assistant. Keesay, you're her bodyguard." He winked at Agent Vingee. "In these days of war and corporate strife, bodyguards are coming into vogue."

"So we may come across some hunted persons, like Falshire Hawks?" I asked Agent Guymin. "Or that interrogating lawyer, Heartwell?"

"Possible, but unlikely."

Vingee asked, "What if we run across them, and they ID Keesay?"

"There'll be bounty hunters there," Guymin said. "Those on the run'll be keeping out of sight, I'd imagine."

"Bounty hunters," pondered Agent Vingee, adding a sideways glance my direction.

"I get your point, Agent Vingee."

"There may be other agency operatives there on the trail of any number of folks," Agent Guymin said. "Including the ever popular Falshire Hawks. Others gathering information on abducted persons, like our Director Simms. If we're able to nab Hawks or Heartwell, or any other big names, we'll do that. But our primary purpose is to get and follow leads on captives."

"Understood," I said. "I'd like nothing better than to secure Director Simms' release."

"Agent Keesay," said Agent Guymin, "you may get a bonus. It's possible that individuals taken by Capital Galactic on Tallavaster may be housed with or near Director Simms."

"Janice Tahgs?" I asked, recalling my last vision of her, a bruised and broken captive. "Do you have information on her?"

"No." He shook his head. "I saw from the *Documentary* that you two became close. The Agency believes that Capital Galactic is holding captives in large groups in as many as three locations." He took a breath and continued. "In the end, some like Simms they may use to negotiate with, if they get trapped and desperate. Administrative Specialist Tahgs, they may believe she has knowledge as to the whereabouts of the wife and son of Dr. Maximar Drizdon. But otherwise, for bargaining purposes, she has negligible value."

"Thanks for the grim analysis," I said. "I could've figured that one out."

"Keesay." He paused. "Since we'll be working together, I'll call you that, and you can call me Guymin, okay?" He grinned mischievously, which seemed out of character, at least for this meeting. "Until we begin using our established covers."

"The same here," Agent Vingee said to me.

I nodded as Guymin continued, saying, "In any case, Keesay, I relayed the possibility of Tahgs to illustrate the urgency of the situation for many involved." He gave me a half smile. "From what I've seen, it's better to be straight-forward with you."

"Understood," I said, and sighed. "I won't write Janice Tahgs off, but any information she might've had is long past use."

Vingee placed a hand on my shoulder. I looked up at her and said, "Reality enjoys rearing one of its ugly heads."

"There's always hope," she said. "You're one of the luckiest people I've ever seen."

"I'll pick up an MP pistol and laser carbine," I said, knowing ammunition for my equipment was unlikely to be found on Io. "But don't expect me to carry them unless the situation clearly dictates the necessity." I caught Guymin's smile. "Or I'm given a team leader's directive."

"Actually," Guymin said, "among a few agents, brass knuckles are making a resurgence. Who knows, shotguns with bayonets may be next?"

That statement didn't have the intended effect. "Just how many people have seen the *Documentary*?" I growled.

"Not many," Guymin assured me. "But you know how fads are. Nobody ever knows the source. Plus, stories spread. The *Kalavar*'s survivors. With some you made a lasting impression."

"Relics in space aren't common," Vingee added.

"Back to the assignment," Guymin said, resting his hands on the table. "We'll have plenty of time for idle banter." He checked the chronometer above the door. "The *Evanescent Thunder* is scheduled to arrive here later today or early tomorrow. She's assigned to trail us and render whatever assistance a patrol gunboat can."

"The *Evanescent Thunder* transported me here, to Io," I said. "Will she be able to range and follow an upgraded—converted exploration shuttle?"

"My understanding is that she's completing a short patrol to work out any technical issues from her most recent upgrade. New cascading atomic engine, so she'll condense space roughly thirty percent less effectively than a military escort, such as a destroyer. Still, with her more powerful thrust engines, she'll be nearly as fast as us. Plus, she's added more fuel stores, and improved life support and reclamation systems for longer patrols."

"What don't you know?" I asked.

"The name of our support engineer. Agent Vingee, would you look into that, and when the *Nuclear Pitchfork VII* is scheduled to arrive?"

"I will," Vingee said, while getting to her feet. "Is that really the name of our shuttle?"

Guymin shrugged. "Don't look at me. It was assigned to us."

"Who did you annoy recently?" I asked.

"Remember, we're working for the hydroponics division. Their motto is: Combining advanced science and modern agricultural technology for a profitable combination."

"Doesn't exactly roll off the tongue," I said.

"Don't complain," he replied with a smile. "I requisitioned your duty coveralls. Equal to the ones damaged on Tallavaster." He paused. "Gray-green of security, with a Mayfair logo and ID."

Thinking of our shuttle's name, and of the name patch that would be affixed above my coverall's left pocket, I asked, "Who picked my cover name?"

Guymin leaned back in his chair. "I did."

I didn't know whether to be relieved or not. "Care to elaborate?"

Still standing, Vingee cut in, saying, "Keesay, I'd be happy to requisition your MP pistol and laser carbine."

"If you like," I said, gazing up at her. "Also, a stun baton. Be sure it's medium duty and retractable." When she nodded, I added, "And armor piercing and standard jacketed .357 rounds, and .22 caliber for the backup on my ankle. Fragmentation and stun grenades, too."

She shook her head. "Forget it," she snapped. "You can requisition your own equipment."

I shrugged as she strode out. "Kind of moody," I said with a look of confusion after the door closed. "I thought we were having a light moment." Maybe because I mentioned the old-style .22 caliber pistol, an antique that Deputy Director Simms had lent to me before being taken captive.

"This is her second field mission," Guymin explained. "Her specialty is records and information. Her first field mission was safeguarding you." He began tapping at the computer screen. "I'd say your earlier assessment was almost right. She's nervous."

"And I'm not?"

"You've been under fire." He lifted the bowl from the table and offered me a fruit strip. "So have I."

The strips *were* strawberry. "So has she," I said. "Remember, Vingee knocked me down before that lawyer could nail me with acid rounds?"

"I'm glad you have faith in her, Kra. I do, too." He deactivated the table's computer. "Vingee suspects she was assigned because no other field agents are available. And she's right."

"She'll measure up, Caylar."

"Let's just hope we all do." He stood. "Go look into your V-ID and equipment requisition." He tapped the metal box next to the table with his boot. "After examining what's in here."

CHAPTER 4

I sat in front of a computer preparing to review the mission file. I'd finished an electronic message thanking Special Agent Guymin for his foresight—what the metal case he'd brought to our meeting contained. Weeks ago he'd requisitioned a variety of shotgun shells and ammunition for my duty revolver, an MP pistol, stun baton, a case containing six flash-stun and three fragmentation grenades, and a set of brass knuckles made of hardened stainless steel. After all, he'd seen the *Documentary* and knew my preferences. I could've dictated my entry, but voice recognition protocol is a hassle, especially since I only had a guest user account on the system. Typing was more efficient.

I rubbed the updated V-ID's tattoo-like geometric pattern beneath my left ear. It reflected my series of inoculations that now permitted travel even to the most remote outer colony. Also, according to the Intelligence medical technician, she'd altered my V-ID such that it couldn't be used to trace me. I didn't think alterations could be done. I guess it couldn't be done *officially*, but I worked for Intelligence. The contract I signed wasn't as good as I had with Negral Corp. Better pay, but more restriction clauses and incarceration penalties. Nothing I ever intended to do, and better on average than what a 4th Class Security Specialist could expect. In any case, I'd be safe from V-ID tracking, unless CGIG or their bounty hunters obtained a record of my updated V-ID pattern.

The computer screen went yellow and flashed an emergency warning. A corresponding claxon sounded in my room, emphasizing it wasn't a drill. The yellow flashing continued across the top of my computer screen even though the claxon ceased after twenty seconds.

I slid on my com-set before grabbing and checking my shotgun. The yellow warning indicated a regional danger, one not directed at the Io research colony. I expected information over my com-set, explaining the warning.

Without an assigned duty station or frequency I switched my com-set to Marine Frequency priority, and Io Colony General Information as secondary and decided to head toward the colony's primary landing bay to see what was going on. Two steps from the door, I received a call from Agent Guymin. "Agent Keesay, report to the medical research lab. Consider the current yellow warning status to be orange. Await further directives."

The link terminated after I said, "Understood." What did Guymin know that he wasn't sharing? More likely, he didn't have the full picture yet.

I took a moment to change into my new coveralls. Even though they bore the Mayfair Mining and Industrials Logo, and my cover name, Bleys, they offered superior protection. My gut told me it was going to be a rough day, so I threw a bandoleer of shotgun shells across my shoulder and pocketed a box of .357 magnum rounds. I looked around and decided to slip the MP pistol into my belt, recalling the times I'd lacked adequate firepower. Simms's .22 holstered at my ankle was something but wouldn't count for much.

Firepower for what? Nothing new flashed across my computer screen. Of course, I only had a guest account.

Yellow, I thought. Yellow within the colony would've meant some sort of engineering or environmental emergency, but under control. An orange threat? Orange indicated an outside threat, such as an incoming meteor shower. Except in time of war. Guymin said to consider it Orange. That indicated an enemy ship, or ships, detected and approaching. Red meant attack imminent. I slipped a fragmentation grenade into each of my thigh pockets, thinking it'd be better to have them rather than wish I had.

The yellow emergency claxon sounded again and echoed down the hall. I fidgeted with my com-set, toggling between the Io colony's information system, Security, and the previous frequency settings.

Instead of a modern subterranean settlement, the Io Colony's corridors reminded me of ancient caves and catacombs, their gray walls showing signs of tunnel-cutting tools. Many of the shaft-like corridors must've begun life as lava tubes. Stepping out of the anti-grav driven transport shuttle after it stopped at a major junction, the intense fluorescent lights reminded me how artificial the colony's environment was. Installed gravity plates supplemented the moon's weak gravitational pull. I suspected the plates cancelled out Jupiter's fluctuating gravitational influence. Physics wasn't my strong suit back in school, so I wasn't sure.

I fell into line with eight white lab-coated scientists and three technicians. "Any idea what's going on?" I asked.

"Unexpected gravitational disturbance in the solar system," answered a tech between breaths. "Not near Jupiter," she said with unconcern and shrugged. "Someone said it could be a Crax raid exiting condensed space."

The rest of the march continued in silence, at least for me. The techs were monitoring their computer clips or communicating via their links. I stood aside, allowing them to pass, and took up post outside the double doors. "Special Agent Guymin," I called into my com-set. "Posted outside the Level Two Conference Entrance to the main medical research area."

Fifteen seconds later Guymin responded. "Proceed to the Cranaltar Research Lab. Secure the area. Coordinate with Dr. Goldsen. It's been confirmed, one or more Crax combat vessels have tripped the warning beacons, believed to be vectoring toward Pluto. They've not yet exited condensed space." He paused and I noted my com-set switching to secure random encoding-decoding. A preprogrammed precaution initiated by Agent Guymin. "Keesay. Intelligence expects something similar to occur around Jupiter. Plan for the worst, expect the worst."

Caylar Guymin never struck me as a pessimistic person. "Understood. Out," I replied.

Within two minutes I descended the two levels, using the shortest route. A Colonial Marine stood outside the entrance to the Cranaltar research area. He held his laser carbine in challenge.

I stopped and said, "I've been directed to coordinate with Dr. Goldsen in securing the area."

Private Velasquez and I knew each other, mainly from working out in the training area. He eyed my gray-green security coveralls, looking at the name patch that read Bleys.

"Ignore the patch," I said. "This set of coveralls was just shipped to me. Computer messed up the labeling. You know how they treat R-Techs." I shrugged. "My other set is in the middle of a cleaning cycle."

Velasquez gave me a sideways glance then smiled before speaking into his collar. "Captain, I've a Security Specialist Keesay here." He held his hand to his ear before stepping aside.

"Thank you, Private," I said as he turned to leave.

"Dr. Goldsen," I said into my com-set, staring up at a security camera recessed into the stone wall beside the door. "This is Security Specialist Keesay." I didn't know if she knew I'd been recruited by Intelligence. Besides, I was armed and my coveralls were the color of a security specialist. "I've been assigned to your facility during the alert."

The double-doors slid open. After marching through, entering the well-lit lab, they closed with a pair of security doors dropping afterward, sealing the front entrance. That seemed odd for an official yellow alert. Someone in the lab expected the worst, just like Guymin.

Dr. Goldsen was in her electronic equipment-filled lab, speaking to one of her assistants. After approaching I waited for the research director's attention. She dismissed the assistant and took my arm. "Specialist Keesay, come with me."

I politely disengaged my arm from her grip. "I've been directed to report to you and assist in securing the area. What's the situation?"

She led me toward her office, past a row of carts filled with what looked like the guts of various sensors and computer systems. They must've been in the middle of some sort of maintenance or upgrading project. Once in her office, Dr. Goldsen moved to her desk but remained standing. She pushed aside a computer clip and a neat stack of file folders before initiating a security sequence through her desk screen. I moved a larger file stack to a nearby shelf. More paper than might be expected in a modern research lab.

She frowned and finished tapping in the security sequence.

"May I?" she asked, and detached my com-set. She plugged it into a port on the side of her desk, I guessed to synchronize my communication gear with her station. Maybe enabling me access to…the Umbelgarri network? Would Guymin—Intel approve?

Her console enacted a security verification facial and retinal scan, and followed up with a scan of her index finger as she pressed it onto a red square along the bottom right corner of the screen.

Dr. Goldsen pursed her lips, and looked around to see if anyone was listening. I stepped away to close the office's metal-framed glass door, but she signaled me back toward her. Satisfied that everyone was too busy to pay attention, she whispered, "A Crax fleet may be on approach. That is all I know."

Fleet? That meant a lot of ships. Agent Guymin might've relayed a bit more concern if that was true. I reminded myself that Dr. Goldsen wasn't fluent in military jargon and didn't question her statement about the Crax. Instead I asked, "Can you lower the intensity of the emergency alert?"

She tapped a screen, dimming flashing the yellow lights. "Astute suggestion," she said. "I am enabling your access to the command frequency. Security is your expertise. Any recommendations you may have are more than welcome."

"I'll assist any way I can. Have your people secured this area for possible enemy bombardment?"

"My colleagues and staff are doing that as we speak," Dr. Goldsen said. "We are securing and isolating in safe mode all files and equipment."

"Until the situation is clarified, I have no other suggestions." My mind raced, trying to isolate reason—or reasons—the Crax would mount a raid on Io, or one of Jupiter's other moon-based colonies.

She returned my com-set. "Routed through the Experimental Research Network, you have temporary access to the Io Colony Command Frequency."

"Understood," I said.

Dr. Goldsen was uncommon in her varied level of technology usage. She preferred old-style glasses and used an informal bedside manner, even if sometimes a bit cold and distant. Probably due to her focus as a research scientist.

"Doctor, can you call up a diagram of the Cranaltar Research Area?"

She spoke to the computer. "Provide layout to Cranaltar Research Area. One to one-hundred scale. Minimal technical details."

The diagram showed the main area with its second tier overlooking the main computer-filled work area, including Dr. Goldsen's office, and scattered attached side rooms and alcoves. To the left of the main double-door entrance, a hallway ran a short distance.

"Seven offices and a lounge along this hall," I said for confirmation. Dr. Goldsen nodded once.

Using the main lab entrance as north, I ran my finger across the screen, to the south end of the east wall. "Beyond this door, two storage rooms jutting off this dogleg hallway with stairs down to the left and a bay holding an auxiliary life support system, a bank of batteries, and a compact backup fusion generator." I knew where the other exit led: To the facility housing the Cranaltar device, and beyond one of the walls, the computer hardware supporting the experimental brain-probing machine. There wasn't any information on the screen beyond that—probably Umbelgarri territory. In any case, I verified what I remembered. "This room beyond is where the Cranaltar device is housed, with an observation section above."

"Yes," she said, following to where I pointed. "The Cranaltar area has an upper observation level. The processing and data transfer equipment is housed in a large room beyond."

"That's where the heart of the device is located?"

"That is where," she started, then shook her head once. "*Essentially*, you are correct."

"Is there access to the Umbelgarri sector through that room?" I asked, recalling an encounter with a crab-like Bahklack there prior to being hooked up to the Cranaltar device.

"Yes. But it is *secure* and only accessible if they allow."

The way she said 'secure' indicated her belief in that route's impenetrability. Maybe to humans. Maybe not to Crax. "Is there an external entry to the observation area?" I asked.

"There is," she said, "via an isolated hallway. Or was. There are two reinforced blast doors. They appear steel, just like the main entrance." She tipped her head, looking over the top of her wire glasses toward the entrance to the main work area, and whispered again. "Umbelgarri alloy. Very few people are aware of that fact. After your recovery and the *Documentary* viewing were complete, the stairwell leading to that portion of the medical research area was filled with rubble fused into place. Although there is no direct evidence, I believe the Umbelgarri requested that access route be closed."

That might explain why Guymin shifted me to the Cranaltar facility instead of my initial posting outside the main medical research facility. I figured some colony personnel might suspect that certain doors had been reinforced with an Umbelgarri alloy, despite the fact it wasn't advertised.

"Understood," I said to Dr. Goldsen before holding up a finger while listening to Colony Command. "Switch your computer to command frequency two."

I quickly assessed the tactical situation that appeared on her desk screen. "See here?" I pointed. "We've one gunboat and two police cutters forming up with what I'd bet is an Umbelgarri battle cruiser." The sleek planarian-shaped vessel dwarfed the human ships, not only in size but also in firepower. "They appear to be expecting trouble, sooner rather than later."

Dr. Goldsen nodded. "I suspected they had a big ship hidden on the surface. I believe there is also a number of our smaller spacecraft." She paused, searching for the names. "Fighters and attack craft."

"They're up there," I said, showing the squadron on the screen, leading the gunboat and cutters. I kept my voice just above a whisper. "I just hope this moon is packed with ground-based firepower." Why would the Umbelgarri reveal their cruiser? Maybe a show of force to deter an attack?

"There are a multitude of weapons," said Dr. Goldsen, "but my knowledge lacks specifics."

"Keesay," Agent Guymin said over my com-set, again running with secure random encoding-decoding. "The Cranaltar facility is considered a possible target of the oncoming raid, either through bombardment or ground assault. The latter of the two determined to be unlikely." His voice was rote, as if concentrating on a half-dozen other tasks. He probably was.

"This colony," he continued, "has limited security and military personnel and wasn't built with defensibility in mind. Colony Command *may* send several Colonial Marines your way, but don't count on it. Notify Dr. Goldsen that Communication Lockdown Protocol, Alpha Nine One will be enacted within the next two minutes. Then, do what you can to prepare the Cranaltar Research Facility to resist capture or destruction."

"Understood."

"Guymin, out."

I turned to Dr. Goldsen. "Communication Lockdown, Protocol Alpha Nine One will be enacted in less than two minutes. I'm not a part of the colony security team, but I can guess the lockdown's objective."

She began tapping at her screen. "I have sent a summary of the lockdown's parameters to your com-set's ocular display."

I flipped the switch that turned on my ocular. The mic-mounted device was supposed to project a display into my right eye. I'd gotten used to the setup while serving aboard the civil transport *Kalavar*. With effort I could shift visual focus, reducing projected images to background shadows when not of primary concern.

The received text image was blurry, reminding me of Agent Vingee's earlier comment. "My ocular hasn't been calibrated."

"That can be resolved, Mr. Keesay," Dr. Goldsen said, retrieving my online medical file. "I have the exact facial measurements, dimensions of the relevant eye, including the lens, which is the main variable." She smiled as she relayed information from her files to my com-set, accurately calibrating the ocular device.

"Thank you," I said, beginning to read the text display.

The communications lockdown protocol limited communication to within pods, except for select individuals. The medical research lab was a pod and Dr. Goldsen would have external access.

I checked my com-set. We both could send and receive external communications. Otherwise, nothing outgoing and only incoming sources routed through and approved by Colony Command. Like me, I figured Agents Guymin and Vingee wouldn't be restricted.

The lockdown would be enacted in less than a minute without forewarning, with the local leader tasked to determine if, when, and how the lockdown would be announced. In addition, movement from the immediate area was to be restricted, unless urgent circumstances necessitated it as determined by the local leader—Dr. Goldsen—and Colony Command authorized it.

Those attempting to circumvent communication lockdown or restricted movement were to be prevented, through any means necessary, as determined by the local leader. And I was Dr. Goldsen's enforcer, should it come to that.

Gazing out at the group, most in view, still busy checking and securing secondary computers and systems, I didn't see treachery as likely. But I didn't anticipate Tech Marshner's attempted assault upon me. Apparently nobody did.

The lockdown protocol might hinder communication should the Crax bombard Io's surface and damage subterranean areas. That didn't consider electronic jamming. Relays were hardwired to wireless hubs, as backup, but that redundancy could be severed. It was similar to the setup I remembered from my stationing on Pluto—which was soon to be, if not already, under attack. But, if there were others compromised like Marshner, or strongly sympathetic to CGIG, Colony Command's effort made even more sense, especially if a surface to subsurface assault occurred.

Thinking about that, and considering the diversionary attack on Pluto, the Crax might believe they'll have more than adequate time for bombardment from space before a counterattack could be mounted. Or a ground assault to achieve their objective, whatever that might be. Having fought the Crax, my gut said they'd attempt a ground assault.

The facility's warning lights shifted from yellow to orange and the claxon sounded again, at a faster cadence. My watch indicated two minutes had passed since Guymin's last contact.

"Dr. Goldsen," I said, "get your people in here."

CHAPTER 5

I watched the concerned and frightened faces as Dr. Goldsen's people crowded into her office. The only one I knew was Dr. Chahal, a dark-haired neuro-chemist, with a trimmed mustache who stood only an inch taller than me, something pretty rare for an I-Tech. He worked with me during my recovery from the Cranaltar procedure, demonstrating a sharp mind and wit, and a friendly sense of humor.

After announcing my presence as her security advisor, Dr. Goldsen addressed her staff, including Dr. Lundox, like her a biochemical engineer with a PhD in neuropsychology and wearing a white lab coat, two information systems analysts in peach-colored coveralls, two white-clad med tech lab assistants, and two maintenance technicians in standard tan coveralls. All except for Dr. Lundox hung on her every word.

"My information concurs with that of Security Specialist Keesay. A Crax force of unknown composition is or will soon mount an attack on the outpost colonies and the associated spaceport and industrial facilities on Pluto, and possibly Charon."

Those weren't my exact words, but close.

"Though I cannot confirm it, Specialist Keesay believes the Crax are preparing to mount a similar attack on this research colony, potentially land assault units here on Io. If the Crax do attempt a military assault, a logical target is the adjoining Umbelgarri outpost. Conceivably, this facility may be considered a conduit to such an end. As such, I am placing Specialist Keesay in charge of formulating a defense strategy."

Anyone with a pair of eyes could read the skepticism on all but a few faces. They either believed that Io's facilities were too insignificant to merit Crax attention, or they believed the A-Tech Umbelgarri defenses would repel any attack. Didn't they realize that the Primus Crax were equally tech advanced, and out to eliminate the Umbelgarri and all of their allies? And succeeding? I'd read news reports of people who didn't believe there was even a war going on and that the Crax invasion was little more than a clever ploy to manipulate resources and incur larger corporate profit margins. I'd have bet that one or two of Dr. Goldsen's staff doubted Pluto was under attack.

All except the biochemical engineer glanced at me before looking back to their project leader. He crossed his arms and glared at me with his broad brown eyes. "What qualifies a fourth class security specialist to assess Crax intentions and to formulate counter tactics?" Dr. Lundox was a dark-skinned man with short, curly hair. He'd cosmetically added graying to his temples.

Dr. Goldsen started to speak, but I interrupted her and met his eyes with my own hardened stare. "Unless a squad of Colonial Marines shows up I'm all you've got. My guess is reinforcements aren't coming and we don't have time for debate."

Dr. Goldsen stepped between us. "I have placed Specialist Keesay in charge of securing this research facility."

"That shouldn't be difficult," the PhD said, continuing his stare-down. "The blast doors are a 9.6 centimeter thick Umbelgarri alloy. It'll take time for the Crax, even the Primus Crax, to get through that...should they even attack this facility, let alone initiate a ground assault. If that remote possibility comes to pass, Earth will have mounted a counterstrike."

Addressing more than Dr. Lundox, I said, "I've fought the Crax. They're skilled and tenacious. They'll be well equipped, both in space and on the ground. More than we can handle." I gazed beyond Dr. Goldsen's staff, into the main lab area. "Maybe my information is wrong, *maybe* I'm wrong. If so, we'll have wasted some time and resources, and have a mess to clean up. If I'm right, it might make the difference between surviving and not." I paused. "Poorly equipped to repel such an attack, it might mean that we'll die anyway, but we'll go down taking some of them with us."

I turned my back on Dr. Lundox. "Dr. Goldsen, this is what I need your people to do." I tapped at the desk screen. "They'll make for this facility once they get past the outer defenses. If for no other reason than it may provide access to the Umbelgarri area."

Dr. Lundox cleared his throat. "What makes you think they'll know where this facility is and its proximity to the Umbelgarri complex?"

"Dr. Goldsen," I said, "either you shut him up, or I will."

Dr. Goldsen turned on the PhD. "Dr. Lundox, the number of Gar Crax this man has killed surpasses your scientific publishing credits, twofold." She stepped back. "If you have overlooked his propensity toward effective violence, that fact should remind you of it. If he determines it is in our best interest to incapacitate you, I will not interfere."

I didn't wait for a response. I'd witnessed carnage inflicted by the Crax and their allies. Even if the scientists didn't fully realize their peril, giving them time to imagine it wouldn't help. Keeping them focused on fortification tasks would keep me busy, too. "We need to set up a layered defense to delay them." I took a breath, searching to rattle loose any feasible trick or tactic. "Dr. Goldsen, do you have access to any highly combustible liquids?"

She nodded and started to list them off, "Acetone, isopropyl alcohol, oxygen, hydrogen."

I cut her off. "No time. Dr. Chahal, select a volatile one that'll react to an electric current." I pointed to one of the medical assistants and a maintenance tech. "Remove eight or ten florescent light tubes in the hallway outside of this facility and fill them with it."

Before anyone could ask why, I made eye contact with the selected maintenance tech after reading her name tag. "Tech Gorgio, the lights in the hall. There's a conduit to them?"

She nodded, her round face held taught while her curly hair bounced.

"Good. Run wiring and set a switch in the lab. Disconnect them from established circuitry." I looked at the assistant next to Gorgio. "Med Tech Yaley, that jell that you fill the tanks to immobilize patients for the Cranaltar, it's pretty slick?"

"It is," she said. "Especially when a small amount of the jelling agent is added. But it's not flammable."

She'd guessed the purpose of the lights.

"Didn't think so," I said. "If it was, it might tip our hand. After the lights are rigged, coat the hallway floor with it." I recalled being placed in the gel prior to my experience under the Cranaltar. "And add a little something that will make it conduct electricity."

"How much?"

"Cover as much of the hallway as you can. Walls if you have extra. I pointed to the other med tech. "You, Corbett, assist her."

That left Dr. Goldsen, Dr. Lundox, one maintenance tech, and the two systems analysts. "Dr. Goldsen, I recall the lab area having sound dampeners. Can you adjust them to counter the Stegmar sounding?"

"There is an experimental program which has proven up to seventy-five percent effective within a confined area. Do you want me to access, calibrate, and enable it?"

"Yes, Doctor. And you're in charge of the blast doors. Opening and closing them. There's three hallway security cameras. Deactivate the one twenty yards—meters down the hall."

When she nodded, I turned to the PhD. "Lundox, your skills are needed." He'd watched me while I'd given directives, but was looking away when I addressed him.

He stepped forward. "My apologies," he began, but I interrupted him.

"We can patch things up later. Stegmar weapons fire needles coated with a paralyzing toxin. The Colonial Marines have a broad spectrum antidote. Do you know anything about that?"

"Actually, Specialist, I possess a cursory knowledge. The chemical components should be in our stockroom nearby. As a senior research coordinator I have access to the components and the necessary details."

"Be about it," I said. He darted out of the office faster than I expected.

I made eye contact with the remaining maintenance tech. "There's a backup generator down the hall." I recalled from Dr. Goldsen's diagram identifying it as a micro-fusion 250 megawatt generator. "Can you fire it up, Tech Yin? And direct its power to an outlet—better yet along a cable to reach inside the lab near the door?"

He thought a moment, then nodded.

I wanted to set a trap similar to what a lieutenant commander did aboard the *Kalavar*. In desperate combat to defeat the Crax boarding, Commander Devans urinated on a plastic tarp and killed a Gar Crax by thrusting a hot cable onto it. Devans died, electrocuted in the effort. Just as I finished explaining the plan to Tech Yin, Agent Guymin contacted me via my com-set.

"Keesay, estimate no more than ten minutes until the enemy drops out of condensed space. How long before it comes to combat depends on how far they appear from Io. Anticipate our def-sats and the few combat capable spacecraft in the area won't be able to fend them off. They'll certainly have anticipated Umbelgarri ground to space weapons. My guess is that we'll have to hold out three hours for Earth forces to organize and mount a counterattack."

"Are we the only ones in the solar system targeted?"

"Negative. Pluto is under attack as well. Small scale, but more than the local defense can handle."

I'd been stationed on Pluto. Ethane collection operations and layover for ships harvesting ice in the Kuiper Belt, some warehouses. Several tri-beam defense lasers and a handful of orbiting def-sats—unless it'd been upgraded in the past couple years.

"Any chance for reinforcements down here?"

"Negative, Keesay. Sorry."

I looked around, with two systems analysts and Dr. Goldsen watching me. I only had my shotgun, duty revolver and backup pistol, newly obtained MP pistol, stun baton, bayonet, two grenades, and a set of brass knuckles. Not good. I spoke into my mic again. "Any chance I might send someone to pick up some weapons? MP or laser carbines?"

"Actually, Keesay, Special Agent Vingee should be arriving with a supply of small arms."

"Will she be staying?" I asked, trying to keep hope from seeping into my voice. Medical doctors and systems analysts? Earnest as they might be, they'd be about as effective as Conscript Moorsheen was, a marketing and sales analysts who died on Tallavaster just after the Crax attack began.

"Negative, Keesay."

"Understood," I said. "Better have her hurry. We're setting up a surprise or two in the hallway and more for our potential guests."

"Acknowledged," he replied, still in a flat voice, still focusing on a dozen concerns at once. "Will let her know. Out."

He finished the conversation before I could ask specifically what Vingee was bringing. I decided not to contact her. She was certainly tasked with a half dozen simultaneous demands, too. Plus, a concerned audience was listening to how I responded, paying attention to more than just the words. Making eye contact with Dr. Goldsen and then the systems analysts, I said, "They're sending us some weapons, just in case.

"Dr. Goldsen," I continued, "watch for Special Agent Vingee, and let me know when she arrives."

After she said, "I will do that," I pointed to the two systems analysts.

"You two gentlemen, with me. Let's move some equipment and see if we can find a plastic cover or tarp of some sort."

A few minutes later, after moving the carts filled with computer equipment to form a barricade across from the main door, Dr. Goldsen called to me from her office, "Special Agent Vingee is just down the hallway."

At the same time, Maintenance Tech Yin rushed up to me. "Specialist," he said, "the reactor is out of service."

I turned to face him. "What does that mean?"

"I don't know," he said, wide-eyed, brushing his straight bangs aside. "I ran through the startup procedure twice. That was the response."

I called to Dr. Goldsen, "Can you find anything on your system about the backup generator being out of service?"

Agent Vingee pushed an aluminum cart around a ladder in the hallway and into the research lab. She had a medium duty laser carbine slung over her shoulder and two replacement battery clips affixed to her belt. "Keesay," she said, trying to catch her breath.

I looked her way. "One moment," and returned my attention to the maintenance tech in front of me.

Tech Yin said, "Tech Gorgio has a class two maintenance rating on fusion reactor systems."

Frustrated with myself for assuming since both were Class 2 Maintenance Technicians it wouldn't matter, I asked, "Can you handle the electrical and lighting contingency?"

Tech Yin nodded, so I said, "Tell Gorgio of the problem and then trade off."

The tech trotted past Vingee and her cart overloaded with laser carbines, MP rifles and several MP pistols.

"Thank you, Agent Vingee," I said, forcing a smile.

She wiped sweat from her brow. "Five Magnetic Pulse carbines, four medium duty laser carbines and three Magnetic Pulse pistols. The MP carbines are military issue and hardened against EMPs. The others are vulnerable."

"Understood," I said.

She pointed to the plastic crate underneath. "Charged battery clips for the lasers and powered ones for the MP carbines. The pistols only have one clip, loaded, set on safe." She smiled. "I also tossed in some bottled water and nutrition packs."

"Thank you. I have nothing to report other than Dr. Goldsen has directed me to prepare to resist intrusion by enemy forces with resources on hand."

From her office, Dr. Goldsen called, "Specialist Keesay, there is no record of the backup generator being down for maintenance. Maintenance records indicate it was checked three days ago."

Agent Vingee looked from Dr. Goldsen's office to me. "If you find something abnormal or suspicious, Agent Keesay, report it to Agent Guymin."

"Understood," I said. "Again, thank you. I suspect you have plenty to do and not enough time to do it."

Vingee nodded once. "I do. And don't think I didn't see that modern pistol tucked in your belt." She winked before turning and striding out the door.

As soon as she left, I directed Systems Analysts Frist and Bowser to get the plastic tarp spread in front of the main entrance and ready for the specially prepared gel that was already being spread in the hallway, except for a narrow path where Tech Yin, Dr. Chahal and Med Tech Corbett were on ladders working on the lights. Both analysts were heavy set, but Bowser's dark hair was cropped short, while Frist's was red, long, and straight. Bowser was older and appeared more knowledgeable with the systems than she was.

The carbines weren't loaded, and I wasn't sure how knowledgeable or experienced Dr. Goldsen's staff was with firearms. I decided to load and set them on safe. The laser carbines were the most fragile but just as easy to use as the MP firearms. As long as they were pointed in the right direction—away from friendlies—it shouldn't be a problem. I looked around the room and up at the balcony-like second tier. I wouldn't distribute the weapons unless a ground assault was imminent. It'd take a little time for the Crax and their allies to get from their drop ships to the surface and fight their way down to us in the experimental medical facility. Surface bombardment would be the first threat to survive. But, if they did come, and in numbers, I feared they'd reach us—if we were an objective.

My com-set picked up general chatter as it switched from frequency to frequency. It became obvious that we weren't the only areas preparing for the Crax penetrating Io's defenses and invading the colony.

Tech Gorgio almost ran into Med Tech Yaley pushing another cart filled with gel into the hallway. I set aside a loaded MP carbine and said, "Report."

"The backup micro-fusion generator is online." Her voice vacillated between confidence and concern. "I was able to bypass circuitry, making it ready for temporary service."

"What does temporary mean?"

"When it starts up, it'll be under condition yellow. I don't know how long that'll last before it trips to red and goes into automatic shutdown. My tech rating and security clearance can't override that."

I met her eyes with a hard stare. "Was the malfunction due to tampering?"

She thought for a few breaths before answering. "Yes."

"Explain," I said.

The Class 2 Maintenance Tech glanced down at my Class 4 rating, which only Relic Techs were given, and appraised me with a raised eyebrow.

Ignoring her skepticism, I grinned before saying, "Layman terms will suffice."

She smiled back and nodded. "The only reason it was detected is because Tech Yin interfaced directly with the computer. The standby signal it was sending out to the energy control systems was green. But if it would've been signaled to start up by external command, it would've gone into automatic shutdown. My guess is that it would've sent a false signal. A containment fracture or something."

"You need to report this to Colony Command." I glanced back over my shoulder. "Dr. Goldsen will get you communication clearance. I'll help pave the way for that."

Tech Gorgio looked hesitant, but nodded once.

"Dr. Goldsen!" I called into her office, above the din of her busy staff. When she looked up, I continued. "Tech Gorgio needs to report sabotage of our generator. It may be widespread. See that it gets done."

I gripped Gorgio's shoulder. "Good job!" When she began trotting over to Dr. Goldsen's office, I added, "Then get back on connecting that cable."

When she was in the office, I adjusted my com-set. "Special Agent Guymin, this is Keesay."

"Go ahead," he said after a five second delay.

"Maintenance Tech Gorgio has determined that the Cranaltar Research Facility's backup micro-fusion generator has been tampered with. Probable sabotage. I've directed her to report it to Colony Command, through Dr. Goldsen."

"Understood. Will coordinate with Colony Command and Control. Out."

With that taken care of, I assisted the systems analysts in their task and helped Yin run the high power capacity cable behind some panels before jutting out and into the conductive gel spread across the plastic tarp.

Gorgio was in Dr. Goldsen's office, installing the first of two hard switches to it. This particular trap was predicated on the Crax not proceeding down the hallway to take out the generator. Some of it would depend on how much detail of the colony's layout they had, and their priorities. If the tampering was coordinated with their attack, the likelihood that they'd attempt to disable the generator should be remote.

The staff stood around me behind our barricade set up ten yards from Dr. Goldsen's office, leaving roughly twenty yards between it and the main entrance. While I reviewed the basics of safe handling and use of the MP firearms and laser carbines, Dr. Goldsen remained in her office, monitoring reports and communications. I'd already established who would stand with me behind the barricade of toppled carts and piled equipment and who'd be posted in along the second tier, and who'd remain in the office with Dr. Goldsen.

The delivery of the weapons, the discovered tampering with the backup generator, and knowledge that the entire base was preparing for attack, including a possible ground assault, had galvanized them to a unified purpose. They'd been a team for some time, many for at least a decade, and they realized that I was the only one among them with any combat experience. Dr. Lundox and Analyst Bowser had some experience with magnetic pulse sidearms, but that was it. And the fact that Med Tech Marshner had tried to assassinate me, a colleague of theirs for three years, wasn't lost on them. Nor on me.

Were there CGIG, and thus potentially Crax, sympathizers still among them? Or somewhere critical on the base? At least one individual in Maintenance or Engineering had tampered with the backup generator. I didn't share the communications received over my com-set indicating at least three other micro-fusion generators were similarly affected.

The muted orange alert switched to a pulsing red, accompanied by a claxon, sounding three blasts that reminded me of a chain saw trying to cut steel plating. It was followed by an authoritative female voice, announcing, "Vessels of unknown origin, believed to be associated with the Crax, have been detected dropping out of condensed space on the far side of Jupiter. Communication lockdown will remain in effect. Report to assigned stations, follow assigned leader directives, await further orders."

With a flick of my head toward Dr. Goldsen's office, I signaled everyone to follow me in there. Other than the limited capabilities of my com-set, she had the only direct link outside our pod.

Everyone crowded around Dr. Goldsen's desk, staring down at the computer display.

"We're tied into Umbelgarri sensors," I said, "or we wouldn't be getting this clear of a reading on their vessels."

Leaning forward, I traced my finger to three ship icons colored in emerald green, and accurately depicting the ships' outer structures. The display showed them closing on Jupiter, opposite Io's current orbit. Maybe they hoped to come in undetected, or at least delay detection. A more detailed representation appeared on the screen's sidebar. "Those three spherical ships are Primus Crax medium cruisers."

Dr. Goldsen squinted as she gazed down, studying the screen as I touched each of the remaining representations, bringing up visual and support data. "I recognize them," she said, "from the combat you survived near the Zeta Aquarius Dock." She frowned and met my gaze. "Their technology is equivalent to the Umbelgarri."

I nodded, pointing to the other icons. "And the Primus brought plenty of firepower. A Selgum Crax heavy carrier, five heavy cruisers, and two other capital ships." I recalled reading about strike raids against the Shards during the Silicate War. "No escorts. They don't have the range of capital ships…it's going to be hit and run."

"Mr. Keesay, they must know that reinforcements are on the way."

I shrugged, and said what I didn't believe. "This could be a distraction, similar to the attack on Pluto." I stared at the display and listened to the radio chatter. The two unidentified capital ships were the same size as the Selgum Crax cruisers. But where the Selgum ships resembled two capital Hs welded together at the crossbar, the unknown ships resembled single Hs, with the leading beams far longer than the trailing engine-bearing sections. "Dr. Goldsen, can you call up information on those two trailing ships?"

She did. "Reports a non-standard configuration. What do you hear over your set?"

I surveyed several channels. "Our ships are forming for a defense. Responding to Umbelgarri ground control directives. Wait," I said, "tie your computer into command frequency alpha-three."

While she did that, Dr. Lundox said, "All systems and equipment are deactivated and in safe-mode. Should we drop security doors and activate security systems?"

"Good reminder, Dr. Lundox," I said. "Give us a moment." Even before I finished, Dr. Goldsen had raised a direct Umbelgarri feed onto a corner of the display.

I expected a translation to appear. It didn't. I didn't require it. During the process to ensure my brain's neural functions emerged intact after enduring the Cranaltar, the Umbelgarri had inserted the ability for me to read and interpret their visual language. One of their thralls said it was necessary for the process to succeed. So, I watched, interpreting the shifting mosaic patterns of colors that comprised Umbelgarri communication, and felt my stomach tighten. *Ground assault imminent*. That's what the Umbelgarri said. The two trailing capital ships must be troop transports. Assault ships equipped with ground assault pods or shuttles.

My thoughts shifted from surviving a bombardment to surviving invading waves of insectoid Stegmars backed by reptilian Crax. I recalled their defense screens and armored elite Crax warriors. "The Io colony has fourteen security specialists. How many Colonial Marines. A platoon?" I was pretty sure, but wanted verification. Asking Dr. Goldsen wasn't likely to provide an answer, and contacting Guymin? Well, we had what we had. None were going to show up and support us here.

"Not very many, Mr. Keesay," Dr. Goldsen responded, still not using my proper title. "Military stationing is not my area. Why do you ask?"

"Assault ships," I said. "The rows of giant rivets lining those two unknown capital ships are drop pods."

"That verifies what you had suspected?" she asked, bracing herself, knowing the answer. Until that moment, I think she'd intellectually recognized the possibility, but the consequences just struck home. Not only for her, but several others huddled around the desk screen.

"They're upgraded Stegmar assault ships. That means Stegmar Mantis shock troops. They intend to invade the colony."

Dr. Goldsen adjusted her wire-rimmed glasses with one hand while absentmindedly searching through a lab coat pocket with her other hand. "To what purpose that bombardment couldn't achieve?"

"We're pretty far underground. Umbelgarri construction. Ensure destruction of the Umbelgarri sector, this research facility. Capture scientists and critical personnel, both human and Umbelgarri?" I shrugged. Thinking of Pluto, I said, "Or a diversion to draw ships in the solar system from a primary objective. Not counting Pluto, we may be the recipients of an additional, secondary attack. A diversion."

Over my com-set, Dr. Goldsen's system, and the public intercom, the same female voice of Colony Command announced, "Enemy ground assault imminent. Enact Delta Four Four. Prepare to repel ground assault."

Dr. Goldsen reached over to a corner of her desk screen and cancelled flashing red lights throughout the research lab. "Security Specialist Keesay," she said with grim resignation, "I am placing you in charge of our defense. Defense of this research facility."

CHAPTER 6

There was time before our ships, few that they were, engaged the oncoming Crax taskforce. Engaged as opposed to intercepted as it appeared the defenders were willing to risk Jupiter's gravitational pull, limiting their speed and acceleration, in exchange for Io's defense satellites and surface-to-space defenses. Either way, I figured they were outgunned. We had one capital ship, an Umbelgarri battle cruiser. It was probably superior to any single Crax ship on approach, but it was our only capital ship. The support ships—two police cutters and one gunboat—couldn't even be classified as escorts along the lines of a frigate or destroyer. The technology they employed, including engines, maneuverability, targeting and firepower was woefully outclassed. And our fighters and attack craft? They'd be outnumbered by those launched from the enemy heavy carrier. Beyond that, ours would be like World War II era propeller-driven fighters facing early 21st century jet fighters.

No messages from Pluto. The early warnings had to be from message rockets that could condense space, delivering the information faster than the speed of light. It'd be four hours before any old-style radio transmissions would reach Jupiter and the colonies on her orbiting moons.

The battle around Pluto was already over. How long would the battle for Io last? Would it be over before reinforcements arrived?

I'd assigned everyone to their defense positions, paired with people they knew best, hoping that would encourage them to stand and fight.

The Cranaltar Research Facility was pretty far down, so we wouldn't be the first area in the colony attacked. Maybe the enemy would focus on penetrating the Umbelgarri sector, and ignore us? I shook my head, knowing that wasn't in the cards.

"Have we missed something?" Dr. Chahal asked, standing to my right as we gathered around Dr. Goldsen's desk.

"Probably," I said. "We'll know, doubtless when it's too late to do anything about it."

Dr. Chahal rubbed his chin with his forefinger and thumb, and gave me a half smile.

"Nonsense," Dr. Goldsen said, standing across from me.

Dr. Chahal had suggested stringing glass containers holding acids above the door and a short distance into the main room, which could be shot by any defender, catching any attacker beneath them in a debilitating, if not deadly downpour. Having shotgun rounds, I was considered the primary defender to target them. In the end, we decided against it. The spray might damage the plastic and cable placed to catch any Gar Crax in an electrical discharge.

Instead, Tech Yin and Gorgio strung some trip cords across the area, several carrying a current like an electric fence, one strong enough to drop a bull.

We each had two syringes filled with a broad spectrum anti-toxin to combat the Stegmar Mantis needle projectiles, and Dr. Goldsen had configured the research facility's audio system to emit sound waves to nullify the anticipated Stegmar sounding. We didn't have access to any pathogens to spread in the air and infect any of the enemy that might survive—if they retreated or, more likely, overwhelmed and defeated us.

I tied my com-set's frequencies to Dr. Goldsen's desk computer to coordinate information on enemy movements. I thought it better that everyone witness events rather than stand at their posts, uninformed, nervous, and confused. A combination promising lowered effectiveness. None in Dr. Goldsen's staff had ever been under fire. While some would stand up to the challenge, odds were several would freeze up, hopefully not crippling our already woefully inadequate defense.

"Engineer Carvascious has been detained," came over the Colonial Marine frequency. "He's been turned over to an Intel rep."

They'd repaired the sabotaged generators and they were ready to go online. The interrogation tied Carvascious to the sabotage effort. I figured it was now up to Guymin to determine extent of guilt and if Carvascious knew anything else. And he didn't have much time to do it. I imagined him right now pumping drugs into her veins to get her to talk.

Heartwell, a sadistic CGIG lawyer had tried that with me. Fortunately, months before, Deputy Director Karlton Simms had injected me with a drug cocktail meant to counter such measures. I hoped Carvascious didn't have a similar cocktail running through her veins. Or a latent Crax device imbedded in her body that might be activated by interrogation drugs, or something else—I didn't know the parameters or how they worked—that would release a catalyst, turning her blood into a caustic fluid able to devour her body in a matter of seconds.

A horrid way to die. There was no question about that. I'd seen it more than once. It reminded me how life and death our struggle against the Crax was. Battling against enslavement, if not extinction, of the human race.

I smiled and nodded to Gorgio and then to Yin. I didn't have to say anything. They knew they'd contributed to the colony's defense.

The next call over my com-set came from the defending gunboat. "Colony Command, this is *Thor's Thunder*. Crax jamming has commenced. Unable to reach Alpha Squadron. Communication Protocol B19 in effect."

Everyone looked to me for a translation. "I don't know Protocol B19's specifics. Unquestionably it dictates countermeasures for set levels of communication disruption without openly detailing it." I looked around. "Communications are encrypted but there might be another traitor willing to transmit intelligence info to the approaching enemy."

Scratching behind my ear, I added, "My guess is that Colony Command is sending and receiving with Umbelgarri assistance."

The captain of *Thor's Thunder* reported, "Enemy rounding the horizon. Thirty-nine seconds, they will be within extreme weapons range."

"Alpha Squadron, remain in reserve," Colony Command ordered. "Wait for the Umbelgarri to fire, then open up along with them when you get a targeting solution. If communications are severed, implement Combat Protocol Gamma Three Delta."

The captains of the two police cutters, *Blue Star 3* and *Solar Wind 9*, and *Thor's Thunder* acknowledged, as did the fighter and attack craft squadron leader. The latter's reply came through distorted by enemy electronic warfare efforts.

Dr. Lundox asked Dr. Goldsen, "May I?" gesturing toward the command corner of her desk screen.

She nodded and placed her finger on a square green icon. "Enable temporary Level Two access to Dr. Rogo Lundox."

Dr. Lundox then tapped a few icons and selections, providing a four view display, including the overall tactical display supplemented by what had to be live views from two satellites and one identified as that of *Thor's Thunder*. The three latter views experienced fluctuating distortions. The interference wasn't significant, but I suspected it'd increase as the enemy closed.

The Crax fired first, launching three waves of caustic canisters in ten second intervals. Those came from the welded-H-shaped ships manned by the Selgum Crax. Although reptilian like the others, they were the most manlike, being bipedal and erect, their scale pattern a splotchy yellow and green, like a ripening banana. The Coregar or Gar Crax were less advanced technologically, but the warriors, being between 400 to 700 pounds resembled a cross between a human and a prehistoric ground raptor. I'd read a description suggesting a Deinonychus-human crossbreed, eighty percent favoring the reptilan parent. Their shields and combat armor were certainly designed and built with Primus Crax support. The Primus Crax, very few humans have seen, but they're reported to resemble five-foot chameleons with bulbous foreheads. Theirs were the spherical ships. I'd seen their firepower, shearing emerald energy beams that tore through the armored hulls of human ships like .22 caliber rounds through an old-style aluminum beer can. Our only armored ship was the gunboat, sturdy but small, less than ninety yards in length. The police cutters were even smaller and unarmored.

Only the Umbelgarri's silver energy beams could match the Primus ones. While serving aboard the civil transport *Kalavar*, I'd seen an Umbelgarri frigate slice into Selgum Crax vessels, before being overwhelmed and destroyed by superior numbers.

The Umbelgarri battle cruiser returned fire. Three silvery beams lanced from the front of the planarian-shaped ship, striking two of the five Selgum heavy cruisers leading the assault. The damage was minimal, but the scarred hull allowed less-advanced human targeting systems to get a lock.

Within seconds, a wave of nuclear-tipped missiles raced from their launch tubes toward the damaged enemy cruisers. The lightly scarred ships could either turn away in an effort to break target locks, or weather the onslaught, counting on the taskforce's multitude of point defense pulse lasers.

I counted two missiles each from what I guessed to be five defense satellites, one from each police cutter, and two from the patrol gunboat. Not very many. It'd be easy for the Crax defensive weapons to wipe them from space. On the other hand, the Crax heavy carrier's canister launch, added to that of the five heavy cruisers, meant 660 canisters, each capable of eating through any of our ships' hulls. Even with its energy shielding and superior point defense weapons, the Umbelgarri battle cruiser wouldn't be able to survive that.

"If they want to live," I said, "their best option would be to fire once, then turn and run."

That statement garnered me a round of stares. Most were angry, with clenched jaws and narrowing eyes. Tech Yaley's bob haircut framed her open mouth and wide eyes. She was surprised. Dr. Goldsen and Chahal simply nodded, their eyes never leaving the screen.

Colony Command must've had target lock confirmation as the order came, "Launch interceptor rockets."

Three missiles, far larger and faster than those launched from the def-sats and ships, rose from their silos hidden on Io's surface and raced toward the enemy.

"The Umbelgarri must have something to help," Med Tech Yaley said.

"I believe they do," Dr. Goldsen replied.

I started to say something but Dr. Lundox said, "I believe they will wait for a better shot. Once revealed, their weapon ports can be targeted and destroyed."

The three Primus medium cruisers opened up next. Lancing emerald energy spears lashed out, not at the opposing ships or fighters and attack shuttles, but at Io's surface. The target wasn't the Io colony. They sheared into the immense Umbelgarri metal towers, each lined with wavy strips of sandwiched metal alloys. I knew the Umbelgarri towers gathered energy from Jupiter's magnetic field. Our alien ally harnessed subsurface thermal energy, and probably used nuclear generators, but losing the towers would hurt. Lightly shielded, each collapsed wherever a green shaft sliced into them.

That overrode any doubt. "They won't be satisfied with bombardment," I said. "They're coming."

CHAPTER 7

"**They have to** get through our ships," Maintenance Tech Gorgio said, just above a whisper. "That big Umbelgarri ship, before they can try to land. That won't happen."

Nobody believed what she said, even the Systems Techs Frist and Bowser. The way their eyes met said everything. Probably the same way mine met Dr. Goldsen's.

I took a deep breath. "We'll know soon enough."

While serving aboard the *Kalavar*, we'd dropped out of condensed space just as a large Crax taskforce was approaching the Zeta Aquarius Space Dock. There we, the human defenders, had more firepower in ships and a space dock, but still not enough—even with an Umbelgarri frigate and a Chicher battlewagon.

And I'd seen what waves of Crax canisters, caustic or acid-filled, could do, and how many of our missiles the Crax vessels could take out. Io's defenders had launched too few. Not nearly enough to overwhelm and get through, even if they split into multiple warheads before impact.

"Whatever happens will be decided in the next fifty seconds," I said, pointing at the desk screen, first toward the missiles, and then the three waves of Crax canisters. Before coming into range of effective defensive fire, the missiles split into multiple warheads. The fourteen ship-launched and defense satellite-launched missiles divided into three, and the three fired from silos beneath Io's surface split into twenty-four total. In the terminal targeting phase, they all raced toward the lead Selgum Crax heavy cruiser.

Colony Command ordered, "Defending flotilla, maneuver and enact self-defense measures as you see fit. Fighter squadron, remain in reserve."

The Crax taskforce opened up with their point defense pulse lasers. With impressive accuracy they destroyed every warhead before even one got within range to detonate using a proximity fuse setting.

Groans and frustrated muttering filled the office.

Analyst Frist said, "They're launching more!"

I didn't pay attention to the launch she announced. Instead, I focused on seeing if any of our ships survived.

The Crax targeted the majority of their canisters at the Umbelgarri battle cruiser. Barrages of silvery energy beams zipped out like flashes of static electricity. Each time one struck, a canister flashed out of existence. But they weren't easy to target, shifting trajectory as they closed. Some from each of the three waves got through, only to impact on the battle cruiser's energy shield. Flashes of energy erupted like miniature thunderstorms wherever a canister released its destructive force.

Humanity didn't have A-Tech targeting. Nor did we have energy shielding.

Scores of canisters passed by the Umbelgarri battle cruiser and raced towards the gunboat and two police cutters. Turreted dual and tri-beam pulse lasers fired first, taking out over half coming their way. The police cutters maneuvered behind a def-sat, enabling the satellite's single-beam defensive pulse laser to come into play. The fighter and attack shuttles added long range sniping fire.

A third of the canisters that survived the laser onslaught collided with the metallic contents of the gunboat's debris pods fired to intercept them. The resulting premature detonations sprayed caustic contents ineffectually into space. Humanity had adopted the Chicher tactic.

The police cutters lacked such defenses. Three canisters impacted *Blue Star 3*'s hull and two survived to strike *Solar Wind 9*. Their hulls breached, they didn't survive the second wave. The third left the two police cutters nothing more than drifting hunks of metal, pitted and holed, resembling sheet metal blasted by buckshot. *Thor's Thunder* continued to fare better, having more defensive firepower and reactive armor plating that exploded away from the hull wherever a Crax canister struck.

Before the third wave reached our ships, the Crax had launched three new canister waves. The three Primus medium class cruisers began firing their emerald energy beams at the Umbelgarri battle cruiser. The battle cruiser's defensive screen absorbed those that were on target.

"They're draining the Umbelgarri shielding," I said. "Softening them up for the oncoming canisters."

The Umbelgarri returned fire, targeting the trailing Crax assault ships.

"Why are they doing that?" Med Tech Corbett asked. "Firing on those ships in the back?"

Everyone looked to me, as if I knew what the Phibs were thinking.

Through my com-set relay, routed through Dr. Goldsen's system, we heard Colony Command say, "*Thor's Thunder*, initiate offensive fire as you see fit. Enact Protocol Gamma Gamma Nine, in conjunction with the *Yellow Nine Green Three*."

The captain of *Thor's Thunder* replied, "Acknowledged. Out."

Within two breaths, the *Thunder*'s single beam offensive laser reached out, scoring a near miss on one of the trailing assault ships.

After absorbing a second round of emerald fire, the Umbelgarri again sent silver energy, targeting the assault ship missed by *Thor's Thunder*. Due to the extended range, the repeated hits did minimal damage to the armored hull.

Before *Thor's Thunder* could fire again, the Crax boosted their electronic warfare efforts. Three views on Dr. Goldsen's screen distorted digitally, then went blank. All that remained was the tactical display. Even that showed increasing signs of inaccuracy, going fuzzy in pulsing digital bursts, frustrating efforts to track the Crax ships and their oncoming canisters.

Colony Command ordered, "Slave defensive systems to Umbelgarri control."

Who exactly was ordered to do so...Io's missile defense and def-sat command? I had no idea. Was there a reason for the omission? Why relay that in the open, not a coded protocol?

Dr. Lundox enlarged the remaining display and pointed. "They're moving away. Retreating."

"What?" Analyst Frist asked. "They're leaving?"

Dr. Lundox said, "The Umbelgarri ship and our gunboat are using Jupiter's gravity to speed their retreat."

The fighters were pulling away too. Dr. Lundox must've had the same question as me. He tapped the screen.

"Ceres," he said. "The dwarf planet might be in range, if they launched with boost tanks."

Ceres had a small ice harvesting operation there. If they could reach it. While aboard the *Kalavar*, I'd had the opportunity to participate in simulations as an attack shuttle rear turret gunner. I closed my eyes, trying to recall life support parameters.

"They're abandoning us?" It was Tech Yin's concerned voice.

I opened my eyes. "There's nothing they can do to change the tide of this battle." I didn't add that there was no sense dying with us. The Crax were on a hit and run raid. Even if nothing was left of the Io colony, military ships would show up, eventually. The retreating ships and fighters could return and form up with them.

Reinforcements were supposed to be on the way. Originally I'd estimated three hours. My wrist watch showed over two hours remained, if that timeline held true.

Most of the Crax canisters vectored after the retreating battle cruiser and gunboat, gaining fast. The Umbelgarri ship might survive, being shielded, having better defensive fire, and moving faster. If even a tenth of the canisters were chasing *Thor's Thunder*, it was doomed.

Colony Command ordered, "All colony sectors, take up defensive stations. If communications are severed, resist to the last. The cavalry is on the way."

My eyes met Dr. Goldsen's.

"Let's get to our assigned positions," I said. "Dr. Goldsen will keep us abreast. Relay to computer clips, via hardwire plug in." When eyebrows raised, I added, "If there are any enemy sympathizers, we don't want to broadcast what digital info the Umbelgarri are sending to Dr. Goldsen. Remote as that possibility may be."

No one argued.

Dr. Goldsen asked, "Specialist Keesay, before we separate, I would like you to say a few words." She looked around at her staff. "Dr. Chahal and I have seen portions of the *Documentary*." She paused, adjusting her wire-rimmed glasses. "Unfiltered confrontations with the Crax and the alien races that have allied with them. They bear no resemblance to the news vids provided by our government.

"Until today, the war has been distant. Already brave men and women perished while in Io's orbit. Died defending us."

She took a steadying breath. "I believe it likely that some of us...maybe each and every one of us gathered around my desk, may be joining those brave souls lost aboard *Blue Star 3* and *Solar Wind 9*."

I nodded once, thinking back to those that died aboard the *Kalavar*, on and around the Zeta Aquarius dock, on the quarantined planet Selandune, and at the Tallavaster Colony. Dr. Goldsen was right. Within the next hour, we may all be dead. Captured or dead.

I knew what Dr. Goldsen was requesting so I combined two scriptural quotes committed to memory in my childhood. "Every kingdom divided against itself is brought to desolation," I said. "And every city or house divided against itself shall not stand. Though they stumble, they will never fall, for the Lord holds them by the hand."

I met the gaze of everyone around Dr. Goldsen's desk, focusing on her last. "May He watch over not only us, but every defender in the battle to come."

A few said, "Amen," before everyone picked up their issued firearm, paired up, and silently moved to their positions.

I stayed to remind Dr. Goldsen that she needed to remain out of harm's way. Of everyone, her brain and knowledge was the most valuable. I didn't mention that fact when she argued, keeping her voice down to a harsh whisper.

I gripped her shoulder. "You put me in charge of security, right?" Without giving her time to answer, I grabbed a nearby laser carbine and adjusted the sling for her. "Just in case they get past us." I shrugged, forcing a grin. "I'll fight better knowing you're not up on the line."

My grin shifted to a lopsided one. "Don't fret. When they get past us, hunker down behind your desk. It'll give you a few additional seconds to fire from partial cover." When she began to object, I said, "Don't worry, it won't provide enough time to drain your carbine's battery clip."

She tipped her head forward, looking at me over the rims of her glasses, unsure how to take my last statement.

Dr. Lundox asked me, "You're thinking they won't make it?"

He stood on my left, behind the barricade facing the entrance on the main level of the research lab. Dr. Chahal stood on my right, checking over his laser carbine for the seventh or eighth time. Right on cue he checked to make sure he could easily pull a replacement battery clip from his pocket should the inserted one get drained. My reassuring nod acknowledged his common sense precaution. The positive gesture appeared to relieve a small fraction of his nervousness.

"Who?" I asked Dr. Lundox while listening to the radio chatter Dr. Goldsen broadcasted throughout the lab. "The Crax down here to the lab?"

Dr. Lundox shook his head. "No, ships from Earth, to drive off the Crax."

"Oh, I think they'll make it, Doctor. Just not in time for us down here in the lab."

Dr. Chahal flashed a smile. "But it is your intention to make it difficult for them anyway?" It wasn't a question.

"We will, Doctor." I glanced over my shoulder, toward the office. "Or that's the plan."

From behind, Systems Analyst Bowser shouted, "They're opening up!"

My com-set picked up feeds from several surviving ground colony cameras showing the enemy on approach. Purely optical tracking hardwired to computers was hard to jam at the source.

The Primus medium cruisers fired several emerald energy bursts. They struck just beyond the landing bay.

"That's where they housed the tri-beam laser," Bowser said. "I was part of the team that installed it six months ago."

Not good, I thought. Good chance some Crax sympathizer had provided them intel. Through my ocular I watched the Umbelgarri ground defense exchange fire with the closing Primus cruisers. The fire was hot and fast from both sides. The Umbelgarri silver beams scored several hits that penetrated both shielding and armor, crippling one of the cruisers before the ground stations were silenced.

"Special Agent Keesay," came over my com-set, a frequency not set for general broadcast.

"Go ahead, Agent Guymin."

"I have obtained information indicating a beacon has been planted in the research lab. Although dormant, it will go active once the Crax gain entry to the colony."

"Acknowledged. Any additional information. How to find or foil it?" I looked around. "Wait." Knowing that finding such a device was beyond me, I grabbed Dr. Lundox's shoulder and then pointed to Systems Analyst Bowser, and waved him toward us. "Special Agent Guymin, coordinate with Dr. Rogo Lundox and Systems Analyst Eric Bowser."

"Acknowledged, Keesay. Out."

Lundox and Bowser both put their hand to their ear, indicating incoming communication. "More fun," I said to Dr. Chahal. He gave me a half smile and then checked the safety on his carbine.

Analyst Frist moved up to take Bowser's place. He and Lundox moved into Dr. Goldsen's office.

I nodded to her and glanced at Med Techs Corbett and Yaley up on the left-hand second tier and then to Maintenance Techs Yin and Gorgio up on the right. Everyone on the second tier was armed with MP carbines. Corbett and Yin each had one of my fragmentation grenades. They'd have the best angle—above and to the side—to get behind any Crax personal energy shields.

One by one, all four second tier defenders met my gaze and gave me a thumbs up.

The radio chatter increased as the Crax bombarded the surface. In addition to the ground defenses, they destroyed the def-sats. Selgum Crax canisters rained down on the landing bay, eating through its metal shielding. Primus Crax sent emerald beams down, presumably slicing through ground and metal, creating access to the Umbelgarri area.

The radio chatter went offline for several seconds. "EMPs," announced Colony Command. "Effects negligible."

I knew a little about electro-magnetic pulses. I used to carry two shotgun-fired popcorn nukes, calibrated for enhanced EMP effect. Military equipment was always hardened against it. Civilian computers and equipment generally wasn't. But orbiting Jupiter and the magnetic field it generated, just about everything on the Io colony had to be shielded. Hopefully the Crax wouldn't be able to reconfigure their EMPs to take advantage of any gaps in the protection.

The massive enemy assault ships took up station over the colony area, spitting out pod shuttles that were tiny in comparison. The riveted, bell-shaped assault craft divided equally between us and the Umbelgarri areas.

"Ground assault shuttles and pods incoming," Colony Command reported. "Main landing bay, Surface Maintenance Corridors Two, Five and Nine, prepare to resist entry. Types and numbers unavailable due to enemy interference."

Dr. Chahal smirked and rubbed his thin mustache. "Types and numbers? Just say 'More than you can resist.'"

The size of the Crax assault ships meant at least 4000 enemy soldiers, based on human assault ship standards. Probably more. Although the reptilian Gar Crax were twice the size of a human, their shock troops, the Stegmar Mantis, were only three feet tall. Still, with their exoskeleton structure, one could tear my arm from its socket if it got ahold of me. The Crax might bring bulldog beetles, flying insects the size of a basketball, with a double set of pinchers coated with mild venom.

Without warning, a spray of rockets sped from the surface to intercept the enemy's ground assault shuttles and pods.

From within Dr. Goldsen's office, I heard Bowser ask, "What are those?"

The assault ships were the only capital ships in range to bring their point defense lasers to bear on the rising hail of rockets. The ground assault shuttles had lasers, but they appeared unable to accurately to track and lock on.

Emerald energy bursts from the two undamaged Primus cruisers lanced down. Again and again, and again. Wherever the rockets were being fired from must've been heavily armored, or shielded.

Images from mid-20th century multiple launch rocket systems firing off dozens at a time came to mind. They exploded among the scattering enemy attack shuttles and pods. The mini-nuclear detonations would've been blinding if viewed directly. We'd used similar systems during the Silicate War to break up Shard swarms attacking ground installations. In space, the nuclear detonations still gave off heat and radiation, but lacked the destructive shockwave an atmosphere enables. To counter that weakness, the military packed grape-sized depleted uranium pellets around the nuclear warheads. Specially coated, they survived the intense heat. During the Silicate War, the resulting heat and radioactive bursts not only cooked any Shards in near proximity, the pellets shattered the enemy in a wider circle of destruction.

Although not as effective as the nuclear-tipped rockets had been against the crystalline Shards, dozens of the current enemy's landing vehicles tumbled, damaged and out of control.

I only had a few seconds to ponder the fact that such ground defense systems placed on Io didn't make sense. The range of the rockets was short. Even if their range might've been extended, their targeting and destructive potential against large, space-faring vessels? It'd be like trying to penetrate steel plate at fifty yards with birdshot...unless someone expected a ground assault, and coordinated it with the Umbelgarri, and kept it a secret—at least enough that the Crax hadn't learned about them.

"Squad Three," Colony Command began, "move up to—"

Not only did Colony Command's frequency cut out, all radio chatter did.

I checked my com-set before running a quick diagnostic. Everyone looked at me expectantly, including Lundox and Bowser, who'd opened a panel beneath a monitor screen outside Dr. Goldsen's office.

"Specialist Keesay?" Dr. Goldsen called from her office.

"Electronic warfare," I replied, scanning for Colonial Marine frequencies. If the hardwired communications were down, I didn't have much hope this far from the transmission source. Not without node relays boosting the signal, especially with electronic warfare raging.

For a moment, the lights and other electronic systems shut down. The battery backup kicked in. Everything flickered back on. Dr. Goldsen called from her office, "Specialist Keesay, it's more than communications. Io's computer network is down. I've switched to isolation mode."

Dr. Chahal met my concerned gaze with one of his own.

"I am receiving Umbelgarri text on my screen, Specialist," added Dr. Goldsen. "My system is not translating it."

Even though I didn't know much about programming or computer systems, it seemed odd. In any case, whatever the Umbelgarri were sending was probably critical. "Can you transmit locally to my com-set?" I asked. "My ocular's still functioning."

While I could interpret the Umbelgarri communication based on color patterns shifting across their skin, combined with low-frequency sounds—the latter provided the emotion behind the words or statement and which unaided I couldn't hear—reading their communications was comparatively easy. Their written language was based on nine dots, in rows of threes. The different color patterns gave the words, and lines that might connect the dots, emphasis or deeper emotional meaning. While nuances were difficult, a simple computer program should've been able to translate the basic meaning, especially if they were sending a simple message.

Of course, maybe it was a coded transmission.

I read it aloud, directly translated. "Violent class ground, forebrain activity exchange, situation condition ongoing, electronic message route, 95.701, subordinate length tenth."

After speaking it, the signal repeated. By the second time through, I translated. The current Colonial Marine radio frequency is..." Then I got stuck. "Can you calculate the frequency, Dr. Goldsen?" I thought for a second about what I could say to help. "They use base ten, but their measurement system is different than ours. Like converting inches to centimeters."

"No," Dr. Lundox said. "They already did the conversion. But Dr. Goldsen doesn't have access."

I adjusted my com-set to the frequency. It wasn't within the bandwidth normally used by the military.

A deep voice hurriedly said, "They've broken through the perimeter defense, spreading beyond the landing bay." In the background MP fire and shouts, cries of surprise and pain. Explosions and the Stegmar Mantis sounding. Even through the radio transmission the vibrant, agitating clicking caused me to clench my teeth. Up close and live it was like nails scratching down a chalkboard to a factor of ten.

Scientists believe the Stegmar sounding originated to flush or herd prey. It didn't herd humans. It unnerved and disabled them. Most fell to the ground, covering their ears in the fetal position.

Even the muted sounding emanating from my earpiece caused Dr. Chahal to instinctively step away from me.

"They've broken out of the landing bay," I said, loud enough for everyone in the research lab to hear. "Stegmar are sounding."

I listened some more to the radio chatter. "They're using EMP grenades." A minute later I added, "Chemical weapons. Grenade released. Inhalant. The Marines have filtering masks."

The chatter remained sporadic and confused. "We're hardly able to slow them. Overwhelming numbers. Mostly Stegmars with carbines firing needles coated with paralyzing agent, backed by Gar Crax with energy shields. Some armored elites. Standard Crax combat halberd, firing acid projectiles.

Molecular saw blades."

I kept my voice steady despite my growing concern. "Available antidote to Stegmar chemicals appears moderately effective."

Then the signal began breaking up before ending. "I've lost it," I said, adjusting my com-set, trying to reacquire or acquire another signal. "Probably Crax interference."

Everyone looked worried. Anxious and worried.

"What can we do about the chemical weapons?" I asked. "Do we have any surgical masks?"

Dr. Goldsen and Lundox exited her office. "It is doubtful that will offer any protection," she said.

Dr. Chahal spoke up. "What about the cascading ionizers? There are two mounted above the Cranaltar IV's probing apparatus."

"If we keep an overpressure of air," Dr. Lundox said, "what doesn't get ionized should get blown out."

"What's the point?" Analyst Frist asked. "The Marines can't stop them. What makes you all think we can?"

Before I turned to face her, I said to Dr. Lundox, "Get Gorgio and Yin, and anyone else you need. Get on it!"

He signaled to Bowser and hurried to the room housing the Cranaltar, our final fallback position. If any of us made it that far.

"Systems Analyst Frist," I said, "the point is that we go down fighting. Every enemy we kill is one less faced by the next group of humans they attack. Call it attrition. Call it desperation, call it being dumb sons of bitches who don't know they're beat. Going down fighting."

She fought back tears. Tears of fear, maybe regret, maybe resignation.

Dr. Chahal chimed in. "They want to make humanity an extinct species." He gripped his carbine. "I am not a violent person. My belief system instructs me to avoid killing and avoid war whenever possible. But war is permissible when confronting evil. The Crax, they are evil."

Even as Dr. Chahal spoke, I thought about Agents Guymin and Vingee? They'd fight, but were they already dead? I thought of my mother and brother on Earth, and my cousin Oliver, serving as a gunner aboard an armed freighter.

We didn't have long, that was certain. "Hurry up!" I shouted.

Analyst Frist slung her carbine and quietly said, "I'll go help."

"Dr. Goldsen," I said, "I need you in your office. We may only have an instant of surveillance when they reach the hallway."

She nodded once, and fiddled with her glasses before hurrying back to her desk.

Tech Yin ran past me, lugging a toolbox. "They've almost got them. I'm working on electrical hookups. Where do you want them?"

"How do they work?" I asked.

Dr. Chahal said, "If I may, Specialist?"

"Yes, go ahead."

"To the right and left of the main entrance. In the corner, far away from the tarp and electrical discharge."

Tech Yin grinned and nodded. "The stone floor isn't a good conductor, but there'll be an awful lot of juice flowing."

The cascading ionizers reminded me of big, old-style bug zappers with vented intakes.

A few minutes later Tech Frist handed me a surgical mask. "Just in case."

I took it and continued fiddling with my com-set until it captured a signal. Caylar's.

"Keesay, are you receiving?"

I double-checked to make sure Agent Guymin's transmission wasn't set to broadcast. "Guymin, receiving you. Weak and distorted, but receiving."

"Switch to random frequency protocol Blue Three. I'll be quick."

"Guymin, I don't know Intel communication protocols yet."

"I know, Keesay. *Kalavar* Blue Three."

"Understood," I said, recalling the civil transport's protocols and making the adjustment. "Ready."

Guymin said, "The *Hornet Nest* just dropped out of condensed space. She brought along *Soul Scorcher* and *Spine Crusher* as part of her battle group."

"That fast?"

"The Crax aren't recalling their troops. They're making a stand. Vingee and I are holed up in hydroponics. They've pinned us, those of us that are left, and moving on toward you, and our allies."

"Understood. What are they sending?"

"Close to everything."

"How long?"

"They may not know the most efficient way, but they'll find you."

"Understood. We'll hold. Out."

I relayed everything I'd learned to the lab's defenders. Knowledge of Earth's powerful task force buoyed hopes. "Any last questions?" I asked.

"Specialist!" Dr. Goldsen's voice cracked. "They're down the hall. Surveillance just went down."

"What did you see?"

She sent it to my ocular. A Gar Crax with a halberd and battle harness holding varied equipment, including bulbs that I guessed were grenades. A bulldog beetle clung to the leader's left shoulder. He was leading a squad of fifteen Stegmar Mantis. One, holding a fist-sized computer, pointed up at the camera. The Crax pointed its halberd at the camera, releasing at least one burst of acid pellets. On target.

CHAPTER 8

We had two surveillance cameras left. Once we brought one on line, if it hadn't already been detected and destroyed, we'd only get a few seconds. Waiting blind was nerve-racking to me, and I'd been in combat before. Each second that ticked past felt like a week. I checked my watch. One minute and twenty seconds.

Adjusting my ocular, I said, "Dr. Goldsen, do you have the sounding-nullifying audio file ready?" Nobody had one of the contact lens oculars. Ones that could function despite the fluctuations in the Jupiter-influenced magnetic field around Io were prohibitively expensive.

Calm flowed through Dr. Goldsen's voice as she answered, "Affirmative, it is."

We didn't want to start the audio to nullify the Stegmar sounding until necessary. A trial run proved to be annoying. Thuds, like a fist on a refrigerator door, coupled with an undulating squeal. Listening to that, tense as everyone was, would be bad on multiple levels.

In addition to the surgical masks, we each inserted ear plugs, those used around loud machinery. Everyone's I-Tech communication chip implants would still function. I had my headset, so I could only plug one ear. But I'd faced the sounding before. That's what I told myself.

I rechecked the sound dampener attached to my watch. It was set to muffle my shotgun and revolver's blasts. One minute forty seconds since the first camera had been shot out.

"Okay, Dr. Goldsen. Activate Camera Two."

She did. Her computer relay showed a Gar Crax using its shield to push the slippery gel aside. There were three other Gar Crax with combat harnesses and weapons, and at least thirty Stegmar Mantis warriors standing against the walls. A Selgum Crax stood near the entry door, affixing some sort of metallic boxes and tubing on it. A Stegmar stood on each side, holding their sub-machinegun-like weapons ready. The Stegmars resembled mottled green and gray praying mantises wearing leather harnesses, standing on their four hind legs, holding their guns with the front two appendages. They had wings and could fly for short distances, which might allow them to reach the lab's second tier. Prepping the defenders, I warned about that possibility three times. But I'd warned about many potential threats.

Shoulder-mounted personal lights illuminated the hallway.

It took less than three seconds to take that all in. "Shut it down." A Gar Crax was already raising its halberd toward the distant camera. I should've just had it flicked on and off and reviewed what was captured in that instant.

"Gorgio," I called. "Turn on the corridor lights, now. All of them." I wanted to get the Selgum technician near the door. Maybe burn up its equipment too.

"Dr. Goldsen," I said, "turn on Camera Two again."

After a few breaths, she replied, "It isn't responding, Specialist."

Thinking that the Crax would be busy dealing with flames, I asked, "Can you flick Camera Three on and off and capture something. Fast enough that they won't detect it."

"I shall try, Specialist."

Dr. Chahal glanced at me before checking his laser carbine again. Dr. Lundox glared at the door, jaw clenched and his laser carbine's barrel resting under the open drawer of a steel cabinet. It provided a portal in our barricade to shoot through.

Above to my left, Med Techs Yaley and Corbett leaned close to each other, talking, their MP carbines held loosely. And across from them, Maintenance Techs Gorgio and Yin both had their MP carbines trained on the door. I turned and nodded to analysts Bowser and Frist, standing beside the entrance to Dr. Goldsen's office. They were our reserves, armed with MP pistols and carbines. Dr. Goldsen had her laser carbine sitting within reach on her desk.

Not very much firepower to hold back all I saw, undoubtedly with more on the way. It would take time for the *Hornet Nest*'s task force to punch through. If it could, it'd take time for Colonial Marines to fight their way down to us—if the task force brought Colonial Marines in sufficient number.

"I have something, Specialist. Shunting it to your ocular."

What I saw, I didn't like. The Selgum was on the floor, writhing, as were a dozen Stegmar Mantises. But I also saw two elite Crax, in body armor. They were like plate armored medieval knights, and immune to my shotgun and revolver, even my AP rounds. Medium duty lasers and MP rifles wouldn't penetrate the armor. Even the eye crystals, I suspected, were protected by a localized energy shield.

"We took out a Selgum tech and a bunch of Stegmars," I shouted. "That'll delay them. There's also two armored elite Crax. We need to save our door surprise for them. Other than my bayonet, we've got nothing that can penetrate their armor." Awkward as it might prove to be firing from behind the barricade, I pulled and fixed my bayonet. "Unless any sharpshooters can hit their helmet's eye crystals in quick succession."

Three or four minutes passed. Dr. Chahal wiped several beads of sweat from his brow. "Waiting is always the hardest," I told him with a friendly grin.

"While my knowledge on the topic may be limited, Specialist, newscasts suggest dying while fighting the Crax isn't all that difficult to achieve." He winked at me and then returned his attention to the doors.

"Let's not be achievers," I said, thinking about asking Dr. Goldsen to attempt another flash view of the corridor.

Dr. Lundox chimed in, "Agreed." His voice held strain, detectable even through his surgical mask.

"Every minute we wait," I started to say to everyone, but never got to finish my thought.

A hole the size of a softball punched through the bottom of the armored door. A faceted sphere the size of my fist shot through immediately after, rising in a zig-zag motion.

"Take it out!" I began firing my shotgun even as I shouted. It had to be some sort of surveillance bot.

Caught in our hail of fire, the small bot shuddered before dropping to the floor. Yin or Gorgio must've scored more hits. A splash of light formed around it as Lundox's laser was on target. Buckshot from my third shotgun blast penetrated its depleted shielding, slamming it against the wall near the door. It sparked two or three times before coming to rest, now covered in slick gel.

"Doctor," I said. "Start up our new wall hangings." They might hear me outside, and Dr. Goldsen would know what I meant.

"Started, Specialist."

How much of a picture they got, I couldn't be sure. "Shift your positions a step or two," I said into my com-set, hoping their ear implants continued to receive despite the Crax's proximity. I reloaded three buckshot shells.

Everyone including me moved to our secondary forward position.

Chahal sent a laser blast through the hole in the door. "Just keeping them on their toes," he said.

A buzzing, sizzling sound came from the entry. Smoking outlines showed where acid was eating through the doors.

"We don't want those falling inward," I said, more to myself than anyone else before firing my shotgun. Everyone else opened up on the doors along with me.

Their fire, especially the lasers, wouldn't help much. It didn't matter. We'd run out of living bodies long before we ran out of bullets or battery power for the lasers. After a few seconds the carved-out door sections lurched back, tipping away from us as they fell. Micro explosives, timed with the acid cutting, detonated a second too late for the Crax's purposes, sending them spinning and slamming into the frames before dropping in the doorway.

Everyone stopped shooting, waiting to see what would happen next. I hated reacting instead of causing the Crax to react, but we weren't in any position to change that.

Two grenades were lobbed in. The first was cylindrical and metallic. The second was bulbous with an opaque plastic covering. I'd already targeted the first and hoped someone got the second. Buckshot wasn't good for shooting small targets. Still, one 00 shot struck the cylindrical device, sending it spinning to ricochet off the door frame. Before hitting the floor it detonated with a flash.

The lab's lights dimmed, but only for a half second. Maybe the lab's hardened wiring and equipment was able to resist. Maybe I damaged the EMP grenade before it released its pulse. The bulbous grenade in front of us was hissing, spraying its chemical contents.

Chahal and Lundox were firing at it, hitting it twice and silencing it. Another bulbous grenade came in. This had shielding that resisted several laser bursts and one of my shotgun blasts.

I held my breath, thumbing shells into my shotgun and feeling the overpressure of air going past, carrying the enemy's aerosol chemical through the doorway and into the corridor. What wasn't blown out was being captured and zapped by the cascading ionizers. Or so I hoped because I had little faith in our surgical masks.

Involuntarily, I tensed and gritted my teeth. The Stegmar predatory sounding. The intense, agitating clicking tore at my concentration, calling for me to panic—to run.

I unsteadily held my shotgun ready, aimed toward the opening. To my left and right, Lundox and Chahal were trying to do the same. The enemy was coming.

Dr. Goldsen's audio program reverberated through the room, deadening most of the predatory sounding's effects. When fighting the Stegmar on the *Kalavar* and on Tallavaster, I had a CNS modulator affixed to my neck and spine. It cancelled the effect. Eighty percent effectiveness would have to do. If we could break the Stegmars, their sounding would falter.

A wave of the mantis warriors rushed into the room, at least a dozen, most running, with a few flying. They fired their Uzi-shaped guns, spraying the room with needle projectiles. Those on the ground skidded and slipped on the gel, slowing them and causing their aim to go wide and high.

Goldsen's staff returned fire, pouring it on. I emptied my shotgun. Dr. Lundox fell beside me, clumsily plucking at several needles buried in his face and left hand. A flying Stegmar made it to our barricade. I caught it on the end of my bayonet as it dove, and tore through its thorax, sending it flopping to the floor behind us.

After injecting himself with a dose of Stegmar antitoxin, Dr. Chahal gave two injections to the fallen Lundox before helping him pluck the dozen needles buried in his skin.

Analyst Bowser raced forward and took Lundox's place, holding his carbine ready. I'd reloaded my shotgun, this time alternating slugs and buckshot. "Yaley's down," he said. "Frist is taking her place."

No more reserves, I thought, hearing the sounding in the corridor building again. "Chahal, we need you on the line."

This time two Gar Crax came forward, through the door. Along with my shotgun blast, laser and MP fire impacted their shielding. Unlike the Umbelgarri, Gar Crax energy shields faced only one direction. For now, toward us. They lowered their halberds and sprayed caustic pellets our way while striding deeper into the lab, using the bottom of their shield to scrape the slick gel and fallen Stegmars out of the way. It was like an invisible squeegee being pushed across the floor.

Ducking and hearing the pellets sizzling into the metal of our barricade and the wall encompassing Dr. Goldsen's office, I shouted, "Grenades!"

To distract the Crax, I shut off my sound dampener, stood and opened up with my shotgun. *Blam*! *Cachunk, blam*! They'd shifted to form an obtuse angle with their shields to better cover each other's back as they deliberately advanced. I guessed they'd even angled it to cover from gunfire from above.

Bowser stood next to me as I ducked and shifted left. I popped up again and fired, seeing the grenades both bounce off the wall above the entry and clatter to the ground.

After getting off two shots, Bowser took an acid round to the face. He dropped, clutching his cheek, screaming once, then nothing. I ducked as the grenades went off amongst a group of sounding Stegmars moving to reinforce the Gar Crax. We had to take them out without resorting to the electricity trap.

After two explosions I stood again. The grenade blasts had scattered the Stegmars and caused one of the Gar Crax to stumble forward.

Gunfire from above took the fallen Crax in the back, leaving the other one vulnerable. It panicked, turning to spray a line of caustic pellets at Gorgio, who'd taken his partner down. I opened up on the vulnerable Stegmars staggering back to their feet.

Yin took up a new position, five arm lengths from Frist, but went down under a spray of Stegmar needles and Crax pellets. Nevertheless, the maneuver allowed Frist a shot. She took the Crax in the leg, crippling it. The alien hunkered down and called into a wrist communication device as the four remaining Stegmars crouched, returning fire, their sounding broken and silenced.

I emptied my shotgun and drew my revolver. There were only four of us up and defending. Me, Chahal, Gorgio, and Frist.

Chahal went down with a grunt, taking both a Stegmar needle in the throat and a Crax pellet in the shoulder. The former kept him from crying out in pain as he collapsed.

An elite Gar Crax, protected by its overlapping bands of armor, leapt into the doorway and raced forward, halberd lowered and firing.

I fired one armor-piercing round and ducked, shouting, "Jolt them now!" Even though the conductive gel had been scraped away from most of the tarp, flowing alien blood filled it. I prayed Goldsen was fast because the charging elite would be off the tarp in less than a second. Without a sound dampener, my ears rang from shotgun and revolver blasts. What if Dr. Goldsen couldn't hear me?

Before I'd finished that thought, flashing electrical fireworks commenced near the door. Buzzing energy surged up from the floor and through my boots. Brief clicking cries and screeching roars preceded a metallic clunk. Then everything fell silent, including the electrical current running through the stone beneath my feet.

I peered over our damaged barricade. All of the aliens were down, dead with signs of charring. No worry of smelling the cooked flesh as wafts of smoke rising from them flowed into the hallway or disappeared within the cascading ionizers.

On the ground next to me, Lundox was stirring, trying to get to his feet, while Dr. Chahal writhed on the floor. There was nothing I could do for Chahal. I'd experienced the pain a Crax weapon inflicted, and short of a major trauma center, nothing could save him. There might be something in the lab to knock him unconscious so he could escape the acid-burning pain coursing through his veins.

Guilt tore at my guts for not at least kneeling to comfort him, but the enemy could make another push any second. My only option was to shoot him. End his agony.

"Lundox, help Chahal if you can," I shouted, thinking his ears might be ringing like mine. While scanning the room and watching the doorway I reloaded my shotgun. I didn't know if there were any Stegmars or regular Gar Crax still out there, but there'd been two elite Crax warriors. Only one was on the edge of the tarp, armor locked in place like a fallen statue.

Plus reinforcements could arrive to bolster their numbers at any moment.

Above, Gorgio and Frist were still standing. Both were wide-eyed and shook up, but they still had weapons in hand, aimed toward the entry. When they looked my way I nodded and gave a thumb's up.

"Generator's offline!" The ringing in my ears was receding, allowing me to hear Dr. Goldsen. She continued, reporting, "The Crax have cut our power. We're on battery backup."

She dialed down the lab's audio system that was still broadcasting to counter the now-silenced Stegmar Mantis sounding. Without announcing it, she turned on our third and only remaining security camera mounted in the hallway. My ocular showed the back of an armored elite Crax warrior exiting the room housing the generator, heading back toward us.

I looked at the long bayonet mounted on the end of my shotgun. It was the only thing we had in the lab that would penetrate the advanced armor. Experience told me the medium duty lasers and MP carbines might leave a scratch. My shotgun's rounds wouldn't even do that. My revolver's AP rounds might pierce the crystal eyes. A next to impossible shot. If I could stab between the overlapping layers, my bayonet would reach flesh. But how much would that do to a 600-pound Crax warrior, already stronger than me, not counting what its armor added.

Dr. Chahal lay unmoving, dead like the systems analyst next to him. Lundox stood up and took position two strides to my right. I ordered, "Take

Dr. Goldsen and retreat to the Cranaltar room."

I started to speak into my com-set to give the fallback order. He grabbed my shoulder. "No," he said. "He'll just follow. We have to stop him together."

The verse from John 15 bubbled up in my thoughts: *Greater love hath no man than this, that a man lay down his life for his friends.* How many Colonial Marines had done that, fighting to keep the Crax and Stegmar from reaching us? Resolve drove all fear from me.

"I just hope to wound and delay him," I said, removing my communication headset and climbing over the barricade. "Single combat. My bayonet can pierce his armor. Otherwise we have nothing here that can stop him."

I didn't see Gorgio, but Frist stood, looking down at me with mouth open and eyes wide.

As they'd only hinder me and not the armored Crax, I sliced through several of the surviving trip wires and said, "There's only an armored Crax for the moment. If I stop him, we'll get a breather."

I stood in the middle of the floor, holding my shotgun forward, presenting my shining Umbelgarri alloy bayonet. "If I can't stop it, it'll be up to the rest of you."

Somewhere, from the hidden depths of my mind came the word, *Sit-thid-zzah.* I shouted the alien phrase as the elite Crax stepped into the doorway, halberd leveled, shimmering monomolecular blade whirring.

It raised the barrel of its weapon and repeated in a synthesized yet reptilian voice, "*Sit-thid-zzah.*"

I'd tried single combat twice before. The first time, such a warrior clipped off the end of my bayonet with a flick of its blade. If it hadn't been for the Chicher diplomat jumping on its back and stabbing it with a poison-coated blade under the arm, I'd have died. That Crax had been busy crushing me down to the floor. The second time I'd faced an elite Crax in armor, with my current blade, I managed to surprise and stab him between the tail and leg. An armored personnel carrier's auto cannon then opened up on him, allowing me to escape. The 25mm auto cannon didn't kill it, just knocked it down, giving me time to run.

We didn't have anything like an auto cannon, so I stayed where I was, away from most of the fallen Crax and Stegmars. Tripping over one of them would end things for me that much sooner. Behind me, I heard Lundox moving, saying something into his collar's micro communicator. I couldn't worry about him, or anyone else. Even so, an image of Janice Tahgs, an administrative specialist from the *Kalavar*, flashed in my mind.

I shook my head once to clear it and shouted, "Come on, Crax bastard. Let's see what you've got." Surprisingly, my voice hadn't cracked.

It stomped forward, kicking its dead allies aside, issuing a synthesized gurgle that I knew was laughter.

He was apparently able to translate my words so I called over my shoulder, "Since you all decided against retreating remember, this is one-on-one combat. Just this Crax and me."

"*Sit-thid-zzah* go short," the elite Crax said. He tipped his halberd toward me and then swirled it, gesturing to everyone else in the lab. "Nest troops, few life beats."

I laughed heartily. "Yes, *you* are going to die fast."

He stood up straight, towering above me, and then lowered into a combat stance. I hoped to anger and get him to rush me, but this Crax elite must've been too experienced to fall for that. I kept my bayonet extended, swirling it in a tight circle as I braced myself, prepared to spring. A Gar Crax could run twice as fast as any human. And his backward knee joints meant he'd be lightning-quick with forward leaps, despite his armor. I figured it had powered gears that not only increased his strength, but enabled him to move faster.

The Crax took several steps forward, hissed, and flicked his halberd, striking the end of my bayonet. I'd experienced this intimidation tactic once before. This time, instead of a few of my bayonet's sixteen inches being sliced off, the molecular blade slid along my blade's length. I used that instant of surprise to surge forward and drive my weapon into his shoulder. My blade's tip pierced where the banded layers merged and creased, allowing his arm's movement. I yanked my bayonet free while moving left, backing away. Four inches of blood showed on my blade.

Knowing my foe wouldn't underestimate me again, I went on the offensive. The crenellated sheath protecting my shotgun's barrel was made of a similar advanced alloy, but the rest was vulnerable to his halberd's blade. I'd seen flatscreen vids of one slicing through a half-inch of hardened steel as if it were cardboard. My flesh and bones? They'd resist like tissue paper.

He parried and redirected my attack, causing me to stumble.

Out of the corner of my eye, I saw Lundox climbing over the barrier. I couldn't worry about him.

Getting to my feet, I raised my shotgun, locking my elbows and blocking a downward swing. The elite alien soldier pressed down, the scintillating molecular saw of his halberd's blade biting into my shotgun's crenelated sheath.

"Hey, Crax bastard!" Dr. Lundox was standing next to one of the cascading ionizers, holding one of the fallen Crax's halberds. I wanted to shout that they wouldn't work in human hands, but if I didn't maneuver and escape the blade pressing down on me, it'd bisect me easier than a knife passing through air.

If I slid left or right, I'd lose my fingers. If I stepped forward, I'd be within easy reach of my faster, stronger, armored enemy. If I lurched back I might have a chance, or die, split wide open from head to crotch.

My shoulders ached and my knees were buckling.

"Come on, take me on instead!"

We both ignored Lundox, until I heard a *plunk*, followed by *fizzing*.

The Crax spun and I ducked, not fast enough. His armored tale slammed into my shoulder—a glancing blow that knocked me skidding across floor.

Dr. Lundox screamed. He fell to the floor, doubled over, clutching his stomach.

Dr. Goldsen shouted, "Commander Devans' folly is reset!"

I climbed to my feet, thinking, Devans' folly? Reset?

My shoulder hurt but it wasn't broken. I'd have a nasty bruise, if I survived long enough for it to form. Already the elite Gar Crax warrior was turning to face me again. With Lundox's interference, the single combat, halberd vs. bayonet was over. I flicked my shotgun's safety off and fired, hoping the buckshot might damage my foe's weapon.

From above a hurled office chair slammed across the Crax's back. More annoying than anything else, the alien ignored Frist's failed bid to hurt him.

I fired again and dove to avoid a spray of caustic pellets. My 12 gauge slug slammed into his faceplate, causing his head to jerk an inch or two. It must've thrown off his aim as the floor and barricade behind me sizzled as the pellets dissolved both stone and metal.

Devans' folly—the high voltage trap spread in front of the lab's entrance had been reset.

I emptied my shotgun, alternately hitting with buckshot and slugs, hoping to drive him back. He stood, jerking a little with each strike. My steel shot and lead slugs didn't even scratch, let alone dent, his armor. He simply held his halberd steady, prepared to keep me and my bayonet at bay.

Something like a lobbed baseball with nubby protrusions struck the elite Crax across the side of its face plate. A second hit it in the chest. Both splattered, spreading what looked like white paint across its armored face and chest.

At the same time, from above, Frist opened up with a laser carbine. Two blasts struck it in the leg and tail. No damage, but another distraction.

I charged. But before I could close the distance, the armor's crystalline eye slits glowed, vaporizing the white paint. The Crax saw me coming and swung its halberd. I ducked aside while shifting my shotgun's sheathed barrel to deflect the monomolecular saw blade.

The strike knocked my shotgun from my hands. I rolled, stood and ran, trying to put distance between me and the Crax. MP and laser fire hit the advanced armor, unable to penetrate. MP rounds ricocheted off its back as it turned to close on me.

I turned and stood in front of a cascading ionizer with revolver in hand. I thumbed back the hammer, waiting to get nailed with a hail of caustic pellets.

They never came. The elite Crax warrior strode toward me, confident of its invulnerability to our weapons. It intended to cut me down—or slice me up. Didn't matter. I took aim with my revolver, hoping to hit one of the eye crystals with my armor-piercing round.

When the Crax was two steps onto the tarp, stepping over the gory, half-cooked fallen Crax and Stegmars, the lab's lights dimmed. The whirring buzz of the ionizer slowed. The Crax stopped, jittering and awkwardly balanced.

My shotgun was on the tarp, out of reach.

"Kill it, Keesay!" Gorgio yelled. "We're down to sixty percent power. Falling fast."

I stepped forward, feeling the electric tingle coursing through the stone floor. Taking aim, I fired an AP round into the shoulder I'd stabbed. The bullet penetrated, and toppled the six-hundred pound alien.

"Fifty-two percent!"

I aimed again, for an eye. Maybe the energy field around it would be drained, or at least weakened. My first round missed by inches, deflecting off with a *dzzthing*.

From outside the lab, down the corridor, Stegmar sounding reached my ears. It wasn't very far off, closing.

"Fall back to the Cranaltar room," I shouted before gritting my teeth and trying to keep my hand steady.

Gorgio's strained voice shouted, "Forty-one percent!"

I held my revolver with two hands, took a steadying breath and fired. The crystal shattered, the head jerked back, and red blood began to pour from the penetrated armor's eye socket.

"Shut it down, Gorgio."

The sounding was getting closer.

The tingling along the soles of my boots stopped. I raced forward and grabbed my shotgun. Climbing over the barricade, I saw Dr. Goldsen still at her desk, tapping and holding her thumb against the inset computer screen.

I grabbed her by the arm, just as she unplugged a memory backup drive the size of a shoebox. "Load Unauthorized Access Virus Package One, commence," she said. "Full memory wipe and Overwrite Protocol One." I nearly dragged her out of her office and raced down the short hallway to the Cranaltar's room.

As soon as we were in, Gorgio keyed a pad and dropped the security door. The Stegmar sounding didn't penetrate the door.

Frist said, "Let's hope they don't have any more elite Crax with them."

"Let's hope they don't have any Selgum Crax either," I said. "Weapons?"

Dr. Goldsen held up her MP pistol. Gorgio had an MP carbine and MP pistol. Frist was slipping her last battery clip into her laser carbine. I pulled my MP pistol and handed it to her.

I looked around. Except for the banks of computer screens and inputs, and the Cranaltar chair and metal parabolic dome above it, there wasn't anything in the room to hide behind. Everything had been hauled out to build the main barricade.

"Only the four of us?" Dr. Goldsen asked as I slid on my headset and adjusted the mic-ocular combo. Hints of despair hung in her voice.

"See what communications you can stir up in here," I said to her.

I pointed. "Frist, take up position behind the chair. Gorgio, that alcove over there." I started walking over to the wall-mounted computer where Dr. Goldsen stood. "Tell me if you notice anything."

"What?" asked Frist. "Like them blasting the door open?"

"Yeah. Something like that." Watching Dr. Goldsen bring the backup station online, I loaded shells from my bandoleer into my shotgun. Reloading my revolver came next. My bayonet? I left it fixed to the end of my shotgun, Crax blood coating the end of its blade.

CHAPTER 9

It didn't take the enemy long to find the main lab's only exit, if it could be called that. There was little doubt the door led to us. The single activated security camera showed an estimated thirty Stegmar Mantises taking up position, preparing for an assault.

All communications were down. Dr. Goldsen couldn't reach anyone via her auxiliary station and my com-set gave off only digital static, including the Marine frequencies. Were we the only ones left? Was the counterattacking taskforce still fighting its way through? Was it repelled, or destroyed?

A pair of Selgum Crax technicians hurried forward, presumably with acidic explosives to breach the door. Eight Gar Crax soldiers stood near the entrance, waiting. Several were bloodied with bandages applied to varying types of wounds. One directed six of the Stegmars, hauling bodies of their fallen to the side of the room.

Maybe the Gar Crax's shields were drained. In addition to them, there were more Stegmars showing up. But they'd all have to fight their way through the bottleneck, and we'd take a lot of them down before they got us. Unless they used a chemical grenade.

No sense worrying about that.

I signaled Gorgio over to me. She'd been steady and resourceful under fire. Everyone on Dr. Goldsen's team had. It impressed me. They'd just lost six colleagues and were soon to die violently themselves. Nevertheless, they stood ready. Determined as any veteran I'd ever met. Not nearly as skilled, but equally determined.

We positioned ourselves ten feet from the door. Since the enemy was going to breach it anyway, maybe we could make that objective more difficult.

"Dr. Goldsen," I said, "when I say, raise the door halfway, then drop it immediately." I signaled Gorgio to kneel next to me. "As soon as it's up, you open up. Just shoot."

Gorgio nodded. Frist came up on my right and knelt on one knee, shouldering her MP carbine. "Got it," she said.

"It will take one point three seconds to raise," Dr. Goldsen warned, "and equal time to close."

We needed to delay them, even if the risk meant only a respite of a few minutes.

I said to Frist and Gorgio, "No recoil from your carbines. Take a prone firing position. You'll be able to shoot sooner and offer less of a target."

They complied without question and I helped them adjust to get into the proper position, offering the best chance for accuracy.

"Take out the Selgum Crax technicians," I said. "They're the ones trained to breach the door "

I checked my ocular. "One is placing explosives now. One is further back, to the right. "Ready, ladies?" They had to know some armed Stegmars were facing the door, weapons ready.

"Ready," they replied in unison.

I said, "On three, Doctor," and counted.

As soon as the door was six inches off the ground I sent a slug round into the Selgum Crax's boot. The Stegmars had stopped their sounding. The wounded Crax curled into a ball after falling to the floor.

I pumped, chambering the next shell while Frist and Gorgio finished off the wounded alien technician. I sent my second blast toward the nearest pair of Stegmar Mantises, already squeezing off return fire.

Frist, to my left, released a sharp cry. Her head dropped, strands of red hair covering her face. She was down, maybe dead, but Gorgio kept squeezing out rounds.

The door should've been down already.

I fired a slug at another Stegmar and missed wide. Luckily I caught a Gar Crax in the calf.

No shield.

A needle took me in the hip. Gorgio took two in her shoulder. The door started dropping. I managed one more buckshot blast before it closed, most of my last shot knocking the downed Selgum's body back a few feet. If it wasn't dead before, there was no question about it now.

Dr. Goldsen shouted, "Down and locked!"

I set my shotgun aside and placed a hand on Frist. I had an anti-toxin syringe prepared. Gorgio was struggling to tear out her needles before I injected anti-toxin into her affected shoulder. They were in deep, biting into muscle like porcupine spines.

Instead of doing the same for myself, I rolled Frist over, knowing what I'd find. She was dead, a needle through the left eye, into her brain. Nerve deadening toxin there—she died seconds after her head dropped.

I injected the anti-toxin into my hip. It was already going numb.

I moved to assist Gorgio. "Doctor, do you have pliers, anything to remove Stegmar needles?"

She was already hurrying toward us, first aid kit in hand.

And then there were three, I thought.

If they got through the door, no way we'd stop them. Probably wouldn't even slow them. But, with no energy shields? Few numbers? Unless they got reinforcements, after they took us down and found the entry to the Umbelgarri sector…their chances of getting very far were close to nil. Unless the Crax had already penetrated from another direction.

I focused on my ocular still tied into the lab's security camera. That was when I saw two Selgum Crax rolling something in on a cart. Cylindrical and steel, half the size of a coffin. On the end facing the camera was a square control panel with buttons and some sort of digital readout.

"Is that a bomb?" I said to myself. Dr. Goldsen, working on Maintenance Tech Gorgio's shoulder turned her head. Maintenance Tech Gorgio looked at me as well.

Dr. Goldsen adjusted her glasses. "What did you ask, Specialist?"

"I think they brought along a portable nuke."

CHAPTER 10

Gorgio dragged Frist's body into an alcove and covered her with a white lab coat. My anti-toxin injection had mostly worked, leaving me with the gait of a recovering stroke victim. I could walk, and maybe manage an unsteady trot without falling. I'd improve with time. Time we didn't have.

"All communications appear to be down," Dr. Goldsen said.

"If you've got any way to get through to our A-Tech neighbors, you might wanna do that," I warned.

Dr. Goldsen adjusted her wire-rimmed glasses. "I shall try again." Her fingers began tapping at screen icons, followed by typing and voice commands.

The Crax hadn't bothered to take out the surveillance camera in the lab area. Maybe this group didn't have the sensors to detect it. Or maybe they didn't care.

They were no longer preparing to breach the door leading to us, and had cannibalized our barricade to create one of their own. Seven Stegmar Mantises and one Gar Crax stood behind it, ready to fire on us should we open it.

Behind them a Selgum Crax had a panel open on the four-foot long nuclear device. I'd extensively read about the Silicate War. We and the Crax were allies, along with all carbon-based intelligent life. I recalled a journal article with a partially digitized picture of a portable Crax nuke. It resembled what was in the other room. The one they had now was smaller, but that's what it had to be. The Selgum technician was inputting commands through a small computer clip with a wired connection. A Gar Crax observed over the Selgum's shoulder.

I pulled my revolver from its holster and checked it. Six AP rounds. If I could get one into the nuke, maybe it'd do enough damage that it wouldn't detonate. Or maybe it'd go off but not fully. Just spread radiation around without the associated heat and blast.

But they'd moved it into Dr. Goldsen's office, meaning that I'd have to fight my way through just about all of them to get a shot. And if anyone was coming from the other direction, Colonial Marines, or even Guymin or Vingee, they wouldn't have a clear shot. If they or anyone were still alive.

I tried my com-set again, simultaneously broadcasting to Guymin's, Marine, and Colony Command's frequencies. "This is Special Agent Keesay. We're holed up in the Cranaltar room of the Cranaltar Research Facility. There's only three of us left, with a mixed platoon-strength force of Gar Crax and Stegmar Mantis in the main research area. No elites in view. They appear to have a nuclear device and appear to be preparing it for detonation." I took a long breath. "Device is in the main office, Dr. Goldsen's office, straight ahead, about forty yards from the main entrance. Will attempt to reach and disable the device in one minute. Estimated chance of success, as close to absolute zero as can be calculated by your standard mainframe quantum computer."

That last part sounded pretty unprofessional. But the only ones hearing it were Tech Gorgio and Dr. Goldsen.

Even if the Crax managed to fend off the counterattack taskforce, they may not have gained access to the Umbelgarri sector. This might be as close as they were going to get. Certainly Fleet was arranging for a follow-on relief force.

And, if our taskforce did destroy or force the Crax assault ships to retreat, Colonial Marines were on the way down, and the Crax and Stegmars were doomed anyway. Setting off the nuke, even if it only destroyed the human sector of the colony? It's what I'd do in their place.

From all I'd read and experienced, the Crax and Stegmar were brave and determined, along the lines of our Colonial Marines. Both groups, better soldiers than me.

Dr. Goldsen was still at her computer, trying to contact someone—anyone. Tech Gorgio stood next to a wall panel with a wrench in hand. She was hammering a plain section of wall with purpose. Morse code.

Was that where a Bahklack had accessed this area of Dr. Goldsen's lab, just before I went under the Cranaltar IV? Gorgio was a maintenance tech. If she didn't know the exact location of the hidden access, she could make an educated guess.

Did the Umbelgarri or their thralls even know Morse code, and if so, was there even anyone within earshot? I shook my head. The Bahklacks resembled four-foot tall fiddler crabs. And the low-slung amphibious Umbelgarri resembled salamanders, but the size of an alligator. Technically, I didn't think either had bona fide ears.

I'd seen one Umbelgarri from a distance. They had small hand-like manipulative limbs that extended from under their jaw, just like their thralls had extending from the front of their exoskeleton. The Umbelgarri used very low frequency sounds as part of their communication, like pachyderms. I was trying to recall if Dr. Goldsen had spoken to the Bahklack I'd seen. I remembered exchanging signals with it using the universal sign language I'd learned while training to be a security specialist.

"Dr. Goldsen," I said, "can you cut the power out there? Put'em in the dark?"

She looked away from her computer screen. "That is something I should have already done."

"Wait," I said. "Maybe it'll give me some element of surprise."

"You sure that's a nuke?" Gorgio asked.

"Odds are it is. But I can't be one hundred percent sure."

She came up next to me. "Want some help?"

"It's a suicide mission," I said.

"Maybe," she replied.

"With your numbed shoulder and my gimpy hip, it'll be interesting." I handed her my MP pistol. "The plan is for us to make it to Dr. Goldsen's office." I patted my holstered revolver. "And for me to put as many AP rounds into it as I can."

"Better to die trying," Gorgio said, "than to just stand here."

Dr. Goldsen came up next to us, holding her laser carbine. "I have set the computer to accept our voice commands." She blinked before adjusting her glasses. "There is no reason I shouldn't accompany you."

"Okay," I said with a reassuring nod. She might prove little more than a target. Maybe improve the odds all the way to a micro-fraction above absolute zero. "Let's lower the lights in here and let our eyes adjust a few seconds. Earlier Stegmars had shoulder lights. Those in there now are sure to have some, but if not, I have a penlight in my breast pocket for taking final aim. If I go down, my revolver's the only thing that'll penetrate. Thumb back the hammer and pull the trigger."

Gorgio nodded. Dr. Goldsen removed her eyeglasses and slid them into her lab coat's breast pocket. Both were wide-eyed, breathing quickly.

"I'll l-lead," Gorgio said. "Be the pin cushion, so stay right behind me."

I nodded. They were being far braver—more resolute than expected. Maybe it was a sense of fatalism, something I understood. "Good plan. Doctor, you're in charge of the voice commands. Have the door drop behind us. My sound dampener will be off. Hopefully the gun blasts will cause some confusion."

Dr. Goldsen looked at me and our eyes met. "It is as if I'm one of the individuals that played a part in your *Documentary*, Specialist Keesay."

"I'm sorry," I said, trying to think of something else to say. "Not very fun, is it."

She shrugged, her grip tightening on her laser carbine pointed at the floor. "A depressing aspect is that it appears unlikely I shall have the opportunity to share the experience with my colleagues." She frowned. "None stationed on Io, at least."

I made eye contact with Tech Gorgio and then back to Dr. Goldsen. "This is what it's like to fight on the losing side." I stood up straight. "*Nemo me impune lacessit.*"

Dr. Goldsen took a deep breath and ordered the lights off in our area.

I took a quick glance through my ocular before shutting it down. A Gar Crax and the Selgum appeared to be conferring next to the portable nuke. I gripped my shotgun and made sure the safety was off. All 00 buckshot shells. There wouldn't be time to aim anyway. My hip was even feeling a bit less numb. Right.

"What's that?" Gorgio asked.

From behind came clicking on the stone floor. I spun, my shotgun leveled and ready. Rectangular patches of colors like splotchy rainbows on computers screen approached.

Umbelgarri thralls. "Bahklacks," I said.

"That they are," Dr. Goldsen agreed.

Umbelgarri communicated through shifting colors, something like chromatophores used by squid native to Earth's oceans. I always figured their thralls' major claw bore the color shifting region due to genetic manipulation.

I translated what the lead Bahklack's claw stated for Dr. Goldsen and Tech Gorgio. "Cut energy to scaled and chitin-skinned enemy intruders. Eight and five tenth Earth seconds. Open door we installed for the masters. Six and four tenths seconds. Close door. We do not succeed, you three humans of three different worker classes succeed. Understood, sub-warrior class Keesay?"

I hand-signaled, "Understood," even as I said it, not knowing if the ambient light from their claws allowed the aliens to observe my gestures. By my count there were eight Bahklacks. We stepped aside as their claws' light faded. With a whisper and a gentle nudge, I made sure three humans wouldn't be in the line of the enemy's fire.

I set my ocular on standby. After a few more seconds Dr. Goldsen said, "Cut all power to main laboratory." After a breath she ordered, "Door to main laboratory, open. Shut after six point four seconds."

The Umbelgarri thralls were already clicking forward. Confused chittering clicks and hissing Crax commands commenced in the main lab area, followed by grunting squawks, and hissing cries of pain. Then silence after the door dropped.

I turned on my ocular as Dr. Goldsen and Gorgio made their way to the computer wall screen. The doctor had called for it to turn on but kept the lights off.

The fight was over in less than thirty seconds. With their fully encompassing shields and hand—claw—held beam weapons, the enemy didn't stand a chance.

All of the Stegmar warriors and Crax were down, severed and seared. The walls and equipment showed biting slashes and scars of the Bahkack's energy beams. The Umbelgarri thralls ignored one of their number that didn't survive. Its corpse, toppled against our former barricade, had several fist-sized holes still frothing from where the Crax caustic pellets had eaten through both energy shield and exoskeleton.

While the two of the Bahklacks were busy disassembling the Crax nuke and the other five formed up in a line blocking the entrance to Dr. Goldsen's office, a squad of Colonial Marines reached the lab. Blood and scattered contusions attested to how hard they'd fought to reach us. Their military grade MP rifles with 20mm grenade launchers, and heavy duty lasers held ready. There wasn't an enemy left standing, at least not in or around the research lab.

Gorgio said, "We sure could've used that kind of firepower…" Her voice held no emotion as it trailed off, but her eyes held buckets of tears. She turned to Dr. Golesen and they embraced.

My com-set came to life, filled with chatter. It settled on a frequency. "Special Agent Keesay." It was Caylar.

"Here, Agent Guymin," I said.

"You made it then."

"Correct," I said. "That's affirmative."

"Excellent," he replied. "Agent Vingee did too." He paused. "A lot of people didn't. Report."

CHAPTER 11

The aging military ground assault shuttle ascended from the Io Colony's heavily damaged landing bay. Its nose was smooth and polished while the boxy body displayed multiple battle scars and patching. Just like I remembered the *Evanescent Thunder*'s assault shuttle when she transported me down to Io on my way to being hooked up to the Cranaltar, but she'd gained a few more gouges and patchwork since.

Guymin, Vingee and I sat, buckled down on a padded bench, with laser carbines and armored vests secured to the walls behind and across from us. It was nice to travel aboard her sitting upright.

Someone higher up in Intel must have influenced the patrol gunboat's orders, possibly changing them. She was to take us to the new rendezvous point with the *Nuclear Pitchfork*, our long range shuttle. Intelligence no longer wanted us to be seen, and possibly reported, departing in the *Nuclear Pitchfork*. The chances of that, I thought, were pretty slim. Eighty-five percent of the colony's personnel, including the Colonial Marines stationed there, died resisting the assault. Another five percent were injured. Rumor had it the Umbelgarri and their more numerous thralls had taken the brunt of the assault, but managed to resist far better than we did.

Cleaning up, eight portable nukes had been found among the destroyed Crax ground assault ships scattered across Io's surface. Destroyed by our nuclear-tipped rockets. We'd gotten lucky.

Eight collaborators had been identified. Two were still alive, including the one who'd taken down the colony's communication system. I hoped they'd get what they deserved. If anybody would've asked me, my recommendation would include Dr. Goldsen hooking them up to the Cranaltar IV to sift their minds for information. Amazingly, her lab wasn't nearly one of the most damaged areas, at least with respect to the human part of the colony.

Guymin, next to me, was reading something on his clamshell computer clip. Vingee, to Guymin's right, leaned back with her eyes closed, maybe trying to catch twenty minutes' sleep.

Guymin commented, "Dr. Goldsen's after action debriefing has some interesting content."

"If you recall, Special Agent, I was there."

He mirrored my smile. "Did you know that everyone but Dr. Chahal and Analyst Frist were recommended for the Cranaltar project by Dr. Maximar Drizdon Senior?"

Dr. Drizdon was the famed military strategist credited with every major success in the campaign against the Silicates. His wife and daughter had taken identities as R-Tech colonists aboard the *Kalavar*. I'd helped them escape the civil transport during a Crax assault and boarding. I'd gotten Maximar Jr. to Tallavaster, where he and his mother escaped before the Crax established a blockade, followed by an all-out assault.

Some believed Dr. Drizdon had precognitive abilities. I didn't put much stock in such things, although I'd seen some odd coincidences during the time his son had been in my company.

"They all stood and fought," I said. "Fought hard. Every one of them went down facing the enemy."

"Maybe ultimately that was why Dr. Drizdon recommended that they be part of Dr. Goldsen's team."

"Did he recommend Tech Marshner?"

Guymin shook his head.

I looked up from our compartment to the pilot. From my angle I couldn't see through the forward windshield. I was sure it wasn't called that, but being an R-Tech, I'd never learned what the official name of the pilot's window in a space-faring shuttle was. Maybe it *was* pilot's window. Or view port?

Instead of asking Guymin what it was called, I asked, "Did Dr. Drizdon plan the counterattack?"

He shrugged. "He's chairman of the Strategic Tactics and Planning Committee. That's common knowledge. Whether he predicted a Crax attack into the solar system, specifically here and now? That wouldn't be knowledge shared."

I thought about the taskforce that showed up. The heavy carrier *Hornet Nest*, supported by the battleships *Soul Scorcher* and *Star Splitter*, and battle cruiser *Spine Crusher*, eight light cruisers, nine destroyers, and eleven destroyer escorts. *Yellow Nine Green Three*, the Umbelgarri battle cruiser returned to the fight, as did *Thor's Thunder*. A significant taskforce to be organized on emergency notice considering the war ravaged condition of the fleet.

All of the Crax ships had been destroyed, with two self-destructing to avoid capture. The cost of the victory? *Spine Crusher* was a pitted hulk, and only two of the light cruisers, the *Red Bison* and *Red Rhino*, survived. Over half the destroyers and smaller escort ships appeared to be miniature versions of *Spine Crusher*. Not one capital or escort ship escaped some amount of damage. How many fighters and attack shuttles survived to launch again from *Hornet Nest*? I'd have wagered fewer than a dozen.

That's what happens when I-Techs go up against A-Techs. That's why humanity was losing the war.

What happens when humans turn on their own kind? Nearly ninety percent casualties among the Io Colony defenders in less than an hour. Such treachery precipitated the rate at which humanity was losing the war.

But the taskforce did arrive with a troop transport capable of combat dropping a light regiment of Colonial Marines. They're the ones who exterminated every surviving Stegmar and Crax in the human sector of Io—

except for those few that had fought their way down to and wrested the main research area to the lab from me and Dr. Goldsen's staff. And except for the handful captured for interrogation.

Maybe the best news was that the Umbelgarri battle cruiser chased down the three Primus medium cruisers when they tried to disengage and escape. It was clear from several videos Guymin had shared that *Yellow Nine Green Three* got shot up pretty good in the process.

Being an Intelligence agent had some benefits, and I was sure that Guymin shared only a fraction of what he knew. That didn't bother me. It was more than I'd learn as a 4th Class Security Specialist.

Guymin also implied that those on Io caught collaborating were to be threatened with a session attached to the Cranaltar IV if they didn't cooperate. Something I wholeheartedly supported.

Dr. Goldsen always seemed more academic in the way she viewed the universe, isolated from harsh realities, including violence. A determined bitterness crept into her demeanor after losing most of her research team. Whether it'd last, I wasn't sure. What I was sure of was that her bitterness would affect how aggressively she employed the Cranaltar in probing the traitors' minds for secrets. To hell with how it might cause suffering while it scrambled their brains, resulting in near certain death.

The *Nuclear Pitchfork VII* was to dock on *Evanescent Thunder*'s starboard side while the patrol gunboat orbited Ceres. Those in charge of our itinerary believed the dwarf planet had fewer unreliable eyes than Io, if any of those unreliable eyes knew what to report.

We stood down the corridor from the docking hatch with our gear packed in duffle bags.

Standing with her arms crossed, Vingee asked, "Special Agent Guymin, in your experience, how often do ship captains wait in the landing bay to welcome aboard a specific member of an Intel team?"

She was referring to our boarding the *Evanescent Thunder*, and Captain Hollaway greeting us, specifically me. The meeting had been brief, professional, and I enjoyed shaking hands with an accomplished captain genuinely happy to see me again.

"If the leader of the team is who you're referring to?" Guymin began but stopped with a grin. "Personal acquaintance. You know as well as I do that Captain Hollaway met Keesay on his journey to Io." The plain-faced Intel man shrugged. "He had to meet with us anyway, finalize plans for them to trail us."

I listened without comment, knowing what she was getting at, just as Guymin certainly did.

"You know my point, Agent Guymin," she said. "Keesay was listed, by name."

"He'd have recognized our team member when we eventually met."

"Right," she said. "However, the ship's captain made a special point to greet him, because he saw and recognized the name. Who else may we come across on our mission that might give special attention after recognizing Keesay, or his name?"

She'd gone far enough. "Agent Vingee," I said, "our handlers, higher ups in Intel, approved—or at least didn't stop me from…being me. Take it up with them, because I'm not changing unless specifically directed to do so." I pointed to my coveralls' patch, identifying me as 4th Class Security Specialist Bleys.

This mission might be a long one. Maybe it was good that I'd spend a portion of it in cold sleep. And cold sleep was *very* unpleasant to wake up from. It was like suffering from the flu while getting whacked all over with a rubber nightstick.

"Speaking of *Documentary* observations," Guymin said to me, "I expected you to comment on your cover name."

I thought about it a second. "Right. While in confinement aboard the *Kalavar* I read Roger Zelazny's *Chronicles of Amber.*"

Viewers of the *Documentary* saw what I saw, and had access to many of my thoughts at the time. Guymin was one of those viewers. It was a minor aspect in the big scheme of the *Documentary*, but no reason he wouldn't know Bleys was one of my favorite characters.

"You could've picked worse," I said. "What're your cover names?" I glanced up at Agent Vingee, standing next to me with her arms still crossed. "If you have them."

Guymin said, "None literary based. A pattern might be detected." He pointed to himself. "Mr. Ronald Chaney." He pointed to Vingee. "I'm her assistant. She's Ms. Amy Long, mid-level executive for Mayfair Mining and Industrials. She'll be wearing Mayfair's company colors: turquoise and emerald green, with an orange scarf only forty percent covered in black. My tie will have sixty-five percent black."

Professionals, such as lawyers, politicians and business representatives had a visual system to identify their area, where males wore ties and females wore scarves. The more black patterned into the identifying accessory, the lower ranking the individual. Vingee's orange scarf would show she had some authority, but wasn't yet approaching the upper echelon of power and influence. It made sense, as someone higher up would be better known. Even so, with an assistant, Guymin, and a bodyguard, me, it'd demonstrate she had clout within Mayfair. The more I thought about it, the more I figured our posing as Mayfair reps might backfire on the company, causing repercussions I could only guess at—if word got out they authorized Intel reps to use their corporation as a cover. Of course, maybe they didn't know, or maybe they were paid well to compensate for the risk. Maybe Vingee actually had the authority to set a preliminary deal in motion. My hope was that Mayfair's board and executives were loyal to humanity's struggle, and didn't care about the consequences, financial or otherwise.

"So," I asked Vingee, "are you really negotiating on behalf of Mayfair?"

She nodded once. "Agent Guymin and I have been given parameters for an acceptable deal. My father designed hydroponic components. Oxygen mixers and UV filters and intensifiers. A mechanical engineer, responsible for three patents."

"So you know some of the jargon and business?"

"During summers and for a year after college I helped my mother manage an arboretum that orbited Mars. Hosted business conventions, upper scale weddings and funerals."

"Isn't your specialty numbers, personnel, information management?"

She shrugged.

"What about you?" I asked Guymin.

He said, "I was a fleet corpsman, before studying corporate law."

My education compared to theirs? Pretty limited. That didn't mean they were smarter than me. More knowledgeable in different areas. Different skill sets. They'd probably had Intel training, whatever that comprised. Probably study in relevant areas of corporate law, human and alien psychology and sociology, and advanced study in computer systems. I knew corporate law, where it related to my area of training, and I was competent with computer systems, especially for an R-Tech. They both knew who I was and what I was capable of, almost as much as me.

I'd have to get used to that.

A slight gravitational shift announced we'd reached our rendezvous point. As the *Evanescent Thunder* slowed, my com-set picked up Captain Hollaway's transmission. "IFF authenticated, *Nuclear Pitchfork VII*. You are cleared to dock. Starboard hatch. Follow the lights."

Two armed crewmen arrived, apparently to back us up, should something go awry.

I imagined the *Evanescent Thunder*'s guns targeting the disguised exploration shuttle. The *Nuclear Pitchfork* probably had at least a single beam pulse laser, and was returning the favor. But the civilian-grade weapon was designed to defend against missiles and slow-moving asteroid bodies no larger than an old-style bus. Even with a direct hit, the pulse laser would do little more than scratch the patrol gunboat's armor plating.

"Acknowledged, *Evanescent Thunder*. Maneuvering to attach, starboard hatch." The feminine voice carried a nasal tone.

A metallic *thunk* sounded against the gunboat's hull, followed by several *clank*s. The computer console's screen mounted next to the pressure door flashed green, indicating a successful docking maneuver. A synthetic voice announced, "Long range shuttle *Nuclear Pitchfork VII* has docked. Security codes match. Environmental scans identify zero threats. Voice command required to open this ship's hatch."

The shorter of the two armed crewmen responded. "Initiate sequence to open Docking Hatch Two."

After three short warning beeps, the metal hatch shifted inward and then slid to the left. A second riveted door rose like a curtain, into a slot above.

A final set of warning beeps sounded before the crewman ordered, "Complete sequence to open Docking Hatch Two."

A smaller, rectangular section, with obvious reinforcing metal bands, clicked and then opened inward on three hinges, like an old-style naval vessel door. Four-inch thick, layered armor plating was evident.

I hefted my duffle bag.

Guymin asked, "In a hurry?"

The *Nuclear Pitchfork*'s pilot stood in the doorway, hand resting on a holstered MP pistol. Her hair, the color of fall wheat mixed with strands of gray, was bound with a glowing neon-green band into a single ponytail hanging over her left ear. She was maybe an inch shorter than me, which was far below average for an I-Tech. The crow's feet around her hazel eyes indicated the gray wasn't cosmetic—unless the wrinkles were cosmetic, too. A fashion rarely seen, and usually indicated someone who was either uncaring of revealing their age, or someone interested in drawing attention to themselves. I was hoping our pilot was the former, rather than the latter. The glowing green band made me wonder.

The burly man behind her could moonlight as a bouncer. His dark skin complemented his orange coveralls, identifying him as the shuttle's engineer. His thick eyebrows provided the only hair on his head—besides eyelashes. He held a medium duty laser carbine.

Were they expecting trouble?

The pilot pulled a rectangular, metallic object from her belt. Despite the deft movement, I spotted a small screen filled with icons before she presented the optical scanner mounted opposite it.

"You're apparently eager to be first, Specialist." I recognized the pilot's nasal tone from the previous communication. After a shrug I stepped forward with my shouldered duffle bag and shotgun and turned my head, exposing my V-ID.

A quick scan and a nod. "Welcome aboard, Specialist Keesay." She signaled me past. "Who's next?"

The *Nuclear Pitchfork* was about the length and width of an old-style mobile home, boxy in shape, but it had two levels. Most of the bottom front housed the cascading atomic engine needed to condense space and the rear held the engine area, consisting of fuel tanks for the two standard thrust engines, and their accompanying controls. A small room housing environmental controls and the backup systems took up space nearly equal to our storage area. A tiny closet of a room with four sleeping shelves and associated medical support caught my attention during the brief tour. Otherwise there was a small recreational area above the engineering and fabrication room, near the kitchen. Other than several private quarters and the pilot and copilot's seats, there were ventral and dorsal turret mountings, each housing a single-beam pulse laser.

I didn't catch all said during the engineer's hasty tour, but I did note the disguised shuttle's cascading atomic engine's condensation factor. If she had high quality standard thrust shuttle engines, and the 525k to one condensation engines, she'd travel equivalent to almost 110 times the speed of light. By my basic calculations, with the *Evanescent Thunder*'s superior thrust engines but inferior condensation of space factor, she might be barely over 100 times the speed of light. Unless the *Evanescent Thunder* also had upgraded thrust engines.

Guymin probably knew.

In any case, I figured we'd arrive at the 70 Virginis System in about 28 weeks, with the trailing patrol gunboat arriving about two weeks later.

"Still has that new shuttle smell," I mentioned to Vingee as I unpacked my duffle bag.

She was busy doing the same. "Technically, it's a refurbished smell. But yeah."

"Maybe Pilot Dvoracek keeps some of it in a spray bottle."

"Spray bottle?" Vingee shook her head. "Thanks for giving me the top bunk."

Our room, or compartment, was cramped and she'd have to hunch over to sit in her bed. "Easier for you to climb," I said. "And less likely you'd bump your head sitting up." When she didn't say anything while hanging her two suits adorned with Mayfair insignias in her locker, I added, "Plus, I consider dangling feet as desirable decorative accoutrements."

"Careful, Keesay. Your use of big words like that, especially when my 'decorative accoutrements are dangling,' might cause my leg to twitch, earning you a fat lip."

Our shared quarters sported light gray walls with metallic trim, and less than fifty square feet. Good thing the beds folded up into the wall.

"Right," I said. "Better than hot bunking."

After securing my shotgun on a wall mount next to my bed, I asked, "Can this shuttle's environmental system and stores support five for thirty weeks?" It was a little more than I calculated to reach 70 Virginis.

"Why?" asked Vingee.

"I didn't see any cold sleep facilities. No chemicals, setups, and tubes. Just that shelved closet with medical support devices." I unbuckled my belt so I could remove my bayonet and its scabbard. No need for it aboard a shuttle. I'd keep my revolver. I felt somewhat naked without it. "Not that I'm complaining. Waking up from cold sleep never gets fun."

I'd been through it several times.

"Vingee turned and smirked. "Those are supplemental beds, should there be additional crew. We're scheduled for hybersleep." She pointed to herself and then to me.

"Hybersleep?"

I knew a little about hybersleep. It placed a person in a state similar to hibernation. It slowed down the body's metabolism to almost $1/70^{th}$ its normal rate. But the latest research I'd come across said it altered brain chemistry, causing severe depression for weeks after awakening. Thirty-nine percent of the test subjects attempted suicide. Even while under observation, several succeeded There were other problems, but messing with brain chemistry and function? Not something I cared to be a part of.

"I've read about it. Some serious drawbacks."

Vingee glanced at me with a raised eyebrow. "Official information on hybersleep. What's released remains rather limited and obscure."

"I read a lot of obscure journals and reports, or at least I did when on warehouse duty." I was pretty sure she was also thinking advanced technology related sources, and that I was only R-Tech. I buried that thought, and hopefully any hint that I'd had it.

"What do you know about it?" she asked, and I relayed what I knew.

"While you were recovering from the Cranaltar," she said, "Agent Guymin pointed me to a report that hybersleep travel had been approved for those serving in Intelligence. A diluted dose that slows the metabolism slightly less, and keeping someone under for fewer than thirty-four days reduced incidents of the potential adverse effects by over ninety-nine, closing in on one hundred percent, making it safer than conventional cold sleep."

"Oh," I said, shrugging. "I'll need to get back into the habit of reading again."

"You wouldn't have found the information in question, Keesay."

I smiled. "Maybe not. Or maybe I'd have pieced it together by combining information from several sources." I was stretching it, as anything Intel wanted to keep quiet, they generally did. But it was my firm belief that widespread reading of disparate sources including news outlets, journals, even governmental and corporate releases offered the best chance of getting a complete picture. Still, pieces of the jigsaw puzzle might be missing, even critical ones, leaving me unable to fill in the gaps.

After a few breaths where I didn't say anything else, Vingee rolled her eyes and then checked the digital chronometer mounted above the door. "Come on, Keesay, or we'll be late for the pilot's meeting."

Pilot Dvoracek's hazel eyes remained intense as she continued listing her expectations while we sat around the common area's small conference table. What stood out to me was how infrequently her eyes blinked as she spoke. Looking up from her computer clip, after tapping once to check another item off her list, she said, "In the unlikely case it comes to combat, Guymin, your primary station will be the dorsal turret. Keesay, you'll take the ventral turret. Vingee, you'll assist Axin."

Engineer Axin glanced up from his computer clip resting on the table. The central piece of furniture reminded me of a Formica table my grandmother had in her kitchen. He offered Vingee a wink of confidence.

Pilot Dvoracek continued, saying, "Secondary stations, Guymin, engineering with Axin, Vingee, copilot, Keesay…" She paused and glanced down at her clip. "Dorsal turret. My understanding is that's what you're most qualified for with respect to my shuttle."

Pilots were always possessive of their shuttles.

I nodded once. She must've learned of my training and turret gunnery aboard the *Bloodhound 3*. Aboard the exploration shuttle I'd had moderate success in fending off traitorous Capital Galactic fighters and attack shuttles supported by Crax fighters. Before it was damaged and eventually destroyed on the surface of a quarantined planet.

"However," she continued, "for the majority of the interstellar flight to 70 Virginis, the three of you will travel while in a state of hybersleep."

She relaxed her arms before leaning on the table. "If you're unfamiliar with hybersleep," she said, mainly focusing on me, "it is a less invasive and lower risk method of inducing sleep during long flights as compared to cold sleep. Until recently the adverse effects have outweighed the benefits of its use."

She checked her computer clip, thought a moment and then continued, again focusing on me. "A countering medication administered before thirty-seven days is recommended." Her eyes then tracked along her clip, indicating she was reading. "A minimum of thirty-six hours, twenty-five of which the individual must be awake and active, both mentally and physically, before an additional maximum span of thirty-seven days of induced hybersleep is deemed safe."

Her reading the guidelines didn't instill confidence. I thought Vingee had mentioned thirty-four days. Vingee was extremely accurate with numbers. New guidelines, I decided, as Vingee didn't dispute the number of days. That hinted at how new the drug was. Still being field tested?

Pilot Dvoracek made eye contact with her engineer.

Axin cleared his throat before saying, "Both Pilot Dvoracek and I are trained and qualified in administering the hybersleep inducing and hybersleep recovery drugs." His deep, confident voice held a hint of boredom as he spoke. "Once we initiate condensed space travel, it will take one-hundred two days plus several hours to reach our destination. As such, each of you three will spend three periods spanning thirty-one days in induced hybersleep. This will minimize use of supplies as we do not know when the opportunity to replenish any of our used stores will present itself."

Agent Guymin interrupted. "Do you believe resupply at our destination will be unavailable?"

Pilot Dvoracek spoke up. "Our destination, having declared independence, is now somewhat isolated from regular traffic. Critical supplies, although likely available, the cost is expected to be at a premium."

"A responsible company wouldn't want to spend in such a manner," Guymin said, his voice showing agreement.

Engineer Axin cleared his throat. "The inducements will be staggered to balance utilization of the shuttle's life and environmental support systems." He smiled at me and winked at Vingee, before pointing with a flick of his wrist at Guymin. "That schedule will also maximize the time the pilot and I will have an individual besides us awake and in the mix during what we hope is a quiet journey."

"The *Evanescent Thunder* has already departed," the pilot said, deactivating her computer clip's screen. "Even so, they will arrive roughly a week after we do."

She stood. "Guymin, Vingee, Keesay, make yourselves at home. Discuss among yourselves the hybersleep rotation preference and inform my engineer."

Guymin nodded in response.

"Departure from Ceres in three hours. Condensed space travel to commence in nine."

With that said, the pilot scooped up her clip and departed the common room.

I sat in the common room with Engineer Lamar Axin as he called up an old-style flat-screen program. He said it was a short-lived old school science fiction series I'd couldn't help but love, once I'd seen it.

"Do you think Pilot Dvoracek will ever play another game of euchre?" I asked. We'd had to play it three-handed since both Vingee and Guymin were in hybersleep. Dvoracek played well. It wasn't her competence or strategy. She'd just had rotten luck, rotten hands, and couldn't win.

He shrugged. "I haven't known her long," Axin said. "First time I've flown with her."

"What'd you do before?"

"A stint in the Colonial Marines. Made it to first lieutenant, repair company for a squadron of ground assault shuttles. Was making it a career until Intel came recruiting."

I shuffled the deck of cards Guymin had given me, along with all of my other gear, including my specialized protective cup with a spring loaded syringe. He'd obviously learned about it, if not seen it used in the *Documentary*. I wasn't wearing it now, but would have to thank him when we were awake simultaneously.

"My goal was to get recruited by the Relic Army Ground Assault Support Force. Tried to get security postings that would gain me experience and get me noticed." I dropped the deck on the table. "See where that got me?"

"Recruited by Intel, same as me." Axin laughed as the wall-mounted screen began to display the old television program. First thing I noted was that it wasn't a black-and-white show. I liked the ballad at the beginning. It spoke toward life as I saw it. The old program didn't quite get space travel right, but the varied socioeconomic levels based on who had technology and who didn't wasn't far off from how things turned out. If they'd have paired their government with all-encompassing corporate entities, the creators of the show would've been even closer. There weren't any aliens. Lucky them. No Crax.

After watching two episodes of *Firefly*, Axin went to make his rounds and check on things. I'd already clocked over six hours in the ventral turret, running simulations. Instead of more turret time, I looked up an old American western, *Big Jake*, to watch. My father had enjoyed those old shows with John Wayne and Clint Eastwood.

Pilot Dvoracek joined me and Axin watching the John Wayne western. We ate vitamin and protein fortified pudding—Axin had chocolate, I had vanilla, and Dvoracek, strawberry.

After the western was over, I told Axin I thought that the writers of *Firefly* had just moved the western genre to space. Dvoracek, who'd watched the entire space western series with her engineer agreed with me.

"Once owned a shotgun like Jacob McCandles had," I said.

"What happened to it?" Axin asked.

"Lost it aboard the *Kalavar* when the Crax boarded."

"I know another show where a fella has a double-barrel shotgun," Axin said with a grin.

Pilot Dvoracek groaned. "Not that one."

Axin frowned.

"You call it up, I'm leaving." The pilot's threat carried some mirth, but her eyes said she was serious.

I reached for the deck of cards. "Have you ever played Hearts?"

When the pilot scowled, I said, "It's totally different from Euchre. Heck, you can even attempt what's called 'shoot the moon.'"

"Anything's better than *Army of Darkness*," she said, intrigued, and held out her hand for the deck. Beginning to shuffle, she said, "How do we play?"

An hour of grogginess was better than hours feeling like you're suffering from a triple case of the Nelgaranian flu.

Hybersleep would definitely affect how people viewed interstellar travel. Whichever corporation held the hybersleep drug patents was destined for sizeable profits, at least until some other group managed to discover a comparable drug regimen. Any military contract alone promised that.

Pilot Dvoracek was in the pilot area performing system maintenance. I was in the common area, on the treadmill, working on my third mile. Axin was next to me working his upper body on the weight machine.

I asked the engineer, "What got you interested in old-style flat screen programs?"

After finishing his ten chest press reps, he replied, "Nostalgia, more than anything else, I guess. A reflection of better times. Simpler times."

I thought about what Axin said until the treadmill's angle of incline lowered. "It wasn't all good," I said, taking breaths between sentences. "More primitive medicine. Fatal diseases were more common." I pondered while Axin pressed through another set of ten. "Hundreds of sovereign governments. Adversity and one big war could've, or probably would've, ended it all for humanity. Wiped out the world."

I thought times were better when people didn't spend most of their time interacting with computers at the expense of interaction with actual people. Implanting microchips. Becoming more and more dependent on technology. At least humanity hadn't been tempted down the cyborg route, yet.

"We didn't have the Crax or their allies to face," I continued, focusing on the main thrust of what I'd said instead of getting off track. "Only ourselves. But we only had Earth. All our eggs on one big round basket."

The treadmill elevated the angle of incline and I couldn't afford any breath to say any more and hope to keep pace.

"Not what I expected to hear from a Relic." Axin got up and tapped in commands, adjusting the weight machine for bicep curls. "Only got interested in flat screen shows during my Intel training. Need something to distract you during interstellar travel. Break up the routine."

"Makes sense to me," I said between breaths. "I used to read a lot."

Axin did his first set of ten curls. "Might have a surprise for you after your next hybersleep session."

"What?" I asked as the incline flattened out. "Discover a card game Dvoracek can win at?"

Axin stopped halfway through his rep of ten, trying not to laugh. "I'm an engineer, Keesay, not a miracle man."

I sat in the common room using the shuttle's computer to review information about my cover as Corbin Bleys. Memorize the details. Become fluent with them. For me, going at memorization for thirty minutes at a time as opposed to longer stints proved more effective.

I could've done the studying in the quarters I shared with Vingee, but she was in there. In hybersleep she reminded me of a porcelain statue, unmoving. Not quite like a corpse in a casket but it made me uncomfortable. I'd have felt the same way with someone in a cold sleep capsule with tubes running out of every body orifice. It was just creepy—not so much that I couldn't sleep. Just too much for me to fully concentrate on the files.

Axin suggested I pull the cover over Vingee's head. She wouldn't notice. I told him it wasn't necessary, but didn't tell him I didn't care to do anything to remind me even more of a funeral corpse.

After it was all over with, I'd ask Vingee if she pulled the covers over my head while I was in hybersleep. I wondered if she'd tell me the truth. The way

Axin shrugged after stating my choice against pulling covers, I already knew the answer.

Once every day a person's hybersleep position needed adjustment just like a hospital patient needs to be moved or suffer bed sores. Although I watched once, the job was left to Axin or Dvoracek because they'd been trained in the proper repositioning rotation.

Several hours before my third session of hybersleep both Pilot Dvoracek and Engineer Axin strode into the common room. I was in the middle of reassembling my duty revolver after cleaning and oiling it.

Axin held a huge grin and was obviously concealing something behind his back. Dvoracek even had a sparkle in her eye, which I'd never seen before, leading me to believe it had to be quite rare.

With a tap I closed the computer file playing instrumental hymns. "What's got the both of you revved up?"

"Revved up?" Dvoracek asked.

Before I could reply, Axin said, "Remember that surprise I'd mentioned a while back?"

I recalled the surprise he'd talked about, but with me being asleep most of the time, seemed like no more than a couple days had passed. I nodded. "Yeah, I do."

His grin widening, Axin brought his arm around and presented a shiny side-by-side double-barrel shotgun. "Not exactly like the one in *Big Jake*. Stainless steel and no external hammers."

"You made it?" I asked, knowing long range shuttles carried fabrication equipment in case a critical part failed while in transit.

He nodded, continuing to grin from ear to ear. "Always looking for something to do. Most of the work was in research and calling up files, and the setup for each piece. Its springs were a bitch, but assembling it? Not close to a challenge for a trained engineer like me."

Axin shifted his grip on the shotgun and nodded toward the shuttle's cabin area. "Guymin told me about your bayonet. Made this from stainless steel as I don't have access to anything but small cubes and slats of Umbelgarri alloys.

I thought about Pilot Odthe and the bayonet he'd made for me to replace the one clipped by a Gar Crax's molecular blade.

"She's all yours," Axin said, breaking it open to show it was empty. He closed it up, extending it toward me. Then he drew it back. "If you do one thing for me."

The engineer struck me as someone who wouldn't ask for something out of line. "Sure," I said. "Name it."

"You have to hold it above your head." He demonstrated by doing so. "And shout, 'This, is my boom stick!'"

The pilot shook her head and laughed.

He held out the shotgun and I carefully took it. "I'm guessing, Axin, there's some significance to that statement?"

"There most certainly is, Keesay," Axin replied. "We'll show..." he started. Then, after glancing at Dvoracek who met his eyes with a stone-faced gaze, he continued, "Let me amend that. I'll show you shortly before your last run at hybersleep."

"Fair enough," I said, looking around at the shuttle's standard recording camera. Raising the finely crafted shotgun over my head I shouted at the top of my lungs, "This, is my boom stick!"

Getting used to my cover name, Agent Vingee asked me, "Would that be called a holster, Specialist Bleys?" She was referring to the faux leather strap and sheath holding my new double-barrel coach gun across my back. With a good stretch I could pull it from over my shoulder. I'd asked Axin about the possibility of a lug for my bayonet, but he said it'd interfere with my ability to pull and replace the shotgun in its sheath.

We were about an hour from dropping out of condensed space on our approach to the 70 Virginis system. Guymin was with the pilot and Axin was monitoring the cascading atomic engine.

I shrugged. "Sheath is probably more accurate, but I think naming it a holster is better. In some situations it may be better than carrying my pump-action shotgun, even with it slung."

It was Vingee's turn to shake her head. "If you requisition a carbon-based fueled chainsaw," she said, "I will personally petition a full mental health battery on you."

"Axin shared a few of his old films with you too?"

"He did," she replied, checking her equipment before placing her computer clip and other gear in a fashionable, authentic leather satchel. Part of her cover as an important up-and-coming Mayfair executive.

"No concern on the chainsaw front, Ms. Long."

Her turquoise bodysuit and emerald green jacket certainly clashed with her orange scarf decorated with black squares, a pattern distributed over forty percent of the surface area. The jacket's turquoise pockets with triangular flaps made it worse. I'd have suggested black triangles to match the flaps, but what did I know of fashion. My experience said, where shipboard attire was aimed at ease of identification through conservative conformity, business dress was aimed at standing out. At making a statement.

I sat in the common area with Agent Vingee, watching our approach on the view screen. Guymin was with the pilot and Axin was monitoring the engines.

The dock complex orbited the Jupiter-like gas giant, most recently named Bonnisbin. Great swaths of solar panels were arrayed across the dock complex, presumably to supplement its nuclear energy stations. The sun seemed brighter than Earth's, so that made sense.

Naming the Virginis dock a complex might have been an understatement as it appeared to have a core rectangular structure, as well as a multitude of additions attached seemingly at random. Some were spherical. Others were boxlike, while a few resembled clusters of crates welded together. Those sections reminded me of the few Chicher interstellar ships I'd seen.

Metallic braces and conduits formed a spider web connection between the various dock additions. Those appeared both planned and sturdy, obviously necessary to withstand gravitational forces experienced as the dock followed Bonnisbin in its orbit around the sun.

Studying the exterior, I guessed the solar panels might've been installed by inhabitants to avoid paying the dock for power. 70 Virginis wasn't that far from Earth. Even so, the orbiting colony was a relatively isolated one, even more so now that it had declared independence. What rules and balance of power governed it was probably still in flux.

The Troh-got vessel stationed nearby, probably a battle frigate based on its size, reinforced the colony's independence. It resembled two thick horseshoes welded together at right angles along the apex of their arches. Beautiful compared to the hodge-podge space dock it protected.

Vingee pointed to the shaft lined with spinning disk structures. They reminded me of varying sizes of wagon wheels. Their rate of rotation appeared to decrease as they extended away from the top of the main dock. Of course, 'up' or 'top' would be relative to where the inhabitants might be in relation to the dock's main gravity plate. The spinning wheel sections probably used centrifugal force to create artificial gravity as opposed to the energy intensive plates. Actually, the spinning structure was probably there before the main dock section, and the older form of gravity generation had been necessary. Maybe it hadn't been fitted with grav plates, yet. Except for energy consumption, they weren't expensive. Most vessels, even shuttles, had them.

"That would be the Celestial Unicorn Palace," Vingee said. "The place you accused Falshire Hawks of visiting." She winked. "But of course you knew that."

I did recognize the multi-disked structure. Who didn't? The Celestial Unicorn Palace's marketing commercials remained a staple, from appearing in online magazines and journals to holo-cast vids and electronic billboards. Some men, enough men, willingly travel dozens of light years to vacation with seven-foot blondes built like exotic dancers. Frequent advertisements paraded dozens of the enormous, voluptuous blondes chanting the slogan, 'Come be a stallion on our range.'

I hadn't heard of an equivalent exotic establishment to lure women. Maybe that said something about women. It definitely said something about men.

Agent Vingee knew that my accusation during my pretrial had been aimed at getting under Falshire Hawks' skin. At the time he was representing the Capital Galactic Investment Group. Initially he was also 'representing' me, as CGIG had largely succeeded in wresting control of Negral Corporation's assets. That included my contract.

Through divesting myself of Negral Corp and some legal maneuvering with the assistance of an Umbelgarri diplomat and the Criminal Justice Investigatory Squad representative, I managed to have myself hooked up to the experimental Cranaltar IV to prove my innocence. But, at the time, I had no memory of what had happened, no knowledge of the host of crimes of which I'd been accused. The only reason the criminal justice system went along with me being connected to the Cranaltar was that any accomplices I might've had would be revealed, if I was guilty.

I leaned closer and stared at where Vingee pointed. "Really, Ms. Long? Exactly what is the Celestial Unicorn Palace anyway?"

She rolled her eyes, stifling a laugh. "I hope you're a better actor than that."

"Who's acting?"

CHAPTER 12

I stepped ahead of Special Agents Vingee and Guymin and submitted myself and my equipment for a security scan to gain access to the Bonnisbin Space Dock. My cover as Ms. Long's personal guard made it appropriate that I go first. I could then observe and ensure that my ward wasn't mistreated.

Having my V-ID scanned in addition to my person and equipment, then inspected by trained security specialists went quickly, but not necessarily effectively. My equipment carried what would be classified as espionage-related contraband. My com-set matched standard model specifications, although a few components had been modified by Intelligence. If they removed the screws to my double-barrel shotgun's butt plate and examined the stock, they'd find an imbedded cylinder encasing sensitive electronic signal gathering gear. The dura-polymer that Engineer Axin used when building the shotgun appeared solid with no cavities.

Those were the only 'questionable' items I carried.

A problem the 70 Virginis colony had that would continue to worsen was their V-ID and other records becoming more and more outdated. A price of declaring independence. They could purchase updates. A constant expense, but one they'd eventually find necessary.

A reflection in the frowning security specialist's left eye showed my modified V-ID caused a corner of the monitor screen to flash yellow.

"When was your last vaccination regimen?" she asked.

Ready with my answer, I replied, "Six months, two days from today." My identity now occupied a ghost file established years ago.

"Specialist Bleys, please present your thumb."

Knowing they were creating a file on me, I placed it on a desk screen before moving it to a metal panel where a needle prick occurred, taking a drop of my blood for DNA identification.

"Thank you, Specialist Bleys." She looked over to her partner, another Class 3 Security Specialist, who nodded. "You and your equipment are clear for entry to the Bonnisbin Orbital Colony."

I nodded once and took several strides over to the conveyer that held my equipment. I buckled on my belt before examining my revolver and sliding it into its holster.

The male security specialist commented as I slid my bayonet into its scabbard, "Fine blade there, Specialist."

"That it is," I said. "Cost this Relic a barrel full of credits." I then turned my attention to Agent Vingee who was placing her gear on the conveyer belt so that it could be scanned before she walked through the scanning arch. Guymin, in charge of Ms. Long's dolly cart, would take longer. He'd have to catch up if they didn't detect the espionage gear both it, and he, carried.

Axin and Dvoracek would do their part, remaining aboard the *Nuclear Pitchfork VII*. One of the things we'd do aboard the dock is collect electronic files and communications. It was their job to break the encryptions. The *Pitchfork* didn't have all of the advanced or A-Tech equipment the exploration shuttle *Bloodhound 3* did, but it did have some, supplemented by state of the art I-Tech software and equipment. At least from what I could determine based upon my limited knowledge.

After they cleared Vingee, posing as Ms. Long, she pulled out her computer clip and turned back to Guymin. "Mr. Chaney, notify me when you have arranged for our rooms."

Without waiting for acknowledgement, she activated her clip and began striding down the sterile corridor. I took my place to her right, following one step behind.

We made our way through one of the older additions to the Bonnisbin Orbital Colony. Behind were the metallic walls painted white and the speckled white laminate floor. Occasionally Vingee and I passed plain, unmarked sliding doors framed by flat strips of polished steel. No conduits. Recessed LED lighting. It was like walking through well-maintained ductwork. Every thirty paces I spotted discrepancies in adjoining panels near the flat ceiling where surveillance cameras and other monitoring devices kept track of those entering the main colony area. The recirculated air was cold and dry, but somehow still managed to feel stuffy. Maybe too much volume pumped into the confined area. My limited experience on space docks suggested it should have been the other way around. Not the cold and dry, but lesser amount of air. Less pressure.

Using her clip, Agent Vingee switched between downloaded directions for navigating the upcoming corridors and files outlining her meetings and agendas. Whatever she viewed, whatever we did, was being recorded and sifted through artificial intelligence software programs. They'd flag any images or snippets of conversation deemed questionable, threatening, or otherwise of interest.

Nobody was heading back toward the docking facilities. Vingee's determined pace enabled us to pass around a pair of men toting metallic briefcases. They could've been fraternal twins, both tall and lean with jutting chins and deep set brown eyes. As we passed the pair I placed myself between them and Vingee, observing over my shoulder the yellow-tied lawyers wearing tie pins indicating they worked for Naill and Trapp Environmental Systems. They ignored me and Vingee, caught up in their own quiet conversations, speaking into collar mics and listening through the micro receivers implanted in their ear canals.

After ten minutes and several turns we reached an entrance to the main colony facility. A holographic image depicting a cursive-lettered, pink neon sign read: Welcome to the Bonnisbin Orbital Colony. In smaller letters just below it read: Follow all regulations and enjoy your visit.

As we walked through the holographic welcome sign, the security-glass double doors slid aside. I followed Vingee into an open area that reminded me of an old-style mall with speckled tile floors polished to a sheen, pastel walls and gray posts, potted trees, bench seats, small shops with window displays, and several restaurants, each with their own holographic sign.

This area held scattered men and women attired similar to Vingee, with business jackets over bodysuits. Various colors depicted the corporation they worked for.

Off to the left, beyond a bench, I got my first view of a Troh-got—actually, a pair. The thirty-five pound aliens could best be described as a scaly yellow centauroid cross between a centipede and a reptilian chipmunk. They were damn ugly, but not quite the level of a V'Gun, which were Chihuahua-sized aliens with a tentacled squid-ish torso resting atop a tarantula-like body and legs.

Even if they were ugly, physically Troh-gots weren't intimidating, even if their saliva was said to be mildly venomous. But, with instinctive tactical skills and advanced technology, their military prowess was another question, both on the ground and in the vacuum of space.

My reading indicated that Troh-gots breathe methane, or at least originated on a planet with methane prominent in its atmosphere. No supplemental breathing apparatus appeared to be part of the equipment clipped to the synthetic straps that adorned the aliens, and pouches that reminded me of small saddlebags.

Straps and harnesses seemed to be the norm among intelligent space-faring species. Of the aliens that I'd encountered, the Gar Crax, Chicher, Umbelgarri, Stegmar Mantis, Bahklacks, V'Gun, and now the Troh-gots, didn't wear clothing like humans. The Gar Crax elites did don full body armor. I recalled one Selgum Crax on the quarantined planet Selandune that wore a bodysuit similar to an average I-Tech human.

The Troh-gots' yellow scales resembled withering flower petals, but were certainly more sturdy and durable. The dull color stood at odds with their neon green harness straps. Their slitted eyes, each with a dozen facets, certainly took in the light spectrum differently than my eyes did. No reason their brains wouldn't interpret what their eyes gathered in ways I hadn't even tried to imagine. Alien thought patterns were so...alien. That their vision would parallel their thought patterns only made sense.

Humans held pariah status among most alien species. Our superior immune system protected us from alien diseases, especially when supported by vaccinations. The Chicher might be considered a greater risk. The two Troh-gots didn't appear to be concerned about the potential health risk.

A quick turn of her head indicated Vingee saw the centauroid aliens too, but that didn't slow her stride. Whether they caught her interest or not, she portrayed a determined business executive. Her taller than average stature and long strides did turn a few heads. I made eye contact with those that took notice of Vingee, and they quickly turned away, back to their meals, computer clips, or other business.

Vingee took a seat on a high stool outside one of the kiosk cafes and nodded for me to stand off to the side. Another executive sat at a tall round table next to Vingee's. He glanced up from his computer clip, apparently unimpressed, figuring she was one of the Bonnisbin Orbital Colony's estimated 38,000 mundane visitors. Last records indicated the colony maintained just over 11,000 residents. Those included engineers, technicians, administrators and support staff, business owners and workers and security personnel. Two of the security types were on patrol, wearing gray-green coveralls under plasticized body armor covering most of their torsos, and armed with medium duty laser carbines, MP pistols, and stun batons. The armor and lasers were certainly meant to say something to visitors, especially as a number of them, like me, were armed.

Both security men fixed me with what they thought were intimidating stares. Having faced elite Crax, I felt like a bobcat observing a pair of puffed up tomcats. I'm sure my indifferent yawn wasn't what they were accustomed to. One security specialist slowed but the second, the older of the pair, muttered something and they continued on with their patrol.

A valet serving bot on wheeled feet approached Vingee. It reminded me of the Tin Man from the near ancient *Wizard of Oz*. That film, along with a few others, somehow had remained popular through the decades and was probably on Axin's play list. The valet bot's wheeled feet and overall boxier shape showed that the designers weren't trying to replicate the old film character, at least not to perfection.

Many I-Techs, advanced as they professed to be, still carried a spot of nostalgia for the less complex and tech-ridden times within them. Some might call it a hidden blemish.

I kept an eye on the serving bot while remaining aware of people moving around. Just what a personal guard was expected to do. By tapping at icons on the bot's chest screen, Vingee selected tea and crackers with coconut paste.

Patches, and painted over welds, along with minor fractures in some of the support structures, emphasized that we were in one of the colony's older sections.

Several minutes after the metallic bot delivered Vingee's tea and crackers, Agent Guymin passed by with our cart. His next task was to secure quarters for our stay, and detect any surveillance equipment installed: standard or auxiliary but always nefarious. It wasn't that anybody, including the colony's administrative wing, knew we were with Intelligence. Rather, corporations and government entities, and presumably alien diplomats and their entourages, spied upon anyone they could. Uncovered secrets meant leverage, power and, for us, maybe imprisonment. Or death.

The same for those we hunted.

Down near the end of the line of shops and cafes, my eyes caught sight of a man I recognized. Or thought I did. It wouldn't do to keep looking, let alone leave Vingee to verify my suspicion. My ocular was in record mode. Reviewing the sequence would settle the issue—if the brown-haired man proved to be who I thought he was. The scene replayed through my mind. Gray-green security coveralls with an orange armband, identifying him as an auxiliary business associate, but for who—if it was him?

The more I thought about it, the more I was sure it'd been him. We'd met on the Mavinrom Dock while I was on layover. Then we crossed paths again, serving in the same company of conscripts, fending off a Crax invasion of New Birmingham, one Tallavaster's three colony cities. The last time I'd seen Kent O'Vorley he was speeding away on an ATV, trying to evade a Crax ground assault shuttle. I was on foot with a mixed squad of Crax and Stegmar hot on my heels as I sought escape, or at least a final stand in an abandoned quarry.

CHAPTER 13

Our suite consisted of two rooms, plus a small bathroom containing a toilet, sink, and shower with both a water and a sonic cleaning head. Two twin beds for me and Guymin. One queen-sized bed for Vingee.

The furniture consisted of a desk with an outdated computer built into it beneath a wall screen for entertainment and interfacing with colony information and services. That was in the room Guymin and I were to share. We weren't high-end, so the single holo-cast projector was in Vingee's room, along with her bed, chair and desk.

The suite's walls were dull blue with a shag carpet that had seen wear but not enough to require replacement. The padded chairs in each room matched the gray bedcovers, and white sheets.

The white ceiling reached just under eight feet with no conduits showing. That meant the suite had once been a premium one. Space dock design engineers normally avoided excess vertical space, considering it wasted space in a limited environment. Vingee was tall, even for an I-Tech, but nowhere close to bumping her head, unless she chose to wear platform-heeled boots. The ceiling's random collapse was more likely than Vingee opting for the unsound fashion choice.

Guymin had placed black tape over one spot in a corner near the ceiling in line with the entry door. Fiber optic camera, probably standard in all rooms so that the dock's security could keep track of who entered. I agreed with Guymin. Cameras in the halls would suffice for Security's needs.

In Vingee's room he'd disconnected the holo-cast projector and affixed thumb-sized devices to the walls, ceiling, and the floor under the carpet. His remote control activated them; their purpose was to foil sound receptors placed on or pointed at the opposite side of our room's walls, floor, or ceiling. Such devices could capture sound waves striking surfaces, especially waves created by speaking. Sophisticated software could convert the captured data back into conversations that resembled any standard recording.

I'd always been on the other end, trying to keep track of what visitors on Pluto and passengers and colonists on the *Kalavar* were up to but, unless there was cause, only in public areas. Ship and colony security teams expected corporate visitors to have equipment to foil basic surveillance efforts. From parts carried in two of my shotgun shells, in Vingee's personal computer clip, and within the cart, Guymin assembled an A-Tech device, probably Umbelgarri in origin. That was something Security wouldn't expect. The assembled device looked like a ceramic toadstool but with tiny metallic studs scattered across its surface.

When Guymin turned it on with his hand-held remote, a pulse wave strong as a light breeze passed through me. It probably disrupted sound surveillance as well as foiled monitoring efforts within the electro-magnetic spectrum.

Guymin shut the door leading to our room, affixed a sound scrambling device to it—which was probably unnecessary—and said to me, "You look a little twitchy today."

"Used to having my pump shotgun," I said. "And I saw someone I recognized." With a few adjustments, I transferred my ocular's files to my com-set so that it'd be easier for the three of us to view my flagged observation together.

After Vingee called up a program on her clip, Guymin pointed his remote at me, instructing the collector in my double-barrel's stock to dump its contents, what it'd already gathered. "This first," he said.

Vingee looked up from her screen. "You'll have to step closer to the clip, Keesay. Even with our equipment's compatibility, the scrambler's degrading the data transfer."

It surprised me that they seemed disinterested in who I'd seen. "O'Vorley," I said, knowing they'd seen him in the *Documentary*. "I think he's here."

"The young security specialist?" Vingee asked.

I nodded.

Her left eyebrow rose. "Let's see."

Instead of the wireless transfer, I pulled the retractable cord from my com-set and plugged it into her computer clip. With a few adjustments I sent the proper time frame. When it showed, I froze it in the middle of the half-second instant.

Guymin nodded before scratching his cheek. "That's him." Then he added, "Good work, Keesay. Not doing a double-take. Any recordings or anyone observing you won't have detected any interest in your young friend."

Young, I thought. O'Vorley was only a few years younger than me. After what he'd survived on the Zeta Aquarius Dock and on Tallavaster, he was anything but the green security recruit I'd first met.

"Since neither of you has spoken up," Vingee said, "that means none of us knows why he's here."

"If it matters," I said. "Shouldn't be a problem to find out who he's working for."

"Might not be prudent for you and O'Vorley to cross paths," she replied. "At least until we discover that."

Agent Guymin nodded in agreement.

CHAPTER 14

My main duties consisted of escorting Vingee and Guymin to business meetings and standing outside the meeting room, sometimes with other security personnel, usually personal guards, or conveying files to the *Nuclear Pitchfork* for Axin and Dvoracek to decrypt with the assistance of the shuttle's computers. Several times Guymin or I relieved the engineer and pilot so they could escape the shuttle's confines and explore the dock.

Most of the food to be had on the dock consisted of carbohydrates and proteins derived from various strains of algae and bacteria, much like what the *Pitchfork* offered. It was just that the dock stocked a different assortment of base microorganisms, resulting in synthesized meals that provided a different taste, along the lines of corn-fed vs. wild grazing cattle. Both beef but with subtly different gustatory characteristics.

Appearance, smell and taste were aspects seemingly easy to manipulate. Consistency and texture, those were more difficult to mimic, especially with meats and certain fruits and vegetables. One thing that docks did have that interstellar vessels lacked, especially the smaller ones, was bread. Fresh bread. Slices were expensive, but worth it, whether part of a sandwich, or simply spread with margarine, artificial jams, or flavored pastes.

After a meal, where I enjoyed a synthesized chicken patty sandwich and Vingee selected synthesized vegetable soup and crackers, both of us with fruit juice with vitamin supplements, we made our way to another meeting. This one was arranged to discuss the specific number and types of hydroponic systems desired, and a cost estimate for installation and maintenance of the systems. The length of the contract, Vingee believed, would be a key sticking point. The orbital dock intended to secure the equipment, observe and learn how to use and maintain it. Then they'd dismiss Mayfair Mining and Industrials' services. A cost-saving measure for the dock, but not acceptable to the corporation Vingee, in the guise of Ms. Long, represented.

Nobody from the *Pitchfork* had spotted O'Vorley. Maybe he'd departed. Nor had we seen many Troh-gots. Thinking about the centauroid aliens while we made our way to one of the older additions to the orbital dock, I asked Vingee, "During the Silicate War, it was believed that the Troh-gots' home planet had a methane atmosphere. The several we've seen here seem to have no problem breathing in an oxygen-nitrogen atmosphere. No supplemental breathing apparatus that I could see."

"Mr. Cheney," she said, referring to Agent Guymin as we traversed a public corridor, "told me that the mechanism which controls their cellular development is much more flexible than our DNA." She paused. "I think he specifically said 'malleable.'"

A pair of tan-clad maintenance techs approached from the other direction, observing the conduits running above our heads. The visual assessment was supplemented by a handheld scanner. Their tromping boots were louder on the sections of metal grating than mine.

I moved in line to the right ahead of Vingee as the corridor was only comfortably wide enough for three across.

The notion that a Troh-got's respiratory physiology could change so drastically was intriguing. I wondered if the aliens manipulated themselves through drugs, through exposure, or selective breeding, or something else. Maybe the same process enabled them to resist human-borne infectious microbes.

Guymin, who might know, had gone ahead to set up for the meeting.

This dock section, known as the After Dawn Annex, suffered from inconsistent gravity control. Not terrible, but it made for interesting elevator rides. Vingee and I were waiting for one to arrive and take us up three levels. We'd waited about thirty seconds. I figured she was going to direct me to press the call button again when the metallic doors slid open.

A burly security man stepped out, armed with an MP pistol and heavy-duty stun baton. The short-bearded fellow grunted at me when we made eye contact as he passed.

His ward, a tall, lanky man, followed him out. Upon seeing him, something stirred in the back of my mind. Anger. Bitter anger. I met the man's gaze. Something about his blue eyes was familiar—but his face wasn't. Whatever it was screamed vigilance. With effort I refrained from moving a hand toward my revolver. The tall man's gaze lingered on me as he strode past. That stride—something rattled my caged memories. The lawyer's personal guard slowed and turned, sensing something was amiss. Latent hostility emerging. His hand was on his holstered pistol.

Confused and angry, without knowing why, I followed Vingee into the elevator. "Take us to Level Nine," she ordered the computer-controlled elevator.

As the lift began to rise a familiar odor penetrated my nose. Lingering musk-scented cologne mingled with wintergreen breath mint! I hadn't taken a breath during the brief encounter. After the elevator closed, in that instant, everything fell into place. A curse fought to erupt—a burning desire to curse his name.

"What is it, Specialist Bleys?" Vingee was staring down at me.

I stiffly glanced up at the surveillance camera. Teeth gritted. I couldn't say anything. Not in there, knowing someone would overhear.

Hawks! The man, it didn't look like him. Tall and angular, but olive skin instead of white, a broad nose instead of long and narrow. But it *was* him, his arrogant, cruel eyes. Falshire Hawks! "Elevator, stop!"

Thoughts ran through my mind. Go after him? Hawks recognized me, but he doesn't know I recognized him. He could be gone—I might never get another chance.

I ordered, "Elevator, return to previous level." Maybe Vingee was right. Plastic surgery might've helped—No, it wouldn't have. *I* recognized *him*.

"Elevator, stop," Vingee said. "Bleys, what is it?"

Every second meant more time for Hawks' escape. I flicked up the snap of my holster's holding strap. I used to wear my holster cross draw, but Guymin had gotten me one for my strong side. It meant I could draw faster, should it come to that.

"We need to retrace our steps without delay," I said, trying to keep my voice even. "Elevator, return us to level six."

"Why?" she asked, again countermanding my order. We locked gazes and she relented. "Elevator, level six."

I glanced up at the security camera. Its presence was obvious. The microphones weren't, but they were certainly there within the elevator, recording.

When the elevator came to a stop I strode out, reminding myself I had hollow tip rounds loaded in my revolver and one slug and one 00 buckshot loaded in the double-barrel.

Vingee put a hand on my shoulder, gripping it. I shrugged her off, continuing down the corridor. When I made it to the first cross hall, no one was in sight. "Remember my lawyer?" I said over my shoulder. "The first one who didn't really have my best interest in mind?"

While I listened for any hint of his presence, it took Agent Vingee several breaths to recall. "*Him?* Are you sure."

I checked down the corridors again, seeing a pair of maintenance techs with a dolly bot toting conduit. That was all. I even tried to sense his cologne and breath mint odor. No luck.

Nodding stiffly, I said, "Ms. Long, I apologize for the delay. I wanted to relay a few words to him." Shrugging stiffly, I continued. "He might've recognized me and already knows what I'd have said anyway."

At that point there was nothing to do but return to the elevator and hope he hadn't recognized me. Once we reached the ninth level and stepped out of the elevator, Vingee said over her shoulder to me, "If Mr. Chaney has everything set up, show him your ocular's downloaded data so that he can troubleshoot the problem you mentioned this morning. Corrupted files shouldn't be tolerated."

"I will, Ms. Long."

We approached the scheduled private conference room. My thoughts vacillated between anger and frustration. I tried to tell myself the delay caused by Vingee wasn't the reason Hawks got away. "Engineer Axin might be more efficient than Mr. Cheney." Most of my agitation didn't register in my voice. It wasn't true but it'd give me a chance to move about the space dock.

"I believe not, Specialist. Remain with me until after the meeting."

I took a deep breath and unclenched my fists. It was better than giving Vingee a brass knuckle sandwich. Lucky for her, Intel agents aren't supposed to do that sort of thing to their partners.

After eighty-seven minutes, the conference room door slid open and the Bonnisbin Orbital Colony representatives filed out. I'd stayed outside the meeting room, doing my 'job.' It'd given me time to think. What was Hawks up to? Preparing to leave? Whatever his plan, it now included contacting CGIG loyalists and putting them on my trail.

For eighty-seven minutes I'd been tempted to abandon my responsibility as Ms. Long's personal guard and hunt for Hawks, or at least assist Guymin. I knew it wouldn't take lawyer Falshire Hawks long to send anyone who might be effective—bounty hunters, CGIG loyalists, or security officials to arrest me on trumped up charges so that I could be dealt with later. He'd done it before.

Tempting as it was, I worked for Intelligence and, as an agent, my responsibility was to the assignment, to picking up trails that led to Deputy Director Simms and others. Guymin was on it. He could track Hawks better than me, better than any R-Tech. Better for me to continue with our Mayfair representatives ruse.

Such justifications didn't satisfy me, or the urge to take action. But they kept me in place, anger and frustration brewing.

The three men and two women ignored me as they left the meeting room, smiling and chatting among themselves. Odd behavior for I-Techs, unless they felt they'd made a breakthrough in the negotiations.

I stepped into the room. "Door, lock."

Vingee looked up from her computer clip, detaching the display projector. Her smile fled as she met my gaze.

"Is this room still secure?"

She glanced where Guymin had placed the sound wave disruption devices on the walls and floor, one on the ceiling, and in one of the recessed lights. And, she carried one that scrambled electronic espionage measures. The rooms were supposed to be secure, but what if that proved inaccurate? A competing corporation might learn something. Lodging a complaint if that happened? Who'd bother to listen? Just part of the way corporate entities worked.

"Good," I said, "because I've got a thing or two to say."

"Oh?" she responded, a bit of condescension in her voice.

"Listen, Agent Vingee—"

"Ms. Long," she interrupted.

I strode forward and stared up at her from across the meeting table, polished black with matching chairs, all pushed in. "How about," I said, pointing a finger at her, "you listen." Before she could say anything, I continued. "What's our mission's objective? It isn't selling hydroponics equipment. That's the cover. And you are *not* my corporate superior."

She eyed my finger as I jabbed it her direction. "Being a team member means following my lead," I said. "Not countermanding it. And this team is here to find—"

She tried to cut me off, saying, "Not here, Bleys."

I kept talking over her. "...leads to captives. Remember? Might not Falshire Hawks, a mover and shaker in the Capital Galactic hierarchy—or at least he was. Bagging him might prove to be a giant step in that direction?"

"If he believes you didn't recognize him," she said, hands on her hips. "Following through on our established schedule will keep that illusion in place."

"You thought of that afterwards, Vingee. You had no idea why I stopped the elevator and ordered it to return. You, without knowing my purpose or reason, countermanded me. Took away my initiative. Why?"

I switched hands pointing at her. "Because you had a meeting. Because you don't think of me as anything more than a grunt bodyguard. Do that again, and you'll be spitting teeth."

She smiled, showing me her perfectly straight, white teeth. It was a fake smile, exactly what she intended. "Are you finished?"

"For the moment."

"Didn't take long for that Relic chip to reappear on your shoulder."

I refrained from rolling my eyes, first, and laughing, second. "Think what you want."

"It was *you* who insisted on remaining yourself. No effort at even the most basic of disguise. If you would've done that, the situation would be different. Don't try to lay the blame of being recognized at my feet."

"Justify your warp screw-up however you like, Vingee. *Your* action, delaying my reaction after recognizing Hawks. Your insistence on following through with *your* scheduled meeting, insistent on maintaining the corporate ruse—which would've remained. Meetings are delayed all the time." I shook my head. "Bad judgment. No, inept judgement."

That got her. She stepped around the table, closer. "Make your move, Keesay. Try it and we'll see who's spitting teeth."

"Intel knew what it was getting when offering me a contract," I said. "Did Intel know what they were getting when they moved you from analysis to this job in the field?"

"You weren't so critical of my decision-making process when you were flat on your back, Keesay."

"Right. I was busy dying. That sort of thing happens when you fight the Crax. You only know a fraction of what I do about that." She started to reply but I continued. "If I recall, you didn't really understand what I'd survived." I shook my head. "You still don't."

Agent Vingee spoke into her collar, "Mr. Chaney, our meeting is over."

Her collar mic didn't have the strength to reach Guymin, so her message had to be relayed through the orbital dock's com system. It was encrypted, but it still told anyone listening in that she was speaking to her assistant. It pinpointed where she was and where he was, presumably on board the *Pitchfork.*

Her hand went to her ear. Receiving through her ear's microchip receiver, attuned to penetrate the electromagnetic scrambling field, I couldn't hear Guymin's reply.

She picked up her computer clip, and pointed for me to detach and deactivate some of the wall mounted sound transfer dampeners. "Let's go, Specialist Bleys."

Instead of immediately moving to do as she directed, I pulled my revolver and switched out three of the hollow point rounds with armor piercing. "Where to, Ms. Long?"

"The shuttle."

While adjusting my bandoleer filled with a variety of shotgun shells, I reverted to my cover. "May I choose the route?"

"Expecting trouble?"

I pulled the MP pistol from its spot along my back, including the holster. Holding it out to her, I said, "Yes."

"That fast?"

"It's Falshire Hawks. He hates me—all of Capital Galactic hates me for bringing them down. What do you think?"

She took the sidearm and holster, and affixed it to her belt, leaving it concealed under her jacket.

"If they come for me," I said, "make a break for it. As far as they know, I'm just a hired gun."

"Bleys?"

"If they've come for me, it means my appearance has flushed them. Should provide buckets of data." I walked over to the far wall. "A panacea of leads to follow."

"You're sounding awfully morose."

I'd stood for an hour and a half, thinking about it. "I hope I'm wrong, Ms. Long. But I doubt it." Venting my anger at her was pointless. It was my fault for thinking and not taking action.

"You should've said something," Vingee said, her eyes momentarily wide.

Analysts are rarely rushed and have time to examine possibilities. Vingee was smart. Smart and methodical, and used to the paced paradigm. It reminded me of a dead marksman assigned as a bodyguard for a hunted politician. She hadn't learned to redirect her skillset for the new conditions. I watched the reassigned marksman die.

Me? Was I cut out to be a special agent, working in the field? Maybe not. And in a short while, maybe I would no longer be.

I wanted to say to Vingee: Would you have listened? Remind her about the surveillance in the elevator and hallways. Instead I said, "That moment's passed.   Let's   get   moving."

CHAPTER 15

Why Vingee didn't object when I took the lead, I wasn't sure. We had to make it through two modules added to the main dock section, traverse it, and then complete the jaunt through the old section of the Bonnisbin Orbital Colony that led to the *Nuclear Pitchfork*.

I planned to stick to the most populated sections on the theory that if Hawks' compatriots intended to make a move on me, they'd hesitate doing so in front of witnesses, especially if violence ensued. The Capital Galactic Investment Group wasn't outlawed on the newly independent Bonnisbin Colony, but CGIG'd been broken up and auctioned off to mostly hostile competitors. It was no longer a functioning corporation, lacking both significant assets and its former influence.

I strode down the unoccupied, narrow corridor. Metal grating ran down the middle of the floor, allowing easy access to conduits encasing wires, carrying water, waste and other things I didn't have time to care about.

Trying to fit the mold of an Intel agent, sticking with the cover, with the plan was a bad move. My gut told me that. I should've listened to it.

The alternate stairwell was closer than the elevator, and a better choice. We didn't even make it that far.

"Bleys," Vingee said as I checked my com-set.

"Cheney, Code 14F," I spoke into my mic, not sure the message transmitted before the energy damper took full effect. I'd faced a damper powerful enough to shut down my com-set before on the Mavinrom Dock. A-Tech equipment. Probably meant Crax shields, maybe more.

The lights faded to darkness. I pulled the double-barrel shotgun and placed my back against the wall. Whoever cut the power would have functioning dark-vision gear. Knockout gas came to mind. Switching out the slug and buckshot for flare shells, I whispered, "This is going to be loud."

Blam! Blam! I sent one shot each way down the hall, broke open my shotgun and reloaded the previous shells. "Down on the floor, Ms. Long." I said. "They're after me."

Being a moving target was preferable to being a stationary one. The forward flare round's spattered paste shed a flickering yellow light. It revealed a man stepping out of the elevator, laser carbine leveled and ready. I loosed both barrels at him, turned, and ran. Ahead of me a man rolled on the floor, caught between cussing and crying out, trying to smother the orange flare round.

Still on the run, I pulled my duty revolver and sent a hollow-point round into the burning man. He didn't have a shield, unlike the man behind me who did. A laser blast struck me in the back just above my left kidney. It must've been a light duty laser because I felt the searing heat, but my protective coveralls kept it from penetrating.

Looking over my shoulder, I saw Vingee on the ground along the wall, hands over her head. The man, wearing narrow pants and jacket came on. With the yellow light flaring behind him I couldn't see much more than that.

I dodged left as the shielded man fired from the hip, grazing my right shoulder. Back pedaling, I fired another round his way. He flinched but kept coming on, ignoring Vingee.

The corridor ran straight for at least fifty yards. With a powerful damper going none of the doors would open. I hurled my shotgun at him. That forced him to duck. It gave me time to reach the smoldering dead man and lift him just in time to catch the next laser blast intended for me.

Vingee was up, behind the closing attacker. I shouted, "Who hired you?" to keep his attention and raised my revolver, thumbing back the hammer.

He stopped, shouldered his laser carbine, and took aim. He never got the chance to fire. Vingee struck him from behind. The way his head snapped to the side before he crumbled to the floor said her blow must've broken his neck.

"Thanks," I said, hoping she heard me. My ears were ringing from my gunshots in the confined corridor, my sound dampener having been disabled.

She checked the man at her feet, picking up his carbine before unclipping something from his belt. I couldn't tell for sure with the flare's remaining light, but I guessed it to be his shield generator.

"The damper?"

She shrugged, then checked pockets and felt along his arms and legs. "Check your man?"

He had an MP pistol with what looked like a crystal barrel shroud attached. I pocketed it. With much of his chest burned I couldn't find anything else except a small clamshell computer clip. I pocketed that too. "No damper."

"That means it's nearby or someone else is controlling it."

I nodded to Vingee. "Let's get moving."

"Which way?"

I was about to answer when a voice from down the corridor, near where Vingee's meeting had been, said, "It's Kent, Kra. Kent O'Vorley." I saw a shadowy form approach with arms held away from its sides.

The voice, I knew it, but wanted to be sure. "Stop," I said. "Field rations."

"What?" the voice asked. "Conscript Potts' worn out joke?"

That was it. Only O'Vorley, who'd shared a bunker in the trench line, along with me and salesman Moorsheen and Colonist Carver Potts would've answered as he did. Someone who'd seen the *Documentary* might, but not that fast. Kent had actually lived it.

"Come forward, Kent."

"Actually, Kra, we should leave the area before Colony Security shows up, or power is restored."

"Or both," I agreed. "Do you have a plan?"

Vingee came up next to me, holding my shotgun. I holstered it and my revolver. Flashes from my dying flare round caught a doubtful frown across her face.

"I was told you were out here," Kent said, extending his hand for a brief shake. He had on a gray green set of coveralls and jacket. It identified him as a security specialist, but no corporate affiliation. Just his name patch. Not even a ranking. "Quick, this way." His short-cropped light brown hair reflected some of the flare light.

"I saw you not long after we arrived," I replied. "Who told you about me?"

"My partner," O'Vorley said. "The engineer that brought the admin specialist to visit you and reprogrammed our company's tank bot."

We were heading down the corridor. McAllister, I thought. Vingee would certainly know who O'Vorley meant.

"Whoever recognized and reported you," O'Vorley said, "stirred up an ant nest of communications. Fleshed out the skeletal connections."

There was so much I wanted to know, but there wasn't time to get a detailed explanation. "Hawks spotted me," I said to O'Vorley. "Falshire Hawks, Capital Galactic lawyer."

At a trot, we made a turn and stopped in front of a maintenance access door. Lights further down the corridor were beginning to turn on.

"No more talking now. Not here." He flicked open a clamshell computer, tapped a few times, examined it. He punched a code into the panel next to the door the instant it lit up. Power was coming back on everywhere.

Vingee and I followed O'Vorley in. The maintenance room housed a hub where conduits split off from main ones that continued up and down. It was like a long, narrow walk-in closet, dark and cramped except for tiny LED lights and several monitor screens. As we watched, they shifted from yellow to green, indicating renewed electronic traffic.

O'Vorley climbed around two maintenance shafts. I clicked on my pen flashlight before Vingee and I followed. He paused at the third shaft, looked up and down, and descended using the plastic-coated aluminum ladder.

One level down, we stopped. O'Vorley pulled out an electronic communication's scrambler. "This is where we split up," he said. "Long, is it?" When she nodded, he continued. "Step out next level. As far as you know, someone took Bleys. You escaped."

"That's it?" she asked.

"We'll be in contact."

Vingee cocked her head skeptically. "Who are you working for?"

He paused before saying, "An ally. Who are you working for?"

I glanced up at Vingee. She said, "We're with Intelligence."

O'Vorley's eyebrows shot up and looked to me for confirmation.

"New data point, they actually hire Relics."

He smirked. "Who'd've thought?"

Vingee asked, "By ally, you mean?"

"The ones who she, his partner, was with," I said, meaning McAllister. Vingee'd know from the *Documentary*. "Think about it." I handed her the clamshell computer clip I'd taken from the fallen bounty hunter, and the faceted gun barrel shroud.

Vingee handed me the shield generator she'd taken from the other dead bounty man. "Has only twenty percent power. It's not Crax. Probably Troh-got. Not as effective."

"Was almost good enough," I said.

Vingee held out the laser carbine. "Trade for your shotgun. Troh-got shields stop kinetic projectiles. In and out."

I pulled my double barrel. "Hope I didn't rattle its delicate components too much," I said as we exchanged weapons. The laser carbine slid well enough into the shotgun's holster along my back. "Here's a few shells, too." Picking up my shotgun would be one thing if I was on the run. My whole bandoleer of shells would be another. She gave me a spare laser battery clip. "Didn't see you pick that up."

"It was dark and you were busy."

"Those two you took out jumped the gun," O'Vorley said. "Wanted the reward for themselves."

I frowned, knowing it seemed too easy. "So there's more of them out there."

Even though it wasn't a question, he nodded.

Vingee offered him the computer clip. "Will this assist you in making more connections?" The offer surprised me.

O'Vorley shook his head. "We'll share resources soon enough, I think."

I shut down my com-set so that there was no method of tracking it. And, even if Dock Security attempted known frequencies we used, they wouldn't get anything, even passively. "I'll give them a merry chase," I assured Vingee, not knowing how it would end.

"I have no doubt you will," she replied. "Just be sure you get away."

"If we do this right," O'Vorley said. "This won't be a permanent goodbye."

"That's a hint," I said to Vingee. "Tell the rest of the team to keep my pump shotgun clean and oiled."

Even with the dock's haphazard construction there might be places to hide. I had a few ideas, but they weren't good ones. I was hoping O'Vorley had better ones.

"Take care of yourself," Vingee said. "Make contact when you're able." She exited, using a maintenance door. The corridor light shined in and then disappeared with a metallic clunk.

O'Vorley rested a hand on my shoulder. "Come on, Kee—Bleys."

Pulling his hand away, he emptied his jacket's pockets. "Put this on," he said, offering me his jacket. "It'll cover your damaged coveralls."

"It'll kind of clash. I-Tech style mixed with R-Tech." After removing the holstered carbine, I slid the jacket on. Its sleeves were a little long. He was right. The laser burns marring my coveralls would turn heads. That was the last thing I needed.

O'Vorley led me through a narrow maintenance corridor. How he'd learned such a route, I wasn't sure. How long had he been on the orbital dock? In my short time, I'd only made casual friends with two maintenance techs. Not enough that I'd trust either to assist me, especially if it might've become common knowledge that there was a bounty on my head.

I wondered how much the bounty was. How much CGIG could afford—and what back channel ways they'd pay it. My training in security provided the basics of how such transactions took place, but I didn't have any firsthand experience.

Those were some of the channels that Guymin and Vingee—and Axin and Dvoracek, and McAllister were attempting to monitor and crack. I figured McAllister was working alone, except for O'Vorley. She was pretty egotistical, and not good at playing with others. O'Vorley was smart and loyal, like me. But easy-going, unlike me.

We'd made it into a conduit between dock sections. This one was cold, dirty and dimly lit. Pipes lined the low ceiling. Wheel tracks cut through the grimy dust covering the narrow paths indicating automated dolly bots regularly traversed the route we were taking.

I didn't like being hunted. This narrow tube-like corridor struck up the image of a hollow log. A fox running through it being chased by hounds. Like any fox, I didn't like being chased. And wanted to be caught even less. My immediate control over that was limited. This isolated dock, largely unfamiliar to me, harbored few friends, and an apparent host of enemies, or potential enemies.

I took a relaxing breath to refocus on the situation and move forward. I'd been in more dire situations, most recently on Io.

There wouldn't be much security surveillance in this area, if any. I looked around, checking recesses and other likely spots, and confirmed my belief. If there was any, it wouldn't be hidden. The entrance surveillance camera, which O'Vorley temporarily overrode, was transmitting a video loop of an empty corridor while we passed through.

"It's harder to hunt," I said to O'Vorley as he stopped at a control panel and pulled out his clamshell computer, "if you're being hunted."

"What?" O'Vorley asked.

"Wait." I placed a hand on his shoulder. "Two things—no, three. I need to know more about what you're doing here, where we're going, and if you, or really McAllister, can direct me toward who's organizing this hunt."

"Why, Kra?"

"Why, to which question?"

"The 'Can you direct me toward who's organizing this hunt' question."

My thoughts flashed back to my time spent in the *Kalavar*'s brig. In between reading several articles on corporate law and the Chicher's contribution to the Silicate War, I'd read a fantasy novel, part of a series that I'd started while performing warehouse duty on Pluto. A novel by Steven Brust, a contemporary of Zelazny. In it, the main character, relentlessly hunted by a ruthless crime organization, came to the conclusion: Just because you figure that one of them is going to get you eventually is no reason to make it easy for them.

My plan was far less complex than that of Brust's Taltos character. I replied to O'Vorley, "Take the fight to who's organizing the hunt. I probably won't make it to them, but maybe shake them up. Rattle their cages, and they'll reveal more to my partners, and to yours."

"I can't shut down dock surveillance like they did," O'Vorley said. "You go after them, it'll give the dock's security a reason to arrest you."

"I'll let them shoot first," I said, pointing to the Troh-got shield generator attached to my belt. "Then it'll be self-defense."

O'Vorley's eyes narrowed and he shook his head.

I could guess what he was thinking. "You just get me close and point me in the right direction, and don't get involved. Even if there aren't fewer of them left to hunt me, they'll be more cautious. It'll slow them down."

"This is a bad move, Kra. Strategically and for your health."

He was thinking CGIG and their operatives would get me. They might. "It's the right move," I assured him. "For me. And for you."

After sucking in a breath between his teeth and releasing it, he said, "Okay, Kra." He gave me a lopsided grin. "You know, McAllister will love this."

"Be sure to tell her, 'You're welcome,' for me."

CHAPTER 16

We stood in a busy corridor two levels below an apartment wing, more accurately described as mid-upper expense quartering. The newer addition to the orbital colony had chrome trim and fittings that still shined, and the tiles hadn't been worn away by foot traffic. *Or* the tile'd been replaced, and the chrome fittings were well cared for.

Following O'Vorley, I'd come to realize how much he'd matured. We first met on the Mavinrom Colony. He was a green security recruit. Then we crossed paths again on Tallavaster where we fought the Crax. Through desperate actions and experience, he'd become a competent soldier. Together we survived the Crax overrunning our company, before splitting up.

On the Bonnisbin Orbital Colony he was demonstrating insight and savvy moving about the colony, avoiding Security and those seeking me. Sure, communications with McAllister and her software applications helped, but it was more O'Vorley's decisions. We stopped and stood along the wall. The corridor was wide enough that we didn't impede foot traffic or passing dolly bots.

"This is far different from the time I showed you how to use a public com-system and get your bearings on the Mavinrom Dock." I shot him a crooked smile. "Our roles are just about reversed here."

He grinned before shaking his head. "Not quite. I never understood why you helped me, got me connected with those Colonial Marines—you didn't even know me. Especially after Security there thumped you pretty good." His grin faded. "That was a long time ago. So much…"

We had to be careful what we said. This corridor contained active security surveillance. Plus, O'Vorley had relayed to me that McAllister said Security was interested in speaking with me.

I gripped his shoulder. "Thanks for returning the favor."

"Do you have brass knuckles?"

"That, I do."

His grin returned. "Well, that means we're certain to cross paths again," he said, referring to two rendezvous points in case something went wrong.

"Keep out of trouble," I replied.

"Uh, right. I won't bother suggesting that to *you*."

"*Nemo me impune lacessit*," I replied. Smiling at his questioning look, I offered my hand. "I'll explain later."

After we shook hands he turned and fell in behind a trio of tan-clad maintenance techs. I strode the other way, running scenarios through my head, preparing to shift the odds a little more in my favor. At least that was the plan, if McAllister had successfully ferreted out a location that met my expectations.

I switched on the Troh-got shield generator before reaching the T intersection and turned left. The corridor was wide and bright with recessed lighting. No floor grating was visible but four-inch conduits ran along the ceiling. Gray walls with slate gray sliding doors staggered every four yards from one side to the other, all closed.

I managed to blend in with the crowd on the elevator. The fact that everyone had been taller than me allowed me to slip by a posted security specialist. As the crowd split off, entering their quarters, I kept pace ahead of two maintenance managers assigned to the life support recycling system. Their complaints detailing how their day had gone said as much. After a moment there remained only one person behind me. Hopefully he continued straight.

I slipped on my headset and clicked on my com-set to record only, and kept moving, observing the new hallway. It was narrower than the previous, being a little less than three yards wide. That was still wide by most standards, which made sense since it was a more affluent section. The doors alternated every five yards, meaning larger quarters. There were also three guards in the hallway: two men and one woman. I knew they were auxiliary guards—personal guards—by their pale green uniforms with gray-green armbands, their placement in the hallway, and the fact that they were openly armed.

The woman, stocky with short-cropped hair and a strong chin, was nearest to me, holding an MP carbine. It had a strap for sling carry but, like the other two guards, she held her weapon in the two-handed carry position. The furthest guard's main weapon was a laser carbine. Whether a light or medium duty model, I couldn't tell. The third guard had an MP carbine, like the woman. Each also had a holstered sidearm, probably an MP pistol.

I put my hand up to my ear, over my com-set's head gear. It wasn't necessary, but it's what I-Techs did to signal others that they were receiving a message via their micro receiver implant.

The environmental systems manager hadn't made the turn with me, so the three guards only had me to focus their attention on. I stopped, and spoke into my mic, "Go straight? I already turned like you said." My eyes shifted to each of the guards, giving me a better look at them while I came to an abrupt stop. I stood twenty yards from the female, stationed to the left of a doorway. A tall, dark-skinned man stood across from it, and a burly, big-eared man with the laser carbine, who could've been the woman's fraternal twin, stood to the right of it.

The man across from the door spoke into his collar while the woman turned to face me. "Stop!" she ordered, recognition registering in her eyes. That made sense if the information McAllister had relayed to O'Vorley was correct.

Right, I thought. Not many folks questioned McAllister's competence. She was always right. Just ask her.

The truth was, McAllister had only been wrong once—the one time she crossed me and thought she could get away with it.

I'd already stopped. Instead of remaining so, with wide eyes, I began backing away. I kept my hand away from my revolver. The corridor was certain to have security monitoring—at least until those hunting me interfered with it.

She levelled her carbine, as did the dark-skinned man, having finished his radio conversation. The burly guard toting the laser carbine glanced the other way down the hall before turning back toward me.

"I said, HALT." The woman's order rippled with threat, tinged with menace.

"I just made a wrong turn," I said, slowing a little. "I'll retrace my steps—"

She answered my unfinished sentence with a three round burst. The bullets were not quite the size of a .22 caliber round, but travelled at more than twice a .22's speed. The bullets arrived before the snapping *crack* from them being fired. One of the intercepted rounds would've struck me in my left eye if the shield generator hadn't stopped it inches from my face. It, like the others, fell harmlessly to the floor. The close impact caused me to flinch, even as I reached over my shoulder for my laser carbine. My revolver would've been faster but, for as long as the shield generator lasted, it'd be useless. Firing it would do nothing more than drain the shield. I just hoped the shield energy lasted through this gunfight.

Both MP carbine-armed guards opened up on me using textbook perfect firing stances. I fired back, less textbook perfect, sending a searing blast that charred the laser-armed guard's left cheek and ear. He'd moved to the center of the hall to get a clear line of fire. Turning away while crying out in pain, he was out of the fight—at least for the moment. His firearm was the only one that could penetrate the Troh-got shield, while the alien device's energy lasted. It'd take a couple seconds for my carbine's capacitor to recharge, so I trotted forward. By closing the distance I was sure a hip shot would be on target.

My com-set clicked off and the hallway's recessed lights faded. A large-scale energy damper. It'd affect surveillance too.

As before when wielded by an attacker, my laser carbine resisted. It had hardened military components, as evidenced by my second blast. It took the female guard in the throat an instant before near darkness cloaked the hallway. Traces of light from further down the hall framed the third guard hurling his MP carbine at me while charging forward. Ambient light from behind probably illuminated me as well.

The woman was down. The first wounded guard's cries turned to curses. I couldn't worry about him. My laser wouldn't recharge before the closing man reached me, so, ducking the hurled carbine, I dropped my laser and pulled my bayonet

The bigger man barreled into me. Even braced for the impact, his bulk knocked me to the floor. I landed on my shoulder, keeping my head from rebounding off the tile. The guard never got to follow up. My long blade pierced deep between his ribs. It took the fight out of him, his life quickly following.

I grabbed my laser carbine without shoving the dying guard off of me. The clomping of the laser-burned guard's approach gave warning. We exchanged shots. Half-guided by the shadowy silhouette's appearance and half on instinct, I took him in the groin. His shot missed, melting the tile floor inches to the left of my head.

His coverall's protective properties proved inferior to mine and he fell to the ground, groaning and clutching his crotch.

I pushed the dead guard off of me and ended the writhing man with a searing headshot.

Despite the darkness, I knew blood covered O'Vorley's jacket. I pulled it off and replaced it with the dead guard's jackets. By feel I also secured two charged laser battery clips from his belt.

Before departing I stopped in front of the door that the guards had been protecting. Turning off my shield generator, I pulled my revolver and sent the three loaded armor piercing rounds through the door. While doing so my mind fixated on a portion of an old-time nursery rhyme: *All around the mulberry bush, the monkey chased the weasel. The monkey thought 'twas all in fun. Pop goes the weasel.* It didn't fit the original meaning of the rhyme, but I saw CGIG loyalists as the monkey and me, the weasel. Each shot through the door was a 'pop.'

I didn't think I'd hit anyone, but figured it'd give those directing the hunt a bit of a scare. Plus, the echoing gunshot blasts would deter nearby residents from sticking their noses in the hallway to see what was going on.

With no more time to spare, I hurried from the area before a dock security team arrived.

I handed O'Vorley back his jacket. He saw the blood on it and mouthed the word, "Whose?"

I pointed at myself, shook my head and mouthed, "Not mine."

He signaled for me to precede him up a ladder and through a maintenance crawl that offered access to several rectangular ducts. Despite the yellow insulation, humming vibrations caused by the recycled air pumped through caught my ear. My penlight revealed a spot where I could lay stretched out with room enough to stand.

O'Vorley closed the door and climbed up next to me. Pointing to a fancy black synthetic sack with a shoulder strap, several tan blankets and a plastic canister, he said, "There's food and water in the bag, and a change of clothes. The blankets should help you keep comfortable, and the can is…well…it'll seal up tight after using it."

"How'd you get to know every unwatched nook and cranny?"

"I don't know every one, and McAllister pointed out to me most that I do know."

If I managed to stay out of sight for a day or two, Dock Security might figure someone had snatched or killed me. Those hunting me might suspect someone else had taken me for the bounty. Anyway, that was the notion behind the plan.

"So, hide out here for at least forty-eight hours," I said. "Then make my way to the Unicorn Palace, and ask for Colossra?"

O'Vorley nodded, handing me a tattered paperback book and a mini LED lamp to supplement my flashlight. Paper books are pretty rare. "War of the Worlds," he said. "Alien invaders killing humans. McAllister said you'd find it to be both new and refreshing."

I smirked.

"My team. Guymin knows?"

O'Vorley nodded once. "They've been questioned by dock authorities. They're being watched. Not just by Security."

I looked around the cramped area. "You being watched too?"

"Not especially. Not yet, at least." He started to descend the ladder. "Hey. *Nemo me impune lacessit?*"

I grinned, remembering I'd mentioned it to him earlier. "Latin for: No one injures me with impunity."

O'Vorley shook his head. "That figures. Just stay hidden with impunity."

CHAPTER 17

Long hours of warehouse duty on Pluto helped me endure waiting in the maintenance crawl area. Waiting, silent and inactive while my trail went cold, seemed wise. That didn't mean it was easy. I wanted to be after Falshire Hawks. Thinking about how close he was to me and I didn't get him left my blood boiling. I missed my chance. He was gone, and out of reach. Stewing on it wouldn't change anything.

I managed a few hours of sleep before deciding to read the novel O'Vorley left with me. It was a short one, very old and obviously written before humanity had an inkling of the nature of alien races, especially those populating the Orion Arm of the Milky Way galaxy. H.G. Wells did, however, have an understanding that humanity would be at a technological disadvantage, but that our immune system would be a great advantage.

One small aspect in *The War of the Worlds* that especially piqued my curiosity was the *Thunder Child*, a steam-driven naval warship. It battled the Martian alien walkers by ramming them.

Two patrol boats, *Calling Thunder* and *Thunder Child*, played a key role in the *Kalavar*'s survival and escape. After *Calling Thunder* was destroyed, the *Thunder Child* managed to ram the damaged Primus Crax frigate. Unlike in the novel, our *Thunder Child* didn't limp away from the confrontation.

Although tradition held that all patrol gunboats have 'Thunder' incorporated into their name, I wondered if the captain of the *Thunder Child* knew of H.G. Wells' novel, and the part the fictional ship played. That question lingered for only a few seconds. Without a doubt, the captain had.

My thoughts remained on the captains and crews of the *Thunder Child* and *Calling Thunder*, lost defending the *Kalavar* and the Zeta Aquarius Dock. The dock survived the first Crax wave, losing all but a few escort ships and defending fighters. Thousands of Colonial Marines died fending off the boarding attempt. A Chicher battlewagon and Umbelgarri frigate fell too, as did all but a handful of the *Kalavar*'s crew.

I switched off the LED lamp and leaned back against the foam-coated wall, thinking on all those people lost. And were still being lost. Dying in the war. Concern for my own troubles receded. Whispering a prayer, I allowed my eyes to slip closed. My hand fell to my holstered revolver.

Unexpected, rest and slumber found me.

The secondary entry door clicking open jolted me awake. A sliver of light sliced through the darkness. My hand automatically pulled my revolver, but then I thought better of it, and grabbed the laser carbine from the floor next to me. Other than that, I didn't move from lying on my back, feet nearest the entryway.

Someone slid a sizeable red toolbox across the metal floor. A male voice followed, saying, "I've got a pair of brass knuckles wrapped in a shop rag."

I recognized the voice, or thought I did—a dead man's voice. I didn't move, or respond.

A hand reached in and placed a bundled rag on top of the metal tool box. "You shoot me, I'm gonna be pissed. It's not like I'm Gudkov or something."

"Step in," I said. "Slowly, and tell me who you are."

A dark-haired, mustached man entered, hands held away from his sides. "Segreti. I'm still a maintenance tech."

"The Maintenance Tech, Segreti, I knew is dead," I said. Just about everyone aboard the *Kalavar* died fending off the boarding Crax and Stegmars. Neither Colonist Potts nor Admin Specialist Tahgs listed Class 2 Maintenance Tech Segreti among the few survivors.

"I should be but I'm not, happy to say." He slowly reached back. "Mind if I close the door?"

"Close it," I said.

The enclosure returned to inky darkness. "I thought you were dead too, Keesay."

Switching on my penlight, I trained it on the man's face. "I should be, but I'm not." The man looked like Segreti, wavy dark hair, skin tone marking him as someone from the Mediterranean region—if he hailed from Earth. Not taking my eyes from him, I sat up. "As reported to me by two reliable sources, the Gar Crax got you."

He chuckled. "Actually, it was the Stegmars. Pumped me full of needles and nearly tore my right arm from its socket. The neural toxin antidote kept me alive, but left me in a coma. I survived the cold sleep process, and well, here I am."

"Cold sleep? How'd that go?"

"Having two of those three-foot mantises playing tug of war with my limbs was more pleasant than waking up from cold sleep."

"I hear you there," I said, flicking on the LED lamp. "Glad you're alive. Now, what're you doing out here, and specifically in here with me?"

He knelt down to open his tool box. I kept my laser carbine trained on him. "I'm not convinced I should trust you yet. There's a lot of credits on my head."

Segreti chuckled, but didn't move his hands any closer to the box's latches. "Don't I know it, Keesay. Got a lot of the dock here in an uproar. Most think you've been captured and secretly whisked away. Some think you were wounded, crawled into some vent shaft to die. A few don't believe you were ever here. More theories than I have fingers and toes." He paused. "I heard about you taking down Crax and Stegmars on the *Kalavar*. A lot of them. That told me these few bodies attributed to you here meant you weren't even trying."

I ignored his flattery. "And?"

"And, I knew Engineer McAllister was on the dock here. If you really were here, she'd know." When I raised a skeptical eye, he responded, "She knew pretty much everything that happened on the *Kalavar*. Why wouldn't she know what's happening here too?"

Segreti was one of only a handful of trusted friends I had while serving aboard the *Kalavar*. But it seemed all too convenient. "So, how'd you get here?"

"Here, on the dock?"

"That'll do for a start," I replied.

"Was on a hospital ship. Negral was in disarray, facing a hostile takeover. Me, work for Capital Galactic? They're a bunch of assholes. The first corporate recruiter that offered anything, I jumped at. Here I am."

I refrained from shaking my head. While his story could be true, could be just that simple, I didn't believe it. He wasn't with Intelligence. He'd have said so.

Segreti glanced down at the tool box. "I'm here to do some work on your behalf."

"Go ahead," I said. "So you went to McAllister and she told you where I was?"

"Not directly." He removed the bundled rag from the top of his tool box, unwrapped it, revealing the copper-colored brass knuckles. Sliding them out of the way, he continued. "And she contacted me. Arranged a drop. I didn't talk to her, nor that young guy I've seen with her."

"She did?"

"Sort of," he said. "Surprised the hell out of me, Keesay. Thought she hated your guts." He flicked the latches and lifted the lid of his box.

"She does," I said with a shrug, deciding to tip my hand a bit. "She just hates the Crax more."

"She knew you and me were friends on the *Kalavar*. Knew you *might* not shoot me on sight."

"Who do you work for, Segreti?"

He pointed to the brown and purple, octagonal logo on the left shoulder of his tan coveralls. "Rift Valley Consolidated Services, a subcontractor for this colony."

"Really?"

He smirked and eyed my shoulder patch. "And you work for Mayfair Mining and Industrials?"

I didn't want to lie so I shifted the conversation's direction. "Remember Agricultural Laborer Potts?"

"Yeah, one of those colonists Negral hired who turned out to be not much more than a thug." He sighed. "Fought pretty hard against the aliens. He was one of the few that survived."

"He turned out to be okay," I said, frowning. "Died fighting in the trench line against the Crax. On Tallavaster. They overran our position. Hand to hand, he took more than a few down before a Stegmar tore out his throat."

Segreti pulled a few shrink-wrapped packages from his toolbox and sat them on the floor before grabbing a fist-sized metallic box with a number of wires emerging from both ends. "You made it, Keesay. You're a survivor. Heard a little how you killed more than your share of Crax and Stegmars before escaping the *Kalavar* on that exploration shuttle. Before the Stegmars took me down." His voice held no malice.

"Potts told me what happened on the *Kalavar*," I said. "Crossed paths with Janice Tahgs too, on Tallavaster." I met Segreti's eyes. "I was ordered to leave the *Kalavar*."

"You don't have to convince me. Orders are orders. I considered you a friend. Still do. Would've preferred you there helping us exterminate the boarders." He shrugged. "That Capital Galactic put a price on you before they were dismantled tells me you've done more than your share."

"Glad you survived, Segreti."

A crooked smile emerged under his thick mustache. "I'm going to do what I can to help you survive, at least a little while longer." He held up the box. "I'm going to splice this into one of the power cables. You can use it to re-charge that shield generator."

It took a conscious effort to keep my hand from sliding to the nearly drained A-Tech device attached to my belt.

He pointed to the packages. "There's a bodysuit, jacket, tie and tie-tack. If nobody looks at your boots, you'll be mistaken for business rep. Junior rank, not even midlevel." He tossed me a smaller package. "This has a pair of contacts. They'll fool the dock's facial recognition software—if you don't give them reason to look too close. Also, a chit with some credits and a temporary ID." His mustache twitched with a smile." You're a Mr. Virgil Deering." He scratched behind his ear. "That ID won't stand up to scrutiny so, if you can manage, maybe don't draw too much attention."

I knew about the type of contacts he'd given me. They distorted what the cameras picked up, measurement between the eyes. That said the Bonnisbin Orbital Colony's security systems were somewhat antiquated. It also meant I couldn't look anyone eye-to-eye for long or they'd notice the contact-induced distortion, especially anyone from Security.

"Understood," I said. "Where'd you come across these…items?"

Segreti shrugged. "Let's just say I have interesting friends." He'd begun attaching the recharging device to one of the cables running along the wall.

"Would you list me among them?"

"Yeah, Keesay, you're on that list."

I laughed. "I'm not on many friend lists."

Maintenance Tech Segreti must've been working for Military Intelligence. I didn't know much about them, other than their primary focus was to watch and ensure corporations weren't breaking laws, like using prohibited military grade equipment. I always figured they did more than that. Much more. No reason the military would trust Intelligence to provide them with everything they needed. Knowledge, even if it only verified what was shared, was important.

Yes, I thought. A competent, unassuming maintenance tech who paid attention to detail would fit that need. He'd never verify my suspicion, just as I'd never verify that I'd been recruited by Intelligence, something he certainly suspected.

Segreti pulled a long tool from his belt. It looked like a screwdriver, but I knew that it fused wires. "Me neither," he said, referring to friend lists. "There's also a masking device you can affix to your revolver. You'll have to leave the carbine and any other weapons behind. I'll come by in a few days to pick the carbine up, and anything else you leave, and this." He pointed his fusing tool at my belt and then to the charger. "It draws slowly so electrical grid monitors won't notice. Probably take twenty hours. Might want to be on the move by then."

He started closing up his toolbox. "I'll pass through my next shift. Drop off some cleansing wipes and deodorant."

"You know where I'm going?"

"I have an idea."

"Thanks, Segreti." I stood in the cramped area and offered him my hand. "I was saddened when Potts said you weren't one of the *Kalavar* crewmen that survived. Seeing you here made my day—no, made my month."

He laughed as we shook hands. "Considering your past few days…" His grin faded. "Keep taking it to them, Keesay."

"As long as I'm drawing breath, my friend."

"Me too," he said, and quietly departed.

CHAPTER 18

I was cleaned up and ready to go. The charcoal black I-Tech bodysuit felt uncomfortable, but not as bad as the red tie filled mostly with black geometric shapes. That garment around my neck felt constricting, like a noose. I knew how to wear a tie, owing to my days as a youth when my mother held dinner parties. The narrow cut black jacket with flecks of red was comfortable by comparison.

I'd thought about stashing my revolver in the large satchel, along with my tightly wrapped uniform and bayonet, but figured it'd hide well enough beneath my jacket and the satchel riding on my hip. The scrambling chip affixed to the frame below the cylinder should defeat cursory electronic scans, especially those performed with older equipment and software.

Leaving my old set of brass knuckles behind for Segreti, I pocketed my new set on the satchel's side as a decoy if the scans turned up something, such as large bits of metal. My bayonet in the satchel was of Umbelgarri alloy and might not trigger concern.

The shielding device clipped opposite my revolver would render my handgun ineffective anyway, once activated. I did have my medium duty stun baton. By removing the internal battery it should appear to be an inert object, not worth a second glance. It'd also be useless unless I had twenty seconds to disassemble, insert the battery and reassemble it. If it did get a second glance, I could discharge the battery, if necessary. But, again, a potentially useful distraction should I be called aside.

The contacts designed to foil facial recognition software left my vision a little blurry, especially close up. Even so, with a determined effort I could bring into focus my purple octagonal tie tack identifying me as working for Rift Valley Consolidated Services. Because of the contact lenses, I wanted to avoid eye contact with anyone for more than a few seconds. Fortunately, being a low level business associate, avoiding eye contact was the norm.

The trip to the Celestial Unicorn Palace proved a long one, especially since the best route was indirect, requiring extensive foot travel and only a few elevators.

The Palace was one of the oldest structures comprising the orbital dock, attached to the initial main hub section. The shine reflecting off the walls, floors, railings—everything—bespoke of extraordinary maintenance efforts. Vines bearing blooming pink and purple morning glories climbed the pillars leading to the Palace. A nearby restaurant whose high-ceilinged dining area held various colorful, free-flight songbirds caught my attention. The posted guard at the elaborate triple door entrance ensured none of the exotic avian creatures escaped from the marble-tabled courtyard. Several authentic trees offered an expansive leaf-filled canopy and supported semi-transparent netting.

Only a few customers dined in the fancy Wellington's Roost. Business executives and high-powered attorneys, all with very little black in their orange and yellow ties or scarves. I wondered how they dealt with bird droppings plopping in their soup. Expensive exclusivity had its price.

Needless to say, nobody paid me much attention, even as I approached several old-style neon signs outlining shapely women and even a muscular man. Just beyond them stood a screening area manned by several corporate security guards wearing a shoulder patch depicting a rearing white unicorn in front of a stylized split rail gate resting half open.

I fell in line behind a pair of tall businessmen, both from Cardinal One Intrasolar Corporation. They ignored each other, eyes focused on their computer clips. Lacking a computer clip made my disguise less effective.

I pondered the chit encased in a plastic card from Segreti. It'd have to suffice. Any financial transaction accessing my account would send up a red flag for anyone monitoring it. Even a small purchase, such as a meal or cocktail. I didn't have any idea how many credits the chit contained—at the time I didn't think to ask Segreti. But it'd have to hold a substantial amount if I hoped to gain access as a patron at the Palace. By all accounts, it was an exclusive, expensive establishment.

Some visiting executives and government officials might not want their accounts attached to the Unicorn Palace, so chits probably wouldn't draw attention. But would there be enough on the chit to get by?

Placing a hand in my pocket, making sure the plastic card was still there, my fallback would be to count on my contact, Colossra. Trust O'Vorley and Segreti? Taking a deep breath while the two business men in front of me were questioned, I realized that I trusted O'Vorley and Segreti more than just about anyone else from my past. They wouldn't steer me wrong.

Both executives ahead of me went through the scanning arch, then answered a question about intent, each saying, "An evening of personal entertainment."

As I walked up to the arch, I noted that it was hooked to a very simple screen, a type that had minimal memory and processing capacity. I didn't recognize the scanning arch's model. While it could provide superior sensing ability, I didn't think it had any directed EMP ability. Not modulating and focusing an electromagnetic pulse when coupled with computer hardware available. There were other possibilities, but they didn't concern me, much. Besides, there weren't a lot of options. Moving forward and keeping alert was all I could reasonably do.

The two Unicorn Palace guards were armed with bulky medium duty laser pistols. My shield generator wouldn't be of any use, and my current attire offered virtually no protection. I thought about my duty coveralls compactly folded into the satchel as one of the security men signaled me forward.

I nodded once and stepped through the arch, looking up and around as if I hadn't been through one before. It gave a plausible reason for not looking either of the security officials in the eye. It took a little longer for the floor ribbon to signal green than it did for the businessmen who preceded me. Maybe because I carried a large shoulder satchel. Maybe because of what it held, or what it concealed on my hip.

"Your purpose tonight, Mr. Deering, sir?" one of the security men asked.

In a straightforward voice, I answered, "An extended evening of personal entertainment." I shifted my gaze from one security man to the other, then to the green ribbon on the floor.

With a grin and shake of his head, the older of the two said, "Move ahead, and enjoy your extended evening."

I mumbled, "Thank you. I believe I will."

Beyond the thick sliding doors I found a dimly lit room about fifty-feet-wide and half that deep. Scattered mostly to the left were twelve tall circular tables. Half had one or two men standing at them, along with a scantily clad hostess cradling a computer clip. I wasn't sure who had more teeth showing, the smiling hostess or the grinning men staring at the holographic images that appeared on the tables, slowly rotated a full 360 degrees before shifting to another image—different women of widely varying proportions. One distant table had a male lawyer observing holographic images of other men, again of all varieties—muscular, thin, dark-skinned, bearded or clean shaven, and more. One table had an elderly female business executive examining the same selection of holographic males, and attended by a muscular, topless male host.

Along the right-hand wall were what I guessed to be full-sized images of what the Celestial Unicorn Palace's customers were examining at their individual tables. Prominent were the nearly eight-foot voluptuous blondes from the commercials, enticing visitors with the slogan: Come be a stallion on our range. There were also women of every conceivable size, shape and color. The most disgusting holographic image appeared to be a little girl—but her figure suggested she *might* be a midget.

Thinking about what that meant turned my stomach. I looked around with a glare that was anything but friendly. A powerful urge to just turn and leave set in. At that moment I might have left, no matter the consequences, except for the dark-skinned, brunette hostess with a sincere look of concern approaching me.

She was about as tall as me, which was a little on the short side for an I-Tech woman. But what she lacked in height she made up for with overflowing cleavage. It threatened to burst free from the skin-tight white shirt under her open black jacket. She carried an oversized computer clip under one arm and maintained eye contact as she stopped in front of me.

I glanced away, remembering my contacts. The room's darkness probably masked their distortion, but better to be safe. I could've stared at her cleavage, something she was probably used to. Instead I looked around, pretending to be distracted by the sights and activity.

"Hello, I'm Brandi, your hostess." Her voice remained light and bubbly as she continued. "May I direct you to a table?" She gestured to her right. Her smile revealed straight teeth whose whiteness captured and reflected the room's purple and turquoise fluorescent advertisements.

When I didn't immediately respond, she added, "There we can begin crafting your experience with us."

I nodded and looked toward a table that wasn't adjacent to any of those occupied. Hostess Brandi took my meaning and led the way. Her stride was both businesslike and playfully seductive, until that moment something I didn't think was possible.

Once at the chest-high circular table, one which rested on a dull metallic post that matched its surface, she extended her hand toward me. As we shook, she asked, "Is this your first visit to the Celestial Unicorn Palace?"

Her handshake was firm and assured. As I released from the hostess's grip I noticed the smoothness of her skin. Her training probably directed her to recognize what I'd find appropriate, what would put me more at ease.

Before the shapely hostess could go into her spiel, I asked, "Is Colossra available?"

The hostess's eyebrows rose. Somehow I'd caught her off guard. Then her face transformed one of questioning contemplation.

I briefly met her eyes and nodded. "Might she be available?"

Brandi tapped her oversized computer clip, prepping the table's hologram program. While she did so, she took in a deep breath. Somehow the synthetic fabric held.

"Are you sure, Mr. Deering?"

Realizing her deep breath had been a test to see if it'd draw my attention, I kept my voice low and even. "I believe so, Miss Brandi." It made me wonder about my request. Instead of assuming Colossra was one of the buxom blondes I'd seen in the advertisements, I should've gotten more information from Segreti. "Is there a reason I shouldn't request Colossra, Miss Brandi?"

"Brandi is fine," the hostess said, tapping a few places on her computer clip's screen before resting it on the table.

I wanted to suggest she call me Virgil, my cover's first name but, based upon my experience of business executives, even mid to low level ones, that would be out of character. Besides, in my experience as a security specialist, formality and titles felt more natural. And I wanted to appear natural.

"No, Mr. Deering." She flashed her wide, teeth-shimmering smile. "We're trained to provide our visitors with options, guiding them toward an enjoyable experience." She shrugged. "You're a challenging client to read."

I wanted to ask why, but could guess. My lack of eye contact. An R-Tech trying to blend in as an I-Tech. Instead I shrugged.

"Your initial profile doesn't match her usual clientele."

They couldn't have had much information on me, with a fake ID. All they had was observations. It made me wonder about Colossra. Was she a midget? Was Colossra not a she, but a he? My mind raced, trying to recall. I did refer to Colossra as a 'she' and Brandi hadn't disputed or in any way indicated that assumption was in error.

I took my own deep breath, realizing I'd discover the mystery of Colossra soon enough.

Hostess Brandi escorted me from the entry to a waiting area filled with several plush white couches and intricately carved end tables. Being someone skilled in working with wood, creating carvings, it was easy to tell that what the imported furniture was expensive. String orchestra music played in the background. Otherwise, it was quiet, especially since we were the only ones in the room.

Brandi offered me a seat and sat next to me before attempting small talk. Rather than continuing to provide evasive answers, I questioned her.

"Has the war interrupted business?"

"Here, at the Celestial Unicorn Palace?" It was her turn to be evasive. When I nodded, she continued, saying, "There's been some interruptions, mainly due to travel difficulties encountered by some of our regular clientele."

"How do the owners of the Celestial Unicorn Palace view the colony here in the 70 Virginis system declaring independence?"

"An interesting question, Mr. Deering." She smiled tightly. "As long as it doesn't affect business and our ability to please our clientele, it doesn't matter."

"Do your employers have faith in the Troh-gots? How will professed neutrality serve them if humanity loses the war?" I immediately regretted asking the questions. A hostess wouldn't have such knowledge, and even if she did, wouldn't reveal anything of interest to me. "I apologize," I said. "Forget I asked."

Another moment of silence reigned while the hostess checked her computer clip. She offered a nervous smile, demonstrating her discomfort. Something she probably wasn't used to.

I ran a hand across the end table next to me, its polished top etched into leaves and roses. "Beautiful cherry wood." Brandi leaned forward as I slid the table around. The thick carpet offered some resistance. I pointed to the legs, depicting thorny vines climbing them. "They appear to be hand carved by an expert."

She nodded in appraisal. "Your company deals in woods and furniture?"

"No," I said. "In my youth I carved busts in authentic wood to help pay for schooling." It was a half-truth. "I couldn't help but notice."

She nodded, her confident grin returning. "We here at the Celestial Unicorn Palace spare no expense to provide a positive experience for our visitors."

A small corner of her clip's screen flashed yellow, then green.

"Your escort will be with us in a moment."

We both stood. After I slid the table back into place, Hostess Brandi directed me to face a door to our left. She leaned close, her chest lightly pressing against my shoulder as she whispered in my ear. "If your choice is not what you expect, don't hesitate to share the fact with Colossra, or any member of our staff. The sooner you do so, the more satisfying your experience will prove to be."

I slid a few inches away. "I will be sure to do so, Hostess Brandi, should it be necessary." I returned my focus on the doorway so that I wouldn't have to maintain eye contact. "I appreciate your concern, but I believe Colossra as my choice is the proper one for my needs...and desires."

"The client is the boss," she said with a hint of smugness. That worried me.

CHAPTER 19

The door, apparently to an elevator, slid open and out stepped a mound of muscles masquerading as a woman.

She wore a single-strapped, shimmering bronze dress that stopped mid-thigh with matching bronze-studded heels. Everywhere bulging, rippling muscles stretched the dress tight. The Celestial Unicorn Palace's escort put every weightlifter I'd ever met to shame. Her biceps and triceps were so large she couldn't rest her arms comfortably at her sides, and the bulk of her thighs and calves caused her to walk with a more masculine than feminine gait. Whereas the hostess's fluid walk reminded me of a seductive rippling stream, the approaching woman's stride reminded me more of a raging river, one barely contained within its boulder-strewn banks.

The shape of her eyes and her long, straight black hair suggested an Asian bloodline. Her brown eyes sparkled as much as her inviting smile.

"Segreti, if I ever see you again," I mumbled, but finished the thought to myself: You're gonna pay for this.

"I beg your pardon?" the hostess standing next to me asked.

"Nothing," I said, and stepped forward, extending my hand to who I assumed was Colossra.

"I'm Mr. Deering," I said, "Virgil Deering."

The name Colossra certainly fit. Her grip was bone-crunching, even though I gripped far up along the web between her thumb and forefinger.

"The bronze fingernail polish," I said, wincing, "with silver roses is a nice…touch, Colossra."

She was only a little bit taller than me before the shoes, allowing me to maintain eye contact without craning my neck too much. A slight tightening of her grip before she released told me she'd been holding back.

With a smile on her lips she brought her left hand up and around. Before it could collide with my shoulder, I brought my arm up to interpose my satchel. The maneuver gave me a chance to duck under her arm while grabbing hold of it. She shook me off before I could place her in an arm lock.

I stepped back, out of reach, making sure my sidearm remained concealed under my jacket.

The hostess nodded to me with a contemplative look across her face. "Enjoy your extended stay, Mr. Deering."

Offering the hostess a brief glance, keeping most of my attention on the brutish hulk of a lady in front of me, I said, "I'm anticipating a span of time not quite like any other I've experienced before." Although I had no intention of following through, I'd apparently demonstrated aspects of foreplay the hostess expected.

Colossra said, "I shall do my best to see to that, Mr. Deering." Her voice was smooth and feminine, and stood at odds with her size and strength. Despite her excessively muscled frame, feminine beauty lurked in her face and demeanor, echoing what resonated in her voice.

Hostess Brandi retrieved and handed me my satchel. "Thank you again," I said to her before offering my arm to Colossra. Nodding toward the elevator door I said to my escort, "I take it you know the way, and possibly what I'm about?"

Flexing her bicep after taking my arm, she replied, "Rest assured, Mr. Deering, I'm prepared to cater to your needs." She laughed as we strode forward. "This isn't my first rodeo."

"Hmph," I said, certain the hostess could still hear. "That's reassuring." I looked up at Colossra, her jaw clenched in determination. Sliding my chit card into the computer access panel next to the elevator, I hoped my escort knew what I was really alluding to.

CHAPTER 20

Instead of using gravity plates, the levels or disks that made up the Celestial Unicorn Palace generated artificial gravity through spinning. Relic technology, and a type that resulted in significant energy savings. It also meant the central shaft housing the elevators lacked gravity. By properly orienting to correlate with the direction travelled along the shaft, movement offered some gravity, until slowing to a stop. Then, the floor or ceiling mounted—depending on your direction—foot and gripping straps proved their value. I imagined the Relic technology used offered a minor exotic experience, but nowhere near what any zero gravity *activities* might.

My tie and satchel floated up a bit, as did my jacket. Unlike Colossra, who was pretty solid all around, some of the Palace's escorts could emphasize their *floaty* parts in zero gravity, making such rides…interesting.

My result was Colossra observing my holstered revolver.

She made a kissing motion with her lips and winked. I smiled nervously, and checked again for signs of surveillance cameras. I hadn't seen any, anywhere, which surprised me. With the somewhat antiquated scanning equipment at the entrance, and the outdated gravity generation system, signs of such equipment should be obvious. Fiber optic lenses are small, and not necessarily visible, but walls, panels and lighting offer hints. A structure's layout points to where such lenses might be mounted to obtain full, unobstructed surveillance.

Microphones could be mounted out of sight and still gather sound, down to minute levels. Low energy sonic scanners could be mounted behind panels and provide outlines and data on movements, but such setups offered inferior detail when compared to proper optic lenses.

The elevator reoriented before its door opened to deposit us on a limited area grav plate. I politely declined my escort's offered arm, preferring not to be entangled. Exiting an elevator provides an excellent opportunity to be ambushed. While Segreti might vouch for Colossra, it was better to minimize the risk and be free to react.

Nobody was lying in wait. Instead, the narrow hallway bathed in soft blues, pinks, and deep purples held two Class 2 Security bots. The model resembled an old-time globe resting on a squat aluminum podium. Their lights flashed yellow, meaning they were in standby/observation mode. They'd been painted deep purple to match the décor, including their tracked wheels and four-pronged appendage arms. They were an offshoot of the models often found in trendy establishments and in medical facilities. The spherical portion could spin and rotate to bring weapons to bear, from CO_2 fired needles laced with knockout drugs to ports for light duty lasers. Advanced models mounted a stun net with the launch mechanism hidden behind a body panel.

Automatically searching for security sensors and identifying the sec-bots reminded me how out of my element I'd ranged. I was a trained security specialist, not an Intel agent. I'd proven to be an effective soldier fighting against the Crax. Posing as a mid to lower level business executive, a Virgil Deering, originally posing as a personal guard named Bleys. I thought I'd settle into the varied roles of an Intel agent, but that wasn't happening.

Agent Vingee suggested surgery to alter my looks. But even that wouldn't have kept me out of trouble on the orbital colony. I recognized Falshire Hawks, despite his plastic surgery. He'd have ID'd me just the same.

Then, entering the Celestial Unicorn Palace, an establishment for rich and high-powered executives to play out fantasies with unique, if not very peculiar prostitutes? It felt like playing quarterback in old-time American football, getting sacked by the entire defensive line, and then having the linebackers pile on.

Colossra was already a step ahead of me and she slowed down so I could catch up. "My suite is around the corner. I believe what I have to offer will prove beyond your expectations, Mr. Deering."

Her voice wasn't as deep as I'd expected, and now it carried a mischievous lilt. That concerned me, even though she smiled reassuringly.

"They're security robots," she continued. "I don't think they've ever moved from their positions since I've been here. Except for cleaning and maintenance."

The sec-bots could record persons and conversations. It's what I'd have them do, in addition to disabling intruders or troublemakers. I didn't mention that as we turned right at the T intersection.

Several yards down the hall, we stopped at a pair of doors placed across from each other. The lighting and colors transitioned to deep violet, almost like black lighting and continued down the corridor and then doglegged to the left. Colossra waved her right forehand in front of the access panel the door on the right, the wider of the two doors. It clicked and slid open.

"What's across the hall?" I asked.

"My personal quarters," she said, stepping aside and gesturing for me to enter.

I nodded politely and said, "After you."

She held back a frown while entering first.

Compared to the hallway, the room beyond was brightly lit, with floors, walls, furniture, and exercise equipment all in combinations of white, accented by cobalt blue, and polished metal. The ceiling reached almost ten feet, giving a more spacious feel, especially as several areas had mirrors reflecting down from it. There were free weights and weight machines, treadmills and climbing machines.

A squat, oval cleaning bot, attending to a padded floor mat along the left wall ceased activity and rolled out of sight into the next room. Opposite the wall with the floor mat—probably a wrestling mat—stood an open doorway the cleaning bot had used, leading to a shower room and, by the small-windowed door visible beyond, possibly a sauna. Across from the entry door rested a large bed covered with a white, puffy bedspread. That stood at odds with its gothic wrought-iron framing, posts, and intertwined design that formed the headboard.

Colossra closed the door behind us with an oral command. A lock clicked into place. A red light in the panel next to the recessed door handle verified it was indeed locked. The green button below the red light would presumably unlock it, as would an authorized voice command.

So would my bayonet and revolver.

"This room should do as good as any," she announced. "Assuming you are not interested in any of my services."

"Thank you, I'm not," I said, trying to keep the sound of relief from my voice. I didn't know what she knew or suspected, nor what her expectations might be. But engaging in *services* wasn't on my list, and having to say it first might've been insulting. "How secure is this place?" I asked, examining the walls and mirrors a little more closely.

Nothing obvious. Maybe behind the mirrors, or behind some of the cobalt paneling that wasn't as opaque as similar instances of decorative accenting.

"From whom?" she asked. "Visitors, intruders?"

"That," I said. "And surveillance?"

She nodded, signaling for me to follow her across the room to the bed area. "Restricted from accessing this section of the Palace. I'd be informed of anyone entering this floor. Pictures and recordings? Those only happen if clients specifically request, and then only through entertainment recording bots authorized entry into the room or suite. The Palace is known for its discretion, especially as some influential clients don't want *any* record of their visits, electronic reservation, audio, visual, or otherwise to exist. Or ever to have existed."

That last statement reminded me of a lie I'd told just prior to being attached to the Cranaltar IV. I was on death's doorstep at the time, and the experimental device was supposed to have scrambled my brain, even as it downloaded my memory in order to translate it into a visual and auditory presentation. One intended to prove my innocence, and turn the tables on Capital Galactic, on Falshire Hawks, their representative accusing me.

I hinted to Hawks during my pretrial that I'd glimpsed a vid of him enjoying himself at the Celestial Unicorn Palace, and that the memory might become part of the official record, what had later become known as the *Documentary*.

Well, at least by seeing Falshire Hawks here on the Bonnisbin Orbital Colony, there might've been some truth to my blind assertion. And, such an assertion made by me, if reported by Hawks, or at least shared with his circle of trusted friends and associates…

Maybe I blushed or betrayed my thoughts as Colossra shifted her stance and put her hands on her hips. With a frown, she gestured to a padded chair along the wall not far from the bed, angled to face it.

"You know who I am?" I asked, unshouldering my satchel and preparing to sit.

"I do, Relic."

The way she said 'Relic,' more than using the word, caused me to bristle. A list of derogatory retorts lined up to cross my tongue, ready to be shot back at her. In the past, I'd've been ready to fight for less, but I managed to keep my hands from balling into fists. It wasn't that she was a mountain of muscle. I'd been beat down by Colonial Marines that could wipe the floor with Colossra—unless she was some unarmed combat expert. And even then…

No. Instead, I took a deep breath, and said, "Yep, I'd say you've got me pegged." Figuring that sitting down would further diffuse the situation, I did.

She followed suit, sitting on the edge of her bed, one hand resting on the iron trellis-like footboard. Her eyebrows narrowed as a scrutinizing look crossed her face. "I think Maintenance Tech Segreti doesn't know you as well as he indicated."

I thought about that a second. "What? Because I'm not issuing you a bruising?"

Her left eyebrow arched before a playful smile stretched her lips. "You really think you could?"

"You realize I have a set of brass knuckles in my pocket."

Her arms flexing, Colossra said, "If you think they'd help."

I shrugged. "Usually they do. But there was this Colonial Marine named Pillar, and this Five-Time Platinum Ring Kickboxing Champion. I did manage to bruise them a bit—while they proceeded to clean my clock."

"Segreti said you weren't one to be intimidated."

"I've decided to focus my aggressive tendencies on the enemy."

"You mean the Crax?" she asked.

I nodded. "Them, the Stegmars, the V'Gun."

"What about the trail of bodies you left behind recently? Human bodies."

It was my turn to shrug. "I have to be alive to continue killing Crax. Besides, anyone allied with Capital Galactic *is* the enemy."

"No one that works at the Palace thinks much of the Capital Galactic Investment Group. At least not anymore."

"I can imagine," I said with a smirk.

"No, Keesay…or Deering—or Bleys?"

"Let's stick with Deering for now." I leaned back in the chair. "Easier for me to keep track of who I'm supposed to be."

"Okay then, Mr. Deering. You probably can't imagine." She leaned back, propping herself up on the mattress with an elbow, then thought better of it and stood. "We've got time to burn. Would you mind background music, maybe some tea?"

"Authentic tea?" I asked.

She started to roll her eyes. "I can serve you Earl Grey, cinnamon apple, or peppermint. And *authentic* sugar."

"Sorry," I said. "This is a high class establishment. I'm used to getting only the synthesized stuff." I had a stash of gum wraps with authentic sugar back on the *Nuclear Pitchfork*.

Wondering if I'd ever board the shuttle again distracted me while Colossra walked along the wall beyond her bed, over to the corner. She tapped a few places and a panel slid aside, revealing a small kitchenette dispensary. "I take it you'd like sugar then, Mr. Deering?"

"Yes," I said. Then I mumbled, "Whoever picked that name…" Taking a breath I decided on a change in direction. "Just call me Kra."

She giggled as she placed two cobalt blue cups in a microwave. Giggling just didn't seem to fit her. While the water was heating, she returned to the bed and placed her palm on a panel, causing it to lift, revealing a computer console. After a few voice commands, soft harp music began to play.

"So what's the plan?" I asked. "Time to kill—burn until what?" Scratching my neck, I continued, explaining, "Segreti didn't say anything beyond getting here and asking for you."

"Kra, you say?" She returned to the kitchenette, selected tea bags and dipped them in the steaming cups of water. Before she turned and brought them back, I removed my contacts and returned them to the thumb-sized case in my pocket.

With a grin she said, "I'm trusting you without a saucer."

I looked down at the carpet, my eyes now able to fully focus.

For a second she giggled again. "It's duro-sealed fiber. I don't have saucers even if you wanted one." Again, a giggle just didn't match her build and original demeanor. Maybe because I wasn't one of her clients?

I smelled the tea before taking a sip. Earl Grey. With sugar. Leaning back, I asked, "The plan?"

"The goal is to get you back to your shuttle, alive and undetected. The details are still being worked out."

"So then…how much time do we have to burn?"

"Enough for you to tell me why Capital Galactic wants you so dearly, dead or alive."

"If I tell you, will you tell me why you dislike the Capital Galactic Investment Group?"

She sat on the bed, legs crossed in what looked like a yoga position, or how some of the colonist kids from the *Kalavar* used to sit on the shuttle bay floor while I explained game rules to them, like whiffle ball. The seated position didn't appear easy for Colossra to achieve, muscular legs and holding a cup of hot tea. I politely looked past her, toward the kitchenette.

She giggled, almost spilling her tea. "Don't be concerned, Kra. I'm wearing undergarments."

Maybe I was blushing, and tried to mask it with a smile. "Good to know. Should I call you Colossra?"

"Yeong," she said, and smiled back. "Very few men ever ask me that." She gently swirled the tea in her cup. "Have an interest in my real name."

I didn't know what to say to that. Most men, I suspected, didn't pay to have tea and a conversation with Colossra. The men who visit her? They must have some odd ideas of fantasy fulfillment. In all sincerity, I replied, "That's too bad."

She stared at me hard, probably trying to determine what I was thinking, so I added, "Sort of like when I worked as a security specialist. All people saw was my 4th Class rating."

"What's wrong with that?"

"On my duty coveralls, above the right breast pocket is my name patch. Above the left is my C4 Security rating."

"So?" She took a sip of tea.

"Only Relic Techs are assigned an initial Class 4 rating. I-Techs start at a C3."

It was her turn to blush. Maybe she was thinking back to her calling me a Relic.

I shrugged. "Not like a lady like you, at an establishment like this would see many R-Techs—at least not security specialist R-Techs."

"You're right, as far as security goes. But every now and again a Relic Tech client makes his way here." She got up after finishing her tea. "I've heard you also killed more than your fair share of Stegmar Mantis and Crax. I almost expected you to arrive at the Palace carrying your old-style shotgun and bayonet."

She'd probably gotten that last part from Segreti. I finished my tea and started to stand, but Colossra signaled for me to remain seated. While she strode over to retrieve my cup, I said, "I'm not in the class of a Colonial Marine, but I've killed my share."

"It is possible that what I've come to understand isn't accurate," she said, placing the cups in the kitchenette's cleaning compartment. "Or you're a modest individual. One *doesn't* see many of those here at the Palace."

I laughed. "I've been called many things, Yeong. I don't recall modest."

She returned to the bed and again sat cross-legged on it. "You were going to tell me why Capital Galactic wants you so dearly. And then maybe about the war?"

"Will we have time? You're supposed to tell me why you don't like CGIG, same as me."

"More than enough time."

"Okay," I said, leaning back in the chair. Thinking about Capital Galactic, my hand involuntarily slid toward my sidearm. I had to be careful. There were parts of my story that remained classified. To give me a few seconds to gather my thoughts, I pulled out my stun baton and began to reinstall the battery. "Since the Crax and CGIG are tied together, you'll get both stories in one. But, beyond the reason you dislike Capital Galactic, I have a few questions I'd like answered. Primarily how I'm supposed to get back to my shuttle—whatever details you might have."

She nodded. "If the stories satisfy my curiosity, I'll do my best to satisfy yours." The excitement in her voice caused me to look past her equivocation.

I decided to start with my waking up on the *Pars Griffin*, just before my pretrial and subsequent connection to the Cranaltar IV. Then I could skip about here and there, still telling about some of my time aboard the *Kalavar* and the enemy boarding. I made no reference to Maximar Drizdon Jr., and replaced him with the Chicher diplomat where it made sense. I then briefly told of my experience in the trench line, defending against the Crax invasion of the Tallavaster colony city, and getting wounded and captured by an elite Crax warrior, omitting any reference to the secret Umbelgarri subterranean breeding facility.

As I spoke, her rapt interest left little doubt that my tale went far to satisfy her curiosity.

CHAPTER 21

My watch showed that I'd been talking for well over an hour and through two more cups of tea. Close attention as she was paying, Yeong hadn't said a word while I relayed the highly abridged version of my tale. It ended with me on the operating table and Lawyer Heartwell assuring me that, despite the fact that the Tallavaster Colony would be temporarily liberated from Crax control, they'd get control of me again.

Needless to say, my voice was getting a little hoarse, having talked for so long. And, filled with tea, I asked Yeong where I might find the restroom.

Upon returning from the restroom located off the sauna area, Yeong had changed into a white T-shirt and shorts, both stretched tight by her overly muscled frame. She asked, "One question, if I might, Kra?"

"Sure," I said, anxious to discover the plan to get me back to the *Nuclear Pitchfork*.

"What happened to the Chicher diplomat?"

I sighed, and choked up for a second, recalling the moment of the diplomat's death. He'd left the safety of our escape shuttle to help me fight off a burly engineering tech who'd blindsided and tackled me.

"He took a Crax caustic round in the back as I was hauling him up the ramp to our escape shuttle," I said. "He'd just saved my life and I failed to save his." I took a breath. Looked down at the floor. "Racing out of the atmosphere into space we spotted a behemoth class transport, a Capital Galactic ship orbiting the quarantined planet controlled by Capital Galactic. With a Crax frigate exiting its cargo hold."

Absentmindedly, I rubbed the small scars on my throat where the diplomat had bitten me. The bite occurred even as the rat-like alien suffered a brief but agonizing death. Me being a friend and companion to the Chicher diplomat, I served as a surrogate, being the closest thing he had to a pack member. That's why I was bit, at the culmination of the death ritual. Something accomplished despite the fierce pain Crax rounds bring as their fluid spreads, killing the victim.

I hadn't really had the chance to share my story with anyone. Nobody on Io talked about it. Agents Guymin and Vingee had seen the *Documentary*, so there wasn't much to tell that they didn't already know. Even the brief telling I'd just relayed, riddled with holes and inaccuracies as it was, offered some small valve of relief.

I'd always been a loner of sorts. What R-Tech traveling through space wouldn't be? Telling Yeong had given me a chance to unload, like setting down a heavy weigh that I'd been hefting for far too long. Even picking it up again, it felt a small fraction lighter.

But it'd also stirred up anger. Not only at so many deaths—Mer,

Benny…virtually everyone aboard the *Kalavar*, crew, colonists, and passengers, and so many more. And, being reminded of Deputy Director Simms and Janice Tahgs, captives of CGIG. Maybe dead by now.

Except for times of prayer, I suppressed memories of those crewmen, those friends and colleagues. People. And if the Crax get their way—if they win—humanity will be enslaved, or an extinct species. Sure, maybe small pockets hiding on isolated moons, or scattered refugee ships on the run.

My jaw tightened. My nails bit into my palms with my hands clenched so tightly into fists. I took several deep breaths to relax, knowing I wouldn't be one of the few, scattered survivors, hunted and hiding, on the run, as our numbers dwindled. Humanity diminishing to nothing.

We'll win, I reminded myself. And if we don't, I'll take down as many Crax and Stegmar—any of their allies as I could. That promise included human collaborators.

But I'd have to get off the Bonnisbin Orbital Colony, and not as a captive to be delivered into Capital Galactic's clutches. With that notion in mind, I asked Yeong, "So, what's the plan then? For me to reach my shuttle undetected."

"Are you hungry, Kra?" she asked, pointing back toward the kitchenette with a friendly, earnest look on her face.

"The plan?"

"It's still coming together," she said.

"Maybe you could check on the progress?"

She placed a finger on her right ear, indicating her communication chip implant. "I'll be signaled."

Leaning forward in the padded chair, I said, "You must have some idea. This isn't your first attempt at covert activity."

"I would ask that you be patient. I'll get us something to eat, and tell you about Capital Galactic's—"

I cut her off, saying, "Patience isn't one of my long suits, Miss Yeong. For all I know, this is nothing more than an elaborate setup." I held up a finger and continued before she could interject. "More likely than that, those working with you have been stymied, or detained."

Sure, stirring up those memories might've shortened my fuse. But playing at being an Intel agent just wasn't me—and wasn't working. I was a trained Security Specialist, and a good one. My instincts and actions had enabled me to survive thus far. Sure, more than my fair dose of luck, but aggressive attitude, decisive action got things done. Thumped more than a few times, but *being* me kept me alive.

I stood. "The R in R-Tech doesn't stand for retarded."

At the change in my demeanor, Yeong's—or Colossra's—eyes widened, then narrowed, hands sliding to her hips. "All you've got is a stun baton and brass knuckles in your pockets and a knife in your satchel. And you think you can intimidate me, here? In my office?"

"Listen, lady," I said, pointing at the mirrors. "My guess is optical and infrared scanners for tracking. Infrared since much of your *office* work is probably accomplished in the dark. Voice command initiation to execute, means I'd recognize the phrase for what it is. Probably electronically charged needle-darts, fired from ports that'll break through the ceiling panels. My guess is the system installed will take half a second to deploy and another quarter second to acquire. That's more time than I need."

Then I pointed past her, to the kitchenette. "I read about that model in a catalog years ago while on warehouse duty. You've got a modified home defense model. Those decorative knobs house nozzles for 'crete string." Concrete string was a polymer gel mixture that could solidify within seconds upon striking a target. "I won't get within range of that. Nor of the Taser mounted behind the manufacturer emblem."

I didn't tell her that any projectiles would be stopped by the A-Tech defensive screen device mounted on my belt. I could activate it before any harm would come my way.

"Okay, security man. You get away from me. Then what?"

"You forgot my revolver," I said, flicking my jacket aside. "You're probably thinking that scanning arch rendered the gunpowder in my bullets inert? At best the installed null-spectrum rays degraded them so that instead of the impact of a .357 magnum round, they'll only hit as standard .38 special. That's more than enough.

"Those sec-bots near the elevator? Those models I eat for breakfast. Those security specialists? Enough might take me down, but not before I critically damage this facility."

She began to roll her eyes.

"That quarantine planet, the one where the diplomat died? We were in such a hurry because I'd initiated a nuclear accident that, if it didn't blow, would be a hell of a radioactive mess to clean up. Just because I don't depend on technology doesn't mean I'm ignorant when it comes to using and manipulating it."

"That's a lot of bluster, Keesay." Her voice held bravado, but it rang hollow.

"Why do you think Capital Galactic is offering eight hundred million credits for me, or my head? You and your pals want to bring me down? Turn me over for the reward? Just remember, *Nemo me impune lacessit.*"

"What does that mean?"

"My motto," I said, balancing on the balls of my feet. "All you need to know is that when this dance starts, you'll be the first to die."

CHAPTER 22

Waving her hands in front of her, and with a wide-eyed look, Colossra said, "No, no. I'm on your side, Kra. We all are."

"We?" I asked. "Who constitutes *we?*"

Seeing I relaxed some, she put her hands down and sat back on the edge of her bed. "Besides me, there's Marvie. He's out, checking on routes and who's still looking for you." When my right eyebrow twitched up, she quickly added, "Somebody has to be out there. I—I, I trust him more than my brother."

I shrugged. What's done is done. "Who else?"

"That know about you being here?" She took a deep breath and exhaled. "That know the sought-after Specialist Keesay is here?" She held up two fingers. "Violet and Mr. Grosstin."

I knew the name, Grosstin. He was the sole owner of the Celestial Unicorn Palace. No investors, no board of directors. There wasn't an up-to-date audio, let alone visual, image of him. None that I'd ever come across. Although I never put an effort into searching, I recalled several editorial commentaries in the few business journals I followed stating such. That was when I'd had time to read, so maybe that had changed?

"That's all, then?"

"All that I know of. Unless Mr. Grosstin told somebody else. Maintenance Tech Segreti contacted Marvie, who told Mr. Grosstin, who relayed back to Segreti to tell you to contact me, after I was told."

"Who's Violet and why her?"

"She's an entertainer like me."

Entertainer? That job description fit as good as anything else. Then I thought better. Who was I to judge? Like in so many other ways, I was in the minority, especially light years from Earth, out among the stars.

Coloss—Yeong's hands returned to her hips as she stood. She'd recognized the look of disapproval that had crossed my face.

I mirrored her position. "If you haven't already figured it out for yourself, have your friend Marvie verify with Segreti. I'm not a likable person. Never have been, even among R-Techs." I shrugged, keeping my hands on my hips. "The plan? The one that you were going to tell me about? What you know about it?"

A smile crept across her face as she leaned back on the bed, the muscles in her neck, shoulders and arms relaxing. "I thought you were going to break into some psychotic violence a moment ago. You really had me convinced."

"It wasn't an act," I said, sitting down. "If things go wrong…if I'm betrayed by you or any of your friends…"

She looked away, at her finger nails, then at the floor. "Marvie's information is always right. He said you'd left a trail of bodies. It matched what Maintenance Tech Segreti had to say about you."

"Which was?" I kept a straight face.

"Said you were fearless, ruthless. And reckless."

I shook my head. "The last two are on target. The first? I've been afraid more times than I care to admit."

"Really?" Yeong asked, a playful lilt returning to her voice. "Like when?"

"Like when a Marine named Pillar was pounding the tar out of me. Even if he didn't kill or cripple me, I was afraid I'd've been in the infirmary, not fit for duty and my contract with Negral Corp would've been voided. My career ruined.

"When the Crax and Stegmars reached the trench line on Tallavaster. They're stronger, faster, better armed and equipped, and there were more of them than us. Watching men die around me. I was scared.

"The thing is, I refuse to let fear dictate my actions."

"I can see that," she said. "That means Tech Segreti is right about you. What does that phrase, your motto you said mean?"

"*Nemo me impune lacessit?*" I said. "That's Latin for 'Nobody injures me with impunity.'"

Yeong thought about that for a second. "If I recall, there's an old saying. Sort of an archaic, R-Tech one."

"Yeah? What's that?"

"I think they used to say, 'Payback's a bitch.'"

I hadn't heard that one before. After laughing I said, "Wonder how that would translate into Latin?"

After telling me the plan: Transport via a dolly-bot, concealed in a hollowed-out auxiliary cooling system, slated for replacement in the *Nuclear Pitchfork*. Marvie would get me to a meet-up point and Tech Segreti would continue the delivery, and assist with 'installation' if necessary. A backup plan was for me to do a little spacewalk, in a space suit, if external monitoring wasn't focused on the *Pitchfork*. I didn't care for either plan. In the first, I'd be cooped up and vulnerable. In the second, I had little experience in zero atmosphere suits, limited to basic training and two practice sessions prior to my working security on Pluto. Who really expects an R-Tech to suit up and work in space?

As Marvie hadn't reported in, Yeong offered me an energy bar. It was good quality, infused with vitamins, vital minerals, and tasted like graham crackers and peanut butter.

After Yeong finished her own energy bar, she cleared her throat. I was back in my chair and she, back in her cross-legged position on her bed. She still appeared nervous, which kept me a little on edge, not knowing what concerned her. It could've been me, but it could've been something else. A concern that things might not be exactly as she'd presented them, and how

I'd respond once I found out?

I leaned forward, resting my forearms on my knees. "You were going to tell me about why you and so many at the Palace don't care for Capital Galactic?"

She nodded once with a small, embarrassed smile. "That's right, Kra." She extended her arms and leaned back on them. It didn't look all that comfortable, but maybe she was more flexible than she appeared.

"I wasn't born this way. I have to work out, but we at the Palace cater to exotic desires. Unique opportunities." She paused, probably gauging my reaction.

"Mr. Grosstin recognized this business opportunity and turned to genetic manipulation to achieve it. He had to set up his establishment out here around 70 Virginis, beyond the jurisdiction of laws regulating such advancements which were morally and scientifically objectionable to some." Irritation entered her voice as she ended the last statement, but shifted to a more upbeat tone as she continued. "It was early in humanity's expansion, and those that established themselves light years out established the rules."

I nodded, knowing that the orbital colony around 70 Virginis was the first of the distant ones established, largely funded by the owner of the Celestial Unicorn Palace.

"For men and women to explore their fantasies," Yeong said, "some old rules needed to be broken. And setting the bar high, needing to travel seventy-nine light years from Earth would, by default, limit the Palace's clientele to those that truly desired the experience, and could truly afford it."

She paused, looking for some reaction.

"I don't have a problem with individuals spending their wealth any way they want," I said, "as long as it's not aimed at damaging or destroying other individuals. One corporation undermining and conquering another through hostile takeovers. Or through legal maneuvers aimed at depleting the target's financial resources rather than actually winning in court. There I hold some pretty strong opinions."

She took a few breaths to absorb what I'd said. "Me? I came for the opportunity. I'd always been interested in bodybuilding. Mr. Grosstin offered me an opportunity to advance it a few steps further."

She sat up and flexed her right arm, showing off her bulging bicep. "This could never come from weight lifting, not with my frame. Steroids and other drugs, it might've been possible, but they have serious complications. Mr. Grosstin's wife, a genetic engineering genius, altered the myogenesis within my body. Normally this can't be done for adults, but she knew how, just like she knew how to manipulate the genetic composition of many entertainers here."

Relaxing her bicep, she continued, saying, "A reasonable workout regimen keeps me built up, and powerful. I can bench 300 kilograms. But it's not all muscle.

"When we met, that jostling. I always do that with clients to ascertain their unarmed combat skills." She stood next to her bed. "You may have surmised, I'm more than just brawn. Even before I came here I'd studied Judo, and continue to this day."

I nodded, reappraising her. "I thought your vice grip handshake and escape from my arm lock was some sort of test."

Yeong smiled sheepishly, which fit her about as much as her occasional giggle. "My clients tend to be powerful men, not the brawn and muscle variety, but power as in wealth and controlling the direction of their life, corporations and the lives of others. More of them than you might expect are competent in self-defense techniques. A few are experts in one or more forms of martial arts."

She slid her long hair back behind her shoulders. "Most of them come to be challenged. Dominated. Not in a masochistic way. We don't do that here at the Palace. For most, it's an exalting experience. Reinvigorates them."

I shrugged my shoulders and looked away. Seemed odd but, then again, I believed sex with a woman should be within the context of marriage. A view which I imagined was more uncommon than views held by the Palace's clients.

"Okay," I said. "You know why I hate Capital Galactic. What do you have against them? What about the Palace in general?"

Her smile morphed to a sneer. "Somehow, a client paid by a follow-on Capital Galactic client, stuck me. Injected some sort of uber steroid. Not knowing what had happened, I continued my weight and exercise routine. Within days my muscle mass expanded and nobody knew why, and it didn't stop. Imagine a forty-three percent gain in muscle mass on this frame."

She turned left and right, flexing to emphasize before leaning back and sitting on the edge of her bed again. "It was so bad I lost significant mobility. When that happened, the growth slowed. So I went on absolute bed rest while the doctors figured out what was happening.

"In the meantime, I had a very important client scheduled. A mega-leviathan."

Yeong saw my questioning expression. "A leviathan is like a whale for a gambling house. Big spender. A mega-leviathan, well, one can mean the difference between a profitable year and years to follow. Disappoint, and he'll never return, and *encourage* others to withhold their patronage.

"I couldn't cancel. He was already en route. And when he arrived, he didn't care about my predicament—which isn't uncommon among clients." She snorted. "Most are self-important. And consider us little more than a play thing. Disposable.

"This guy was polite but insistent. Nine days scheduled with me at ten times my normal compensation, plus his other expenditures. Each day of vigorous activity resulted in reinvigorated muscle growth. And the guy got off on it. On my distress, as much as I tried to hide it. My suffering."

She crossed her arms, nostrils flaring. "When he left I could hardly stand, barely move about. In his warped mind, he'd conquered me.

"The doctors figured out what was in my blood, filtered it out. They totally immobilized me for six weeks, allowing my muscles to atrophy, along with a new round of genetic therapy. Without the latter, I'd have had to retire.

"I can't prove it, but that Capital Galactic executive arranged it." Momentarily she cussed under her breath before the veneer of an entertainer, a lady, covered her emotions. "Mr. Grosstin wouldn't let me reject all CGIG clients. They, or those that had connections to CGIG made up over half of our client base. But he allowed me to charge double my normal rate."

Yeong took a deep breath. "And they paid my elevated rate. So I took the credits." She looked around reflexively, and sighed. Then frowned. "You understand about bounties. How they work."

I nodded once.

"I could never get the CGIG exec," she said. "The mega-leviathan. But his accomplice?" Her hands balled into fists. "It's my understanding that he encountered an unfortunate industrial accident."

I asked, "*Nemo me impune lacessit?*"

She thought a moment, her hands relaxing. "Yeah, maybe." She paused again. "You and me, Kra. We're not as different as I thought."

I grinned. "We have the same enemies, Yeong, albeit for different reasons. That kind of thing can forge some pretty strong bonds. Maybe even permanent ones."

"What sort of bond do you believe has been formed?"

"I believe you just spoke from the heart, shared something you've rarely shared with anyone." Thinking of McAllister, and the Colonization Riots years ago, where I killed her fiancé, I continued. "I've formed an alliance of sorts with someone who wanted me dead more than just about anything else in the galaxy. Everything except the fact that we had a mutual enemy. The Crax. With them, we're just humans. A race to be exterminated. When confronted with that, our squabbles and hatred have to be set aside.

"You know why I'm fighting, Yeong. And I'll continue to do what I can to see us survive, and the Crax and their allies destroyed."

It was my turn to ball my hands into fists, thinking of the Crax on Io, and the lab and med techs fighting them. Facing the enemy, if only because there was no other choice.

"You know," I said, "the Felgans are defeated, and the Umbelgarri aren't far from it. We're losing on every front, and the Chicher? They're next in line to be, eliminated.

"They'll go down fighting alongside us. If it comes to that. One more dead Crax is one fewer Crax to enjoy the fruits of their victory."

"*Nemo me impune lacessit,*" she said.

"Damn straight," I said.

We spent a moment of silence, each buried in our own thoughts.

Her question, "You wanted to know what the Celestial Unicorn Palace has against Capital Galactic?" snapped me out of my thoughts, wondering what Dr. Goldsen was doing, and what Corporal Smith, a friend from the *Kalavar*, would think of her.

I could ponder where that odd connection of people came from later. "Correct," I said.

"Not long before Capital Galactic's assets were frozen and its board of directors arrested for treason, several of their corporate operatives hacked into the Palace's computer system and stole some important data."

Before I could wonder, she added, "It's common knowledge, at least among corporate lawyers and executives. Mr. Grosstin sent a message rocket containing the confession of the corporate operative that didn't get away to Earth, set to broadcast directly to the Criminal Justice Investigatory Department and Capital Galactic's Corporate Headquarters. The immediate ban of Capital Galactic executives followed, and an increased access fee charged to executives with direct ties to CGIG."

"That must've cut in on Mr. Grosstin's bottom line," I said.

"That didn't matter to him. We lost some business, but the additional fee made up for some of it."

To me it was obvious what Capital Galactic was after. Either lists of clients and associated corporate secrets the Palace's entertainers might've gathered while performing services, or knowledge of advanced genetic engineering, exclusive to the Celestial Unicorn Palace.

I was about to voice my speculations and gauge Yeong's reaction when she glanced toward the entrance. "Marvie's returned," she said, placing a hand to her ear. "This isn't good."

CHAPTER 23

Ten minutes later Marvie was in Yeong's workout room, explaining what he'd discovered, and demanding that I take my clothes off.

By his name, I expected Marvie to be a young man, not thin, wrinkled, and gray. He wasn't much taller than me and moved about pretty well for someone who had to be in his late 80s. He reminded me of an aged errand boy from some old-time crime boss. Alert, quick and smooth talker.

"It won't take long for that bounty hunter to convince someone in Security to back his claim," Marvie said, speaking fast, waving animated hands. "And gain admittance to the Palace here." His suspicious eyes shifted to me. "Especially if he offers a cut of the bounty—which he'll do. Miggs-zel is like that."

Miggs-zel, I gathered, was a bounty hunter.

The old man squinted at Yeong standing next to me. "Remember two years ago, when that lady embezzler was on the dock? He tracked her here when everyone else'd given up. Bribed Ms. Ambleer, manager of the Cluclow Hotel, and Roxort, that S2 Security Supervisor, to look the other way?

"Won't get Mr. Grosstin or anyone here at the Palace to look the other way," Marvie said, his squinting eyes shifting to me, "but Security wants to speak with ya in an urgent way, Bleys, err Keesay…or whoever."

He pulled what appeared to be a form-fitting silk skull and face mask from a pocket. It shimmered with thousands of tiny facets. "Tell'em, Colossra. Tell'em to undress b'cause time's running out. Miggs-zel's got someone watching to see if Keesay leaves."

I knew what the shimmering face and headdress was. A holo-mask, used at masquerade parties and theatrical events. Expensive but it wouldn't fool security cameras, even outdated ones. "Any security camera that spots someone wearing that—it'll red flag you. May not be able to penetrate the holographic disguise, but—"

Marvie cut me off. "So says you. This one's got A-Tech projectors. Sucks energy like a black hole and feels like ants crawling all over your face an' scalp. Uncomfortable as hell." He pointed at me with his free hand. "Only has to work for a few minutes. Long enough for me to lose any that's watching. I can do that, no problem, but it doesn't do more than my face." He looked at his pointing finger. "Well, I got gloves too."

I'd seen a hologram image once fool security cameras and equipment, but it was Umbelgarri design. Marvie's holo-mask appeared to be of human, or I-Tech design, supplemented by A-Tech hardware and software. Motion detectors and pattern tracking sonar would detect an anomaly with visual tracking sensors. The electronic signature emanating from such a device? That was an even greater vulnerability.

When I started to disrobe, Marvie offered me his brown jacket, saying, "Only need your jacket and body suit. Keep your boots." His eyes widened. "And your gun."

He looked up at Yeong. "Colossra, you must have something he can wear besides my jacket." He pulled a set of faceted gloves from his jacket pocket, and an optical scanner. "Violet's been alerted. Should be here any minute."

After I was undressed and standing in my underwear, Marvie said, "Hold still," and circled me, pointing the optical scanner at my face and head. Then he scanned my hands. While he was tapping at the optical scanner's small icon screen, commanding it to download data to the mask and gloves, Yeong returned from the bedroom with a pair of white coveralls and a black shoulder bag.

"These should fit," she said. The black shoulder bag wasn't exactly a purse. She rolled her eyes at my expression. "Whatever you've got in your satchel should fit in this."

I had my coveralls, wrapped up in my satchel, but something other than those colors might prove useful when trying to avoid getting picked out of a crowd. While I got dressed and belted on my gun, Marvie dressed too. He slid on the mask and gloves. With a voice command, the holographic disguise activated. "How's it look?"

I thought it was a pretty good match. Yeong said, "Be sure to keep a straight face, or scowl, Marvie."

Before I could say anything, movement in the bedroom caught my attention. My hand moved to my revolver.

"It's okay," Yeong said. "Violet used the back entrance."

"Back entrance?" I asked.

"Fast as he went for his gun," Marvie said, a look of concern on his—my face, "I'm gonna get going." He deactivated the mask and gloves. "I hate this damn thing," he said more to Yeong than me, especially as my attention was split between him and the woman walking through the doorway, into the exercise room.

She was tall, nearly as tall as Agent Vingee. She had long green hair, a deep jade color. That was less spectacular than her skin. No question where she got her name. Deep violet with occasional rippling flashes of what my mother would call lilac and plum surged along her smooth skin. That told me it wasn't makeup, and it certainly wasn't a body-covering version of a holo-mask. Violet's eyes matched her hair and her lips were black, matching her finger nails.

So focused on her skin and hair, I didn't notice her silky emerald dress right away. It reached mid-thigh and was very low cut, revealing a chest that made Hostess Bambi seem like Violet's younger, undeveloped sister.

When I glanced back, Marvie was already out the door.

"As you might have guessed, Kra, this is Violet."

"Adorable attire," the purple beauty said, eyeing me from head to boot. Her voice flowed in a soft, relaxed cadence. It rubbed me the wrong way.

"Here." I took off Marvie's jacket and tossed it at her. "Use this to supplement your lacking."

She ignored it, letting it strike her and drop to the floor.

"Violet," Yeong interjected. "There's a reason Capital Galactic wants him so badly." The women's eyes met, exchanging unvoiced communication.

Yeong turned to face me and bowed her head. "It was a pleasure to meet you, Kra. I wish you luck and…continued vengeance."

Abrupt as the dismissal was, I picked up Marvie's jacket and extended my hand, "I'm glad I met you as well, Yeong. I don't know your future dreams and aspirations, but I hope you meet them." As we shook, out of the corner of my eye, I caught Violet's emerald eyes widen. Maybe at the use of Colossra's real name.

While I'd wondered in the back of my mind about much of what Yeong had said, the purple entertainer's reaction indicated Yeong had been truthful about her name. It gave me hope she'd been truthful about much more.

With Violet, I had far less confidence.

Other than a request to follow her, the purple entertainer didn't say much, at least until we exited into a tight, cylindrical elevator that reminded me of a narrow closet. She'd entered first and turned to face me. The door closed as soon as I'd stepped in. Immediately I wished I hadn't followed so quickly. It was too tight to turn around so I stood face to face with her ample cleavage, her breasts actually pressed against my shoulders.

I looked up and met her amused gaze. Assisting my escape or not, she was in need of an attitude adjustment. Even as I reached into my jacket pocket, Violet seemed to grow taller, elevating her breasts to frame my chin. Her shoes. Heels designed to elevate or depress as desired.

"*You* may find this entertaining," I said, leaning back against the door as much as possible. "*I* find it annoying." The snarl in my voice was evident.

"I am attempting to ascertain the sort of man you are, Security Specialist Keesay. May I address you as Kra?"

"I am the sort that gets angry when an elevator remains stationary when it should be moving. Address me however you want, especially after I discharge my stun baton into your thigh."

Her shoes stopped elevating. "A normal heterosexual man would be experiencing arousal and prepared to, if I might be so crude, strike with a more organic baton."

While there'd been some arousal, as she intended, my anger quashed any such desires. "I suspect that your genetically altered skin will react colorfully to an electric jolt. Any thoughts you might care to share on that?" Even as I spoke I prepared for any action that might threaten me or my health.

How had I gone from fighting Crax on Io and dodging capture and execution by bounty hunters, to exchanging threats in a cramped lift with a high expense, genetically enhanced prostitute?

Her shoes reversed their elevation. Even so, I depressed the button on my stun baton. A series of clicks sounded as it telescoped to its sixteen inch length. Then I switched it on, the activation hum sounding like a fist full of angry bees.

"You realize, Specialist Keesay, our bodies are in substantial contact. You will receive forty percent of the discharge, at a minimum."

That she knew the expected electrical transfer from body to body said something. "I'm betting your skin, supplemented with some form of chromatophores, will pulse like a purple rainbow as the electrical charge courses through it. I've witnessed Umbelgarri under fire. Colors, like ripples in a pond, flow from their wounds."

An image of the alien, a lumbering quadruped with an energy beam generator strapped to its back, flashed in my mind. It exited a crippled main battle tank, surrounded by Bahklacks. Under heavy fire from advancing Crax and Stegmars, they never made it to our trench line. Our line which was overrun moments later.

Violet leaned back, as much as was possible. Staring down into my eyes, which I imagined were hard and uncaring, she said, "Now I perceive the sort of man you are."

I switched off my stun baton, causing it to emit the fading deactivation hum. "And what sort of man is that?"

"Elevator, return," she said before answering me. As it dropped, she continued. "The sort devoid of humor and passion for life."

"Being hunted sort of saps one's sense of humor. So I'll grant you that. But passion for life? I've fought to live, harder and more often than you perceive."

The purple entertainer noted the sarcasm at the end of my retort. "I suspect you shall need to retain that passion, if you hope to continue." As the elevator slowed, she added, "Unsolicited, I advise you to smile more often, Specialist Keesay. Laughter, even fake laughter, will prove reinvigorating. More than you might expect."

I was tempted to laugh at her advice, but refrained. What she'd said was laced with truth.

Violet's private suite was roughly twice the size of a mid-level military officer's quarters. Not surprisingly, pillows and padded furniture, primarily purple and white, filled her rooms. Her suite was located on the outer rim of one of the Palace's spinning disks, as evidenced by the slowly passing stars viewed through a pair of oblong portholes set into the purple carpet. The floor's almost imperceptible curve reinforced the room's placement on the disk's outer rim.

Watching as Violet stood at a wall-mounted computer console decoding an encrypted message, I had to admit she was quite alluring. The way subtle shifts in color ran along her skin provided an air of rarity, a touch of the exotic. There was little wonder why powerful men might pay a treasure in credits for the opportunity to spend time with her.

Whereas Yeong's entertainer persona seemed to differ from her true personality, Violet's arrogance? That dominant trait appeared to extend from her entertainer persona to the businesslike personality that emerged after we'd departed the elevator. I guessed the latter was a further glimpse of her true self.

"A moment longer," Violet said. "There are seven levels of encryption." She hiked up her short dress and pulled a thin palm-computer from a strap located high on her thigh. Tapping some icons, she observed the screen for a moment.

While she continued working, I inspected my surroundings. The room's wall panel concealing the elevator was very effective. I'd have wagered a lot that the results from a standard structural scan would be interpreted as a wall section, identical to the adjacent wall panels. No obvious cameras or other surveillance devices. It was possible that hidden sonic sensors tracked movement within the suite, but I doubted it. Such sensors normally supplemented other surveillance methods. Besides, simple pressure detection through the floor plates would be less expensive and, in some ways, more reliable.

That was, of course, if the Troh-gots hadn't provided some of their A-Tech equipment. I knew that V'Gun sensors could detect detailed facial features, even through a civil transport's bulkheads. But didn't see a reason why the Troh-gots, let alone the V'Gun—who were race a subjugated by the Crax—would install advanced sensors in the Palace.

While thinking on that, the patrolling Troh-got battle frigate came into view through the left-hand porthole. The warship's horseshoe-shaped curves were spread with knobs that housed pulse ion cannons, backed by turret-mounted lasers. The Troh-got ion cannons were far superior to those mounted on Chicher battlewagons. More powerful and accurate, just like the quad-beam lasers mounted on the tips of their ships' pointed spar. More lethal than any ship-mounted combat lasers humanity could muster.

I'd never seen a Troh-got ship in action. They fought alongside the Shiggs during the Silicate War, and there were few vids, let alone detailed combat reports. Most of what humanity knew had been gleaned from what the secretive Umbelgarri were willing to share.

The Troh-gots weren't quite in the Umbelgarri or Primus Crax league, but close. They outclassed us humans.

"Those seven levels of encryption won't mean anything if Troh-got software is employed against it," I said to Violet as she walked toward me.

Glancing down, she spotted the alien battle frigate. "What interest could they possibly have in my electronic communications?"

I shrugged. "The same interest they'll have in protecting this orbital dock when the Crax come looking to finish the job?"

"You believe that humanity is destined to lose the war?" Before I could answer, she continued, saying, "It is my understanding that we humans *are* losing. The Umbelgarri, as a cohesive military force, is no longer extant."

While I found her phrasing odd, her assessment was accurate.

I thought about the success on Io, but decided against mentioning it. "That doesn't address what will happen here, *if* we lose."

A dark line of purple flowed from Violet's eyes, down her cheeks and neck before fading away. "I am not among those who establish or enforce policy on the Bonnisbin Orbital Colony."

"But your boss, Mr. Grosstin, has influence."

She frowned, narrow waves of purplish gray emanating from her lips and fading before they reached her cheek bones. "Not sufficient to eradicate the residual presence of Capital Galactic remnants, as you have observed first hand." A wide smile crossed her face, her gleaming white teeth standing out against her coal-black lips.

"So what is the plan?"

"The plan is to ensure your survival, based on the assumption that you'll continue to unravel whatever remaining threads of CGIG fabric you discover."

Verbally sparring about the war and local politics wouldn't go anywhere. "They'll get me eventually."

She directed my attention to her computer clip with a quick hand gesture. "It's doubtful, Specialist, that you're going to be pleased with." She paused for a breath. "The plan."

I crossed my arms. Her voice and grim stare said that she was in earnest. I wouldn't be pleased. "Let's hear it."

I stood, wearing a standard emergency evacuation space suit. Despite the 'upgrade accessories' as Entertainer Violet named them, reinforced elbow and knee areas, thicker, tear-resistant gloves and boots actually designed for contact in zero atmosphere, hardly gave me confidence. An emergency evacuation suit was just that. A suit an untrained civilian slips on before abandoning a ship, shuttle or space structure facing imminent destruction. Float in space and await rescue.

Such suits are designed for minimal contact with surfaces, especially those that might have points or right angles. They're essentially a durable balloon roughly shaped like a human body. A broadcasting beacon and environmental support pack completed the kit. Normally such a suit administered a sedative strong enough to put the wearer into a deep sleep to conserve energy and life support supplies.

For an active wearer? Three and a half hours life support, maximum.

This suit was a dull metallic gray, lacking the reflective coating. It'd stand out less when viewed against the orbital dock's outer hull sections, and might not trigger external camera surveillance.

Strapped to my stomach in a sealed bag was my equipment—stun baton, revolver, brass knuckles and everything else. Holstered on my hips were two hand-portable thrust jets. Really, they were little more than construction drill shaped devices powered by CO_2 canisters. Crude devices, even by R-Tech standards. Point and depress the trigger and your body is propelled the opposite direction, for as long as the compressed CO_2 lasts.

Two magnetic rollers, one for each hand, rounded out my zero space travel equipment. They reminded me of ski poles filled with batteries and tipped by a four inch diameter, magnetic wheel. They were designed to help me maintain contact with the orbital dock's surface and propel me along it—for as long as the batteries lasted.

And the best part of it was, the *Nuclear Pitchfork* had already departed. According to Entertainer Violet, "Thoroughly searched by the orbital dock's security, and 'encouraged' to leave, the business arranging for hydroponics installation and maintenance having been successfully negotiated."

Three *rah rah* cheers for Agent Vingee's successful negotiations, effectively reinforcing the crew of the *Pitchfork*'s cover. And possibly pointing to an alternate career, should Vingee tire of working for Intelligence.

My destination was *Loki's Lady*, Kent O'Vorley and Senior Engineer Nova McAllister's long range shuttle.

The purple entertainer circled around me, checking my gear. It disturbed me that my eyes wasted precious time roving over her curves and scintillating skin instead of focusing on my predicament.

When Violet finished her inspection, I asked, raising one of my magnetic rollers, "You have genetically enhanced skin, advanced holographic equipment. And this jumble rig of equipment comprises the best 'plan' available?"

I was having second thoughts. Maybe I could contact Segreti, or get to *Loki's Lady* another way.

Violet must've seen it in my face. "This is the backup plan of a backup plan. Marvie reported Security is still looking for you." She crossed her arms, pressing down her ample cleavage. "If they believe you're still here and still drawing breath, you can rest assured any bounty hunters or Capital Galactic agents on the dock will be seeking you, and the substantial reward capturing or killing you will bring." She stepped back. Her right hand gestured my direction. "At least those with any measure of competence and minimal connections."

After a sigh, she continued, saying, "My suite has an airlock only a few people loyal to Mr. Grosstin are aware of. I already informed you of this. Try getting an emergency evacuation suit with a silenced automatic homing beacon."

I knew McAllister could do it without breaking a sweat, but genius-level programming engineers probably weren't on the Palace's payroll. Their security equipment and supporting software verified it to me.

So, it came down to two choices. Abandon the 'plan' and attempt to make my way inside the dock to O'Vorley's shuttle, or face the vacuum of space and attempt a walk. Either way, my luck was likely used up.

I made my decision. "I'll risk the walk," I said. "If something goes wrong out there, Capital Galactic won't get the satisfaction of knowing I'm dead."

Violet grinned, then raised a hand to her ear. She stared down at me, frowning as she listened to her embedded communication chip. "It's imperative you depart now. A security team is approaching the Palace entrance. A large one."

I nodded as I checked the holstered CO_2 guns and the wrist straps connected to my rollers.

My mind raced again, rethinking my options. Bounty hunters served a valuable slot in society, but those willing to do CGIG's bidding? Sure the wealth offered—if CGIG actually paid—was a powerful incentive to track and capture, or kill me. But it also spoke to their moral character. A willingness to perform a task for a corporation proven to be working with the Crax, a race determined to crush and subjugate humanity. Or exterminate, which was more likely. Humanity was many things, but docile and willing servitude? There'd always be elements of rebellion. Me among them, of that I was sure.

No. Back to the 'plan.' Better odds of doing more damage to CGIG, and the Crax, if I survived.

When I'd asked her, the purple entertainer explained that most of the time, the spacewalk was to an airlock whose sensors and life-support connections had been compromised years ago. Normally the 'plan' for the individual in the emergency evacuation suit was to reach the nearby air lock. What circumstances necessitated such a spacewalk? Even a short one to the nearby airlock? I didn't really care to know.

That wouldn't work for me. I needed to reach *Loki's Lady* directly, and hope Engineer McAllister wasn't in a vindictive mood. I'd killed her fiancé years ago during the Colonization Riots. She never forgave me, and tried to kill me while aboard the *Kalavar*, and then wreck my career and my life as a fallback when the initial goal failed.

Entertainer Violet directed me with a quick hand gesture to lie down in the revealed floor cavity between the portholes. I retracted the shafts of my magnetic rollers and clipped them to my hips. Stepping into the cavity I gripped her extended hands with my suited and gloved ones. Then the purple woman assisted me as I sat, and then laid flat.

"Remember what I told you," she said. "Grab the steel cable when the air lock opens, or the centrifugal force will hurl you into space and you'll deplete your thrust jets just to get back."

I nodded and flipped down my faceplate. While it sealed and the life support system activated, she added, "Follow the bouncing ball." Bending over and giving me an eyeful of her chest, she made a quick check of my placement and gear. "Don't dally or you'll run out of oxygen. Unless your batteries drain first. Freeze or suffocate, either way you'll be dead."

I nodded and mouthed, "Thank you."

"Give the bastards hell," she said, "and we'll call it even."

I grinned and winked. I'd left Segreti's chit with Yeong.

It didn't matter whether Violet meant the Crax or Capital Galactic, or both. Giving any and all of them hell. That was *my* plan.

The floor plate slid shut, enclosing me in darkness. Faint LED lights lining my faceplate activated. The secondary door below me opened. The capsule dropped, allowing a secondary door above to close. It appeared to be thick as a bulkhead. My capsule vibrated as it was conveyed a short distance laterally and then rotated so that I faced out toward space. I felt more than saw the hatch close and seal. Magnetic plates activated, locking my coffin-like capsule into place.

My hands gripped the side bars as the outward gravity, or whatever it was called, caused by the Palace disk's rotation threatened to launch me when the door opened. I watched and listened. My suit expanded slightly as air was drawn out of my capsule. "Five seconds," a modulated computer voice warned, "until airlock door opens. Four seconds, three seconds, two seconds, one second. Door opening."

There it was: black space pierced by twinkling stars. And the cable along the left hand side of the opening.

"Airlock door will close in thirty seconds," the computer voice warned.

Spreading my knees wide to stabilize myself and slow my ejection from the airlock capsule, I let go of the bar with my left hand and reached. I scraped my knuckles along the edge but snagged the cable.

It felt like holding onto an old-style rope hanging from a tree limb while swinging out over a pond. But, unlike that childhood experience, I wasn't going to let go. Rather, I reached across with my other hand as my legs and hips swung out of the air lock. My right hand latched on to the cable, and I dangled a moment. I closed my eyes, taking deep breaths and refocusing my thoughts.

When I opened my eyes, the airlock was closed.

Then, hand over hand, with protected knees and feet, I climbed the cable along the disk and then over the lip, making my way toward the central shaft. Simulated on my screen, a purple glowing ball bounced along the cable, and I followed.

What I really needed was a harness with a latch hook. Losing my grip and falling from a cliff to spatter on the ground was preferable to drifting off into space. Of course, the suit wasn't made for external chafing and stresses a harness might cause. It wouldn't survive someone being arrested after starting to tumble away.

Sure, if I lost my grip and my hand jets ran dry, breaking radio silence and calling for help was an option. Better to pierce the emergency suit and die quickly…or as quickly as suffocating in the frigid grip of zero gravity space would allow.

I kept going, hand over hand, carefully lifting and placing each knee, watching for any rough patches or jagged welds.

Once I reached the main shaft around which the Palace's disk sections spun, the centrifugal force attempting to hurl me away faded. Once stabilized, hanging in basically zero gravity space allowed my arms and hands a moment's rest.

I'm not ashamed to admit the suit's systems had worked double-time absorbing my cold sweat. During the climb my hands cramped twice because I gripped the cable too tightly.

From there I followed the purple bouncing ball projected onto my faceplate, along a groove in the shaft that took me past two of the Celestial Unicorn Palace's spinning disks. Then I deployed my magnetic rollers. They propelled me across the main sections of the Bonnisbin Orbital Colony.

The process was slow, especially as I strove to be methodical, avoiding portholes and areas festooned with antennas and other outcroppings.

Finally, I spied the docking area. The odds were long that anybody would be looking through their forward or side viewing ports, and see me outside. Even if they did, I might be mistaken for someone performing inspections or maintenance.

For a short time I'd been able to see the Troh-got battle frigate, the light of 70 Virginis reflecting off of it. It'd reminded me of radiation, which the emergency evacuation suit was built to resist.

Then I saw it. Or rather the purple bouncing ball directed my attention toward it. *Loki's Lady*, a sleek long range shuttle, or would've been sleek, except for an auxiliary external thrust engine dorsally mounted, and pair of dual-beam pulse laser turrets. One pair ventrally mounted near the aft section, and the other above the forward bridge area. The area near the shuttle's chin, where the cascading atomic engine that enabled condensed space travel was housed, appeared more bulbous than similar models. Almost like the metal was angry and swollen. Like most long range shuttles, she had an upper and lower level, but appeared stretched fifteen or maybe twenty percent longer than others of her class.

Her portside was attached to the dock, and along the starboard in fierce flowing red script was her name: *Loki's Lady*.

Moving carefully toward the aft section, below the main thrust engines, I found the emergency hatch.

Once I reached it, holding my breath, I deactivated one of the magnetic rollers and tapped against the hatch in the prescribed pattern, announcing my presence to whoever was inside.

CHAPTER 24

After two long minutes, and with only forty minutes of life support left, the shuttle's emergency hatch swung open. I climbed in and around the shuttle's spherical escape pod.

While waving to the camera, the emergency hatch closed. Several seconds later the digital readout next to the internal hatch flashed green. The oval hatch opened.

With her mismatched green and blue eyes, Engineer Nova McAllister stared down at me. A genius in software and hardware design, thrust engines, and cascading atomic engines, and more, she looked down on everyone. She was twenty times smarter than me, and equally difficult to get along with. So it wasn't surprising her first words to me were, "Spend a little time on a space dock and people start looking to kill you? Who would've thought?"

She didn't say it with a smile. More of a sneer. Her orange coveralls reminded me of our days serving together aboard the civil transport *Kalavar*. A platinum ring hung from a silver chain around her neck, the ring I pulled from her lover's hand just after a Crax had killed him, and handed to her just before we fled. The blood that had covered the ring was gone. The hard memories between us remained.

I tapped the sequence to release my facemask's seal. "Some things never change," I said. "Abrasive as ever."

She reached down and offered me a hand to climb out. "You must have been desperate to do a spacewalk in that rig."

The pull of gravity, even artificial, felt good. In the narrow corridor couched between compartments, I said, "Thanks."

"For rescuing you?" She shrugged, emphasizing the shoulder padding in her engineer orange cover suit. "There's some killing that needs to be done. Capital Galactic traitors. Possibly some Crax. It's one of the few things you excel at."

With raised eyebrows, I asked, "Really?"

She showed a feral grin. "With luck, there might be Primus absorbing some of your archaic firearm's buckshot."

"In this?" I glanced back toward the thrust engine compartment. "I saw some modifications, but—"

"But," she interjected, ignoring my question, "the really good news is that you get to experience another bout of cold sleep along the way."

That news made me frown. Going under wasn't bad. The process and result of cold sleep wasn't pretty: pale and frozen, with tubes thrust into every orifice. Ugly as it was, you felt nothing. You didn't even dream. On the other hand, waking up sick, enduring suffering like a triple case of the flu, it's something you never forget. That recovery gets easier after your first cold sleep, or even the second, is a lie. Corporate propaganda aimed at luring the poor and ignorant aboard their colonization ships. I knew firsthand and carried the precursor chemicals in my blood and cell tissues to prove it.

The only good news was that if you survived your first cold sleep and didn't react to the injected drug cocktail that ensured your cells didn't freeze and burst their membranes, you were virtually guaranteed to survive the process from then on, barring equipment failure or a medical technician screwing up. Or someone killing you when you were completely helpless.

Those facts ran through my thoughts…the propagated false rumors, the callused propaganda. No, waking up from cold sleep never got easier.

"There's that glum look I appreciate seeing on your face, Keesay."

As McAllister said it, Kent O'Vorley peered into the corridor and waved. "Hey, Kra. Heard you were making your way here."

I gave him a thumb's up. "Hey, good to see you too, Kent."

McAllister laughed. "Your *one* friend in the galaxy, Keesay."

"One friend?" I asked. "I've got more than *one* friend."

"More than one?" She smirked. "I wager you can count the total on one hand."

I thought about it, knowing the difference between a friend and a co-worker, or an acquaintance. After Kent, there was Segreti, and Guymin, and maybe Vingee. Dr. Goldsen? Without intending to, I shook my head. To her I was closer to a patient turned colleague.

"I bet mine number more than yours," I said, "or would, except for the war."

I'd had friends on the *Kalavar*, but the Crax killed most of them. Corporal Smith, always grinning and poking fun at me for being a security specialist instead of a Colonial Marine. And the Chicher diplomat who'd thought of me as a pack member, survived to escape the *Kalavar* with me and McAllister. The alien served as part of the *Bloodhound 3*'s crew, taking Maximar Drizdon Jr. with us so he wouldn't be captured. The boy survived, but the Chicher, in the end, didn't.

Even as the buried images emerged in my mind, McAllister's right hand shot to the ring dangling from its chain. She'd lost Anatol Gudkov on the *Kalavar*.

The short, arrogant and fiery engineer standing next to me had status and respect, and many colleagues, but Gudkov had been her only friend.

Changing the subject, I asked her, "Where can I get out of this suit, and into something else?"

Her hand dropped to her side. "That anxious to strip down for cold sleep?" Forced mirth hung in her words.

O'Vorley must've sensed the jibes edging toward something darker and stepped between me and McAllister. "Your friends from the *Nuclear Pitchfork* managed to send a care package, before departing." He shook his head, eyes widening. "How they managed it, don't ask me. But at least you've got duty coveralls *and* your shotgun."

"Which shotgun?" I asked, hoping it was the pump-action, especially if we were going to be going up against Primus Crax. They were more advanced than the Gar Crax. Not nearly as large and fierce, but superior technology could make up for that.

He tilted his head back with a wide smile. "Right. Not that double barrel you were carrying, like we used in the Mavinrom Dock's range. It looks like the one you fought with on Tallavaster. Titanium alloy, with a bayonet lug. And the perforated jacket, made from metal like your bayonet, protecting the barrel. Not many like that."

"Great," I said, patting the package strapped to my chest. "Because I still have my fancy bayonet."

"Of course," McAllister said, turning to make her way toward the engineer's station near the thrust engines. She finished, muttering, "What Relic would leave Earth without one?"

I tried not to frown and dampen O'Vorley's cheery mood. McAllister and I didn't care much for each other. Well, I didn't like her—her superior attitude, and the way she looked down on not just me, but just about everyone. I'd only met a few people that were as smart as her—her brilliance was why the Umbelgarri had allowed her into their secret underground breeding area on Tallavaster.

No. She wasn't easy to get along with. And she despised…no, hated me. But we'd managed to tolerate each other, and worked well as a team bringing down Capital Galactic, and killing more than a few Crax along the way.

I must've lost some time in thought because O'Vorley was staring at me, a questioning look on his face.

"Just wondering," I told him. McAllister was out of sight but probably not out of earshot. I didn't care. "If we'll be able to work together again."

"She's told me a few things about you and her," O'Vorley said. Putting a hand on my shoulder he directed me the opposite direction McAllister had taken. "Like she said, you'll be in cold sleep. Me, her, our pilot, and medical doctor—or med tech—will be rotating staggered as pairs in and out of hybersleep."

"Hybersleep? I get cold sleep and you get hybersleep?"

"The Troh-gcts will probably scan us before we depart. In cold sleep, you won't be picked up as something living. So our numbers will match the official manifest."

Following behind O'Vorley, I asked, "Are you sure?"

"Sure as anyone can be, Kra." He tapped the side of the corridor before reaching for a ladder rung in front of him. "This shuttle has some Umbelgarri alloy in its hull, just like your shotgun's jacket." He looked back down at me after starting to climb. "Not enough to raise suspicion—new construction shuttles have it incorporated, if the buyer can afford it." When he reached the upper level and made room for me, he looked back down. "One effect is to interfere with security scans of external origin." After I'd climbed up next to him, he slapped me on the shoulder. "Enough at least that your frozen shelf partner wasn't detected on the way in."

CHAPTER 25

Med Tech Devatha was a middle aged man with dark skin, wavy black hair and a small, well-manicured mustache. O'Vorley told me that Devatha was really a medical doctor but felt it'd draw less attention if he served as a med tech. Devatha called me Specialist Bleys. The rest of the shuttle's skeleton crew, McAllister, O'Vorley and the pilot, called me Keesay. And I called him Medical Technician Devatha. That said something about all of us.

The pilot went to catch up on some sleep because she'd just completed days of intense decryption efforts. Repeated references to me as Specialist Keesay had assisted them in breaking the code. That probably influenced her calling me Keesay more than anything else.

O'Vorley said that McAllister hadn't found any decrypting success until she was able to identify references to me in the context of my actions and them being reported, and watched the encryption code alter between the times of my appearances and actions as the enemy on the dock tracked me. That offered McAllister and her team on the *Loki's Lady* the sliver of insight needed.

O'Vorley was back on the dock, securing some last minute supplies before departure. He said he'd be back before Tech Devatha put me under, a process necessary to successfully insert the tubes prior to initiating cold sleep. More than getting supplies, O'Vorley must've been tying up any loose ends.

"So," I asked Med Tech Devatha standing next to me, reading some data on a wall-mounted screen, "my blood tests came back positive?" I already knew the answer.

Smiling, he looked down at me sitting on the examination table that doubled as his bed. "They did, Specialists Bleys." He spoke with a slight, quick-paced accent.

Behind me were the two cold sleep berths. One, more square than rectangular, was occupied. They and their equipment consumed as much space as the cramped medical room did.

"Computer," Tech Devatha said, "based on blood chemistry and entered data, calibrate sequence, settings, and dosages for Specialist...the Security Specialist." He leaned against the wall. "It is my understanding that you and our engineer have a checkered history."

"She prefers chess to checkers."

"That, I know. She excels in chess, like so many other things."

"She's got her flaws," I said.

He turned back to the computer screen. "Such as?"

"Arrogance."

He stifled a laugh. "Specialist O'Vorley is good natured and that enables him to get along with our engineer. Pilot Detter, only once did I detect signs of agitation in her. She's too confident in her skills to be insulted or belittled."

"And you?" I asked.

He gestured, batting a hand at me without turning from the screen. "The medical field is overflowing with individuals imbued with god complexes."

I pointed over my shoulder with my thumb, indicating the Bahklack in cold sleep. "What about him?" O'Vorley told me that after the alien thrall and McAllister had broken the CGIG's communications code, it immediately went back into cold sleep.

"I believe *it* is a, *her*," Med Tech Devatha corrected me. "She and McAllister communicate through computer translations, an interface which suits both very well. The alien is brilliant on many levels, but lacks insight in direct interactions with humans."

"Same with McAllister," I said with a smile. Before he could frown or say anything, I added, "Same with me—except the brilliant part."

That earned me a grin.

"Specialist Bleys, I believe it necessary to inform you that Engineer McAllister monitors what transpires aboard *Loki's Lady*."

I stared into the obvious camera mounted near the ceiling. "She knows what I think of her. And I'm aware of what she thinks of me."

"Are you certain?"

"Some people change," I said, rubbing my palm against my thigh. "I even tried it once, recently. Didn't work out."

Devatha didn't argue. Instead he pulled three long-needled syringes from a nearby wall cabinet and removed their sterile packaging. Then he moved to the climate-controlled cabinet and removed three large vials.

It wasn't necessary to read the labels. Their contents would be injected in a prescribed sequence prior to my cold sleep.

Tech Devatha glanced over and consulted the computer screen. "Roll up your sleeve," he said, drawing 1.35 cc of opaque dandelion-colored fluid from the smallest vial. After injecting it into my vein, he said, "I'll be back in nine minutes to administer the second in your pre-cold sleep regimen." He pointed to the computer console. "Before you disrobe in preparation for cold sleep, use the computer to leave any messages, instructions or other information."

He observed my raised eyebrow, and said, "It is my understanding that despite being a Relic, you are competent interfacing with computer systems. Pilot Detter directed me to establish an account."

He grinned mischievously before saying, "It will prompt you to set your own password."

"I know," I said. "Even if McAllister's computer access didn't grant her access to all of my files, she could hack her way in faster than I could make a peanut butter and jelly sandwich."

"Actually, the pilot has the highest level of access, but your point is well taken." He moved to leave, but turned. "When was the last time you had a peanut butter and jelly sandwich?"

"An authentic one, with genuine peanut butter and jelly?" I shook my head. "Seems like more than a lifetime ago."

He stepped out, commanding the door behind him to remain eight percent open.

There weren't any electronic messages to leave. After undressing down to my underwear and lying down on the shelf that would be my bed, I closed my eyes, expecting to hear the humming of *Loki's Lady*'s computer cooling fans and other equipment. In addition to that, the acoustical nature of the shuttle's corridors enabled me to hear O'Vorley, who must've just returned, talking to someone.

"Separate drops to Segreti and Flannigan," he said.

"Sent the decryption key in a narrow beam to the coordinates where *Evanescent Thunder* should've been, three minutes prior to the *Nuclear Pitchfork*'s departure." The hushed feminine voice wasn't McAllister's, so I surmised it was Pilot Joanne Detter's.

"They'll send message rockets." McAllister said that and paused, before continuing. "We'll drop out of condensed space after a day's travel and send two rockets as well. Double our chances of getting word out about the behemoth class transport."

"Based upon your information," the pilot said, "I'll time our arrival to coincide when the planetary orbital rotation places it opposite the sun from our approach. Roughly three weeks before the behemoth's scheduled arrival."

O'Vorley asked, "What if we're the only ones there to greet them?"

"If Fleet gets the messages," McAllister said, "they won't miss this opportunity."

I didn't hear Med Tech Devatha offer any input, but I figured he was there with the others, and I appreciated him leaving the door ajar. The small medical lab serving as his quarters, he knew I'd be able to overhear.

It reminded me of my days aboard the *Kalavar*, serving as a 4th Class Security Specialist on the civil transport, and often out of the main information loop.

I'd have to thank Devatha for enabling me to have a periphery connection within the loop.

A few minutes later, O'Vorley walked into the small med lab. "Hey, Kra. You just about ready?"

Faking a smile, I said, "Sure."

"If you say so," he said, leaning against the wall. "I think your presence on the Bonnisbin Orbital Colony has slipped from notice."

Before I could ask why he said, "It was announced that a flotilla of Trohgot war ships with support vessels are en route. Some are talking takeover, like it'll be a good thing. Others are trying to book passage off the colony."

"I doubt bounty hunters and Capital Galactic will so easily forget about me."

"Yeah," my friend said. "You're right. We're fortunate Pilot Detter's request for con-gate initiated travel has already been approved and scheduled." He glanced up at the med lab's chronometer. "We'll be departing in just under two hours."

"That means Tech Devatha better get to it," I said, pointing at the tubes and other cold sleep gear hanging in sterile packaging.

"Better him than Engineer McAllister. She is certified you know."

"She never told you, Kent?" I asked, recalling the outdated long transport shuttle and equipment. "I was her second cold sleep patient."

He laughed. "Really? Who was her first?"

"The obnoxious med tech that had just given her a once through explanation on the procedure. It was either that or me shooting him."

Kent raised an eyebrow.

"Straight forward choice for him," I said. "If you had been there it'd make sense."

My friend smirked and shook his head. "I bet."

I awoke to a pair of eyes staring down at me. The left green and the right blue. "McAllister," I groaned, the aftereffects of the cold sleep meds lingering in my body. Every bone and muscle ached, even my eyeballs. Nausea, and a headache that alternated from throbbing to piercing just behind my eyes.

"Damn," the red-haired engineer said.

In the background, O'Vorley laughed while Tech Devatha's quick voice said, "You lose, Engineer."

It'd hurt too much to lift my head, let alone attempt to sit up. Still, I forced a smile across my lips. "Any day McAllister loses is a good day."

"She thought your first word would be 'Shit,'" O'Vorley explained. "I disagreed."

"When it really counts," McAllister said, her voice moving away, "you don't want to be around the day I'm wrong."

Three hours passed and I was starting to feel a little better. Still, I was curled up under a blanket on Med Tech Devatha's narrow bed. "If you give me a hand," I said to him, "I can recover somewhere else. If there's a spare bunk."

"You're not ready to move," he said, shooting me a half grin while tapping at his wall-mounted computer screen. "I know. I've been in your shoes. Besides, once you're up and around, our alien friend is next."

Tech Devatha reached over to tap a switch, activating the shuttle's internal communication. Pilot Detter's voice sounded over the intercom. "Coming up on the mark," she said. "Are you ready to deploy?"

Through the intercom, O'Vorley replied, "Engineer McAllister nods yes."

Why didn't McAllister reply directly? My only meeting with the pilot had been brief. Medium height for an I-Tech, sharp chin, wavy brown hair that didn't reach her shoulders, brown eyes, and a friendly smile. Firm, confident handshake.

Maybe she and McAllister didn't get along. Wouldn't be surprising.

Keeping my thoughts on anything but my aching body, I asked Devatha, "What are they deploying?"

"A communications re-transmitter."

I didn't bother craning my neck to follow as Devatha stepped to the other side of the cramped room. "Why would we be doing that?" I asked. The disconnected feeling flowing through me said we were still in condensed space travel.

"We don't want to be detected as we approach HD 97658."

HD 97658? It took me a moment to think and do a few mental calculations. A mining operation on the single planet orbiting the star. A hot place, not a lot of metals, but a few rare isotopes, useful for forming data storage crystals. Remote robotic mining as the planet's surface hovered around 900 degrees Fahrenheit. The space dock had a name, Bizmith Orbital Dock. But like all CGIG moons, planets, colonies, and space docks, they'd been stripped of their name. I didn't know what name had been assigned, but the dock's orbit kept it in the planet's shadow, protecting it from the nearby sun.

It also served as a refueling depot, mainly for smaller class freighters. The knowledge stemmed from my warehouse days on Pluto. Conversations during evenings I played euchre with members of a methane freighter's crew on layover.

Capital Galactic had owned the mining operation, and the freighter. The operation might still have some sympathizers there.

"No patrol gunboats or police cutters protecting it?" With war losses, it was a dumb question.

Devatha answered it anyway. "Too small of an operation. An early warning satellite and a pair of def-sats. The dock has self-defense weapons. Most current data indicates three turrets mounting dual beam defense lasers."

"Deploy, now," Pilot Detter said over the intercom.

I grabbed onto the sides of the bed.

"Deploying," O'Vorley replied.

The shuttle lurched, causing my weak grip to fail. I nearly slid off the bed and onto the floor. That's what happened when you ejected things while traveling in the wake of condensed space, those objects penetrating the vessel's generated anti-gravity field. And especially when suffering through cold sleep recovery.

"Would you like to be strapped down, Specialist Bleys?"

I craned my neck to see the med tech. Apparently he'd weathered the jolt without a problem. "Not unless we have more drops," I told him.

"I believe your next concern will be our drop out of condensed space travel."

As if on cue, Pilot Detter announced, "Five minutes until we drop out of condensed space."

"Ideally they should have a second early warning satellite and detect what we're attempting. We have a very small window. Fewer than eighty seconds where the local sun will interfere with both the dock's sensors and the single early detection satellite."

It made sense. Warning satellites were costly and in high demand, thus only one. The def-sats wouldn't have the sensor range to detect a ship as small as ours dropping out of condensed space. The enemy wouldn't know the number or exact orbital location of those, or of the detection satellite, or if there were any patrolling ships. Thus, they would have a nearly impossible time succeeding at what we were attempting. An undetected approach.

But there were the treacherous actions of Capital Galactic and her sympathizers.

Tech Devatha retrieved some clamps and straps. "The pilot will be deactivating the gravity plate after exiting condensed space and reorienting our ship."

Carefully, I rolled onto my back. It wasn't the most comfortable position in my condition.

Med Tech Devatha adjusted my blanket and pillow. "We'll be coasting in, providing recon."

"Relayed through the re-transmitter."

Devatha nodded. "We'll send narrow beam, a weak signal that the transmitter will boost and dispatch in a narrow beam to a set of coordinates." He shrugged. "I never bothered to inquire about them."

"What are we expecting?"

"The arrival of a behemoth class transport, carrying at least one, possibly three Primus Crax battle frigates." He ran a strap across my chest. "McAllister believes their goal is to capture the dock and her fuel stores intact. Destroying or stopping the launch of message rockets. Its strategic location and being only sixty-nine light years from Earth, a valuable base of operations, even if temporary."

Something humanity couldn't ignore. They'd made incursions into human space, but all were launched from long range. The attack on Io was a prime example. But if they were allowed to establish themselves around HD 97685? We didn't have enough combat ships to meet current needs. Dealing with it would further hamstring current operations.

Devatha finished strapping down my chest and legs, and taped my pillow to the bed.

Pilot Detter said, "One minute until cessation of condensed space travel, on my mark."

"Will shut down the cascading atomic engine," McAllister replied, "one minute from your mark."

"Mark," the Pilot said.

McAllister replied, "Shutdown procedure enacted. Condensed space will end sixty seconds from your mark. Antigravity field will be collapsed three seconds after. Deactivation of gravity plate to follow, upon your command, Pilot."

O'Vorley chimed in, "Will shut down shuttle gravity plate on your command, Pilot Detter."

"As soon as I verify our trajectory and make adjustments, Specialist O'Vorley."

They had no more than eighty seconds to accomplish all of that. Not knowing if there were any CGIG sympathizers on the mining dock, no communication or contact, no coded requests to alter the satellite or dock sensors, or their reporting protocol could be attempted.

Not now, nor could the military have attempted it. Not with the limited time available. How long had it taken for the *Evanescent Thunder*'s or *Loki's Lady*'s message rockets to arrive and warn the military and Intel of the behemoth transport's arrival with its cargo of Primus Crax combat ships?

We'd raced almost forty light years to reach HD 97658. McAllister had formulated the plan to relay recon, anticipating the military would comply. What choice did they have? There hadn't been time to coordinate otherwise. Based on the small amount known to them, the military would've already formulated a plan to ambush and destroy the CGIG and enemy ships. Fleet and any Colonial Marines they brought along couldn't arrive early, and risk tipping their hand, could they?

There were so many variables. So many ways this could go. So many more it could go wrong.

At least everything aboard *Loki's Lady* went as expected, up until now.

"Ready," warned Pilot Detter. "Shut down cascading atomic engine."

"Shut down initiated," McAllister replied without emotion.

The long range shuttle lurched, and the constant feeling of slight disconnection snapped out of existence. Like the humming of electronic fans you get used to and don't notice, until they're gone. Silence.

My body rocked to the left.

"Adjusting course trajectory," Pilot Detter commented. After a smaller pull the other direction and slightly downward, she added, "On course. Shutting down thrust engines. Specialist O'Vorley, power down the internal gravity plate. Ten percent reduction every five seconds."

"Acknowledged," O'Vorley replied. "Ten percent increments. Complete shutdown in fifty seconds."

"Thirteen minutes from now," Pilot Detter said. "If we've been detected, we should receive a radio contact by then."

That told me how far we were from the space dock. Over 90 million miles. Enough time for them to detect us, and send a radio contact.

After thirty seconds, McAllister announced, "All space condensing systems deactivated and locked down. Proceeding to join you, Pilot."

"Acknowledged. Optical scanners will be yours."

My arms felt lighter. The sense of fading gravity sent a new wave of nausea through my already sick body.

"Are you going to be okay?" Med Tech Devatha asked me.

Pursing my lips, I nodded. After a few shallow breaths I asked, "Can you access McAllister's sensors down here?"

"Shouldn't be a problem," he said, squinting with a half grin. "I'll query first."

There wasn't much to see. A distant planet in near orbit to an orange dwarf star, slightly smaller than Earth's sun. The focus shifted to the planet, and then to an object in its orbit. With manipulation the object appeared in more detail. A large metallic cylinder capped by an octagonal disk on both ends. The fuzziness disappeared further as the computer refined what had been captured of the image.

No ships docked or stationed nearby. Med Tech Devatha released a small sigh. He'd been concerned. Me? I hadn't. McAllister had failings, but in cracking CGIG's secret codes and piecing together disparate information and data, I knew she'd be right. On second thought, I recalled how nothing was assured with respect to interstellar travel and maintaining perfect schedules. But, if anything, delays were to be expected over early arrivals.

Minutes passed. No attempted radio contact from the mining colony as we flew like a bullet at over 190,000 miles per hour toward our target. No activity picked up by our passive sensors. No message rockets dispatched, and active sensors trying to reach and identify us.

We'd monitor and report, sending low energy, narrow-beam signals to the re-transmitter while remaining in zero gravity and under minimum power, until we reached the colony in a little over twenty days.

McAllister floated toward me in the common room. A buckled strap held me in the chair while I read a journal article discussing possible upgrades to standard security robots, hardening them against EMPs, and improvements to their armored covers and ability to resist impact damage. I sided against the move. Too labor intensive and succeeding in only a half measure. If they wanted an improved sec-bot to backup security teams and military troops on colonies, design and build it from the ground up. The additional weight and components would be too much of a drain on the current models' batteries. Plus, there was no room to increase number or size of the battery cells. The added internal support struts proposed wouldn't be as effective as projected.

McAllister placed a hand on the back of my chair, stopping her progress.

I pointed to the article on the table screen. "Have you read anything about this?"

McAllister frowned. "No, this would've been along Anatol's interest."

I refrained from pursing my lips. Bringing her deceased boyfriend—maybe fiancé—to mind wasn't my intention. We'd avoided each other as best we could since my revival from cold sleep. Thirty-six hours was a good run, and our meeting wasn't necessarily the way to keep things calm. It could go either way. McAllister's volatile personality and my stubbornness…

She leaned closer and scanned the screen, tapped to expand several of the diagrams. After skimming another few screens of information, she asked, "What do you think, Keesay?"

I leaned back and shared my thoughts. About half way through her left eyebrow rose. "If a Relic like you can figure it out, Keesay, any competent engineer should be able to come to the same conclusion in half the time."

"Thanks," I said, only offering up a sliver of sarcasm. "My guess is the licensing and patent holders angling to expand…no, extend the life of the product line."

She said, "Some manage to accumulate substantial wealth through military procurement."

"Others pay the price for faulty decisions," I said. "Substandard equipment."

"A vital question is, Keesay, does humanity have the time and resources to develop a new system, establish a new production line and logistical supply for repair and replacement parts? For that standard model, that supply line, familiarity with the systems. Repair and maintenance. It's already established."

"So, you think that's what's going to happen? Upgrade and make due with what's available?"

She gripped the table, pulling herself around to the opposite seat. "Even *you* must be able to read past the hype and propaganda published. We're losing. Getting pressed by the enemy. What you're pointing out is a symptom of a bigger problem."

I tried to keep anger from my voice. "So, you think the bastards at Capital Galactic, throwing in with the Crax. They're the smart guys?"

She rolled her eyes before tapping the screen, and logging into her account. "Say they're right and the Crax win, what use will they be to them after that?" She pulled up a chess program. "They're like you playing this game."

I began unbuckling myself from the chair even as she buckled in. "Who says I'm playing, McAllister?"

She ignored my statement, and activated the holographic imaging program, making the board 3D. "You can be white."

I pushed away, heading toward the pilot's station. Maybe something of interest would be on the optical scanners.

"You never change, Keesay. Never thinking more than three moves ahead."

I stopped in the doorway and turned. "My feeble planning skills on the

Kalavar enabled me to come out on top, McAllister. Remember?"

She grinned wickedly. "Selective memory, Relic. Recall what I'd set into motion with respect to your accounts? Lucky for you, the war interrupted the game, or it would've been checkmate."

I remembered. My accounts would've been drained. Zeroed out without a trace, and probably limited recourse. But, if she thought it would've ended there...

McAllister held up a hand and tipped her head, looking away. "Keesay, I'm sorry." The words were strained, and they surprised me. "I didn't seek you out for this."

After a deep breath, she lowered her hand and said, "You've been avoiding me since your recovery. Not easy on a shuttle in zero gravity. I left something on your bunk."

I didn't know what to say. What would she have left?

"You're welcome," she said. "And you owe me at least one game. You'll see."

I sat in the tiny med lab, staring at the genetically modified patch of exoskeleton on the Bahklack's dominant pincher claw. The alien resembled more than anything else a four-foot-tall fiddler crab. The modified section shifted colors, much like a squid might. It was the way the thrall communicated with its masters, or so it named the Umbelgarri.

Having been under Umbelgarri care while they rebuilt my neural pathways after the Cranaltar IV ravaged them, the advanced aliens inserted the ability for me to comprehend such communications. My eyes were capable, but my hearing was unable to detect the low-frequency sounds that accompanied the colors, sounds which added emotion and emphasis. In producing sound, the thrall was far more limited than the advanced alien race that created the crab-like thralls to serve them.

I spoke into the med lab's computer, which translated my words into colors displayed by the monitor and sound by the speakers. "Yes, Thrall Blue Gray Blue Blue Nineteen. I know how to work with the shuttle's computer systems. Not as well as the others on the crew, but well enough to get by."

I waited a second and observed its reply, even as the computer's optical scanner received and translated. "Why do you persist in remaining ignorant of higher interface manipulation of electronic powered systems that support this miniscule between-star transport vessel?"

I refrained from replying in a similar mode of wording. The point of the exercise was to get the thrall more accustomed and fluent interacting with humans. "It's not necessary to perform my assigned duties."

"Such ignorance sustained inhibits more effective function within the human organizational collective."

I shrugged. "I improve myself in other ways."

"Repetitive physical labor while tethered and restrained to maintain physical strength and endurance." The alien bowed its eye stalks down thirty degrees. A sign of agreement or approval. "Reliance on archaic devices is less efficient and less effective in confronting the enemies of the Masters, even when engaged..." It spread its claw tips. "From afar." Its eyestalks spread slightly, indicating disapproval.

"My training is elsewhere," I said. "I am a Security Specialist. Programming software and maintaining hardware is for others, like Engineer McAllister or Pilot Detter."

"You remove pieces of common polymer cube by cutting and scraping with primitive metal tools instead of reducing ignorance."

The Bahklack thrall had observed me in the common room wearing my protective glove, using gouges and knives to work one of the wood-simulating polymer blocks. Zero gravity made it tricky. I'd rigged a small vacuum to suck in the shavings and carved bits so they wouldn't float away.

The carving tools came from McAllister, a gift to me. She'd use the shuttle's fabrication equipment to make them while I was in cold sleep. Why? I had no idea.

O'Vorley wandered into the room, a half grin on his face, probably having heard some of the conversation through the computer's monotone voice as he approached.

"Don't you have art?" I asked. "The Bahklacks and the Umbelgarri?"

"The Masters do. They create it. I and fellow thralls do not comprehend it. Are you not aligned closer to thralls, having more masters than those you are master over? Yet you create reduced polymer blocks as art."

O'Vorley's eyes shifted between me and the thrall as we spoke, a straight expression maintained across his face.

"They're carved busts," I said. "Artistic representations of individual humans. It is a way for me to relax. I enjoy doing it. I give the creations away. Gifts to make others happy."

After a pause, the thrall continued. "You are comparable to thralls on the hierarchy. You extensively serve more masters than those that serve you. You create the reduced polymer blocks for those that you serve?"

My eyes met O'Vorley's. He hadn't entered more than a few feet into the room. With a slight push off the floor he floated back and gripped the doorframe and held on, content to remain there.

"I carve something that I think others will enjoy. Don't you ever receive gifts?"

"Negative. I am granted use of more efficient software and more capable computers to house and run the software. I am enabled to better serve the Masters. I serve them now by serving you. I remove ignorance by engaging in communication with assorted humans. It is my purpose."

And that's what vexed me. The Bahklacks were created to serve. That's all they knew, and genetically engineered to desire. No interest in possessions or personal aspirations. Its equipment harness and computers—everything directly related to its function, its purpose. Artificial intelligence in organic form, which was pretty smart on the Umbelgarri's part. Every space-faring race, including humanity, discovered the peril of creating artificial intelligence computers, and allowing a measure of autonomy. If they hadn't, they wouldn't have become a space-faring race.

How could I explain to the Bahklack that too much reliance on technology dehumanized us? Creates barriers, making humans more comfortable interacting with a computer than a fellow human.

After all, the Bahklack was the Umbelgarri solution to the rogue AI problem. The Phibs created a race with a single purpose: To serve them.

The Crax conquered races. Those they couldn't subjugate, they exterminated. Were the two advanced alien races, the Umbelgarri and the Crax, really different?

It wasn't something I intended to ask the Phib's thrall. Maybe I'd discuss it with Kent, sometime, out of the Umbelgarri thrall's earshot. They didn't have ears but could hear, at least sounds not too far up the audio frequency spectrum.

O'Vorley opened the door to our shared quarters and floated over me on the way to his bunk while I continued my push-up routine.

"Got you an energy bar," he said. "Salted peanuts and banana."

"Synthetic," I said, knowing it'd been processed from algae grown using onboard lasers and genetically modified bacteria.

He laughed. "Simulated, Kra. We don't get the dining delights they spoiled you with on the *Kalavar.*"

I'd shared what I could about my time there while we served as conscripts on Tallavaster. More recently I shared with him about the battle against the Crax on Io, even as Kent told me about his experiences, some of it working for the Umbelgarri. He and McAllister had actually been in close proximity to several.

I finished my last push-up, unhooked the elastic strap stretched across my shoulders, stood, and brushed off my hands on my coveralls. "The dining delights were once a week," I said, taking the bar. "It's only been six days."

O'Vorley laughed again. "Maybe for you cold sleepers."

"You rotated hybersleep. Which, for my credits, beats cold sleep any light year travelled."

"Look at you," he said, after taking a bite of his bar and shoving the mouthful into his cheek with his tongue. He pointed to the old-style watch on my wrist. "Shouldn't you say something archaic like mile or league or something? Not light year."

"I'm adaptable."

"For a Relic? I'll give you that, Kra." He took one of my carvings from the shelf, floating behind the containment netting. "I recognize McAllister and Gudkov." He tossed it to me. "He was an intra-colony kickboxing champion. Three platinum rings."

"Not my favorite man," I said. "He didn't care for me either." I chewed a bite of my bar and swallowed. "Died well. Brave. Took on a Gar-Crax warrior hand-to-hand. Stood between it and McAllister."

"She told me," O'Vorley said. "Together you and her killed it. She wears one of Gudkov's platinum rings on a chain around her neck. She did say, 'Keesay took it from his bloody hand for me.'"

I remembered. McAllister was in shock from witnessing her love's death. I pulled the ring from his hand and shoved it into hers. Got her moving again, toward survival.

We both finished our energy bar in silence, lost in our own thoughts for half a moment. I was about to ask what maintenance tasks were scheduled for today when the door slid open, without a chime or even a knock.

"Who?" O'Vorley asked, even as McAllister launched past him, toward me. "You bastard!" she shouted.

I pushed aside, out of her path.

She slammed into the bunks, and spun to face me. A stun baton extended in her hand, murder in her mismatched eyes.

I didn't have my own stun baton so I pulled my bayonet before she could launch at me again. "McAllister, stop!" Using deadly force wasn't my intent, but the intense glow across her stun baton's tip said it was at max charge. One successful strike would take me down, painfully. A second and third would do me in.

She wasn't going to get that chance.

O'Vorley intercepted McAllister as she pushed off with her legs, toward me. Both slammed back into the beds. Grappling with her, he shouted into his mic, "All call emergency, my quarters now!"

Kent took a knee to the gut, knocking the wind out of him. But that gave me a chance to discard my bayonet and get McAllister in an arm lock.

All three of us spun, bouncing off the wall, angling toward the ceiling.

"You, bastard." she seethed at me. "You have no right."

Her stun baton discharged against the ceiling, sparking and shorting out the lights. Before they fully faded, the red-tinted emergency lighting kicked in."

My combat experience in zero gravity was nil, but that didn't matter as we tumbled, McAllister trying to push off with her legs and launch me into a wall. My bayonet was floating in a corner, near the floor, safely out of reach. With a further twist, I managed to force McAllister to release the baton.

O'Vorley shifted his grip, earning a glancing kick to his thigh. "Relax, McAllister," he urged through gritted teeth. Between us, we had her immobilized. Our security self-defense and takedown training was more suited to zero gravity than McAllister's kickboxing.

I couldn't figure why she was here. "Just like you," I accused. "Overriding the security systems. Doing whatever you please."

McAllister's response was something caught between a snarl and a scream.

Kent snapped, "Shut up, Keesay."

Pilot Detter arrived in the doorway. "What the hell's going on?"

Straining to maintain my grip, I growled, "With McAllister you have to ask?"

"If all you have are smart ass questions, Keesay, do like O'Vorley said and shut up."

Med Tech Devatha ducked under the pilot and moved toward us, eyes shifting between me and the red-faced McAllister. He snatched McAllister's stun baton floating nearby. Having lost contact with a wielder, it deactivated. Pressing the button to retract, it didn't respond.

Figures. She'd security programmed it for her individual use.

"Engineer," Med Tech Devatha said, "Specialist Bleys is going to release you. Specialist O'Vorley will retain his hold until after Specialist Bleys has departed." The tech's eyes met mine. "For the med lab."

She grunted what I took for agreement, so I let go, reached under my pillow strapped down to the head of the bunk, and retrieved my duty revolver and its holster.

McAllister's burning glare followed me but she didn't make a sound. When I started to go for my bayonet, Pilot Detter said, "Leave it, Keesay."

An hour later in the common room, McAllister sat across the table from me. Pilot Detter sat to my right and Med Tech Devatha to my left. O'Vorley was forward in the pilot's station, monitoring the shuttle's sensors.

The pilot placed my carving of the three busts on the table. Without gravity, the synthetic wood representations of Gudkov, McAllister, and the man I only knew as Steffon, the young man I'd killed, hovered slowly in my direction. The heads rotated to face me as if in accusation.

I focused on the clean-shaven face of Steffon. I'd managed to carve it without his twisted, menacing hate burned into my memory. Deep set eyes, broad chin and wavy hair slicked back. McAllister had risked her life and career to avenge him. Drugged up on Thrust, she tried to kill me. When that bid failed, she shifted to destroying my career while covering up her attempted crime.

Engineer McAllister named me a murderer. No doubt harbored in her mind. I was guilty of many things, but murder wasn't among the list. After Gudkov's death, we managed to work together despite an undercurrent of unresolved hostile emotions.

For being brilliant, McAllister allowed her emotions to rule. Something I thought she'd gotten a handle on. Condescending and arrogant, those would always be with her, just like her brilliance.

Everyone stared at me, waiting for me to speak. Even the carved trio's faces were angled up as if gazing expectantly. I leaned back and crossed my arms. I wasn't in the wrong. They'd be waiting until *Loki's Lady* reached the single space dock in HD 97658's system.

One minute passed, then two. My unconcerned gaze moved between the pilot's and McAllister's. Neither was happy with me. Annoyed detestation showed in Pilot Detter's expression. Seething hatred in McAllister's. She might crack a few molars if she clenched her jaw any harder.

Like on the *Kalavar*, I was the outsider. I should've been on the *Nuclear Pitchfork*, seeking Deputy Director Simms, and maybe Janice Tahgs. Not on *Loki's Lady*, dealing with my past and Senior Engineer Nova McAllister.

No matter how much people think they've grown, how quickly they revert to previous ways, long established patterns. Not just McAllister, but me as well.

After another few breaths, Pilot Detter glanced at McAllister, and then addressed me. "Engineer McAllister would like to know why you felt it necessary to select those particular subjects for that carving that floats before us."

My eyes remained fixed on McAllister's unblinking gaze boring in on me. "If it's Engineer McAllister who truly wants to know, it should be her doing the asking."

"Specialist," the pilot said sharply, "I am asking in her place to keep *this* conversation from escalating to violence."

Warp screw that notion. "It's answers that she doesn't want to hear that'll result in her getting thumped."

Pilot Detter pointed at me. Her eyes narrowed. "Understand this, Specialist. Orphaned, I took you in to be a part of my crew—at considerable risk. Risk to everyone on board, our mission, and the vessel itself. Our mission being one vital to the war effort."

She leaned closer, her pointed finger becoming part of a fist pressed against the tabletop.

My glare weakened. Gesturing to the carved bust trio, I said, "McAllister knew I carved wood. She fabricated tools for me while I was in cold sleep. I thought to return the favor—"

"You bastard!" McAllister interjected. "You murdered Steffon. You have no right—"

I cut her off. "Warp screw you. Lie to yourself. Lie to them. Don't bother lying to me. I was there." I leaned toward her with a sneer. "I did kill your Steffon."

Her face reddened ever more, more than I thought possible. Her freckles disappeared.

"He pulled a sonic blade on me," I said. "His fault for not using it fast enough." I jabbed a finger at her. "If you'd've picked it up, I'd've bayonetted you, too."

I leaned back. "I don't know why you were there and don't care. I was there to draw the mob's ire. We—me and the other security volunteers were supposed to die."

I didn't add that we were too young and ignorant to know it.

"Most of us did. Died by the dozens."

Recalling the moment, it was him, Steffon, or me. I chose me. Deep down I was sorry that he died in McAllister's arms. I was sorry for him and the other thirteen I killed that day. For the others I wounded. For security specialists that died around me. Most only half trained. Sacrificed for a cause, or a reason they never knew.

I snatched the bust trio and turned it to face McAllister, her eyes burning with murderous rage. What kept her from acting on that building rage? It was out of character.

"There's fourteen faces seared into my memory. That ten second encounter with your fiancé and his sonic blade...it was enough to carve this."

I slammed it on the table, everyone but McAllister staring at me, listening. Her narrow-eyed glare, even if she was hearing me, she wasn't listening. She'd once named me an efficient killer. Thing is, the fourteen deaths at my hands, each one blackened a portion of my soul. All those that followed. For right or wrong, it's dealing death.

That dark space inside me welled up and I couldn't look away from it. Couldn't deny it. Something I'd never speak of, never share. Praying for forgiveness was futile. I didn't deserve it.

What drove me now was payback. Hawks, Heartwell, Capital Galactic, the Crax. My purpose. *Nemo me impune lacessit...*

Suppressing my anger, my despair, I grabbed the busts, gripped them tight and snapped them apart, separating Steffon from McAllister and Gudkov.

"Keesay," McAllister seethed, but her fuming remarks certain to follow remained unsaid.

O'Vorley shouted over the intercom, "Detter, McAllister, get up here! You need to see this."

CHAPTER 26

With optical scans, Pilot Detter said we couldn't be sure. I was sure, and so was McAllister.

O'Vorley sat with me at the conference room table, which also served as the dining table. "Kra, You sure those are jettisoned bodies?"

I finished chewing my walnut and raisin flavored energy bar and washed it down with a drink of vitamin fortified juice, green and tasting faintly of sour apples. It was one of Kent's favorites. Not mine. I didn't care for straws, but they were necessary in zero gravity.

Nodding to his question, I added, "You're going to doubt both me *and* McAllister?"

"To what end?"

McAllister estimated at least ninety bodies, but no more than one-hundred and ten. Ejected from the cylinder shaped dock capped by octagonal disks, opposite the planet with enough momentum to resist the pull of gravity. The CGIG bastards wanted them to remain in orbit, at least for a while. Long enough for their Crax masters to witness their continued treachery.

"You know what I think," I said.

Through his straw, O'Vorley took long swallows of his apple flavored drink. "Maybe the Crax are already there."

"No Crax ships. The dock still has its def-sats and satellite. Freight shuttles still coming up and going back down to the mines. Only CGIG loyalists are there."

"Could be the other way around."

I rested my forearms on the table's edge. "You really believe that, Kent? It's loyalists that were jettisoned from the dock?"

He looked away, not saying anything. His first direct taste of betrayal. Humans turning on their own kind in our fight for survival. He'd been close to it on Tallavaster, but no bodies. He'd been tracking, but it was more theory, more cat and mouse. Not space-frozen corpses. Men and women killed to prove a point. To prove commitment and loyalty.

In theory, I could've been wrong, but knew I wasn't. Despite our rift, McAllister and I agreed. "Pilot Detter said we'd know for sure in six hours."

The pilot sent the optical data for retransmission shortly after O'Vorley discovered it. Like O'Vorley, she didn't want to believe what was in front of her eyes.

Kent shrugged.

I unbuckled and pushed away from the table. "Six hours. I plan to get some sleep until then."

Fleet's surprise assault on the orbital dock was both fast and decisive. Every message rocket launched was destroyed before achieving condensed space travel. Rebellion against the dock's Crax sympathizers aided the Colonial Marine landing squads, including hacking of the com-systems, disabling all radio communications. With no radio distress signals sent and no message rockets escaping, the approaching Behemoth class transport should arrive unaware of what happened.

I watched the assault on the wall-mounted screen in Med Tech Devatha's room, accompanied by the Bahklack. Her eyestalks remaining motionless, taking in the scene.

Apparently the dock had retained its official name, the Bizmith Orbital Dock, as determined through narrow beam communications directed toward *Loki's Lady*, still eight hours from reaching the dock.

The captain of the *Star Splitter*, a refurbished battleship still showing hasty patchwork from recent combat, ordered the jettisoned bodies to remain undisturbed. The *Star Splitter* and her three escorting destroyers, and the assault troop transport, departed four hours before we arrived. She left behind a heavy freighter docked to the Bizmith Orbital Dock and presumably a battalion of Colonial Marines along with attack shuttles and breaching pods. They'd also deployed two new def-sats to replace those destroyed in the assault.

What part, if any, we aboard the *Loki's Lady* were to play wasn't clear. Updated information estimated we'd arrive four hours before the Behemoth class transport. We might be ordered to depart. But with McAllister and the Bahklack, and the opportunity to catch some Primus Crax ships unprepared, hopefully board them...I hoped if they went, I'd be included. McAllister could vouch for me, as a personal guard. Capital Galactic's ruthless treachery had pushed McAllister's hatred of me aside. If I didn't ward her, then the Bahklack whose language I comprehended would be a reason for me to participate. On that second point I prepared to argue my case. Electronic warfare could disrupt computers and their translation programs. There was the Official Galactic Sign Language, but it has limitations.

Taking on the traitors, and the Crax. It's what I wanted to do more than anything else. I shrugged to myself. Some decisions were beyond my control. At least Pilot Detter ordered McAllister to energize our shuttle's gravity plate. It made cleaning and oiling my shotgun, duty revolver and bayonet far easier.

CHAPTER 27

O'Vorley and I followed McAllister and the Bahklack down one of the aging freighter's narrow corridors. Since it was occupied by Colonial Marines, I carried my shotgun slung. I'd also brought along my bayonet, revolver, stun baton and four fragmentation grenades. From somewhere on *Loki's Lady*, O'Vorley had found me a combat helmet. It wasn't an exact match to his. Mine accommodated my earphone headgear and gear wired into my com-set attached to my belt. Being grayish green to match my coveralls and unmarred, I suspected he or McAllister had fashioned it for me while I was in cold sleep.

As usual, McAllister knew more about what was going on than I did, and was able to anticipate equipment needs. I'd've wagered credits she was responsible for my helmet. Mentioning that, however, would reopen a nasty wound.

Next to me, and behind McAllister, O'Vorley was checking his clamshell computer clip. He carried a slung medium duty laser carbine, MP pistol and, to my surprise, a sonic rapier.

McAllister's black backpack bobbed with each of her strides. It, like her satchel, was filled with electronic equipment. The Bahklack ahead of me had a number of faceted devices, mainly of opaque gray and whites, attached to its synthetic harness. McAllister had a holstered MP pistol riding on her belt. That didn't impress me. What did impress me was the baton dangling from a clip attached to the alien thrall's harness. I'd seen one used. Its energy beam was more lethal than O'Vorley's, McAllister's and my full firepower combined.

We were supposed to be part of the second wave, and not see direct combat except in an emergency support role. McAllister and the alien were assigned to hack into the Crax systems in support of the boarding attempt. The Fleet knew of her abilities and that she was aboard *Loki's Lady*, and had already integrated her and her alien associate into the plan. O'Vorley was her personal, or bodyguard. I was assigned to the Bahklack. That made sense, since I could communicate with it, at least one way, if computer assistance failed. It to me. Without computers, all I had to respond back with was the Official Galactic Sign Language. My sign language knowledge was basic, but I wouldn't have to read signs from the thrall's small, manipulative appendages. The genetically modified section of its main claw carried chromatophores that conveyed direct communication.

The freighter's metal grates *clumped* beneath our boots and *clicked* at the Bahklack's chitinous steps. Somehow, the crab-like alien kept its six legs and feet from sticking in any of the grates' larger rectangular gaps. They reminded me of jointed table legs

About a fifth of the old-style fluorescent bulbs were out, and many of those still working flickered irregularly. Patches of rust showed through scraped and bubbled tan paint. The Fleet didn't expect the old freighter to survive, or at least not depart the system. The *Iron Oxen*, a write-off casualty.

Resting my hand on my holstered revolver, O'Vorley looked over at me. I winked. "Good thing we didn't leave anything on board."

"What?" he asked, closing his clip and sliding it into a thigh pocket. In addition to our protective coveralls, we each had plasticized armor vests.

Before I could answer, McAllister announced, "Another forty meters."

Ahead a Colonial Marine armed with an MP rifle stood watch. His eyes narrowed in suspicion as we approached the open pressure door. The Capital Galactic murderous treachery had put many on edge.

Orders, conversations and the sounds of activity emanated from the hold.

"Hack Team Four," McAllister said, stopping three paces away from the Marine. "We're assigned to a breaching pod in Cargo Hold Three."

"Hard Luck Hank," the Marine challenged.

"Screw the galaxy," McAllister replied, a wry sense of humor seeping into her voice.

"BP-J-132," the Marine replied, his eyes no longer narrowed, but his baritone voice carried no emotion. He stepped aside. "Aft section of the hold."

A J-series breaching pod. The last update I'd read about was the G-series. It made sense. Being able to cut through a Crax ship's hull, especially a Primus Crax ship, would be a challenge. Then I wondered if the upgrades were along the lines envisioned for the security bots. Rigging and shoehorning an already established model to make due. More cost effective measures coming at the cost of maximum combat capability.

Cargo Hold 3 was one of four dorsal holds, this one was starboard aft. The *Iron Oxen* also had four ventral holds, two running fore to aft, starboard side, and a parallel portside pair. The holds, being large and cavernous, had breaching pods, along with a lesser number of attack shuttles and converted medical shuttles filling the bottom. Closed and sealed above were the pair of massive doors that would swing open like trap doors to release the hold's contents. I always reminded myself of a major difference being in space, was that the freighter's gravity plate, which bisected the ship, dictated what was 'up' and what was 'down.'

Each of the breaching pods resembled a squat cone, reminiscent of an ancient lunar exploration capsule, but on steroids with a trio of powerful thrust engines mounted on the narrow end. Strategically placed around the pod's hull were sixteen maneuvering thrusters, each capable of swiveling nearly seventy degrees. They reminded me of exhaust pipes. I knew the pod's base held both mechanical and magnetic clamps, and a combination of molecular saws and laser torches.

Standing on the small observation balcony encompassed by a single waist-high steel tube, I counted sixteen breaching pods in two rows of eight. Scattered among them were six older-model attack craft. They looked like oversized torpedo fighter bombers from World War II, but the size of heavy bombers of that era, without the propeller and with stubby wings that were nothing more than weapon mounts. There were also four emergency medical shuttles, two converted from ground assault shuttles, and two from obsolete long range shuttles. The presence of converted medical shuttles equipped to stabilize and evacuate wounded both comforted and worried me. Even though they bore the recognizable red cross several places on their hull, the red and white emblems were less than a foot in diameter. Our enemies didn't distinguish between combat and medical ships. That each medical shuttle's single beam laser turret hadn't been removed emphasized the fact.

Why our team hadn't entered at the ground level, I didn't know. We'd have to climb down the aluminum ladder to the hold's floor fifty feet below, after lowering the Bahklack using the hoist bolted to the wall next to the balcony. I figured the alien's synthetic harness was stronger than it looked. Probably strong as the two-centimeter-thick winch cable, plus the thrall had an anti-gravity generator attached to its harness as backup. It'd only use a fraction of its stored energy to arrest the fifty foot drop, should the cable or harness fail. Or if it decided to clamber over the steel railing and leap.

I signaled O'Vorley over to show him how to use the hoist's manual controls.

McAllister managed not to roll her eyes—almost. "Bide, Bleys," she said, before calling over her shoulder, "Private Raynes, are the stairs in operable order?"

"Affirmative, Engineer," the Marine replied. "A moment." He then muttered a request into his collar mic.

Less than a minute later slats built into the wall hinged down, forming a set of stairs to the hold's floor. Several slats hadn't deployed, leaving gaps, and a few rested several degrees beyond perpendicular to the wall. With the steps extending only a meter out, I wasn't sure if the fiddler crab-like thrall could manage them.

There was always his anti-grav device.

With apparent confidence, it followed us, descending sideways with its backside against the wall. Its eyestalks bent and swiveled, keeping track of the gaps, each rapid step like an ice pick tapping a steel can.

We wove our way through the breaching pods and attack shuttles. The Bahklack drew fewer glances and stares from the Colonial Marines and maintenance crews than I expected. Maybe because of the half dozen Chicher scurrying about.

The three-foot aliens looked like brown-furred rats that had maybe an eighth of their bloodline descending from equally large squirrels. While they could walk and maneuver on hind feet, they mainly scampered around on all fours. Their harnesses and equipment belts took this into account, along with their prehensile tails.

The Chicher were directing some tan-clad maintenance techs as they moved and loaded hexagonal crates into some of the pods. They appeared to be constructed from layers of authentic wooden slats, but with unusual swirling woodgrain patterns.

That the Chicher were available to participate in the military action on such short notice said something about how humanity and the pack-structured aliens had integrated aspects of their forces. But assaulting the Crax, especially the Primus Crax? Except for the Umbelgarri, the Primus were arguably the most technologically advanced species known to humanity.

The Chicher were R-Tech, still using vacuum tubes in many of their computer systems. But what did that matter? I was shouldering a shotgun, technology that predated humanity's use of vacuum tubes.

How the Chicher managed to become a space-faring race continued to be debated. My theory was they stole, reverse engineered, and modified equipment for their purposes. The Felgans were the first to encounter the Chicher, about two centuries ago, and tried to conquer them. At the time the Chicher were just beginning to explore their home solar system. Somehow they repelled the Felgan incursion, probably owing at least in part to their tenacity.

Ahead of me the Umbelgarri thrall's eyestalks swiveled about as it clicked across the hold's steel plate floor.

Overhead floodlights came on, supplementing the marginal fluorescent illumination. It created subtle shadows but immediately increased the speed at which the maintenance techs worked. They still used their flashlights and illumination beams attached to headbands and portable halogen lamps.

McAllister snapped closed her clip and called over her shoulder at me. "I imagine you'll be saying, 'It's a small universe,' Bleys. I'll attribute it to the fact that even highly improbable events can occur."

She wanted me to request clarification, so I replied, "If you say so, Senior Engineer."

Her pair of braids bounced as she laughed. Her hint of mirth was drowned out by the hollers, shouted orders, and muttered conversations audible above the mechanical din.

A droning voice over the intercom announced: "Two hours until boarding and button up."

O'Vorley leaned close to me. "In two of the other cargo holds, they're emplacing ion cannons."

The Chicher employed ion cannons on their battlewagons, and the Troh-gots had more advanced ones. Humans had them too, usually as a secondary ship-mounted weapon. More often they supplemented ground-based batteries. Not as powerful as the Troh-gots' but more accurate than the Chicher's.

O'Vorley caught my expression as we sidestepped a squad of Marines followed by a dolly bot loaded down with weapons and ammo. "There's no time for that," I said. "Even if there was, they'd stick out on a freighter's hull like a pair of Gar Crax on a llama farm."

"No, you're right," O'Vorley said. "They would. They're emplacing them inside the cargo holds on tracks so they can slide forward. They're precutting portholes and emplacing shaped explosives to blow out the opening. They'll have a limited field of fire."

"Correct," I said, thinking of the cannons on tracks, poking out like iron muzzles on ancient sail-driven war galleys. O'Vorley must've gotten his information from McAllister, or maybe Pilot Detter. "Even a glancing strike will disable a Behemoth transport. Gives the breaching pods a better chance to close. For us to board."

"Disable the Crax too."

Shaking my head, I said, "Maybe," knowing it wasn't likely. "Disrupt some systems, temporarily. Not disable."

We approached our assigned breaching pod, one of the smaller variants. BP-J-132 was painted in bold black paint across the non-reflective reinforced steel hull. Infused with crystalline and ceramic components, the pods were supposed to be resistant to lasers and energy beams. I'd seen the emerald green weapons of the Primus Crax lance through the armored hulls of capital ships. That said what chances our pod had against the Crax weapons.

Also painted to the right of the pod's number was something reminiscent of nose art on attack shuttles and fighters. A hand-crank can opener with a stylize engine—like an old-style motorcycle's spitting exhaust smoke—attached to the cranking gear. Scrawled in angular script was the pod's apparent name, *Turbo Crank*.

Out of the corner of his eye O'Vorley caught my smile and shook his head.

I said, "Guess you were correct, Engineer McAllister."

McAllister didn't turn her head. "It's even better than paintings of general issue Relic equipment, Bleys."

Two maintenance techs were sealing the armored plate that protected the housing for the pod's auxiliary metallic hydrogen fuel canisters. Next to them stood a Colonial Marine Sergeant. What caught my attention first was his scarred scalp with patches of dark hair cropped short. Thinking of a globe of the Earth, if the scars were oceans, the eighth inch hair resembled continents. Caustic burns from Crax rounds. The Marine must've taken a pellet or two to the head. They splattered and he managed to get his helmet off before it was completely burned through. And he survived the associated toxins that must've reached his blood stream, from even a light exposure. That marked him as tough, even among Colonial Marines.

Something about his build, a little on the thin side, and his stance stirred a memory.

The sergeant dismissed the maintenance techs and ducked into the pod's hatch.

From inside a Chicher's chattering was translated into a mechanical voice after several seconds of delay. "Scarred Warrior Leader, the orb is lowering toward the time when we swarm."

If the chittering language hadn't announced the presence of a Chicher, the hollow translation, along with its odd word selection and syntax, would have. At least for me.

A tightness in my throat arose as I recalled the Chicher diplomat that died rescuing me. Died from a Crax round dissolving his innards. I swallowed hard, rubbing my throat's scar from the diplomat's bite. The last act of his brief death ritual.

McAllister knew I got along well with the Chicher. She probably thought it was because they were R-Techs like me. Maybe there was something to that, but more, I knew what it was like to stand alone, like a crayfish in a pond filled with frogs. And the Chicher were a pack species, most comfortable when in a group of their own. Unfortunately, their assignments often left them isolated, not only from their pack, but all members of their species. Something far harder for them to deal with than it was for me.

Why didn't they pair them up? Did they assign the individuals based on a psychological profile that would enable them to endure isolation from their own kind, or at least bond with humans they named surrogate pack members?

I looked ahead. A Bahklack thrall, single-mindedly driven to serve their masters, and not very empathetic, wouldn't make good surrogate pack members. I doubted the Umbelgarri would. The Chicher didn't trust Felgans, so that left humans. Their only ally that might do so.

Those questions and conclusion raced through my mind as we stopped outside the pod's entry hatch. McAllister whispered back to me, "Quite the homecoming for such an expansive galaxy."

O'Vorley looked a little puzzled, but still grinned. He knew some about my history with the Chicher.

McAllister looked over her shoulder and winked at me, then called into the breaching pod. "Sergeant Justice Smith, Hack Team Four reporting."

I kept a straight face at the shouted name. The stance and build. Corporal Smith, the last time I saw him, he was engaged in a losing battle in the *Kalavar*'s shuttle bay. During my pretrial, what seemed decades ago, I'd been led to believe Corporal Smith died helping Veronica Drizdon escape, while I escorted her son, Maximar Drizdon Jr., to an exploration shuttle. Both hunted by the enemy. Their survival and freedom a priority even as the Crax and Stegmar boarding parties overwhelmed the *Kalavar*'s crew, passengers and squad of Colonial Marines.

The scarred Marine emerged, flanked by a corporal and a private. His eyes, those of Corporal Justice Smith—now a sergeant—fixed on McAllister and narrowed in recognition. "Engineer McAllister."

Smith's two fellow Marines appeared more interested in the Bahklack's presence until their sergeant glanced my way.

His eyes widened as he stepped past McAllister, between her and the Umbelgarri thrall to shake my hand. Patting me on the shoulder, his voice boomed, "Security Specialist Keesay!"

Despite the din, nearby eyes turned our way.

I signaled with my eyes down to my name patch, and he checked out my duty coveralls. "Bleys? You steal some unsuspecting sec-spec's uniform?"

"Nope," I said. "I am who it reads."

Smith's left eyebrow rose for a few seconds until he came to a conclusion. "Right, Specialist Bleys. Sorry." He looked over at Kent. "Specialist O'Vorley, we've met, right?"

"In that you are correct," Kent said. "Briefly on the Mavinrom Dock."

Smith offered his hand to Kent and they shook.

"I thought so," Smith said. He stepped back and shot a glance at the thrall. It stood still as a statue, except for its stalk eyes taking in the Marines and the surrounding activity. "Engineer McAllister, the lieutenant is attending the final mission brief." He swung his arm toward the pod's hatch. "This here is Corporal Pallish and Private Umpernilli. Ignore them and step inside. I'll give you the tour, short that it'll be, and introduce your team to the rest of the squad, unimpressive as they might appear."

"Appear?" McAllister asked sarcastically. "Appearances can be deceiving with Colonial Marines, right?"

"Right," he said, shrugging. "You may not benefit from the tour, but the rest of your team might."

During our tour, Corporal Pallish and Private Umpernilli volunteered to get some additional gear. Smith's eyebrows flitted up in surprise, but with terse directives he sent Pallish to gather some additional first aid supplies and Umpernilli to check on additional battery packs, ordering both not to muck around.

A breaching pod was little more than a capsule with clamping and cutting gear on one end and a pilot nestled up between the engines on the other. A circle of seats with harnesses lined the circular wall. Equipment was stowed in gear boxes and netting beneath the seats with additional storage space in an octagonal locker bay thrust up like a shaft in the center. It reminded me of an old-style roller coaster ride with brown lockers from high school three arm lengths out of reach when seated. That meant room for a boarding squad loaded with equipment to maneuver.

Clear white lettering on the boxes and lockers identified contents, from emergency oxygen tanks and masks to hand tools and spare ammo. The white letters reflected the internal lighting like polished mother of pearl in the otherwise steel gray walls and floor grating, and brown storage and seating.

The pilot, a Fleet lieutenant named Arnold, and Smith showed us our assigned seats, folded them down, adjusting the harness fittings and seat height from the floor. To the right of each seat was a vertical storage bin for weapons and gear, with quick release straps. O'Vorley and I took the opportunity to strap our shouldered firearms into their slots.

The pod was sparse and uncomfortable, but all it needed to do was transport boarding teams from the launch ship to the enemy ship—and back if a retreat was called for.

Two Marines were removing one of the seats while two others installed auxiliary adjustable harnesses for the Bahklack. The alien stood silently along a pair of folded up seats, eye stalks focused on the Chicher as it chattered at a maintenance tech installing a pair of pallets that would hold one of the hexagonal crates lined with wooden slats. In between bursts of the power drill's whine, a muffled *buzz* filled the drill's momentary silence. It reminded me of my Uncle's honeybee hives. The Chicher stood next to the crate, paws or hands resting on it, sounding a rapid-fire clucking.

Pilot Arnold's deep voice sparred with McAllister's as she argued over some obscure computer readout. He scratched the back of his bald head and calmly explained that yes, the software is out of date, but functional, and that she wasn't authorized to install an updated version. O'Vorley moved over to intervene as the pilot warned that if she attempted to interface with the pod's systems he'd shoot her. A hard stare and hand on his MP pistol suggested he wasn't joking.

Smith commented to me, "She's never going to change."

I shook my head, showing my agreement.

Smith rested a hand on my shoulder. "Your partner's got patience, that's for sure."

"Maybe we should name him Saint O'Vorley."

The Marine lieutenant's arrival interrupted Sergeant Smith's laughter. It took a little longer for the scowling pilot and cursing McAllister to notice.

CHAPTER 28

We sat in our assigned seats aboard BP-J-132, nicknamed *Turbo Crank*. Apparently 'Can Opener' was a popular name among breaching pods so Lieutenant Burian and everyone else referred to her as *Turbo Crank*. The lieutenant gave us the run down on our anti-grav equipment and overall part in the planned assault.

Second Lieutenant Burian was a middle-aged lanky man with a cutting sense of ironic humor, referencing to just about everything in this mission. He seemed a bit old to be a lieutenant, but McAllister leaned close and showed me a screen shot of the lieutenant's history on her clamshell clip. He was computer programmer and owner of a part-time gunsmith business, specialized in customizing high-powered MP rifles for hunting expeditions.

Like so many others, the war came and he volunteered. Less than a month out of officer training, he was given this thrown-together squad, now on a hastily organized assault mission. Little time to mold them into a cohesive unit.

The lieutenant sounded technologically astute with a firm grasp of an apparent infinity of details. He also leaned heavily on his veteran NCO's experience. It suggested he and Smith made a good team.

Maybe, just maybe, we all wouldn't die in the next few hours.

The lieutenant glanced up at *Turbo Crank*'s chronometer. "Smith, where are Corporal Pallish and Private Umpernilli?"

Smith reiterated, "I sent Pallish and Umpernilli to get additional first aid gear and batteries after Hack Team Four arrived. I'll check on it." Immediately Smith put a hand to his ear and sent a harsh query just above a whisper to the missing corporal and private.

After widening his eyes in an 'it figures' expression, Lt. Burian spoke over Smith. "*No* sense wasting time." He held up a harness with eight faceted objects attached in a square pattern, four to the front, and four across the back. The objects looked like Umbelgarri technology, each metallic and the size of a sliced golf ball. "Shared Umbelgarri gear," he said, nodding to the Bahklack.

Through its electronic translator, the rote voice emanated from the Umbelgarri thrall. "I recognize and comprehend this aspect of the Masters' innovative ingenuity. Do you require that I expound upon the bestowed boon, lowest echelon of leadership cast directing the contents of this archaic infesting craft?"

The Bahklack rarely spoke. Even so, intuitively I recognized the thrall went out of its way to be both polite and respectful.

Lt. Burian turned and blinked several times before answering, "Negative, but I thank you. Knowing this, my instructions will be easier. I won't have to be concerned with phrasing that might be confusing to you."

"Acknowledged," replied the thrall. "I shall redirect my planning to further the objective of the Masters."

That earned a raised eyebrow from the lieutenant. It did from me too, but since he chose not to pursue exactly what the objective was, I didn't bother either. Sure, capturing a Primus Crax ship might be it, but I doubted that the Umbelgarri were single minded in any venture.

I heard Smith order a Marine next to him, "Pallish and Umpernilli aren't responding. See to it."

Private Villet must've been the squad's communications specialist. With a nod the thin Marine, not even as tall as me, hurried out, making adjustments to the com-gear clipped to his belt and strapped to his left forearm.

Besides Pilot Arnold, Lt. Burian, Smith, me, and the rest of Hack Team 4, that left Privates Brooker, Nollie, Xiont, and the Chicher, who continued lurking near his intermittently humming crate.

The crate was a curiosity, one that I wanted to learn more about, but the lieutenant's explanation of the harness took priority.

The lieutenant began with a frown. "Intel from debris recovered after battles where we've held the field, or space to be more accurate, and our allies, suggest that Primus Crax utilize poles and rails for movement within their space-faring vessels. Owing to their apparent arboreal-dwelling ancestry."

The lieutenant removed a hand remote device from his breast pocket and tapped a few icons with his thumb. Three projector lenses mounted in a section of the pod's ceiling turned on. A second later, images from recovered wreckage appeared a little above eye-level as I sat. Each poorly defined image, roughly two feet in size, rotated and then faded, making room for the next to appear.

Quality optics wasn't a priority on the aging breaching pod. I leaned forward to get a closer look.

It appeared that two pairs of parallel rails, nonmetallic and resembling two-inch-diameter PVC pipes were what Lt. Burian was referring to. I wondered if the repeated color pattern—pink, turquoise, faded emerald, lilac purple—was in some way significant. Maybe a visual label for direction of travel or identifying authorized or prioritized usage?

"For those that may be unaware," Lt. Burian continued, thumb tapping his remote, "Primus Crax most closely resemble terran veiled chameleons, but reaching four to five feet long. The higher caste or higher authority Primus Crax is generally green, with lower castes being tan. Those in the middle having mixed coloration. When stressed or frightened, their colors tend to darken. Aggression, the opposite."

He took a moment while images of the few Primus captives rotated through the holographic display. "They are reported to have a military or warrior caste that are black but shift to gray when in a fighting mood. None of those have ever been taken captive.

"Unlike terran veiled chameleons, the Primus Crax are quick moving with lightning reflexes."

Lt. Burian switched off the projectors and pocketed his remote. "Needless to say, the Primus are smart and equipped with technology that surpasses ours, equal to the Umbelgarri." He held up one of the harnesses with the faceted devices. "While our ally the Chicher might be able to climb and maneuver with only minor difficulty, we humans would be in trouble. This vest will offer anti-gravity maneuverability during the assault."

We humans did have anti-gravity devices, sometimes mounted on bots or even battle tanks, but they were heavy and batteries wouldn't cut it. They required a constant energy supply, a miniature metallic hydrogen generator would be best. A backpack would work, but it'd reduce agility, maneuverability and, unless the power generator was armored, it'd be vulnerable to damage. They'd never proven reliable in combat.

If I was fighting the Primus Crax, and Stegmar Mantis reportedly found on their advanced ships, and my anti-grav generator cut out? The result would be like trying to run a marathon wearing scuba gear: Mask, air tank, diving weights, fins and all.

Lt. Burian glanced over at my stowed shotgun. "Specialist Bleys, you'll need to get yours specially attuned so that recoil doesn't send you slamming into bulkheads. Or worse."

"I'll see to it," McAllister said.

That earned a raised eyebrow from the lieutenant.

"She's the resident techno-genius, Lieutenant, sir," I said. So that McAllister's ego didn't inflate too much, I pointed a thumb to the Bahklack and added, "If Senior Engineer McAllister can't figure it out, her associate should be up to the task."

That drew a snort from Smith.

"Sergeant?" the lieutenant asked.

"Nothing, sir," he replied in an all-business tone.

I raised my hand to get the officer's attention and distract from Smith's faux pas. When he acknowledged me with a nod, I asked, "The poles, will we be issued a lubricant? Something to make them impassible?"

"No," the lieutenant said. "It's in the mission notes being sent to your inbox, but I'll explain it here as long as we're waiting for Pallish, Umpernilli, and now Villet." His eyes shot to Smith before finishing. "The travel poles are designed with a honeycomb structure. Although smooth in appearance, their feel is said to resemble tight-woven burlap. Don't ask me why. Nevertheless, they tend to absorb deposited liquids and gels, or shed them."

"Can't the absorption system be overwhelmed by a thick spread of something like axle grease?"

"Micro lubricants don't work and unless you want to tote a ten liter bucket of grease, Bleys…"

"Understood, Lieutenant. I'll review the mission brief at the first opportunity."

The lieutenant glanced over at the pilot who was watching and listening from his situated area above us. "Arnold, record my oral briefing for Pallish, Umpernilli, Villet." He paused, "Sergeant?"

Smith stood. "Villet's been unable to locate them. Communications non-responsive. I'll track them down, sir."

Lieutenant Burian looked like he wanted to expel an exasperated breath. Instead he simply said, "See to it while I finish up here."

Hack Team 4 was temporarily attached, with file work identifying us as civilian conscripts, to the 3rd Squad of the 2nd Platoon of the 1st Company of the 2nd Battalion, a part of the 22nd Light Assault Division. The mission brief assigned the 3rd Squad to escort and support the insertion of biological pests of an alien arthropod nature. The objective being to disrupt a coordinated resistance against our attempt to board and capture a Primus Crax vessel.

That Hack Team 4's mission to infiltrate the alien computer systems in support of the boarding was secondary chaffed at McAllister as evidenced by her grumbling to O'Vorley, "How long can it take to release a barrel of Chicher-bred hornets?"

She ignored O'Vorley's reminder: "Maximum effectiveness requires that they be released at one of nine anticipated critical junctures. Reaching any of those might take a while."

While en route to the orbital dock, Lt. Burian's company had practiced their part in the assault using virtual reality simulations. All of the Colonial Marines and Fleet pilots had.

That Lt. Burian had been preparing to lead an understrength squad to accomplish the mission, that the breaching pod would've participated in the assault carrying less than a full complement of boarders, until our arrival, said something. And it wasn't good. A mission this important, even on short notice, didn't have enough Colonial Marines—trained bodies—available to participate...

The Chicher Thuckich Handler approached me a moment after I shut down my ocular. There were so many things that could go wrong. Heck, the Crax could open airlocks, exposing us to the vacuum of space. That was just one reason I actually agreed with McAllister. Hacking into the Primus computer systems and disrupting counter boarding measures seemed higher priority than releasing a Thuckich hive. The Marines needed to hit hard, and drive deep into the Primus vessel. Speed meant survival, or a chance at it. Warp screwing the enemy's computer systems would go a long way toward extending that chance. The Colonial Marines had three teams coordinating on that. Even against three teams that prepped for this mission, my credits would remain on McAllister.

Everyone else but the pilot and the Bahklack was outside the pod. Arnold was up checking his systems and reviewing radio encrypting protocol with Assault Command. The Bahklack stood motionless with its eyes closed, asleep. I was meeting assigned duty by watching over her.

Thuckich Hardler, as the rat-like alien ally had been introduced to us, stood on his hind legs before bowing quickly and shifting his tail to the left. "Clawed Slave's Security Man, are you prepared to infest the Long Thinking Scaled Enemy?" The translation followed the Chicher's squeaks and squirrel-like chattering after a delay of several seconds.

I'd seen such a greeting only once. When a Chicher Diplomat first met a Catholic priest, naming him a 'spirit man,' the Chicher bowed but shifted his prehensile tail to the right.

"I've been in the company of a Chicher once before," I said after bowing my head several inches. "Never did I merit such a greeting." After giving the disc-shaped translator clipped to the Chicher's equipment harness a few seconds to translate, I continued. "To what do I owe this honor, Thuckich Handler?"

The three-foot-tall alien sniffed the air and leaned close. "You are a Pollinated Pack Member." His head tilted in question.

I felt at the scars along my neck.

"Pollinated. Marked member traveling outer circle of the Rifted Land Pack. Other circle than mine." Thuckich Handler rapidly nodded his head. "I recognize. All Chicher that sniffs air shared recognize."

"Greater than a surrogate pack member?" I asked.

A moment of silence hung between us long after the translation should've been made by the Chicher's translator. It operated with outdated technology by modern human standards but met Chicher needs. At least I knew more about the Chicher Diplomat, my lost friend, who'd apparently thought of me as more than a friend, much more.

Not that I didn't take friendship lightly. I had few true friends. So maybe there hadn't been much difference between us.

"Pollinated is higher," the Chicher Handler said, spreading the claw-tipped fingers of his rodent paws. That snapped me back to the moment. The handler tipped his head sideways, back and forth. "High, as twig of a tree, does not fall away," he said through his robotic translator. "Surrogate is lower, as leaf is part of a tree that falls away when orb moves lower across sky. When season changes, when surrogate and pack member separate."

That made sense. The Chicher Diplomat was the only one of his kind on the *Kalavar*. With him, I'd been a surrogate pack member. We'd been close. Defeated an elite Gar Crax together, made it to a quarantined planet, survived an arctic trek. Maybe it was my being a fellow Relic that had formed the initial tenuous bond. He'd helped me come out on top when McAllister had tried to frame me. He'd seen me at my best and at my worst. I did what I thought was right by him, but didn't deserve elevated status in their culture's structure.

The bite must've changed my body chemistry. Something in the Chicher's saliva. Maybe I gave off a pheromone now, one that Chicher olfactory senses could detect. I wondered if Dr. Goldsen knew. If she could detect it.

The Chicher Thuckich Handler stood, paws now limp, watching me. I never recalled the Chicher Diplomat demonstrating such nonverbal cues. Even the phrasing between the diplomat and the handler differed. It reminded me that just like humanity, aliens had their own diversity of cultures. Heck, the handler was from a different pack, and I wasn't sure what that entailed.

I glanced over at the secured wooden container. "Tell me about your hive." The mission brief provided details, but it seemed like the right thing to ask while we had a few moments. And I might learn something more than what the military knew, or was interested in sharing.

The Chicher Handler snapped back into motion and scampered on all fours, returning to a bi-pedal stance next to the hexagonal wooden crate. "Thuckich hive. No mountain peak mother. Given scent of Long Thinking Scaled Enemy, fable killing mountain peak mother. Will swarm. Sting and share venom, sever air consumption."

The military's diagrams showed a Thuckich warrior caste as a hornet, colored like a blue bottle fly and the size of my thumb. It had eight legs, pinchers like a stag beetle, and a lancing proboscis that injected a neurotoxin, broad spectrum in its effect on various species. Only the Shiggs and Trohgots are immune, as reported by the Chicher. Immune to the venom, not the pinchers, which were described as painful. Worse than a horse fly's bite.

"So they will ignore us." I pointed to the handler. "Chicher." Pointed to myself and the pilot above. "Humans." Pointed a thumb to the Bahklack, and used the Chicher's naming. "Clawed Slave."

The Chicher Handler nodded his head once. "Fly past," he said, his eyes flicking to me and the pilot and the sleeping Bahklack. "Fable set before forced night slumber." He pulled an aerosol can from a belt loop. "Morning rays, forced rising."

"I can hear them," I said of the humming.

The Chicher Handler shook his head once and pointed to his translator. "Radio communication of labor hive mates there. Electronic fable eases night slumber."

I nodded my understanding. "Good. The Thuckich will help," I said and then chuckled a few seconds. "We're going to need an awful lot of luck too."

Pilot Arnold called down. "You three the only ones down there?"

"Correct," I said. "You want me to fetch someone?"

"Not really," the pilot said, leaning down through his hatch and signaling me closer. After I complied, he asked, "You're really that Relic, Keesay, aren't you. The man who toppled CGIG?"

I shook my head and pointed to my patch. "You must be mistaken."

He grinned. "Sergeant Smith told a few tales about you on the way over. Heard him call you Keesay."

The pilot seemed like a decent guy so I replied with a shade of the truth. "What would be the odds of Sergeant Smith and this Security Specialist Keesay randomly crossing paths out in space?"

Pilot Arnold stifled a laugh. "About the same as Smith confusing a shotgun and bayone- toting Relic Security Specialist with someone he'd shared air with. Sounded like they were friends."

"I think Smith would be a good man to count as a friend."

"I get your meaning, Specialist Bleys." The pilot smiled, then frowned. "Considering Sergeant Smith's tales depicting his friend's daring and thick-headedness…" He paused and locked gazes with me. "Knowing what's coming…what it's going to take to survive, I think we're going to need a healthy dose of Keesay's daring, and luck. Wouldn't you agree?"

Sergeant Smith's curses just outside the breaching pod's entry hatch interrupted our quiet discussion.

Pilot Arnold dipped his head further down, checking the chronometer. "A dress down is on the way. The least Pallish and Umpernilli deserve." With that said, he pulled himself back up into the pilot's seat.

McAllister strode in rolling her eyes but saying nothing, followed by O'Vorley and the other Marines: Villet, Brooker, Nollie and Xiont. O'Vorley tossed me a pair of energy bars and a juice pouch. He tossed the same to the Chicher.

I tilted my head toward the stirring Bahklack. McAllister caught my movement and held up a plastic sack and walked around to the Umbelgarri Thrall. When its eyes focused on her, she said, "Nourishment."

"Necessary for efficient service toward the Masters' objectives assigned to me."

"As to be expected," McAllister said, placing the bag on the grated floor and stretching it open.

The crab-like alien squatted down and began eating what looked and smelled like shredded fish. The Chicher wasn't the only one to notice the smell. A couple of the Marines commented as they went through the gear near their assigned seats. They also watched the Bahklack eat. It was more entertaining for me to watch them watch the alien quickly devour the fish, being less messy than might be expected of an oversized crustacean. It'd finished long before I finished my meal, one bar simulating graham crackers and honey, and the other peanuts and honey. The packaging of the cherry fruit drink and of the bars was edible too, offering extra fiber but no real taste.

Once Sergeant Justice Smith's one-sided shouting and cursing ended, Lt. Burian issued a less audible set of orders, or so I figured.

Corporal Pallish and Private Umpernilli, both apparently cowed, moved to their seats and immediately began reviewing the mission brief. From what I'd overheard earlier, it was much the same as they'd practiced, with only minor bits of new information incorporated. Observing them, I thought of the old-time comedians Abbot and Costello, Pallish being taller and more angular and Umpernilli being shorter and a little stocky. Even so, he was still taller than me by an inch or two.

Thinking of Abbot and Costello reminded me of their comedy routine, *Who's on First*, and Janice Tahgs, who'd showed the old black and white vid to me. My mind drifted to her, and to Deputy Director Simms, and then to Agent Vingee and Guymin aboard the *Pitchfork* seeking them.

I examined my supply pack and its gear, including a first aid kit, portable breathing apparatus, thirty meters of dura-polymer rope, spare batteries for the anti-gravity harness, a CNS Suppressor Modulator, and more. Through my security training I was familiar with everything in the pack, except the CNS modulator. That, I learned how to attach and detach aboard the *Kalavar*. We could've used them to nullify the Stegmar Mantis sounding on Io.

I attached the white, foot-long strip to the base of O'Vorley's neck and partway down his spine. He could activate it by pressing with two fingers along the tip. He could detach it by pinching the same area for several seconds. Attaching was painless. The same couldn't be said about detaching.

After O'Vorley affixed mine, he, McAllister, and I got a brief fifteen minute trial run with our gravity harnesses. We did it inside the breaching pod as air had been pumped out of the cargo bay and our pod, like all the others, was attached to a power and life support umbilical.

As we didn't have time to actually train and allow the anti-grav system's computer to become accustomed to our individual movement habits, we operated under the default setting. It was like being in zero gravity, but the system sensed, by our reaching or leg movements, which direction we wanted to go and made adjustments. It offered some resistance, allowing us to scamper up walls, if we desired. It was fortunate I'd recently spent a lot of time in zero gravity as the breaching pod's interior didn't offer room to practice.

When Lt. Burian caught O'Vorley smiling at our efforts, colliding in such a confined space, the officer called to my friend, "That equipment is both rare and extremely valuable. You'll be returning that upon completion of your mission. No forgetting, no excuses."

Smith chimed in, saying, "In other words, even if you're wounded, drag your dying ass back to the pod so we don't have to recover it, oh, and your dead ass too."

Private Xiont added, "Right, and try not to bleed on it, too."

That drew a round of laughs from everyone, except the Bahklack thrall. Even McAllister and the Chicher Handler let loose, though the Chicher did a little late because of his translator's delay.

Private Villet had even managed to secure a helmet for McAllister, and a customized one that fit the Chicher. Both had sturdy straps and a digitized camouflage pattern made up mainly of blacks, blues, and grays. The Chicher's accommodated his mic and wired earpiece. I'd never seen a Chicher wearing a helmet. It reminded me of a laboratory rat wearing an old-style bicycle helmet.

Ninety minutes passed slowly. I spent most of it chatting with Private Xiont who sat to my left. The thrall on my right was a horrible conversationalist, 100% focused on its actions serving Umbelgarri goals. Most of the Colonial Marines just squinted or shook their heads the few times that the alien interjected a thought into the conversation between McAllister and Lt Burian. Her effort to increase the priority of her task to help foil the Primus computer systems was anything but subtle.

Xiont had turned nineteen the day before and his swarthy-skinned face rippled with smile after smile as we exchanged stories. We discussed my shotgun, and the usefulness of shotguns on penal colonies and in combat. I showed him my bayonet and he showed me his old-style switchblade that he kept in a narrow thigh pocket. It wasn't balanced for throwing or great for hand-to-hand combat, but he'd won it at a church raffle and considered it lucky.

We both laughed while speculating how the church ended up with a switchblade and what led up to it being included in their fundraiser. The topic had come up before with Xiont, and he figured every credit raised was a credit the church could use in service of the Lord. Plus, the switchblade at the time was going to a future Colonial Marine, and God works in mysterious ways.

The whole time Xiont and I were talking, Umpernilli and Pallish kept looking my way. Mainly Pallish. After the twentieth or so time I was about to say something to the angular corporal when Lt. Burian sat up straight and his hand snapped up to his ear.

At the same time, Pilot Arnold shouted down, "Gravitational fluctuation. Someone's dropping out of condensed space travel."

After a moment, the pilot switched on the holo-display, giving everyone a view of the Behemoth class transport. "Well, isn't that special," he said. "They decided to arm her to the teeth." From his controls, he adjusted the holo-display. "Well, lookie there. They slapped on some armor plating. Covers most of the hull." After hearing a few Marines groan, the pilot asked, "Any wagers down there as to whether our itty-bitty rotary cannon will penetrate, or just plink off of that?"

CHAPTER 29

Everything went well for the first fifteen minutes of the behemoth class transport *Jormungand*'s approach. Switching through my com-set's channels, I listened in. Radio communication between the dock and the approaching transport seemed brief but professional. The corpses floating in space didn't appear to surprise or concern *Jormungand*'s captain. Why would it? With four tri-beam laser turrets, two on the portside, one facing forward and the other aft, and a mirror arrangement starboard, that gave them ample offensive firepower. I counted at least eight dual-beam pulse laser mounts for close defense against missiles, fighters, attack shuttles, and breaching pods. But what concerned me most was the dorsally mounted cannon that appeared to have a 360 degree horizontal and 180 degree vertical axis acquisition and firing arc. Both McAllister and Thrall Blue Gray Blue Blue Nineteen identified it as a Primus Crax auxiliary energy beam cannon.

I wondered how much of the behemoth transport's cargo area had been dedicated to housing nuclear reactors to power the additional weaponry, especially the A-Tech cannon. If they had A-Tech targeting and A-Tech sensor arrays as well, we were beyond warp screwed.

I strapped on my helmet, deciding that if they had a complete suite of advanced sensor arrays, the ambush would've been detected already. Matching advanced targeting sensors with the advanced cannon seemed like a better plan, for them…

Still, that they'd armed the behemoth transport meant stealthy missions requiring close proximity to ships, orbital colonies, or planetary objectives was out, at least for the *Jormungand*.

"Detaching from umbilical," Pilot Arnold announced. That meant wired communications had been severed. With strict radio silence except for dock systems sending to the closing ship and simulating normal activity, the next message would announce the balloon going up.

"With their unanticipated firepower," Arnold said, "orders are to execute Secondary Assault Plan D."

I had to stop and think about that change. Closing my eyes, I recalled the alternate plan from reading the mission brief details. Instead of two waves, with fighters and attack shuttles leading, breaching pods were to follow right on the first wave's tail rather than launch after a five minute delay.

Lt. Burian stated the obvious. "She has more firepower than the Bizmith Orbital Dock and this dead-in-space freighter combined. If the add-on ion cannons fail in their objective, the tin can sheltering us'll be Swiss cheese. And soon after Mr. Grim Reaper'll be around to retrieve my life's little claim ticket. And all yours, too."

He was right. The task force would take at least twenty minutes to arrive once the recall signal was sent. Maybe longer. During the Silicate War, it took a Crax frigate twenty-four minutes to cold start its engines, but experience told me they could do it faster. And if they'd been prepping, twenty minutes for the cavalry to arrive might be too late.

A minor shockwave reverberated from the floor grate up through my boots. My seat's construction allowed it to absorb the jolt caused by explosives shearing open the *Iron Oxen*'s hull to provide the ion cannons a field of fire.

"That's our signal," Pilot Arnold said. "If you're not buckled in, now would be the time."

Everyone but the Bahklack double-checked. The Chicher gave a quick visual inspection to assure himself that the hexagonal crate remained secure.

With a few thumb tapping commands via his remote, the lieutenant shifted the holo-projection to give a split view. The *Iron Oxen*'s cargo hold's doors began opening while the ion cannons advanced their muzzles beyond the newly shorn portholes. The view of the closing *Jormungand* diminished in size. Her main engines and starboard side maneuvering thrusters flared to full power.

A slight jolt announced the ion cannons releasing their first blast. Sparkles of white gouted from the exposed cannon muzzles even as they recoiled back within the confines of the freighter's hull.

Each ion blast streaked toward its target like a giant had hurled a fist full of sparklers, old-style fireworks, at the enemy freighter. The lighting effects weren't necessary as ship targeting systems automatically detected origin, hits, and misses. The psychological effect of being fired upon by an enemy, even if the particular vessel you occupied wasn't the current target, carried weight. Thus, the sparkling lights were included because nobody enjoyed witnessing their side taking fire, even if it missed.

The *Oxen*'s opening salvo streaked past, both shots missing by narrow margins.

Not good. Either they rushed their shots, have poor tracking and targeting sensors, or both.

Two of the Bizmith Dock's three turrets must've gotten a targeting solution as they fired next. One pair of dual beam defense lasers struck aft, but failed to penetrate *Jormungand*'s armor. The second pair also failed to penetrate but managed to rake across one of the transport's forward mounted laser turrets.

Fighters and attack shuttles exited the *Oxen*'s hold as we took off. "Hold on to your seats, gentlemen—and women!"

I guess he counted Blue Gray Blue Blue Nineteen as a woman, along with McAllister.

The enemy transport didn't turn but pressed forward.

By the time we exited the cargo hold, the ion cannons fired again, but not before the *Jormungand*'s remaining forward firing lasers opened up. The tri-beams tore through the bay holding one of the ion cannons, and burned deep into the old freighter's bowels. One of the ion cannon's blasts struck the closing behemoth transport in the nose, sending a shower of arcing sparks along its front. Before the signs of the cannon's strike diminished, three small vessels—Primus Crax fighters—rocketed from a portside bay.

Whereas the Crax fighters I'd seen before were wedge-shaped, these looked like two small pyramids stuck onto opposite sides of a slightly larger sphere. They looked odd, but fast. Faster than any fighter or attack shuttle I'd ever seen, even Umbelgarri.

Almost immediately the trio of Primus fighters began pelting the *Oxen* with streams of emerald energy in five round bursts. Each pyramid had a turret. Six energy streams hammered the *Oxen*, zeroing in on the hold housing the remaining ion cannon.

Everyone was watching the holo projection of the battle, just like me. Even the Bahklack appeared to have a look of concern, the way its stalk eyes followed the Primus fighters, excluding everything else.

The lieutenant asked, "What say you, Pilot?"

"Well, I'm glad I'm not a fighter pilot. Which means I'll probably live about ten minutes longer than them."

The orbital dock and the *Oxen* had launched everything. That meant nine fighters, eleven attack shuttles, and twenty-four breaching pods.

O'Vorley glanced at me, eyebrows raised in concern.

I commented to him, and anyone listening, "Emerald is fast becoming my least favorite color."

"Mine too," said Smith.

"Okay, passengers," Pilot Arnold said, "enjoy the ride and the light show. Ignore the jinking, or at least hold your stomachs, as I try a little evasive maneuvering."

The original plan called for breaching pods to follow the fighters and attack shuttles in. The fighters' job was to engage any enemy fighters. Terran were anticipated. The attack shuttles were to silence any self-defense batteries the behemoth transport might have and follow up by taking out her primary thrust engines, and then engage any Primus Crax frigates that might emerge from the transport's cavernous cargo hold. Two of the breaching pods were to latch onto the *Jormungand* and keep her crew occupied until reinforcements arrived. The rest of us were to attach and cut our way into any Primus Crax vessel that was in the hold, the second the doors opened, or were blown open by canister mines launched from some of the attack shuttles.

Private Umpernilli asked, "Will that work, Lieutenant?" A look of concern mingled with dismay filled is eyes. "The jinking?"

Lieutenant Burian returned the question with a grim smile. Rapping his knuckles against the metallic hull plate behind him, he said, "She's nimble as a hippopotamus navigating an obstacle course. That data point should suffice to draw a reasonable conclusion."

As if to emphasize the bad turn the engagement had taken, the *Jormungand*'s eight dual-beam pulse laser mounts opened up, peppering us with long range fire and giving our fighters one more thing to worry about, a minor distraction with respect to the incoming destructive scheme of things.

My com-set switched to Bizmith Dock Command. "Execute Beta Six."

That was all I heard before our fighters launched their short range missiles and opened up with their pulse lasers, hoping to pound through the enemy's defensive screens before being shredded themselves.

There was no hope of out maneuvering or outrunning the enemy.

Spear-wielding Neanderthals charging Nazi SS troopers firing MP 40 submachine guns.

Within seconds, emerald fire turned five of our fighters and their pilots into shattered bits of debris. Only one Primus fighter sustained damage in the exchange.

Before the Primus fighters could fire on their second target, two silver beams struck and penetrated the screens shielding the undamaged Primus fighters, crippling them.

Pilot Arnold said, "That, gentlemen, came from the replacement def-sats, apparently constructed with an Umbelgarri upgrade."

"Might've executed that release decision sooner," grumbled Sergeant Smith as we watched the opposing fighters close to knife-fighting range. The combination of missiles and pulse lasers finished off all three Primus fighters, leaving two surviving fleet fighters, one severely crippled with engines flaring out.

"You're right, Sm—Sergeant," I said. "Should've played that ace in the hole sooner."

Our breaching pod, *Turbo Crank*, swayed in its trajectory as we closed on the oncoming behemoth transport. The best 'jinking' the pilot was able to perform.

"Even if we get there," McAllister muttered, "this ill-conceived calamity can only lead to catastrophe."

"You've been wrong before," Smith suggested before winking at me.

She rolled her eyes.

"I'll just be satisfied if our breaching equipment cuts through," O'Vorley said.

"One disappointment at a time," McAllister replied.

The thrall's computerized translation interrupted McAllister as she took a breath, saying, "The Masters have provided Monn-Gorrium Mwa Moon monomolecular saws to the human caste of allied followers. Data shows one is installed on this vessel designed for controlled rupture to deposit hostilities against the Masters' Swamp Nests World Destroyers. Co-enemies of the human caste of allied followers. The Masters' designs are superior to the Swamp Nests World Destroyers metallic alloys."

It was obvious, in all of the excitement, the crab alien had dispensed with trying to frame his phrasing for clear translation.

One of the Bizmith Dock's lasers found its mark again, but failed to do more than superficial hull damage. In response the *Jormungand*'s forward laser battery took out one of the upgraded def-sats.

The behemoth's Primus weapon hadn't moved. I doubted it was a mockup. Maybe the ion cannon's strike had disabled it. With that in mind, I said to no one in particular, "They recovered awfully fast from the ion cannon strike."

The eleven attack shuttles each launched a pair of missiles. If they made it past the self-defense pulse lasers and found their mark, the nuclear warhead blasts should knock the crew around a bit. Without an atmosphere to carry the shockwave, I didn't think the carbon-coated depleted uranium pellets alone would penetrate the armor. But they might find some cracks and vulnerable systems mounted on the outer hull, like pulse beam laser turrets, sensors, and communication arrays.

Across from me, Umpernilli said in an unsteady voice, "It would be easier on us if there weren't any Crax ships in the transport."

That sounded uncharacteristic of a Colonial Marine. Maybe they were scraping the bottom of the barrel for recruits.

"It'd be a monumental misallocation of assets if the behemoth transport was stuffed with something like cotton balls, Private," Lt. Burian snarled. He leaned against his straps, toward Umpernilli. "I'm sure Capital Galactic renegades slapped on armor and military grade lasers, and a Primus energy weapon just for that. What about the bodies of the dock's crew jettisoned into space for no important reason? Possibly akin to scattering hundreds of rose petals to honor the arrival of Humanity's greatest enemy?" He leaned back and put his hand to his ear.

My thinking was that I didn't want Private Umpernilli covering my back. Meeting Kent's eyes, I knew he felt the same. McAllister? With that sneer, what stopped her from spitting I'll never know.

The enemy shot down all but two of the missiles. The transport's turret gunners knew their business. One of the missiles detonated against a dorsal section, scarring it just forward of the mounted Primus weapon. The other must've had a proximity fuse as it detonated portside, just aft of the ship, damaging one of the main thrust engines.

I wished my com-set had the codes to decipher the attack shuttles' communications.

The *Jormungand* came on despite the surviving def-sat taking out the transport's remaining forward lasers. She sloughed off the attack shuttles' raking pulse laser attacks, destroying four of them with her own pulse lasers in the process.

As soon as the attack shuttles passed and began to form up with the two fighters, the behemoth's armored cargo bay doors blew open. They literally detached and tumbled away. That'd leave the ship's vulnerable interior exposed.

Just as fast, two spherical ships—Primus Crax frigates—emerged from the bays. One portside, the other starboard. It appeared they were using maneuvering thruster power only. At least for the moment.

"That's our cue," Pilot Arnold said. The *Turbo Crank*'s swaying evasive maneuvers ceased as he gave full power to thrust engines.

O'Vorley, sitting between Umpernilli and McAllister, leaned over and asked, "How long until reinforcements arrive?"

I shrugged. "Five, maybe ten minutes at the earliest."

"Look at that," Private Xiont said, pointing at the holo image.

Like popcorn in a hot kettle, emergency life pods ejected from the behemoth transport.

Private Villet, the communications specialist, said, "She couldn't have been damaged that badly."

"I agree," said the lieutenant. "Mighty fast recovery from the ion cannon."

Smith shouted up to the pilot, "Is her trajectory carrying her where I think?"

Arnold was too busy coordinating with Command to answer.

Various types of shuttles, from short range inter-solar system to long range condensed space capable joined, the last few emergency escape pods fleeing the behemoth transport. Who'd pick up those that couldn't escape under their own power? If we won the day, they'd become prisoners, probably executed for treason. If the Primus Crax survived, would they pick up any of the certain-to-be desperate humans?

The Bizmith Orbital Dock fired with all she had, striking the closing transport in the nose. She absorbed the lasers and even the def-sat's energy beam that had the angle. The silver beam lanced into the exposed cargo area, tearing at the internal structure and systems.

The attack shuttles could've given chase and taken out the suicidal transport's engines, but it wouldn't alter her momentum. She had more than sufficient maneuvering thrusters to keep her on course. Instead the attack shuttles looked to the mission's objective, and their own survival. They launched their second volley of missiles at the Primus frigate nearest the swarm of breaching pods, then chased them in.

The *Jormungand*'s imparted momentum carried the Primus frigates along with it. They focused their thrusters on moving away rather than directly opposing their trajectory. One angled away, perpendicular as could be managed. The other, our intended target, perpendicular as well, but at a slightly depressed angle compared to its partner.

Thrice the size of a patrol gunboat, the frigates were thought to have limited range compared to Primus capital ships. Even so, they were armed to the teeth.

Pelting from long-range pulse laser fire, the attack shuttles demonstrated that the Primus had raised their defensive screens. How much we'd find out. Were those easier—faster—to power up than weapons?

Then the Primus frigates opened up. The behemoth blocked the farther frigate from engaging anything but the fighters and attack shuttles. The second frigate followed suit, ignoring the breaching pods and the missiles and went for the two fighters and seven surviving attack shuttles as well. At the same time they both fired maneuvering thrusters to retard their momentum, presumably so that the *Jormungand* wouldn't remain between the frigates and they could offer each other direct line-of-sight fire support. And they wouldn't be engulfed by the collision that was to come.

Emerald energy shot from the spherical frigates. It reminded me of tracers—tracers that blotted every fighter and shuttle from space.

"Watch this, gentlemen and women," Pilot Arnold called down. "Our fate is about to be decided in the next four seconds."

The nearest frigate targeted the missiles that were nearly upon it. Four of the fourteen disappeared in a green impact followed by a white flash. Those that survived fired what appeared to be retrorockets mounted in their nose just before reaching the frigate's hull. The reduced speed apparently allowed them to pass through the defensive screens and detonate! Well, six of them did. Two missiles hadn't slowed enough and disintegrated upon impact with the screen. Nuclear blasts and carbon-coated depleted uranium pellets destroyed the final two before they reached and passed through the Primus frigate's defensive screen.

"Wasn't that pretty?" the pilot shouted down.

"A thing of purest beauty," the lieutenant replied.

The Chicher Handler chattered excitedly, his translator failing to share what he said.

McAllister added, "Let's hope those minor victories aren't fleeting." Her frowning face held little hope.

One breaching pod slowed and tumbled for a moment before righting itself. Com Specialist Villet raised a hand to his ear. "That one took a pair of friendly pellets. Penetrated the primary hull but not the secondary. Sounds like she'll make it."

"Hold on again, gents," the pilot said, the breaching pod veering to keep the massive transport between it and the undamaged Primus frigate for as long as possible, even if that meant only an additional ten seconds. "Diverting energy to hyper-charge our shearing devices."

With that the gravity plate zeroed out. A few unsecured tools began floating, as did the ends of McAllister's braids extending beyond her helmet.

Lt. Burian glanced at Smith, who then barked at Nollie and Brooker. "Secure those. Stuff them in your pockets if you have to."

Poor discipline again, I thought, reaching out and snatching a pair of needle nose pliers. O'Vorley grabbed a micro-capacitor switch, traces of carbon soot showing it'd burned out. The two Marine privates managed to secure five other items, sheepish looks telling me the policing of loose items had been their responsibility.

My experience with Smith, soldiers under him didn't get 'lost' and out of contact. Things were *always* done right. Lt. Burian seemed competent and aware. Somewhere I was missing something. Some variable or changed dynamic.

It concerned me even more. I looked around and counted. O'Vorley and McAllister. The Chicher and the Bahklack. Smith and probably Burian. Those six I could count on. The rest? The pilot wouldn't be going in with us. He'd stay with the pod. Man the external auto cannon, oversee the automated defense systems, fight and do all he could to make sure the *Turbo Crank* was there when we returned. He was a veteran, been around.

The rest? They weren't a unit, bonded to fight for one another. Probably thrown together. Corporal Pallish and Private Umpernilli? Slackers. Villet, Brooker, Nollie and Xiont? I'd wager this was their first mission, first time facing combat.

Biting his lip, O'Vorley was coming to the same conclusion. The look of disgust plastered on McAllister's face said the genius, nearly as socially inept as me, had figured it out too.

Except for Smith, the Marines probably didn't think much of a shotgun-carrying Relic Tech Security Specialist. What they didn't know, might keep them alive. What I didn't know, might get me dead.

A lot of things happened at once.

The damaged Primus frigate used what thrusters it had to distance itself from the closing swarm of breaching pods, or at least delay our reaching it.

The def-sat's silvery energy beam cut into one of the damaged frigate's engine ports.

The undamaged Primus frigate split its fire between the breaching pods and the def-sat.

Emergency escape pods began racing from the doomed orbital dock, despite its lasers scoring hit after hit.

All of the breaching pods, including ours, sent bursts of auto cannon fire at the damaged frigate. The rounds appeared as effective as hail striking an armored personnel carrier. The Primus weapons however, struck like emerald bolts of hot magma against a tin lunch pail.

Pilot Arnold shouted, "Hold on!" At the same time the *Turbo Crank* shuddered like an old-style pickup truck racing downhill on a gravel road, then slammed on the brakes. A massive thump rocked the breaching pod, like that truck got hit by a hurled brick.

A warning claxon went off, along with pulsing yellow lights.

"Outer hull penetrated," Arnold announced. The shuddering stopped as the pilot returned to what was equivalent to full throttle. "Appears to be a one-and-a-half meter gash. Heat damage to the secondary hull…but she'll hold."

The holo-display showed nineteen breaching pods still closing. One of those was damaged worse than us, coming out of a tumble and limping back on course.

The damaged frigate opened up, but with only two firing ports. That left seventeen breaching pods.

I closed my eyes and said a quick prayer, for us on the *Turbo Crank*, all of the other pods, and for everyone—human—dead or dying. Yes, even for the CGIG traitors. Even if they survived now, something akin to karma was going to get them in the end.

I opened my eyes seconds before the *Jormungand* crashed into the Bizmith Orbital Dock.

The transport's captain had aimed to strike dead center along the main structure, but the dock must've shut down its stabilizers at the last moment, jettisoned or blew air, causing her to rise above the transport's trajectory. It wasn't enough as the enemy still had some maneuvering thrusters.

The *Jormungand*, even being a behemoth class transport, was dwarfed by the orbital space dock. The enemy ship's upper third tore away like a twelve-foot-tall bus trying to drive under an eight-foot overpass. The orbital dock buckled as its center was driven up, reactivated stabilizers unable to compensate. The transport continued on with unstoppable momentum, shards of metal spinning away and the emptiness of space snuffing out random gouts of fire.

"Gutless bastards!" Xiont shouted.

"Harness that anger," Lt. Burian said. "You'll be needing it shortly."

Umpernilli said, "I wouldn't count on it, Lieutenant."

The officer turned on the stocky Marine. "You, Private, might think on letting go of that pessimism. Won't benefit you, me, or anyone else—except the enemy—whatever happens."

"This just keeps getting better and better," Arnold shouted down.

Everyone saw what he meant when the undamaged Primus frigate's main engines came online. I held my breath, waiting for the damaged frigate's engines to fire up.

They didn't and we were still gaining on her. A few seconds later and a barrage of emerald blasts, and there were twelve breaching pods left.

"Lieutenant," Arnold said, "all things remaining the same, you have four minutes to give final orders to your men. After that, we'll be clamped on. Things from then on tend to be on the loud side."

Umpernilli had opened his mouth to comment when the holo-projection showed a sparking shot race past the swarm of breaching pods and find its mark. Arcing jolts of energy rippled across what could be called the top half of the damaged frigate's northern hemisphere. Without a defensive screen, she was vulnerable to an ion cannon, just like any human ship.

"That should scramble a few systems," I said, wondering how one of the *Oxen*'s ion cannons managed to survive the early onslaught. The undamaged frigate might at least split its attention, giving us hope of surviving that final four minute run—if it couldn't burn us off like ticks attached to its partner's hull. But those remaining on the *Iron Oxen* had just called the crosshairs back onto them, an unarmored, dead-in-space freighter.

"Private Brooker," said Sergeant Smith, "How long until the cavalry arrives?"

"Five minutes ago is too long for me," he said, staring at the holo-projection. "Marines dying in combat against the enemy is one thing. Being obliterated while strapped down inside one of these tin cans is another."

I shook my head. That was unprofessional.

Smith's retort was interrupted by the pilot. "Well, lookie there," Arnold stated from above. "Speak of the devil."

The holo-projection image provided by the early detection satellite showed the *Star Splitter* drop out of condensed space travel. Behind the battleship appeared her three escorting destroyers. No sign of the troop transport, yet.

The undamaged Primus Crax frigate pelted the *Iron Oxen* with its emerald fire, saving enough to take out the two leading breaching pods, before it turned to intercept the *Star Splitter* approaching from its, and roughly our, ten o'clock high.

The nuclear detonations and ion cannon strike must've inhibited the damaged frigate's ability to get its main engines online as we continued to close, faster as the ion strike had cut its maneuvering thruster speed by roughly a third. And she wasn't able to target us, fire her main weapons, or both. One thing she lacked was close-in defensive weapons. Her main guns were supposed to serve double duty for that.

Bad news for her and her crew. Lucky for us.

I lost all interest in the holo-projection as did everyone else as we closed the distance.

Pilot Arnold fed energy back into the artificial gravity plate just after he spun the *Turbo Crank* 180 degrees to land on the enemy frigate's hull.

"Once again, gentlemen and women," Pilot Arnold warned, "hold on."

The 180-degree spin had proven disorienting enough for me. When he fired the auxiliary deceleration rockets, it felt like we were in a freefalling elevator while its emergency braking system tried to catch.

With a thump that rattled my teeth, we made contact. Metallic slams, clangs, and screeching followed. Vibrations in the floor plate ran up through my boots.

Lt. Burian unbuckled. "Up and ready, Marines," he shouted. I barely heard him. He signaled with his hand, showing three fingers. "Three minutes."

The Chicher immediately removed an aerosol can from its harness, slid open one of the wooden slats and pointed it into a cylindrical hole.

Someone grabbed my shoulder. I turned to see it was McAllister, a fierce gleam in her mismatched blue and green eyes. "Forget the rat and these Marines," she shouted in my ear. "Me and you are going to wreak havoc, like we done before."

CHAPTER 30

With the seats retracted, I stood next to the Bahklack, helmet on, Troh-got defensive screen on my belt activated, and shotgun ready. The oversized crab alien stood rigid, Umbelgarri energy baton gripped in its smaller claw, some sort of oblong hunk of metal in one of its small, manipulative appendages under its jaw. Silvery light glowed like LED bulbs nestled in tiny fissures spread across the otherwise dull, rippling piece of metal.

Private Brooker stood with his own remote device, ready to control the Thuckich Hive's movement. The Chicher was perched on top, hunched down with his prehensile tail curled around one of the straps for additional support. Holstered on his harness were two small firearms that I hadn't noticed before. They were roughly the same shape and size as a .22 caliber pistol, a little bigger than a pocket derringer. He also had a sheathed pair of fighting knives and a tail blade.

McAllister had her MP sidearm holstered and the Colonial Marines each had a medium duty laser carbine with a 20mm grenade launcher, and an MP pistol like McAllister. They also had cylindrical grenades the size of old-style D-size batteries. Smith tossed me a few.

"You know how to use these more modern ones?" he asked, leaning close.

I nodded. "White ones are white phosphorus, brown speckled ones are fragmentation, and metallic are flash stun, of which you didn't give me any."

"That's because we're here to kill, not stun," he said with a crooked, wicked grin.

"And capture the frigate, if at all possible," the lieutenant reminded, still having to shout over the screeching caused by the cutting torches and molecular blades.

Or hack and steal whatever we can get before setting the energy systems to destroy the ship. I didn't say it, but knew it was running through McAllister's thoughts. With only ten breaching pods, the odds were longer. I didn't know what the crew complement was aboard a Primus Crax frigate, as this might be the first time humans managed to board one of their ships. But they were certain to have some nasty internal defenses.

Arnold stepped down from his pilot area holding a four-barreled medium duty laser plugged into a backpack battery. Mounted beneath it was a standard 20mm grenade launcher.

The pilot saw I'd taken notice of his weapon. He leaned close. "Built it myself," he said, patting the top two of the four barrels. "Kit was expensive as hell, but I intend to hold the fort in case you gents have a notion to retreat."

McAllister rolled her eyes, but O'Vorley said, "Good to know, Pilot.

Thanks."

Pilot Arnold nodded to O'Vorley and glanced up at a readout. "Fifteen seconds, gentlemen! They're jamming my cameras. Every pod's for that matter." He walked over to a wall mounted computer while saying to the lieutenant, "Allow the *Turbo Crank* to deploy her area denial welcome mat and then it's all your show."

I wasn't sure what this model had for area denial. Old models I'd read about had napalm jets and automated rotary cannons combined with various timed explosive shells similar to mortars, all of which could be nasty in an enclosed area. They were also used to deny enemy access after the boarding teams exited. If the Primus got past that, the pilot's impressive kit-built carbine probably wouldn't make much difference.

At the lieutenant's signal we all activated our anti-gravity harnesses. Right on cue the screeching from the cutting blades and torches stopped and reverberations from concussive explosions ran through the floor grate to my boots. Lt. Burian nodded to Smith, who signaled with his laser carbine's barrel for Nollie and Xiont to proceed.

Nollie dropped a camera bot. I watched through my ocular as the bot's video transmission digitized then went black.

"Two can play at that game," Pilot Arnold said, tapping at several icons on the wall-mounted screen. It did a retinal scan. "Secure all unhardened equipment for EMP."

I flicked off my com-set and set it for secure. I shut down the sound dampener attached to my wristwatch's band. Nobody messed with their anti-grav equipment and I knew the CNS device on my neck and spine was built to resist EMPs, even those generated by A-Tech equipment. That thought reminded me to flick off the Troh-got shield generator.

"Ready?" Arnold asked, holding his finger over a red switch. "Three, two, one." He depressed it.

No sound or hint of the EMP burst, other than a red warning on the computer screen and the pod's chronometer flashing EMP twice before reverting to displaying the time. Why we didn't do that initially, I didn't know. Maybe it could catch friendly teams unprepared?

This time Xiont dropped a camera bot, also wired into the pod's systems. My com-set was just coming online. Using the *Turbo Crank*'s floodlights, the 360-degree camera showed a shaft corridor with scorched and twisted metal and tubing—probably the walking rails with a nearby shaft angled down toward the bowels of the ship. It was dark beyond the floodlights' reach, at least in the down shaft as evidenced by the shadows. The straight on shot of light reached out along the transit tunnel as it curved with the frigate's outer hull.

Keeping within the mission's radio silence protocol, the lieutenant signaled Private Nollie to take point, showing us he wanted Formation 4. That didn't make me happy as it'd put Corporal Pallish behind me.

Nollie leapt down, his weight mostly compensated for during the eight-foot drop, looked both directions, and then stepped toward the shaft-like corridor. Smith and Xiont went next, followed by Umpernilli, Brooker controlling the Thuckich hive with the Chicher right beside him. Then Lt. Burian and McAllister flanked by O'Vorley, me and the Umbelgarri thrall, then Com-Specialist Villet and Corporal Pallish.

"Good hunting," Pilot Arnold said, his voice jovial while tainted with underlying concern.

We didn't advance in single file, more like pairs with one member a half step ahead of the other, except for Nollie on point. I'd expected a harsh welcoming party. Maybe they were offering up such festivities to the other breaching pods.

Everything was silent, except for the increased hum emanating from the Thuckich hive. Only a faint trace of burnt metal and plastic lingered. No smoke, which said a lot about the Primus life support and air recycling systems. The Bahklack's faint fishy smell was stronger.

Atmosphere felt warm, like on a summer day in the shade with low humidity.

The floor had two pairs of parallel conduits as described, elevated about eight inches from the floor. Pink, turquoise, faded emerald, lilac as described in the mission brief. They were scorched and scarred, like the walls. Evidence of the *Turbo Crank*'s area denial weaponry. Away from the damaged are,a the metal was smooth. Not reflective, but clean, almost antiseptic. The tunnel made even a luxury transport's corridors appear a little cluttered and dingy.

Thinking on the colored rails, I didn't believe advanced aliens would climb everywhere. There had to be an elevator or something. Kneeling, I touched, then brushed my little finger along the porous pipe for a few inches. Dry, although it appeared to have a sheen of dampness. A cloth texture as described, combined with a barely perceptible…buzz of energy, like if you touched a nearly dead 9-volt battery to your tongue. Maybe the rails were for carts, sort of like old-time trollies? Like water pipes, they split off, part of each line going straight, and the other curving down into the dark shaft.

McAllister caught what I was doing, slowed and whispered into my ear. "There's a faint electrical current in them." Her voice carried just above the hive's buzzing hum. The clamshell computer in her hand was collecting data through some sort of passive mode, similar to the remote that Nollie held in his off hand. "We need to move faster."

I nodded in agreement. A pace no faster than a walk gave the enemy more time to respond to our incursion.

Just before Nollie reached the shaft, about twenty-five paces ahead of me, the alien thrall stopped and pointed up, toward the outer hull with it large claw. One of its eye stalks swiveled and focused on me.

Looking up, I didn't see anything, not even a seam in the smooth reflective metal.

McAllister stared upward too, squinting and searching. Color patterns on the thrall's large claw communicated to me: "Obscured varying spectrum observation apparatus."

Lt. Burian looked back at our delay.

I pointed up then signaled using the Galactic Sign Language. "Watching us." After I'd done it, I realized it wasn't a bright move. The Primus Crax could understand the GSL. Not every human could, so maybe the enemy on the other end couldn't either.

"Pierce with your simple severing tool composed of the Masters' alloy," the thrall said through the shifting patterns on its claw's surface.

Pulling my bayonet, I jumped and thrust it into the ceiling where the Bahklack had focused a narrow laser light. The grav harness recognized my effort and compensated. The blade only penetrated a half inch. Figuring it couldn't hurt, I pulled my stun baton, activated and discharged it against the imbedded blade. Twice.

At the same time Nollie, using a telescopic-handled mirror angled down the shaft, shouted, "Armored bot!"

Some of the Marine teams had their own armored bots. Not A-Tech, which I imagined drove the urgency in Nollie's voice, but they had a bot. Not us. We had a Thuckich hive. We were supposed to be part of the second wave, not part of the point of the spear.

An emerald plasma bolt destroyed Nollie's mirror, knocking the melted reflective metal from his hand, and sprinkling the Marine with several droplets of superheated matter. He dropped his laser carbine and fell back screaming, gripping the wrist of his damaged hand. I didn't have to see to know that in an instant, flesh and bone had been painfully consumed.

Plasma at this scale wasn't energy efficient. That meant we were up against something top-of-the-line, probably with a strong defensive screen. There wasn't anything I had that could penetrate that, let alone the certain-to-be armored casing.

To add to our troubles, Stegmar Mantis sounding came echoing down the corridors, by my estimate, from behind and from down the shaft. It put me on edge, but the CNS modulator held the panic it induced at bay.

Smith and Xiont were already chucking grenades down the shaft while Umpernilli dragged Nollie back from the edge.

I slapped the Bahklack on its carapace. "You've got the only weapon that can take it."

McAllister shouted, "The rails are energy conduits."

The thrall pulled the baton from its belt. "Trained human warriors, evade," it said through its translator. I had trouble hearing it amid the din and confusion, so I flicked on my com-set. Through my earpiece came the thrall's next translated message: "Abandon energy rails."

"Marines, down!" I ordered, flicking my com-set to full broadcast strength and getting against the wall. I didn't think they'd hear me above the sounding and concussion of grenades, but maybe through my com-set despite the electronic damping. I made sure my Troh-got shield was off. It wouldn't stop emerald energy bursts and would limit my most effective weapon.

In front of me, McAllister had taken up position behind O'Vorley on the left. Umpernilli cragged Nollie up to Burian ahead on my right. The lieutenant slapped a med patch on Nollie's wounded hand.

The hive dropped to the floor, sheltering Nollie, with the Chicher climbing to position both of his pistols to fire over the top. Brooker stood ready, aiming his laser carbine. That offered the downed Nollie a small measure of cover.

From behind, Villet and Pallish fired off several 20mm grenades the other direction. I was hoping the *Turbo Crank*'s area denial weapons would stymie the enemy's advance on that front. If they had their own plasma-spewing armored bot we were really warp screwed.

Xiont had retreated some and taken a prone position right between a pair of the rails, carbine ready to open up.

"Move, Xiont," I shouted the same time Lt. Burian ordered, "Now, Private Xiont, reposition against the wall opposite Smith!"

Either he didn't hear us, or simultaneous commands confused him, or he was too stubborn or focused to respond.

The bot swung up along the curved railing, wheels clinging like magnets to iron. It was triangular, like a slice of pumpkin pie, where I thought it'd've been spherical.

Even as it came up, over the edge, the Umbelgarri thrall's energy weapon lanced toward its exposed underside. The silvery beam didn't reach where one of the roller's legs disappeared into the bottom of the smooth metallic chassis. Intercepted by a defense screen.

Everyone else opened up, including me with my shotgun adding to the mix. *Blam, ca-chunk, blam!* My sound damper wasn't working.

Through the flashes and projectile impacts the armored bot came on, unscathed. Its surface was smooth as polished steel, with seemingly random bumps, like tiny, sugar-white ant hills. Those projections, probably sensors, didn't concern me. What did? The pair of stout, rotating plasma gun barrels. Imbedded in the armored sides of the pie slice. Evil, stout-barreled eyeballs seeking a target for their consuming emerald fire.

The configuration allowed the barrels a wide range of fire, except to its rear. Worrying about its aft firepower was pointless when it had more than enough forward, facing us. Oddly, one of my thoughts was that it's the right height and length for a coffin.

Nothing we sent at it penetrated the energy shielding. McAllister wasn't firing, but had turned her laser carbine on one of the rails, setting it for narrowed focus continual fire. That'd burn out its components, if it didn't drain the battery first.

Xiont hadn't moved from between the rails. Instead he'd shoved several grenades forward and then tried to shuffle backwards, away from the oncoming armored bot.

Two emerald plasma bolts raced toward the Umbelgarri thrall. Even though that caused me to flinch, I sent a slug round at the compact war machine.

Two plasma bolts proved more than the thrall's defensive screen could handle. Although nearly depleted, remnants of the bolts splattered on the thrall's primary claw, burning through the chitinous exoskeleton.

The thrall staggered back, emitting a primal gurgling screech, its primary claw half dissolved and locked a defensive, shielding position. Collapsing to the floor, the thrall again energized its baton followed by a narrow-arc sweep beneath the enemy bot. The silver beam sliced through the rail conduits behind the enemy where they curved down the shaft. Xiont, lying flat and covering his head—and still between the rails—died instantly, laterally bisected a fraction of a second before his trio of grenades detonated.

The concussive force slammed against the defensive shield, rocking the bot upward an inch or two. Every Marine and O'Vorley poured laser fire into the oncoming machine. McAllister slammed a fresh battery into her carbine and continued the rail cutting. We'd all be dead before she succeeded—if her carbine and battery supply held out.

The bot stopped, and fired again, prioritizing what it deemed the two most dangerous threats. One plasma bolt took the Umbelgarri thrall in the main body. The other raced toward McAllister. O'Vorley must've anticipated this and dove in front of her. The emerald bolt slammed into my friend, turning his chest into smoldering cinders before his body hit the floor.

Just like that, I'd lost a friend. *Blam, ca-chunk, blam!* I didn't need another reason to hate the Crax and Capital Galactic.

The thrall's final action was to follow through with its strategy, using its energy beam to sever both rails several feet in front of it. Maybe it succeeded because of follow through, or on instinct, or a twitch resulting in blind luck. At that moment, just witnessing O'Vorley's death, I wasn't open to the notion of God's hand and mercy.

The armored bot engaged some sort of anti-gravity device and lifted off the section of track isolated by severing, moving toward the undamaged pair on its right.

I shouted, "McAllister," and kicked the Umbelgarri weapon along the floor to her.

Cussing, she threw aside her spent carbine and snatched up the baton. It looked different from the one I'd seen Diplomat Silvre use years ago. Instead of disks along the bottom, the thrall's had sections fit for its claw to depress and activate. But McAllister was a dozen times brighter than me. I loaded more shells while moving forward and dropping to a single knee, ready to fire. She had to survive if any of us hoped to live. I flicked on my shield.

Maybe it would stop a plasma bolt. Lying to myself, saying it counted as a kinetic weapon, made no sense. I flicked it off.

The Chicher had pried open one of the hive's slats, releasing an angry stream of the blue-green hornets. The Marines continued to fire their lasers, the armored bot being too close for 20mm grenades—but maybe not for the Stegmar Mantis warriors climbing out of the shaft, flapping insectoid wings assisting.

The bot was lowering itself onto the undamaged rails. In a flash, the wooden hive erupted in an emerald burst and Lt. Burian toppled backwards, dead as O'Vorley. The Chicher must've seen the blast coming and leapt away, only taking a fraction of the blast and a few wood splinters in his back.

"Keep your head down, Keesay," McAllister shouted over the mayhem. Even before she finished, silver energy lanced out, flashing against the armored bot's shielding before shearing into the rails beneath it.

My shotgun blast slammed into one of the bot's sides, the buckshot deflecting off, but taking two of the sensory bumps with them. Laser blasts impacted, scorching the armor. Smith's shot hit one of the plasma guns, deforming the barrel.

From behind, Villet and Pallish hurled fragmentation and white phosphorous grenades, sending them beyond the armored bot and among the Stegmars before they fired upon us.

I fired again, my slug striking the undamaged plasma gun's ball swivel mount. That caused its shot to miss me high and just to the right. "Torch it, McAllister!" She had to know that last plasma bolt had her name on it.

"Shut up, Relic!"

Several more laser blasts and grenades and another buckshot blast from me impacted the bot before McAllister managed to discharge the Umbelgarri weapon into the Primus Crax combat bot. The silver energy pierced the unshielded bot's armor. She only managed to slice laterally a few inches before the weapon sputtered out.

It was enough. The bot fell silent.

Smith ordered, "Umpernilli, Brooker, advance! Mop up the Stegmar."

He looked over his shoulder. "Relic, McAllister, make sure that bot's dead." He glanced at Nollie with his MP pistol in his uninjured hand. "Contact Arnold. Have him send that little maintenance bot down here to help drag you back, and what's left of the lieutenant, Xiont, O'Vorley, and the crab. Then remain and help hold the fort for our return."

The Chicher Handler scampered unsteadily on all fours up to Smith as I trotted past the sergeant. The alien's translator emitted only a scattering of static. "Warrior Leader's Trusted Hand, now Warrior Leader, I before dawn released the Thuckich upon the lizards, only a morning of a full day's span escaped before their nest's end. I ask to graft...auxiliary member of your infestation pack."

I didn't hear Smith's reply as I'd drawn my revolver and fired two rounds through McAllister's hole and into the bot at slightly different angles. It rocked and bits of smoke that smelled like burnt plastic and seared metal drifted out of the hole. Wisps of smoke rose from a narrow fissure opened along a lateral metallic seam, and where several of the sensory bumps had been.

"If it was set to self-destruct," I said over my shoulder to Smith, "whatever might've controlled it isn't working." Ahead of me Brooker finished off a Stegmar with his MP pistol while Umpernilli cautiously glanced down the shaft, carbine held ready.

"Him first," McAllister ordered, staring at Private Nollie while pointing to O'Vorley's body. A tightness filled my chest and a lump in my throat formed, but I pushed it back. There'd be time later to mourn my friend. The time now was for the mission. Beyond that, whatever measure of revenge in his name I could inflict. Today and every day moving forward.

The senior engineer had picked up the oblong metallic device that the Bahklack had carried and was detaching what I guessed to be the alien thrall's shield generator, depleted as it was.

"Engineer McAllister," Smith said. "Will you be able to complete our secondary mission without the Bahklack's assistance?"

The sergeant knew her answer. Probably asked it to head off an argument. Private Nollie had his burned hand, numbed and hastily wrapped in gauze, held to his ear as he communicated with the breaching pod's pilot. Glancing back, by the shattered Stegmar Mantis bodies, it appeared that the *Turbo Crank*'s area denial defenses had stopped the enemy's advance against our rear.

"The secondary mission should've been the primary, Sergeant Smith." McAllister stood, O'Vorley's laser carbine in hand and his MP pistol stuck in her belt. "And affirmative, my knowledge and skills are sufficient to continue that mission."

Smith shot her an uneven grin. "We could always just wreak havoc, and draw forces from the other teams."

"They should be doing that for us," she replied, tossing Smith several unused grenades, probably retrieved from O'Vorley's body.

"Let's move out," Smith said. "Brooker, take point. Umpernilli and I will follow." He turned and pointed from the Chicher to Engineer McAllister. "You guard her, along with the other Relic. Villet and Corporal, you watch our rear."

I quickly knelt, placed my hand on Kent's forehead. It was still warm. Probably from the plasma bolt's incinerating heat. "Greater love hath no man than this, that a man lay down his life for his friends."

McAllister squatted next to me. "Appropriate words." She stared at my name patch. "Bleys. But I also remember you once quoting: A time to love and a time to hate. A time for war and a time for peace. C'mon. You know which of those it's time for."

CHAPTER 31

We worked our way down, seeking some sort of computer or communications hub where McAllister could connect with the ship's system, even if it meant descending into the bowels of the Crax frigate. We weren't the only ones with the mission and I wondered if McAllister would be stepping on the other hackers' feet, or vice versa. That was if any of them survived and found a connection. Or if we survived. Some Colonial Marine teams were still alive and fighting, as evidenced by Smith's brief communications with Pilot Arnold.

The anti-grav harnesses were effective in allowing us to descend into the dark shaft. Maintaining frequent contact with the wall kept me steady. The point Marines 'walked' along the wall, but that would've been too distracting for me, like constantly falling forward or being suspended, despite the harness's effect.

Shortly after beginning our descent, the Marines activated their helmet LED beams. I could've too, but got better satisfaction from McAllister watching me tape my pen flashlight to my shotgun's perforated jacket. I didn't turn my light on, preferring to use illumination provided by everyone else. The flashlight would be a beacon pointing right to me as a target, as their LED beams did to their heads. The enemy had sensors and hidden cameras, but the Stegmar Mantis soldiers probably didn't, or weren't tied in. So me and the Chicher, the only other Relic, travelled in our small puddles of darkness.

It didn't matter much as about forty yards down we came to a cross section. The one to the left had a lit cross section about thirty yards away. The other was completely dark. Nobody pointed out any doors or hatches. Being A-Tech, maybe the Primus Crax doors were seamless.

Smith moved ahead, then glanced back at McAllister. She tipped her head, signaling toward the lit tunnel.

When we reached the lit corridor Private Brooker took a peek with his own mirror. This one was probably swiped from a dental technician's equipment. Brooker signaled, then whispered into his collar mic, "One downed Primus Crax and six Stegmars attending. Looks like the Chicher's wasps got him."

It was a very low-power direct line of sight transmission. Everyone got the message via their implants, and me through my com-set's headset. The Chicher did too, through the earpiece wired to his translator. He stood up straight, showing his teeth and bobbing his head. Smith went forward to take a look.

Anger still brewing, I stepped up to Smith, tearing the penlight from my shotgun's barrel and fixing the bayonet. "I got this," I said, and moved past him, not waiting for any reply.

My appearance caught the Stegmars off guard. They were crowded around a Primus Crax lying on the floor. It looked like a four-foot long, veiled chameleon turned a sickly mottled gray. Maybe it was one of their normally black warrior caste. Dressed in a harness like the Chichers wore but with more bands and what looked like ceramic-coated electronic gear attached, the reptilian alien's tail twitched while its clawed feet flexed, grasping at the air.

What looked the most dangerous was the Primus's headgear. It consisted of straps holding glass and ceramic-coated goggles that flexed with its independently movable eyes. Two cords ran from the goggles and their straw-shaped fixtures to what I figured was a power pack affixed across its shoulders.

One Stegmar stood, clicking and chittering into a box—what I knew was a radio communication device. Luckily the one assigned to sentry was looking the other way.

Blam! I took out the communicating mantis warrior with a lead slug. Charging forward, I shot from the hip, sending a round of buckshot into the group. One went down and two others staggered back, wounded. As expected, the Primus Crax had an active shield protecting it from the mixture of lead and steel shot. I flicked on my shield. As expected, my Troh-got shield intercepted the sentry Stegmar's spray of needles fired from its compact machine gun. Two laser blasts shot past me. One took out the sentry. The other struck one of the wounded alien's lower legs, causing it to topple to the floor.

The surviving Stegmars appeared confused. Closing a few more strides, I flicked off my shield and exchanged fire with the unwounded Stegmar. It dropped with a slug buried in its thorax. I finished off the last two. One fell to a tight pattern of buckshot. The last leapt at me, thinking its pistol was useless. It wasn't quick enough to evade my bayonet.

Stomping down on the impaled Stegmar, I said, "For you, Kent," and finished off the insectoid alien while extricating my bayonet. Pounding boots approached from behind.

I managed to free my bayonet just as the Primus turned its head my direction, both eyes ratcheting to focus on me. That struck me as more dangerous than two dozen Stegmar Mantis warriors. With slow but deliberate force I drove my bayonet through the energy shield and into its neck. Twisting the blade, dull red blood gushed as I sidestepped trying to keep out of the dying alien's extended line of sight.

Closer inspection showed the alien's body was covered in welts. Scattered along the floor were two dozen blue-green Thuckich hornets. All were crushed to varying degrees, with about half still moving their legs and a few erratically flapping their wings.

Killing the enemy didn't begin to fill the void left by Kent's death.

Revenge was like a canteen with a hole in it. Nevertheless, for that moment it felt good and would tide me over until I could mourn, not only for him but for Xiont and everyone else. If I survived.

"Good work, Specialist," Sergeant Smith said, coming up next to me. Brooker and the Chicher moved past us, watching down the hall for the enemy. The Chicher wore two bandages hastily applied to his arm and shoulder. He or someone had removed wooden splinters driven into him when the plasma bolt destroyed the hive's crate.

Until that moment I hadn't examined my surroundings, being so focused on the enemy. While this corridor had the two pairs of rails in the standard order of pink, turcuoise, faded emerald, and lilac, it also had a series of small platforms with a pole set into the wall next to them, like a railing circling up and around to the other side, reaching the floor where a matching square platform sat. Along the curved railing were evenly spaced square sections, roughly three feet to a side. Sliding doorways? Artistic discolorations adorned the center of each door's metal, like swirling script. The corridor's ambient light didn't seem to have a direct source, and maybe that caused the effect. It might've been skewed away from the normal light spectrum…normal for humans.

Smith said, "McAllister, Villet, see if that Crax has anything of value on it." Then, following my gaze he commented, "Like the Stegmar, they probably see in a broader spectrum than we do."

Without warning, a dizzy spell struck me. Not bad, but it left me with a headache.

McAllister, who'd shoved the Primus's headset and harness with all of its accoutrements into her backpack swayed a little as well. Pointing to the scattered Thuckich, she said, "They all just stopped moving. Died all at once."

"Saw that," Villet said. He yanked an environmental sensor from a pouch on his belt. Adjusting its settings, he removed the probe, waving it around like a miniature wand. The collected data ran down the wire onto the rectangular device's screen.

After ten seconds, Villet warned, "Dangerous carbon monoxide levels, and rising."

Everyone reached back into their pack for their portable breathing apparatus. I was a little slower, and opted for the nostril plugs instead of the mask. It took me a second to string the tube under my com-set's wiring, but I was ready fifteen seconds after everyone else.

Within a few breaths the dizziness and headache began to abate.

Smith was already sending a warning about the elevated CO levels to Arnold to relay to the other pod pilots and to their teams. With the damping within the frigate, the small relay chips he'd been dropping ensured our ability to at least reach our pod. The chips might be like a trail of bread crumbs leading to us, but so were the dead bodies.

Pointing at the doors and their lettering, Smith asked McAllister and Villet, "Can you read any of these?"

Holding up a clamshell computer, Villet said, "Limited resources on their written language, Sarge. These aren't numbers or labels, like Medical or Storage."

"These are personal berths," McAllister said. "Names. That's what your private is attempting to read."

"You're sure," Smith asked. It really wasn't a question.

McAllister's answer was a hard stare.

"Keep moving. Brooker, point. Same order."

Looking over at the Chicher, I saw he didn't have a supplemental oxygen supply running to his nose. "You're okay with the air?" I swept my hand, gesturing at the air.

"Breath from poor burning not smothering to pack of mine like smothers pack of yours."

That made sense. Alien physiology. Excessive carbon monoxide probably didn't affect Stegmars or Crax. It did humans and, looking down at the dead insects, Thuckich.

It made me wonder what else the Primus might have in store. On the *Kalavar* we'd released bioweapons. But aliens didn't always think like us, or act like us. The *Kalavar* had a security team aboard to safeguard against internal takeover or pirates attempting to board. This was a warship. Still, they had Mantis warriors, armed, and armored security bots, and the Primus had a shield and the goggle headset, the straws with wire conduits running back to a power pack, probably a weapon.

Lying under a rail was a four wheeled device, like a narrow three-foot ceramic skateboard with metallic wheels and electronic motors underneath. Maybe that was how the Primus moved around their ships.

How were the other teams doing? Better or worse? They had more Colonial Marines, or potentially did. Probably servo-armor and heavy duty lasers. I'd seen those take down a Gar-Crax screen. But they didn't have a Bahklack like we had. Or McAllister. Would a frigate have enough security bots to send after each pod's team? I wondered how the space battle was going. It didn't feel like we were moving, but that didn't mean anything. The Primus's tech might have superior gravity controls. I didn't think they could disguise the feeling of condensed space travel.

The ship shuddered, as if in answer to my questions. Everyone stopped for a few seconds, looking around.

"Fight out there isn't over," Smith whispered through his collar mic. "Same in here."

We came to a six-way intersection, up and down, plus four ways, with us coming in from the south, at least as I oriented our progress.

When Brooker approached to within fifteen feet of the intersection, with me and Umpernilli ten yards back, a swarm of Stegmar Mantis dropped from the upper path. With fluttering wings they swooped down upon Brooker. He got one with his laser carbine and smashed a second aside with the butt of his gun.

I got one coming for me with a slug and the second with buckshot. Umpernilli wounded one in the side with his carbine and winged another He ducked as it flew out of control past him.

The Stegmar sounding started, but did little more than put me on edge, thanks to the CNS modulator on my spine. I sliced one out of the air with my bayonet, charging to save Brooker who was on the floor with three tearing at him. Although the Stegmars were only three feet tall, their exoskeletal structure made them three times stronger than a human.

They were coming at us unarmed. The Chicher squealed and Smith shouted orders. Out of the corner of my eye I caught flickering laser fire flashes. Firing a slug, I wished I'd loaded all buckshot. My slug burst into a Stegmar's abdomen, covering me in green blood as it tumbled past overhead. But that allowed two following to latch onto me, their momentum driving me back at an angle. My leg caught one of the rails and I fell backwards, clawed hands latched onto me and mandibles biting into my left shoulder and my right-side ribcage.

My helmet absorbed most of the blow when my head hit the floor and my coveralls kept the Stegmar mandibles from biting into my flesh. It still hurt like hell, like vice grips locking onto my shoulder and ribs.

I could bite back. I didn't have many options. An antenna flicked past my mouth and I caught it with my teeth. With my left hand I tried to grab hold of the antenna of the Stegmar on my ribs while my right hand snaked for my stun baton.

I kept my jaw locked on the antenna even as the Stegmar let go with its mandibles. When it couldn't get loose without tearing out its sensory appendage, it reared back a claw, intent on tearing into my face. The other Stegmar easily shoved my left hand aside and went for another bite a little further down. I didn't have time to worry about that Stegmar or the new round of pain it inflicted.

Just as I'd telescoped my stun baton and set it for full discharge, the claw-ready Stegmar's head snapped to one side, then jerked a second time. I slapped a jolt into it anyway, knowing I'd get some feedback. The baton's discharged caused the Stegmar to lose its grip and spasm, already dying from two MP rounds to the head.

McAllister was lining her MP pistol up on my second foe. She got it before I recovered from my stun baton's mild secondary shock. What carried through my body to the still biting Stegmar didn't deter its attack in the least. McAllister's carefully aimed round to the back of its chitinous skull did.

I kicked it off, fearing its mandibles would lock onto me in death instead of releasing.

I sat up, wincing. "Thanks."

"You would've taken them."

While I shutdown my stun baton and looked around, McAllister continued. "Bet that antenna didn't taste like asparagus."

I could move my right shoulder and breathe okay, but I knew there'd be massive bruising. At least they hadn't taken a chunk out of me like they did Brooker. His cheek, just below his left eye looked like a rabid wolverine had gone at it. Umpernilli had his first aid kit out, trying to stanch the bleeding. Corporal Pallish was assisting, applying a medical patch to Brooker's hand. The face wound was only one of Brooker's multiple injuries. The way he was laying, it looked like they'd dislocated his left shoulder and snapped his right knee. I'd have been screaming in agony, if not screaming or unconscious. Instead he grunted through clenched teeth. Probably why I wasn't a Colonial Marine. Hopefully the patch Pallish applied eased some of Brooker's pain.

Smith was communicating with Arnold, and the Chicher watched for more attacks while Villet scouted out the six way intersection.

I got to my feet, wincing and readjusting the tube for my oxygen supply.

McAllister handed me my shotgun. "Sixteen of them," she said. "Fortunate for us they were unarmed." She glanced at my belt. "How much protection remaining on that kinetic shield of yours?"

Taking the shield generator off my belt and examining it I estimated based upon the depth of the gray, white being fully charged and black being empty. I couldn't read any of the alien numbers or lettering. "About fifty percent left, maybe sixty."

"I see one of those nodes we're looking for," Private Villet called back in a restrained voice. He was looking down the right-hand corridor.

McAllister lost all interest in me, turned and strode toward Villet. The frigate lurched again, this time like it'd tried to fire up its engines but they stalled out. I put a hand against the wall to catch myself from falling and wondered why the anti-grav harness didn't prevent that. Or the Stegmars from knocking me down.

McAllister stumbled, but didn't fall. A few seconds later she reached the corner and looked around. "That's what I need," she said through her collar mic and loud enough for us to hear without receiving it electronically.

Everyone heard Pilot Arnold warn, "They just opened about an eighth of the frigate to space. Lost what remained of two squads."

McAllister stepped around the corner, using the railings to assist. "Follow me, Villet."

Smith glanced over at me. "You too, Specialist. Once we stabilize Brooker, we'll follow."

This corridor had the same rail system in the same color pattern. Its walls, however, had large sliding doors on either side about every twenty feet. There was a dome-like node in the ceiling about thirty feet down. It looked like half of a disco ball that I'd seen in old-time videos, but this one lacked any reflective surfaces.

McAllister used her anti-grav harness to elevate and reach it. "Don't watch me," she said. "Watch for aliens or security bots interested in shooting me."

"Right, Engineer," Private Villet said.

"She knows what she's doing?" he whispered to me as we watched opposite directions down the corridor.

With only the background humming of engines and machinery and the faint noises of Smith and the others, McAllister certainly heard the private's question.

"Affirmative," I said, not adding that she'd worked for the Umbelgarri, at least for a while, in one of their secret breeding areas. I still wondered where the light came from. There weren't any shadows. Maybe the glow emanated from the walls, sort of like a glow-in-the-dark paint.

Even though McAllister said not to, I glanced up and over my shoulder at her. She held her clamshell computer with a wire running from it to the oblong metal device she'd taken from the fallen Bahklack. Its tiny lights partially hidden in the crevices flashed on and off in seemingly random patterns. If I had to guess, I'd've said it was some sort of computer, supplementing the software and processing power of McAllister's computer. Although it was physically small, there was little doubt she'd packed it with the latest crystals and microchips, and software—including that of her own design. But brilliant as she was, she was still human, and her knowledge base was derived from I-Tech sources. Although she had spent time working for the mysterious Umbelgarri.

She strapped the computer to her left forearm, tapping keys and icons with her right hand while adding verbal directives to her computer. Then, with her left hand, she manipulated the oblong electronic processor, pressing thumb and forefinger into a groove as needed.

Without looking down, she said, "Com-Specialist, up here. Give me a hand."

I'd never seen her so frantic or stressed.

"Take two of the wired leads from my pouch," she told Villet. "Any two colors will do. Plug them into the thrall's computer."

I was trying to look both ways when the Chicher scampered around the corner.

"You watch that way," I told him.

"Agreed," he said through his translator, standing on his hind legs and drawing both pistols.

There was no way I was going to shoulder my shotgun and fire effectively. The recoil against the painful throbbing wouldn't work. So I switched out slug rounds for buckshot and planned to shoot from the hip. It was either that or my revolver. The shotgun didn't have armor piercing rounds but had more takedown power. If it came to another armored bot, neither would be effective.

"Patch connect where?" Villet asked. He had a blue and a yellow wire with a standard plug on one end and a small octagonal patch attachment on the other.

"Plug," McAllister replied. "Anywhere, one at a time. It'll work. You'll patch where I tell you in a moment."

Glancing up again I observed the com-specialist touch the blue connecting wire's metallic end to the oblong processor. The plug slid in like the alien device was molding clay. "Hmmph," was all he replied.

Without looking away from her screen, McAllister said, "Bleys, eyes on the hallway. You don't want me to get shot or bitten by a flying arthropod."

"Correct," I said. "If you need my input getting past their firewall, let me know."

She snorted. I smiled, watching my assigned corridor. The term 'firewall' wasn't quite as archaic as my shotgun, but the security software structures constituted what was essentially an electronic firewall. Even I knew that.

After Villet placed the patch connectors where McAllister directed, she went silent. Without looking I knew she was tapping at her screen and mini-keyboard. I'd seen her fingers dance across it many times before. Thinking of my mother's museum piece typewriter displayed on a cherry wood pedestal next to the fireplace, I estimated McAllister would've been a 150 words a minute typist. Right. Like McAllister would ever do something so manual, so mundane.

After a moment, McAllister said, "Pilot Arnold, someone managed to reset their main engines. Thirteen minutes until third attempt at cold starting them." She paused. "Damn—damn, damn!"

That caught the Chicher's attention. Standing sentry along the opposite wall, his head flicked up. Out of the corner of my eye I saw his nostrils flare and ears stand upright. Maybe he was smelling some of McAllister's pheromones. That made me nervous, but there was nothing I could do. I'd have wagered my entire savings she was the person best within three dozen light years capable of infiltrating the enemy's system. Maybe more. Everyone onboard, and half the ships in the vicinity, were counting on her, whether they knew it or not.

My ears popped. A change in air pressure, followed by a stiff breeze blowing past, toward the intersection. Breezes don't occur within interstellar vessels.

I pulled the rope from my pack and tied a clove hitch, the fastest knot I knew that might work, might hold onto one of the rails. Then leapt up, counting on my anti-grav harness to assist, and drove my shotgun mounted bayonet into the curved ceiling. My injured ribs and shoulder howled, but I pushed the pain aside. The wind speed was picking up.

"Air pressure dropping," Arnold warned through my com-set. "The Crax are depressurizing our zone."

"No kidding?" I said to no one in particular. I could've just tied myself to the railing, or tried to break into one of the rooms, but McAllister had to be my priority. She was our best chance of survival.

She cursed.

I ran the rope behind my back and then threw the excess to Villet. "Tie her to me before the grav-harness is overwhelmed. As he did I braced myself upside down, leaning against my shotgun, its bayonet dug into the ceiling by less than an inch.

It wouldn't work, but what else was there to do? She was the only one who could override what the Primus Crax were attempting to do to us.

The Chicher landed along the ceiling next to me, rope secured to its harness and tied to a different rail below. He grabbed onto my harness with his clawed hands and pulled back against his rope using his prehensile tail.

Before Villet had finished his knot, McAllister shouted, "Ha!"

The wind died within seconds.

She shot a glance at me and the Chicher. "Creative but flawed solution, Relics," she said.

"Sure, you were our only *real* hope, but I'll accept your 'Thank you' later."

She didn't respond, once again focused on her computer's screen and hacking deeper into the enemy's system.

A few minutes later Sergeant Smith ordered, "Take'em out." A half dozen laser blasts shot through the intersection. "Good job, Marines," he said. "Remain alert." Then he asked over my com-set, "Specialist, anything to report?"

"Negative," I replied back. "No enemy spotted. The engineer and com-specialist are still working." It felt odd, having such limited frequencies. I wondered if it was just a naturally limiting phenomenon built into the Primus Crax ship.

A few minutes later, McAllister said into her collar mic, "Sergeant Smith, command functions are locked in a loop, effectively locking them out of engine control. Main thrust, maneuvering thrust, and condensed space. It should take the enemy and their automated antiviral systems at least ninety minutes to break through my interdicting code. They shouldn't be able to move their ship, so I hope we're not drifting anywhere…bad.

"They won't be able to use the engines to self-destruct, unless they go down there and cause a detonation manually. All other systems slowed to 0.378 percent. They could still interfere with lighting and environmental, or try their airlock safety bypass and expose a section to space, but I should see it coming, or Major Howard, who also appears to be actively interfering with their computer systems. He's got control of the shuttle bay."

Leaning back and observing her computer, she said, "*My* suggestion would be to have Rear Admiral Tallman bring in more troops on medical shuttles and take off the wounded. Strip whatever they want, maybe take prisoners and interrogate, because once the system goes back on line, my educated guess is that there'll be an accelerated countdown to destruction."

"Right, Senior Engineer," Smith said. "Private Arnold, relay the engineer's report."

The pilot replied, "Acknowledged."

A moment later, Pilot Arnold came back. "Major Howard indicates there is a squad of Colonial Marines fighting their way to main engineering. Medical and support shuttles en route. ETA to shuttle bay, sixteen minutes. And our current vector of drift is not defined as, 'Bad.'"

McAllister, still staring at her computer's screen and tapping away rolled her eyes, but with a grin.

Smith cut in, asking, "How many shuttles can that bay fit?"

He didn't specifically address his question to the pilot or McAllister, probably intentionally.

"Room for three shuttles," Arnold replied.

Private Villet added, "Senior Engineer McAllister concurs. She also requests an additional set of batteries for her anti-grav harness."

"Private Villet," Smith said, "remind her that if we cannot fulfil her request, there's a Relic whose shoulders she can stand on."

The Chicher Handler stared from my shoulder, up to McAllister. "Warrior Leader's Trusted Hand, now Warrior Leader," he said into his mic through his translator, "I am shrub to a tree. Select stored drive stones from my hoard to Computation Web Conjurer's hoard."

Laughing, Smith said, "Specialist Bleys, explain it to your fellow Relic."

CHAPTER 32

After ten minutes passed, Sergeant Smith consolidated our position to support McAllister's continued effort to maintain a lockdown on the enemy's computer system. At the same time she was downloading whatever she could that might be of value to both Intelligence and the military. She'd commented to Private Villet when he asked how she'd hacked her way in, that the Primus Crax had protected their system from outside interference, but not very well from an internal attack. It wasn't something they anticipated.

They'd brought Private Brooker over to us after wrapping his shoulder, used an inflatable splint to hold his shattered knee, and pumped him so full of pain meds that he was essentially unconscious.

After Smith sent the Chicher to watch the intersection with Umpernilli, he said to Corporal Pallish, "Once they land shuttles and begin sending additional teams to secure the frigate, I want you and Umpernilli to get Brooker to one of the medical shuttles. Nollie is doing okay on the pod and can wait."

Sending teams to secure the frigate was a bold move, when things could go the other way, with self-destruction as the result.

"I'd rather take Specialist Bleys," the corporal said, tipping his head toward me.

That response surprised both me and Smith. Maybe McAllister too as she took a second to peel her eyes away from her screen to see if the corporal was serious.

"He's not part of our team," Smith said.

"I know, Sergeant. But he's got a shield that's proof against the Stegmars' CO_2 needle guns. If we run into a combat bot or a Primus with a shield, it won't matter if it's the specialist or Umpernilli with me. But if we stumble across one or more Stegmars, we'll be in a better tactical position."

Smith cocked his head, one eye squinting at the corporal.

"It'll be tough to haul Brooker as he is, Sergeant, if we get even a little numbed by the toxin coating those Stegmar needles."

Smith locked eyes with me for a reaction. Pallish saw me charge straight at the Stegmars and not get taken down by their needle barrage. Maybe heard McAllister ask me about my shield and put two and two together. I shrugged my uninjured shoulder. "He'd have to do the carrying."

The sergeant looked up. "He's your man, Engineer. Part of your team."

"He is," she said, still focused on her screen.

"Specialist O'Vorley was assigned to protect you. And he the Bahklack. Seems his assignment now is to keep you safe?"

"The lizards and their insects, and their bots are holed up in Engineering," McAllister said. "If the arriving Colonial Marines aren't able to break through, and if the arriving engineers aren't able to manually disable the self-destruct components. Both the cascading atomic engine and the main thrust engines in the next eighty minutes, if we're not all out of here, our scattered component atoms will be all that's left of us." She took a second to glance down. "No less dead than Specialist O'Vorley."

"That's why the pods are staying attached. Our emergency exit route. Us and any shuttled-in Marines that we can fit."

I asked, "Why aren't all teams challenging the surviving Crax?"

"You mean us?" Smith snorted. "Besides keeping the engineer safe while she completes her mission? Us and our bitty medium duty laser carbines would just get in the way."

"At the moment," McAllister said, "I am observing and keeping their secondary systems occupied. Once they purge my code and restart…"

"Keeping the Crax and Stegmar worried about their safety," I suggested. "Keeping the pressure on might make the difference. Even using lead buckshot and little lasers."

Smith rubbed his chin. "Specialist Bleys, always looking to scrap?"

"Not always, Sergeant. But it's the best way to kill them."

Corporal Pallish, kneeling down next to Brooker stared up at Smith with raised eyebrows. "Bleys or Umpernilli, Sergeant. Either way."

"Sergeant, you and your men should be able to protect me as well as Specialist Bleys," McAllister said. She slid a little finger into one of the lit crevices in the thrall's oblong device. "If you can arrange for him to rejoin me and the rest of our team." She scowled. "What's left of it."

"Engineer, how'd you get here, to the orbital colony?"

"*Loki's Lady*. A long range shuttle."

"You're the ones who contacted Fleet about the behemoth arriving here?"

"That'd be classified," McAllister said. "If we did." Her tone left little doubt.

"Okay, they'll know your shuttle," Smith said, more to himself than anyone else. "They'll know who Specialist Bleys is, or can easily find out." He glanced down at Brooker. "Here's the plan. Won't matter if everything goes right and we keep the frigate, or we scatter before she blows."

He spoke into his collar mic. "Arnold, with all the shuttles and troops arriving I'm assuming the *Brisbane* and the *Gallant* are nearby."

"Affirmative. The troop transport and the medical frigate are nearby, ready to move out of range should it be necessary."

He turned to Pallish. "Get Brooker to a med shuttle. If there's room on a med shuttle or one of the others bringing in heavily armed Marines, get off the frigate. If things go bad, I am guessing we'll need every seat available. You and Keesay get back to the *Brisbane*. McAllister's shuttle should be able to pick up Specialist Bleys there before the fleet departs."

Smith scratched an ear under his helmet. "I'll put Arnold on making the arrangements, contact *Brisbane* to get verified return orders in the system and appraise *Loki's Lady* of the situation." Then he frowned. "They'll probably want to retrieve Specialist O'Vorley and the Bahklack in any case. Corporal, you assist Bleys on that end. Make sure he's there when the *Turbo Crank* arrives."

Smith took a breath, thinking. "The Phibs might be interested in their equipment more than one of their dead thralls. Either way, I'll get Arnold to make higher-ups aware. There's going to be a lot of body bags, both from here and the dock, freighter, fighters, and attack shuttles and whatever ships the other Crax frigate inflicted."

Smith's neck stiffened. "A lot of space burials coming up."

Villet chimed in, "Nothing new, Sergeant."

"We don't want either of them mixed up. Same with Xiont and the lieutenant."

"I hate them, Sergeant," Villet said. I didn't think he'd even heard his sergeant's last statement.

Smith met my gaze while addressing the communications specialist. "Me too, Private. Me too."

Smith and I shook hands. I refrained from shaking my head. What were the odds of him surviving this far? Of me surviving all I'd faced, and the two of us crossing paths again. And surviving?

"Engineer McAllister, listen to Sergeant Smith," I said, "and keep out of trouble, so we can do this again."

"Havoc, Relic," she said, not looking away from her screen, her mood shifting. Her voice trailed off. "Wreak havoc until we are no more."

Smith looked confused, and I didn't have time, or more accurately it wasn't the opportune time to explain.

"If we hustle," I said to Smith, "we might be able to get Nollie on a shuttle too. If not a medical, then a regular. One more open seat, should disaster threaten."

"If he has time," Corporal Pallish said to Smith, "have Pilot Arnold send me and Specialist Bleys directions to the shuttle bay."

CHAPTER 33

Carrying the unconscious Brooker down several long shafts was quickly draining Corporal Pallish's anti-grav harness. Unconscious was the only way to carry Brooker, even with his shoulder wrapped and leg immobilized. We didn't have a stretcher nor the manpower available to traverse a hostile ship's corridors in such a manner, so it was a fireman's carry all the way.

Private Nollie brought up our rear, being about 90% alert, despite the pain meds. I did have my Troh-got shield if the private's aim was off. With me being point, I wondered if protection from the rear was less than forward. Even so, it should stop an errant round from Nollie's MP pistol.

I worked to push O'Vorley's death from my immediate thoughts. McAllister was a loner, like me, and she was egotistical. Back to Kent, I wondered how she'd handle his self-sacrifice for her. Especially after the current crisis, when she wasn't in her element, trying to beat the Primus's computer systems.

I'd been prepared to do the same for her in the past. Had stepped forward to do so to protect a secret Umbelgarri breeding ground. But there, I was going out fighting. It wasn't a straight up sacrifice, taking a plasma bolt for someone.

I didn't dive in front of the Bahklack, who I was assigned to protect. My thought at the time? Avoid getting between the thrall and the target of its energy beam weapon, or I'd end up like Xiont.

Was that nothing more than justification after the fact?

I snapped back to full attention on the current mission. To reach the shuttle bay and deliver Brooker and Nollie. Moving through the Primus frigate was like a pet hamster scurrying through a maze of plastic tubes. Only with us it was roomier, with directions transmitted to my com-set by Arnold.

This corridor appeared to have sliding doors the size of equipment lockers, hundreds of them and all with script on the edge of a human's visual spectrum. I wondered if we could read it by touch, having a different texture than the smooth metal. Maybe a thermal device could read the lettering placed against the metal background. This lettering appeared more straight and harsh, less curvy and fluid. It struck me as Stegmar Mantis in nature.

The lockers were small enough that I didn't think anything would jump out of them and attack us. McAllister had screwed up their computer system, so surveillance devices wouldn't be tracking us. Plus, the enemy was focused on holding main engineering which was directly opposite from the shuttle bay. Our only concern would be a stray Stegmar or Primus.

"Looks like there was a fight up ahead," I said over my shoulder. Seven Stegmar Mantis and two Primus Crax, stripped of their electronic gear, lay scattered about. Laser burns and fragmentation grenades appeared to have been the cause of death. The dead Primus were tan, one of the lower castes.

Passing through them, Pallish asked Nollie, "Pick me up one of those Stegmar pistols, for a souvenir?"

I didn't think such souvenirs followed Colonial Marine policy, but it wasn't my business. The splattered blood and burned remnants of uniforms and equipment about forty yards down told that the fight hadn't been all one-sided. No bodies cr equipment, so it appeared our side won the skirmish.

We made a right hand turn, taking us toward the outer hull. Ahead a Marine stood, looking our way. He'd heard us coming, which said something about both his efficiency guarding the passageway and us, making our way to deliver our wounded.

Broad shouldered and dark skinned, he was armed with an MP rifle and a laser sidearm. He watched us approach while keeping an eye the other direction.

"A security specialist from a penal colony?" he asked as we neared, looking at my shotgun and gray-green coveralls. His baritone voice was just loud enough to be heard, and wouldn't carry far beyond.

"Close enough," I replied, mimicking his volume. "We're heading to the shuttle bay to deliver our wounded."

"First wave's departed," he said. "Second one is landing now. If you move along briskly, you might get there before they pressurize the landing bay." He grinned. "Now that they've figured out how to work the controls." He gestured with his rifle. "Less than forty yards, around this bend, go up one level and you're there. But you already knew that."

"The directions, not the exact distance," I said. "Thanks."

Before we could pass, he added, "More dead than wounded. I'll radio ahead."

We were stuck in a holding area, several nurses in white and corpsmen in mottled blue attending mortally wounded Colonial Marines.

Someone had blown the sealed sliding door that led to the rectangular room. The floor was holed and pitted, like an old colander polished clean. The wall to the left of the entrance had four panels in the same color pattern as the rails. On the wall opposite the colored one, a small tube to the left spiraled upward with a single rail. Several racks were set into the metal walls on either side of the tube passage. The wall across from the entrance had four three-inch-diameter poles set into the floor and a low ceiling next to it. Curvy Primus lettering, again perceived only through an off-coloring of the metal was placed next to various geometric shaped buttons situated into rows of eight. Near the wall, five poles were set into the floor and ceiling. They must've enabled the chameleon-like Primus to climb up to press the buttons

Compared to the large travel corridors, this room, with a seven-foot ceiling felt cramped, even though it was at least thirty feet across and twenty wide. Counting me, Nollie and Pallish, there were only two other men,

Colonial Marines, combat ready. They stood along the color paneled wall, watching as the three nurses and five corpsmen worked to stabilize six of their fellow Marines, all severely injured.

One of the nurses and corpsmen came over to help Pallish lay Brooker out on a floor mat. They began asking the corporal questions. Nurses and corpsmen working with portable emergency equipment, and no doctor. It was equal to a first on the scene emergency squad. Better than it could've been. If they hadn't captured the shuttle bay intact, and figured out how to control it, these men, and the group before, would be on the breaching pods waiting for evacuation.

The corpsman asking Nollie about his bandaged hand told the Marine that each of the corpsmen was from the pods, ordered here for triage. The first wave of med shuttles had taken those Marines that had a chance. Nollie told the corpsman we'd arrived after the first wave because we stayed to make sure Engineer McAllister was secure in her effort to hack the enemy's systems.

The corpsman expected a few more stragglers like us.

I knelt down next to one of the mortally wounded Colonial Marines, made eye contact with the attending corpsman, who nodded solemnly.

Delivered on a makeshift stretcher, the diagnostic computer's readout sitting above his head showed the Marine had lost a quarter of his abdomen. The same with his hip. The mylar blanket covering the Marine's body couldn't disguise it. The way the monitor showed blood circulating, the stench of third degree burns, of freshly cauterized flesh, identified the culprit. Plasma bolts. The same thing that killed Kent.

The pale welts on his exposed hands and face said he'd been hit by at least a dozen Stegmar needles, at least that I could see. I didn't bother to try and decipher more of the medical screen display to get an accurate count. Even a maximum dose of anti-toxin couldn't counter the number I counted. Not for long.

The alien toxin had paralyzed him, and four patches on his neck had hopefully muted most of his pain.

His eyes opened when I took his exposed hand into mine. They tried to focus on me.

I leaned close, gently gripping his hand, trying to think on what to say.

"If nobody told you, Marine, our mission is a success. We control the Primus Crax frigate."

I glanced over at the screen to get the Marine's name since the blanket covered his name tag. "We couldn't have done it without you, Lieutenant Yuxiong. Your dedication, loyalty, and willingness to sacrifice."

I swallowed hard, maintaining eye contact. What I was sharing with the dying lieutenant, I was saying to my departed friend, Kent O'Vorley. "Thank you."

Lt. Yuxiong's grip became firm, shaking. The monitors flashed from yellow to red. The corpsman placed a gentle hand on the dying man's forehead. There was nothing we could do to save him, so I leaned close to his ear and recited the 23rd Psalm.

His grip slackened as I spoke. He was gone by the time I finished.

In a quiet voice the corpsman asked, "That was from the Old Testament?" He was a thin man. His actions demonstrated caring for the wounded and dying. They were measured and meticulous.

I nodded, placing the dead Marine's hand on his chest.

"What if he wasn't of the Jewish or Christian faith, Specialist?"

I shrugged. "Hope," I said, meeting the man's questioning eyes. "The lieutenant's faith, his God will understand, and welcome him none the less."

"His file said he was atheist, Specialist. In his last moments you whispered a prayer in his ear."

"Lieutenant Yuxiong's dying moments, a human voice to see him off, the offer of hope."

"What right did you have, Specialist. You're not even a Marine."

I stood, looking down at the man still squatting next to the lieutenant's body. "Corpsman, if he was an atheist, and he's right, what does it matter now?" I kept my voice low and even. Still anger crept in. "And if I'm right? Just reminding him of an option before his last breath. If I'm right, what difference might that make?"

The corpsman shut off the emergency medical monitoring equipment and removed several leads from the lieutenant's head and neck.

Now wasn't the time or place for a fight. "Hope," I said. "An assurance his sacrifice meant something. That he made a difference. A sincere voice speaking to him. Offering him comfort, and hope. Atheist, Hindu, Muslim, whoever. When it's my time, I hope there's someone there for me."

"Hope you say?" The corpsman shrugged and pulled the blanket up over the dead Marine's face. "In this war, we all need hope."

None of the other wounded Marines died while waiting for the shuttles to land, the bay to close and pressurize. When it did, the floor began lowering. It surprised me—and Pallish and Nollie. The nurses and corpsmen didn't appear concerned, so I just took it in stride. The walls became smooth and featureless, except for the one with the bands of color. Those remained, extending all the way down, as did the poles along the wall opposite the entrance.

We dropped about twenty feet, slowed and stopped. If I hadn't had my eyes open, it would've been hard to tell we were moving.

About two feet off the floor, along the wall with the poles, was a window. It was long, stretched oval. About four feet above the window, a seam ran across the wall.

I hunched down to see what the window revealed.

"What'cha see, Specialist Bleys?" Private Nollie asked. I felt his eyes on me, but not as much as Pallish's.

"Four shuttles unloading Marines in servo-armor," I said. "Heavy lasers and large bore MP rifles. Two medical shuttles, two assault shuttles. Pretty cramped in there." Someone had said there was only room for three shuttles. Probably McAllister. "I count thirty-eight Marines forming up. Female unit."

One of the corpsmen, a Master Chief Hospital Corpsman, moved his hand to his ear, then spoke into his collar. "Understood, sir. Will do."

He pointed to me and Corporal Pallish. "You two, carry your Marine to Med Shuttle NYB-244. Private Nollie, you'll board with Private Brooker."

The master chief put his hand to his ear again and nodded in understanding. "Corporal Pallish and Specialist Bleys, looks like you're the only healthy ones with orders to depart this wave. Report to GAS-448R. Pilot Madeira is expecting you."

"Will do, Chief Gibbons," Corporal Pallish said, a little disappointment creeping into his voice.

As I was checking my gear, making sure all was secure, the window wall slid outward and then up, revealing the bay and its contents.

Securing a pair of telescoping poles, we converted the floor mat Brooker rested on into a stretcher. Pallish took the front and I lifted from the back. We hurried out so the waiting Marines could enter the elevator room and get into the fight. A dozen of them assisted the nurses and corpsmen carrying Marine bodies.

Delivering Brooker to the med shuttle's nurses and doctors, I wished Nollie luck and a quick recovery. Corporal Pallish patted him on the back and expressed a hope the private would be able to rejoin the squad soon.

"Come on, Specialist," Pallish said. "Faster we're out of here, the sooner they can deliver more Marines."

I couldn't argue with that. Nodding once, I followed, whispering a prayer for all those who died fighting the Crax today, and to keep those safe who yet faced danger, no matter their faith, or lack thereof.

Ground Assault Shuttle 448R was a new, short range model that didn't show more than an arcing pattern of patched gouges. The pattern suggested being sprayed by Gar Crax acidic artillery. We strode up the ramp and into the troop compartment.

Pallish stepped forward and called into the pilot's compartment. "Corporal Pallish and Security Specialist Bleys boarding as ordered for transport to the *Brisbane*."

I selected a seat where I wouldn't see the pilot, but had a narrow angle of sight through the pilot's window, normally where a copilot would sit. Why there wasn't a copilot, I wasn't sure.

The entry ramp retracted and the hatch closed while Pallish and the pilot exchanged a few words. I secured my shotgun, placed my helmet under the seat, removed the nostril tubes, and shut down the supplemental oxygen supply.

While shedding my pack and anti-grav harness, Pallish said, "Ninety seconds till departure. Turn around and I'll remove your CNS modulator, then you get mine "

"Sounds good." They were painful to remove, especially if you tried to reach back to do it yourself. I loosened my collar and waited. I was about to ask Pallish what he was waiting for, when he rested a hand on the side of my neck. Did he place something there?

I reached up to check and he snatched my hand while slamming me forward, pressing my face against the wall. The lowered seat caught me just below the knees, knocking my legs out from under me, depriving me of leverage.

The Colonial Marine corporal's right hand caught me reaching for my revolver. I tried to shout to get the pilot's attention, hoping he wasn't in on this, but all that came out was a gush of air. My neck felt slack, lacking strength, and my focus became fuzzy. Knock out—paralysis patches? With his body pressed against mine and his leverage, I'd never pull my revolver in time, or reach my stun baton. I fought to reach my com-set, placing my fingers on the buttons.

Pallish leaned close and growled in my ear. "The infamous Specialist Keesay. You weren't so hard to capture."

I thrust my head back and toward the ear he spoke into, but the weakness in my neck and shoulders blunted the strike. Not even enough to bruise his cheek. To distract him, I tried to yell again, struggling to keep awake, alert. I programmed my com-set for alarm, to *Loki's Lady*'s emergency frequency. Pallish wouldn't detect it broadcasting until...he wouldn't just smash it. Six taps...six...minute delay...or was...it sixty...? Then, I thumbed...the...lock...out.

CHAPTER 34

I awoke, hands bound behind me. Plastic zip cuffs. My ankles as well, and I had a cloth gag tied across my mouth. I was on my stomach, my left arm and shoulder asleep. Sharp needles of pain raced along them when I shifted. It was dark, hot, and muffled, like being sealed up inside a sleeping bag.

Pallish's voice, sounding as if I was listening with my ear pressed against a closet door, asked, "How long will the maintenance crew be fooled?"

"We're almost ready," a female voice said. It had a slight nasal tone, one filled with confidence. Like someone used to giving orders. An officer? "It'll be chaos out there. Everyone scattering before she self-destructs."

"Unless that engineer I was telling you about can do something. She hacked into the Crax system like their code was written by a retarded Relic."

"As long as Fleet is focused on what's going to happen and responding to that, it's to our benefit."

A moment of silence followed before boots against metal flooring approached. Something sounding like a crate next to me was scooted aside.

At the same time, the female said, "Have the dolly bot park it over there. And be quick about it."

"Yes, ma'am," replied an uncertain voice.

This fellow wasn't part of the conspiracy? I took a chance and yelled, despite being gagged. My reward was a boot to the head, twice…thrice."

Darkness swallowed the pain.

Rather than a groggy awakening, the next one was filled with throbbing pain. Like a horse had kicked me in the head. I refrained from groaning and listened. Still cuffed, still in the dark. Hot, and covered in sweat. The air was warm, humid, and stale. The floor was vibrating, like a ship—or shuttle—moving. No disconnected feeling, eliminating condensed space travel, for the moment.

Pallish knew who I was? How? Did he recognize me? The pain and difficulty breathing made it hard to think. Smith named me when we first met outside the breaching pod. Did he discover it then? McAllister had called my name once during the fight. But there was no way Pallish could've planned or organized in that short of time. Pilot Arnold? Was he in on it? Planning on getting a cut of the bounty?

Good luck with that, I thought. Capital Galactic would sooner put an MP round to his head than hand over credits it didn't have to. Treacherous as CGIG was, a round to the head for anyone who brought me in to claim the bounty wasn't out of bounds.

"Captain Sanchez," a new voice said. Male and edged with concern. "We're receiving a radio contact from a shuttle. She identifies herself as *Loki's*

Lady. I think it was that long range shuttle that fed intelligence to the strike group while en route."

The male voice continued after a breath. "We're getting a call from a breaching pod… BP-J-132. Obviously, I'm not acknowledging or responding."

That was *Turbo Crank*'s number. I didn't move, and struggled to breathe at a steady pace so that anyone nearby wouldn't know I was awake.

"Analyze the signals," Captain Sanchez said in her authoritative, nasal voice. "Strength, and are they vectored at us or non-directional?"

"They're on the medical flotilla's frequency, our specific channel," the pilot replied. "Our equipment isn't designed for such intelligence gathering. Give me a moment."

"We may not have more than a handful of moments," the captain said. "The pod doesn't have the range, and probably not the authority to pursue us. The long range shuttle could be a corporate freelancer, or maybe with Intelligence." She huffed. "I wonder if the taskforce refueled and provisioned her. Corporal, go through the Relic's equipment again."

Someone grunted. Sounded like Pallish, but could've been some other male.

"They're continuing to call," the pilot said. "The long range shuttle's is directional, stronger, narrowly focused. The breaching pod's is weaker and not directional."

A *clomp* and then *clatter* of equipment—my gear? It was less than a dozen feet away.

"There's a stray signal emanating from our shuttle," the pilot exclaimed. "Brief."

Sanchez ordered, "Corporal, you did check and secure the Relic's com-set?"

"I did, Captain. It was set on lock out, so I shut the entire unit off. Deactivated it."

"Brief and periodic," the pilot added.

"Yes, it's switched off," Pallish said with assurance. "Completely shut down."

"Captain," the plot said. "If we presume they're from Intel, they'll have sensors that can locate and track us. They probably already have and are. The taskforce could too, but they're still reorganizing."

"That won't take very long. Rear Admiral Tallman will see to that."

"I can alter our vector to place the planet between us and the task force—and that shuttle sooner, but—"

Captain Sanchez cut the pilot off. "Stop, Corporal! Don't destroy it."

"It just flicked on for a second and then deactivated again."

"The signal. It's periodic," the pilot confirmed. "Every twelve seconds. Encrypted burst. Strong enough to reach the long range shuttle, especially if she has sensitive equipment. And knows what to listen for."

"The Relic is known to booby trap his equipment, Corporal."

Shuffling of boots on the metal floor preceded Pallish's question. "What do you want me to do, then?"

"Pilot, assist him," the captain said, moving further away from me. "Attach it to one of the signal rockets, along with this. Its magnetic field will eventually destroy the set's components and software, and any stored data. Set the rocket for a three minute delay, slow burn, toward the planet."

The pilot and Pallish were away from the main compartment. The captain was piloting. I hadn't heard anyone else. Now was my chance. Flexing and straining, I tried to break my bonds. The Stegmar bites ached and burned more than the bite inflicted by unyielding plastic cuffs. The warm trickle of blood told me I'd torn skin and flesh in the effort.

Slowly I tried to bend at the waist and bring the cuffs below my hips, so I might be able to curl my legs and get beyond my boots. That would be a start.

My head and face throbbed, while my ribs and shoulders—their stabbing pain brought tears to my eyes as I clenched my teeth down on the gag in my mouth, struggling to remain silent.

The body bag, as I surmised I'd been stuffed in, magnified the maneuver's difficulty. They hadn't sealed the bag so that sufficient air could reach me. If I could wriggle out, that might provide opportunity. What opportunity I didn't know, but more than what was available inside the bag.

From a distance, probably the pilot's seat, Captain Sanchez called, "Corporal, the Relic is awake." Annoyance more than anger hung in her voice. "Put him back to sleep for a while."

Heavy boots clomped over. Timing his arrival I swung my hips and legs, trying to connect with him. Knock him down.

It'd just piss him off, but it'd make me feel better.

I successfully managed the maneuver, but without adequate surprise or force.

With a quick *shhissing* sound and tug at the bag, light struck my eyes. Pallish's palm slammed down on my forehead, holding me still. With his other hand he slapped a patch on my neck.

My eyes took in the surroundings before returning to glare at him. He grinned down at me without saying a word.

The glimpse of retractable bedding and medical diagnostic equipment said I was lying in the main compartment of a medical shuttle. One of the newer models, unless the military had decided to upgrade the contents of their older ones.

Some of the newer models were capable of condensed space travel.

I tried to think, but my mind was slowing. Would McAllister and the rest of *Loki's Lady* be able to track me? Would Fleet help? Get a vector of travel with the crisscross of ships and fighters and attack shuttles that had arrived, then departed and raced back to gain surprise on the enemy?

My last question before losing consciousness was: Why would they bother?

CHAPTER 35

Dark dreams. Mostly about trudging through mud, or tar, or freshly poured concrete. I awoke feeling exhausted. To the whir of fans and the hum of engines. To the disjointed feeling of condensed space travel.

I listened. Steady breathing nearby.

My arms were at my side. I'd wait, wait for the breathing to move further away.

"I know you're awake, Specialist Keesay." The nasal voice of Captain Sanchez emerged from the direction of the breathing. "You were in hybersleep, and I administered the counter drug. Can't leave you under too long."

I opened my eyes to the dimly lit main area of a standard medical shuttle, this one apparently designed around a long range shuttle. Expensive. I didn't think the military used them, but apparently I was wrong.

My hands were bound to the fold down bed. Breathing deeply, my chest and abdomen were strapped down as well.

"I have secured your legs as well, Specialist Keesay. Across the thighs, and each ankle individually, like your wrists and arms."

"You're mistaken," I said, my throat hoarse and dry. "Corporal Pallish, who I presume brought me to you—"

She laughed and said, "There's been no mistake."

Even as she laughed and said that, I continued. "I'm 4th Class Security Specialist Corbin Bleys."

"Rest assured, Specialist Keesay. Once tipped off to your presence, I verified who you are."

I shrugged and winced. My bite wounds hadn't healed. "I have no idea why you've abducted me," I said, attempting to continue my ruse. What else did I have? "I've committed no crimes, haven't stolen or crossed anyone of wealth that might fund this operation."

A hologram appeared. One of me, lying wounded, bandaged and dying before my pretrial aboard the *Pars Griffin*. "DNA doesn't lie," the woman said with confidence. "Well, it can, but only a fool would alter his DNA to superficially match that of Security Specialist Krakista Keesay. My knowledge, skills, and equipment can see through such measures, if for some reason you might have been posing as a decoy. Anyone foolish enough to do that deserves worse than you'll get."

Okay, so she'd properly identified me. "That last statement's accuracy, I question. Or, if you truly believe that, I question your intelligence."

"Thank you for your candor, Specialist Keesay." She moved a little closer, but still out of my field of vision, unless I craned my neck. "In your position, I would've attempted the same."

"Then why wake me?" I asked, already knowing the answer. I decided to crane my neck to see the speaker.

After I did that, the woman walked within my uncraned field of vision. She was tall. Maybe as tall as Agent Vingee, but darker skinned, a wider nose, and far longer hair, black, which she began brushing. She wore an off-white bodysuit—my mother would've named it ecru—and a white medical jacket lined with pockets, like Dr. Goldsen favored.

"The chemical compounds flowing through your veins indicate you've endured cold sleep, but this just made more sense. Easier to hand you off."

With that said, I did all I could to break free in one violent effort. And failed. Breathing hard and wincing at the pain in my shoulder, ribs, and knotted skull, thanks to Pallish's boot, I noticed she'd stepped back a few paces and pointed a pistol at me. Closer examination indicated it fired tranquilizer darts.

"From your white jacket, you must be a doctor, or a lab tech," I said, "and think what you've got in there will do the job. But if I were to get up, you'd need a .44 magnum to stop me before I broke something on you."

"I appreciate your honesty, Specialist." She gave me what appeared to be a genuine, toothy smile. "I've been informed how dangerous you can be. Corporal Pallish told of your courage under fire.

"If I even suspected you might slip an arm or hand loose, I'd shoot you. That bodysuit you have on won't protect you from a mosquito's proboscis, let alone a high velocity needle. And, to show you how fast it works…"

Click-pfftt. There was a needle in my leg. Three seconds hadn't passed before I was woozy. Another breath and I was out.

I awoke later, still strapped down. I heard music and, from the sound of exertion, someone dancing or exercising to it. A fast beat, with drums and synthesized horns. I was wearing a tan jumpsuit. The other one, I thought had been gray. It was hard to remember.

I'd had a conversation with Captain Sanchez. I worked to recall the details of the brief conversation. Before she shot me, unconscious.

My shoulder and side hurt a little less. I bet they were still deeply bruised. Rolling my head around on the pillow highlighted a small but still noticeably tender knot on my head. With hybersleep's slowing of metabolism, it must slow healing too.

After about thirty minutes of me listening and waiting, the captain ordered the music to stop. She sounded out of breath.

No time like the present. "Miss Doctor," I said, "thank you for shooting me. I needed that extra bit of shuteye."

She strode into view, wearing shorts and a bra, and her hair pulled back in a ponytail. Sweat glistened on her skin, from head to literally her toes.

"A moment," she said, "and I'll provide you some liquid nourishment. Orange, peach, or apple flavor?"

I was thirsty, and hungry. "Orange."

Captain Sanchez, as she'd been called but possibly wasn't aware I knew, ordered a modern orchestra score to play. It was far louder than necessary and looped three times until she returned to my field of vision.

"Computer, stop play," she said, now dressed in her bodysuit, lab jacket and boots. Her long hair was still in a ponytail, but her sweat sheen was gone. In each hand she held a tall glass. One had a long straw, a bendable one.

There was no reason for her to drug my drink. "You've made a mistake."

"How so, Specialist Keesay?"

"What should I call you, Miss Doctor?"

"Doctor Sanchez will do." She took a sip from her glass.

I raised an eyebrow. "Is that your real name?"

She held the cup so that the straw's tip was near my mouth. While I drank, she said, "What's to hide from you? You're strapped down. I've cleansed your colon, and I've inserted a catheter." She withdrew my cup. "Since you won't be loose while conscious, it's to be an all liquid diet."

"You're in more trouble than you realize," I said. "Being cautious now won't help."

She shrugged. "What? You think Fleet will hunt for me?"

"That's just one of your problems on the horizon."

"My shuttle is one of fourteen constructed and leased to Fleet by Yakum-Blost Industrials. As I am an experienced trauma surgeon, they assigned my contract along with the lease." Her nasal voice shifted from matter-of-fact to cynical. "Their added contribution to the war effort, without consulting me."

She turned, walked away, and set the cups on a shelf. "Corporate theft. Breach of contract." She pointed toward what must have been beds beyond my feet. "Them? Corporal Pallish and Pilot Beventi. If the military catches up with them, the punishment will be *far* more severe."

"My training in military-corporate law is limited," I said, "but it might be better if they caught you first."

She cocked her head, with a raised eyebrow.

"It might be better," I said, "if you don't use what you get for turning me over to Capital Galactic—if they follow through with payment. Which might be problematic in itself. The longer you're in prison, the longer you'll live."

"Your thoughts are not tracking," she said. "I detected only a mild concussion inflicted by the corporal."

"Track this," I said, sneering. "When I escape. I'll hunt you down. You might be safer in prison, but the day you're released will be your last."

She grinned as if amused. "Really. In another twenty-nine hours, I'll put you back into hybersleep. When you next wake up, I will have my reward and you'll be earning your reward."

"For what?" I asked, flexing my arms. Alarms went off. She must've placed sensors in the restraining straps. Or activated alarms already incorporated into the design. I continued, straining against the straps while speaking over the flashing red lights and staccato beeping. "For killing Crax and Stegmar? Enemies of humanity? Or revealing Capital Galactic's treachery? Turning on humanity. On their own kind?"

She reached under her white lab coat to the small of her back, and pulled her tranquilizer pistol. "What you earned for killing a good friend of mine," she shouted. "A cousin."

I was having no luck loosening the straps. They were too strong, too secure.

She leaned close, up to my face. Anger twisting hers. "You killed Jammie Jazarine."

With that, she pointed the gun at my eye.

I stared straight at her, still struggling, my lip curled in anger. "Another traitor," I said, "traitor to humanity, like you."

"No," she said, her anger abating. "Capital Galactic loyalists will pay more for you alive, Specialist. They are certain to be more cruel than I could ever imagine."

She moved the pistol's aim from my left eye to my right. "I have imagined this moment for a long time. What, with professional bounty hunters seeking you? The tens of thousands of people keeping a lookout, just in case? I never truly believed it would happen."

Pain spiked through my shoulder and ribs. My head began throbbing. I relaxed. No sense spending myself, aggravating injuries.

"Traitor to humanity, you say", a sense of amusement in her voice. "For earning an exorbitant bounty for turning in a 4th Class Security Specialist? A Relic?"

"I've killed more enemy, more Gars and Stegmars than you can imagine, Doctor."

"And people too, Specialist. People."

"Sure, I've killed people. Enemies, Doctor. But I didn't kill Jamayka Jazarine."

She snorted a laugh. "Save your lies."

"No reason to lie, Doctor. It was Crax acid that got her. An implant. You've heard of them?"

"Lies," she retorted, maybe a little too strongly.

"Believe what you want, Doctor Sanchez." I met her gaze. "I said enemy. Now you're one of them too."

With that said, she shot me in the arm. She tried to make it look casual, but I saw the troubled concern forming in her eyes.

Dr. Sanchez didn't speak a word to me during the rest of my wakeful hours aboard the medical shuttle before being placed back into hybersleep. I didn't have anything pleasant or even neutral to say to her. The doctor's matter-of-fact attitude, from providing vitamin-fortified orange drink to draining my catheter, offered minimal comfort and health maintenance. She did provide an audiobook performance of *Moby Dick* through a nearby speaker, a novel that I'd never read.

The selection hinted at what the doctor thought about Relics, and offered a thematic mix of messages from defiance and death to friendship and duty. She played it twice, giving me additional opportunity to ponder my own direction and situation, if that was her intent. Nevertheless, it was a welcome distraction from boredom, and a respite from thinking about what lay ahead. There was no doubt about Sanchez's belief. Capital Galactic loyalists would not be kind to me. Cruelty was the word that sprang to mind.

In no way did I intend to go down without a fight, little as that resistance might ultimately prove. I'd offer them as little satisfaction and enjoyment as was within my power. That, I determined and promised myself to do.

Dr. Sanchez put me back into hybersleep without a word and a blank expression on her face. Too late for second thoughts.

The next person I saw was one I hoped to one day see again, but not in the circumstances under which our meeting occurred.

CHAPTER 36

I was sitting erect on a metal stool, my back against a wall and my wrists cuffed to rings set into the seat. Bright lights made it difficult to see the man sitting in a padded chair about ten feet away.

"No need to pick up right where we left off, Security Specialist Keesay," pronounced a male, nasal voice. What was it with CGIG and nasal tones? Then it registered. I knew that voice and hatred immediately welled.

"Lawyer Heartwell," I said, reminding myself to stay calm, and not play into any desires he, or any other Capital Galactic refuse, might have.

"It means so much that you remember me after our brief time spent together." Sarcasm dripped from his words. With a hand-held remote he altered the lighting from a spotlight aimed at me to fluorescent set into the low ceiling.

The room was a simple square, about twelve by twelve feet, uniform white walls, ceiling and floor with a single metal door behind Heartwell.

The malevolent man smiled. Average height for an I-Tech, slicked-back, blond hair and what had once been a round face. There was more leanness to it now, a haggard expression. That all fell to the background, behind his malicious eyes and grin. He wore a business suit much like I remembered from our first meeting, but wasn't sporting a yellow tie, which would identify him as a lawyer.

Circumstances change.

"This time, Specialist, we are not under any time constraints."

"You should already know my view on this, Lawyer. If humanity wins the war, you lose. If humanity loses the war, you lose."

"Your information is out of date, Specialist, on a great many things. Your side has lost the war. It's all over, except for the dying." He paused, waiting for my reaction, which wasn't forthcoming, so he continued, saying, "You will address me as Warden."

My Stegmar-bitten shoulder wasn't hurting too much, so I shrugged, deciding to pick my battles. Conflict would emerge soon enough. "Understood, Warden. A demotion?"

With a straight face, he replied. "A lateral career move. My special talents and skills are a perfect fit for this facility's needs." He pointed his remote at me, shaking the end. "This career track offers more opportunities for upward movement. If I recall, you once said that the victors in this war won't have much use for lawyers. On that, I believe we found agreement, Specialist."

His face split into a toothy smile, one like a cat getting ready to pounce might make. "What about you, Specialist? Besides wearing a fictitious name patch, what else has changed? Who holds your contract, and was it a demotion, lateral move, or a promotion?"

First battle.

During our previous encounter, when I was lying wounded and under the care of V'Gun surgeons, Heartwell discovered that interrogation drugs available to CGIG were useless. My body's ability to resist owes to an injection then Field Director Karlton Simms gave me after I'd prevented Representative Vorishnov's assassination. If the V'Gun, a diminutive alien species that resembled a mutated combination comprising a squid and a tarantula, didn't have a countering serum, nothing Capital Galactic might concoct had a chance.

"I prefer not to share that information, Warden."

Heartwell probably had a good idea, if he or his people got information from Dr. Sanchez, Pilot Beventi, or Corporal Pallish when they handed me off. That phrasing hadn't stuck out to me until that moment. Handing me off meant they didn't deliver me to this 'facility.'

Another thing I hadn't paid attention to when I first awoke was where I might be...what this 'facility' might be. No disjointed feeling, so no condensed space travel, or vibration common on a moving shuttle or ship. The facility could be part of a space dock or planetside—or moonside. Actually, except for the fluorescent lights' hum, there was no other noise, except for me and Heartwell breathing.

In those few seconds I hadn't noticed Heartwell's sinister grin reappear. "Wrong answer, Specialist." Thumbing an icon on his remote, he triggered an electric shock.

I struggled to ignore the pain assaulting every nerve ending, the shocks causing spasmodic convulsions. When my stool toppled I managed to tuck my head and lessen the impact when my skull struck the metal floor.

The shocking charge continued. I closed my eyes and drew inward, trying to think, to be elsewhere. A sustained stun baton's shock, but calibrated for maximum pain rather than physical damage or long term incapacitation. A lesson, where I experienced a similar shock during a hands-on experience during Penal Training 101. That instructor-administered shock had been similarly calibrated, but only for an instant and a minute fraction of the strength now coursing from the stool into me. The connecting shackles ensured I received a constant flow of pain.

I didn't know how long it lasted. Except for brief seconds, I couldn't keep my thoughts focused on anything other than the biting pain. When it stopped my jaw ached where I'd clenched my teeth, my muscles were cramped—arms, legs, back, abdomen. I was sweating and gasping for breath.

My bladder had discharged. Fortunately Dr. Sanchez had cleansed my bowels. Otherwise it would've been worse. False result that it was, maybe it suggested to Heartwell that I'd managed to retain a small element of self-control.

Sometime later, maybe seconds, maybe minutes, maybe longer, I realized the intense spotlight was on me once again.

"Your initial pragmatism disappointed me, Specialist." Heartwell's words were clearly enunciated, smug with confidence. "I thought I might actually have to wait to administer punishment. Shall we try that again?"

After a drawn out pause, Heartwell asked, "Tell me, Specialist, who holds your contract?"

Unsure my voice would hold any defiance, I shook my head. Then, I recalled the pain I'd endured, Crax acid flowing in my veins. I stared up at Heartwell. "I prefer not...to share...that," I said with a snarl, and braced for what I knew was to come.

Whether he continued to ask the question or just periodically tap his icon, I didn't know.

The jolting fire continued, burning its way into my dreams. No doubt the bastard watched my body twitch and convulse long after I'd lost consciousness.

My security training aimed at resisting interrogation and torture was limited. Surviving as a hostage? I'd studied it, both in theory and limited scenario participation during training. My plan had always been to go down fighting. Corporal Pallish's treachery, attacking me from behind—after we'd survived combat against the enemy together?

I thought on this as I sat naked in a 1.5 x. 1.6 meter room, shackled to the steel-grated floor. White walls and ceiling. Bright white spotlight shining down on me. It was so bright I couldn't see beyond it to the surveillance camera I knew was up there.

My wrists were shackled as were my ankles. The chains, or more accurately metal cables, that held each limb were only a foot and a half in length. Placement of the ankle cables bolted to the floor beneath the metal grate forced me to sit on my buttocks. I had to lean left or right to relieve the biting pressure inflicted by the grating, which was no more than a millimeter thick with each square in the grid being four centimeters per side. I could lean my shoulders against what I named the rear wall, but it left me at an uncomfortable angle, with my neck and head pressed against the wall. My wrist cables disappeared into the base of that wall, a part of some sort of spool that controlled the amount fed into the cell, releasing or further restricting my comfort, and range of movement.

Three factors made it even more uncomfortable. The first was hemorrhoid burning and itching. That's what I guessed it to be. I'd never been afflicted, and there were effective medications. Security duties can include assignments where sitting for hours on end occurs. From what I'd read and had described, I was suddenly suffering from a severe case.

The second factor was the random surge of direct current electricity released across the floor grid, causing unpredictable instances of pain. Sleep, when it came, never lasted long. And awakening to the jolt was less than the pain from the odd position I was forced to take while sleeping. That was compounded by the pain while recovering from where my body had pressed against the unyielding narrow-gauged grate.

The third factor was the excessive heat and humidity, sapping my strength and causing me to sweat profusely.

Sleep deprivation and constant thirst piled onto my misery. The odor of my urine and solid waste a foot below the grate barely registered. They must've force fed me while I was unconscious. Off to my right, built into the floor, was a hole that I guessed to be there for a prisoner to relieve himself. That would require more freedom of movement than available.

It was impossible to tell how long I'd been in custody. The tube they lowered from somewhere beyond the spotlight offered a bitter liquid and tasteless food paste. When it appeared was as unpredictable as the electric shocks. Sometimes it was nourishing. Other times it caused me to vomit, or suffer diarrhea. Or so I believed its contents was the cause.

The light never dimmed. It wouldn't have mattered. No human or AI contact. Not a friendly face. Not a hostile one.

Careful observation revealed a pattern that provided an anchor. Ships and docks, and even subsurface colonies altered lighting, including UV lighting, to simulate day-night patterns. Cockroaches, German cockroaches, *Blattella germanica*, came and went, feeding on the vomit and waste beneath me. I imagined the time of insect scarcity to be day, and increase in numbers to be night.

Discovering the cockroach pattern offered me a small victory. Something beyond just existing, weakening in body and increasing in despair, spiraling down into depression. I continued to observe the pattern while scraping a section of the cable against the floor grating. It was a futile effort, but kept me focused and busy.

Then they increased the sweltering heat, so humid that I imagined steam floating in the air. Then, they infused the air with bitter cold. It made me shiver for what had to be hours on end. So cold that the cockroaches wouldn't show. And my growing beard? Had they trimmed it back when I passed out beyond all recollection? Or maybe the nutrition tube held drugs that put me to sleep, allowing them to act. My beard trimmed, along with my fingernails? Or was that all my imagination? Or not my imagination, and simply an effort to throw my mind further off any recollection of time's passage?

How long had it been? Five days? Four? Fourteen or twenty four? I decided that days didn't matter. My mind's wandering, circling in on itself…grasping at straws, wondering on what ifs. Would I be here if I'd only have…?

Up until that moment the only thing I'd succeeded in maintaining was my silence. My refusal to cry out, ask for help, for mercy. For death. I was like a hare in a rabbit hutch of torture.

No, not a hare. Wrong animal. A terrier. That fit better.

Despite the pain, despite the growing grate-induced body sores that wouldn't be attended to by my captors…I needed a focus more than I needed answers…answers to unanswerable questions. Pointless questions.

I needed a strategy to survive. A strategy to endure.

There wasn't anything Heartwell or Capital Galactic wanted from me. Any information I might have was out of date. They had no idea of my knowledge pertaining to a subterranean Umbelgarri breeding ground and nursery on Tallavaster. My knowledge of Maximar Drizdon Senior's wife and son, their location was part of my *Documentary*, which CGIG representatives had seen, the primary reason they'd initially wanted me. There was my mission with Guymin and Vingee, but that had likely already come to fruition, or failure.

Now it was all about payback. Revenge for my significant part in revealing their collaboration with the Crax, mankind's enemy. And the company's subsequent downfall, imprisonment of thousands of CGIG loyalists, and auctioning off of all corporate assets—or all that hadn't been swiftly hidden or liquidated before the hammer fell. Before the government, the military and rival corporations came after them, freezing and seizing everything.

As those really important within the CGIG hierarchy knew, or at least suspected what my *Documentary* might reveal, they were able to take action before the authorities could respond, gain a head start. Disappear.

Capital Galactic had been the largest and most influential corporation, with varied assets and interests scattered from Earth to the inner and outer colonies. That worked to their advantage. Wealth can trump morality, loyalty. Right versus wrong? Look where I ended up.

Too many key persons disappeared before they could be detained or arrested, as did ships, financial assets, and valuable data and equipment. They'd retained more than enough credits and influence to offer the bounty which led to my capture.

Heartwell, on behalf of Capital Galactic, intended to simply make me suffer pain and agony. Vids of my capture and the result would be distributed far and wide. And Heartwell would enjoy it. Every week. Every day. Every hour. Every minute. Every second.

Intel would be seeking me, if not on their own, at the urging of the Umbelgarri. Intel was seeking Deputy Director Simms. Why not me as well? The Umbelgarri, with the destruction of their homeworld, or moon, at the end of the Silicate War wouldn't want any of their vital breeding grounds revealed.

I didn't think they had many breeding sanctuaries, and those they had were key to the Umbelgarri's long-term survival. Their hope for recovery, if we won the war. A big if.

I had to hold out, give Agents Guymin and Vingee, and McAllister and crew…I took a sad breath, recalling Kent's death. No longer part of

McAllister's crew, a friend I'd never see again. Another reason to survive until they found me.

They'd come looking. My com-set's coded emergency transmission alerted them, helped put them on the trail of Dr. Sanchez and her crew of two. They'd have to find them to learn about the handoff of me to CGIG loyalists.

McAllister was unrelenting. Guymin too, once he found Simms and maybe Tahgs. Maybe others.

I'd have to survive. Endure, while waiting my turn. They had to come for me. And if I didn't endure?

What would be lost in trying?

The solace of my teen years' favorite fishing hole, a deep channel nestled between rows of cattails where a shallow stream trickled into a small man-made lake. The memory of croaking bullfrogs, glimpses of surfacing painted turtles and reed-rustling muskrats while I fished for bluegill and catfish using my cane pole. Remembering that experience distanced the pain inflicted by flaring hemorrhoids and the biting pressure of the grated floor. But the random jolts obliterated the solace, the memory, making it more and more difficult to reconstruct. The jolts overwhelmed attempts to rebuild distant, carefree memories. Jolts that left me twitching and drooling, alternately grimacing and panting, trying to recover.

I needed something more, and fell back on another comforting memory. One where I wasn't a passive participant, observing within the memory. One where I didn't wait and listen, but could participate in, actively. Better enable me to fend off Heartwell's torture regime.

I felt myself slipping and needed a better place to retreat. Lack of sleep, disrupted sleep, wrecking any pattern. Insufficient food and water. No outside stimulus. Just lights on white walls, indenting, cutting pain from the floor, the smell of my wastes, bowel and bladder and vomit. Alternating hot and cold. And electric jolts.

Mental and physical breaking down brought on depression. Despair ascending.

A comforting memory arose out of those jitters. They reminded me of vibrations, strong sounds reverberating through the air. A massive organ at the front of my childhood church's sanctuary. Bronze pipes reaching toward the arched ceiling, framed by stained-glass windows.

As soon as I was six, in first grade, my mother allowed me to sit by myself in the front pew, a wooden one without cushions. In wonder and awe of the organist, a stern elderly woman who sometimes smiled at me as I struggled to stay awake during the preacher's sermons.

The music, forced out through the pipes, caressed my face as it filled my ears. It vibrated through the hardwood floor during some hymns, touched my feet through black socks and brown dress shoes. I sang the hymns, even though I couldn't read all the words. I learned them by sound and belted them out, even though I had no talent for singing, then and continuing as I aged.

Choir members, sitting in their loft to the left of the massive organ pipes watched me, kept an eye on me for my mother, permitting me to sit every Sunday morning and *feel* the music through my skin and muscles and into my very bones.

Trapped within my cell, I retreated to that memory, of a Sunday where I sang. Where Miss Rita played the organ, and the preacher's Scripture reading reminded me, and where the Lord's roof and walls sheltered me.

A Mighty Fortress, a shield to defend me from evil, from Heartwell, Capital Galactic. Muffle and dampen their blows. *Lord of the Dance*, reminding me Jesus struggled to dance with the Devil on his back, but did. Heartwell was one of the Devil's minions. Miniscule in comparison. Nevertheless, I determined to do the same. Finally, *The Battle Hymn of the Republic*, reminding me that through the centuries, men and women had fought and died for others' freedom. If the same was to be my fate, I found comfort in that.

I didn't belt out the hymns, my throat dry and my voice weak. But they sang in my head, giving hope to my heart. When the shocks came, they melted into the pipe organ's vibrating voice. The pain was there, but I had a measure of detachment from it. Insulation. Over and over again, verse after verse, and sometimes returning to my fishing hole, to relax and catch instances of sleep whenever I could manage.

For how long? The cockroaches came and went, when the cold and heat cycles allowed. Came and went again. During their next return, the nutrition tube appeared. Its contents must've been laced with drugs that knocked me out, put me into a deep sleep. Drifting beyond my sheltering memories and song, but also beyond the pain.

CHAPTER 37

A stream of water splashed against my shoulder. Brisk and steady. At first the sensation was incorporated into my dream. An unexpected storm, a downpour of rain at my fishing hole.

Refreshing, despite the sting as it ran down my scabs and open sores. After awakening to my confined reality, I caught and swallowed mouthfuls until the streaming water switched to a chemical soapy mixture.

I coughed and spat out the cloying, bitter taste. I smiled at a childhood instance where my grandmother caught me cussing and stuck a bar of soap in my mouth. "Let's clean that tongue of dirty words," she'd said, like it was a mutually beneficial project.

Taking advantage of the opportunity, even as I spat, I rubbed what had become sudsy foam along my chest, legs, face, and neck as my cables allowed. My sores burned like peroxide being rubbed into them. A good burning, clean.

Malnourished, dehydrated, and weary as I was, the effort wore me down. Someone must've been observing because the stream of water returned, rinsing my grime and blood to drain away beneath me.

Abruptly the water stopped and the spotlight, my constant companion, was shut off. Dripping wet, I began shivering in the absolute darkness. I'd like to think the shivering was due to the cold and not the darkness, but I'd lost a good measure of my brashness. I couldn't see my hand in front of my face, even after several moments for my eyes to adjust.

Black, silent, closed. A coffin without cushions or pillow.

I sat, huddled as much as my shackles allowed, listening, waiting, braced for the electrical jolt that'd shoot into me from the floor and through my manacles. Like a thousand times before. A thousand times? More than that?

Only then, while shivering dry, did I ponder why they'd allowed me to clean up. Until that moment, the 'why' hadn't occurred. My mind was worn down, my thought patterns frazzled.

Leaning back carefully to inflict as little pain on my stiff and sore-ridden body as possible, I decided not to worry or wonder, but to begin the process of revisiting my sheltering memories. To disconnect, whether the shock or something else came. The cold darkness that surrounded and enveloped me would follow. Could it dim the stained glass windows, even shatter some of the lights? Maybe muffle sounds, but not the organ and its music. I had to believe that.

The chance to determine the accuracy of my hope never occurred. A needle prick in my shoulder came first, bringing with it an alternative form of darkness.

A thudding pain aroused me.

"Want me to kick him again?" asked the deep-throated voice of a thug if I ever heard one.

"Make it twice more," replied a nasal voice.

I recognized Heartwell's voice before the second of two booted kicks knocked the wind out of me. The thug must've known his business because he didn't crack any of my ribs.

I rolled over, trying to breathe. When gasps of air finally reached my lungs I sat up. My periphery vision identified someone in black standing next to me. In front of me, not five feet away stood Heartwell. He wore his business suit without tie, and his malicious grin.

With everything I had, I launched myself at him, expecting the thug to grab hold of me, or at least my daisy-adorned hospital gown. There was no need. The perfectly clear plastic wall proved an effective barrier. Fortunately my hands impacted first or I'd have broken my nose.

Both men laughed heartily as I struggled to my feet.

"Specialist Keesay," Heartwell said, wiping a mirthful tear from his eye, "that was quite amusing. Thank you." He rocked on his black boots' heels and pointed his rectangular remote at the man standing next to me. "I'll thank you even more if you go after Mr. Gillgall, there. If you think you're a match for him."

I obliged Heartwell, turning as I got to my pink-socked feet and went after the hulking Gillgall. He stood well over a head taller than me, his bodysuit and jacket unable to disguise his muscled frame. I faked going for him in the same manner as I had Heartwell, but pulled up, intending to sweep Gillgall's feet with my legs. I must've telegraphed my move, or I was too weakened to change direction with any amount of surprise, because he stepped back, out of my reach. His square face grinned and deep-set, brown eyes sparkled as he beckoned me to try again.

I didn't understand what was going on, but what did I have to lose? They couldn't punish me any worse. I shook my head as if to clear cobwebs and took a fighting stance, protecting my kicked but uninjured ribs.

He took a martial arts stance, not too dissimilar to mine. I moved in to jab at about 80% my current speed and strength. He blocked and laughed, moving away in a circle, trying to draw me forward. I knew I couldn't win. But he could pay.

I sneered, pursuing with caution, and waited. Jabbing again he blocked and sent a left my way. I ducked inside, grabbed hold of his forearm and bit down, hoping to tear through his jacket and jumpsuit sleeves and come away with flesh. I knew what was coming but didn't care.

His laughter turned to a howl of rage. My teeth dug into flexing muscles before his fist clubbed down on my skull. Somehow I lost my grip on his arm. Next thing I knew, my airborne body slammed down against the tiled floor.

I tried to get up, but had spent all of my strength. All of my reserves.

Gillgall's strong hands yanked me up from the floor. "Stand," he ordered.

I did, only swaying a little, ignoring the pain inflicted by the floor. In a few minutes I might have the strength to go at him again. For some reason, the back of my neck, near the base, itched. When I moved to scratch, Gillgall slapped my hand down and batted me across the back of my head. I stumbled to one knee but got back up.

"Pay attention," he ordered.

I didn't even bother to look at him. "I'll get you," I said, staring ahead at the grinning Heartwell.

"Yes, yes, of course," Heartwell said. "*Nemo me impune lacessit*, if I accurately recall." He rocked on his heels again, looking smug. "You must have forgotten the three main tenants of goal setting, Specialist. Specific, measureable, and attainable. You fail on all three counts." He put a finger to his cheek. "The first two, possibly you've internalized rather than verbalized. But for the last, you are guaranteed never to achieve." He shrugged and smirked. "Sorry, but that's the truth."

I shrugged. "We'll see."

"Speaking of that, something else I believe you might be interested in seeing." He stepped aside. So focused on him I hadn't even noticed the man sitting on the floor, along the wall two paces behind him.

The man's bald head was bowed as he sat cross-legged, his attire similar to mine, except for his gown held a pattern of tiger lilies. Two long-healed scars, white and puckered, poorly stitched after something had torn across his skull years ago.

The light-skinned man was emaciated, not quite to the extent of concentration camp victims. My mind flashed to flat screen black-and-white vids from World War II archival footage.

Was I staring at my future?

Something about the man tugged at my memory. With his head drooping forward I couldn't see his face, but something about him. I knew him.

Before I could chase down that memory, Heartwell said, "I believe this counts as a reunion, Specialist Keesay." He walked back and placed a hand on the seated man's forehead, pushing it up for me to see. "Say hello to Deputy Director Karlton Simms. The man you and your friends abandoned."

I just stared ahead and suppressed a smile, before receiving a beat down with fist and boot. Guard Gillgall didn't appreciate being bitten, believing a concussion and severe bruising to be sufficient payback.

While he delivered it, between punches and kicks, I managed to ask him, "What use will the Crax have for you, if they win? Will they enslave, or just kill you?"

CHAPTER 38

My future sat across from me: Deputy Director Simms, unmoving, catatonic, wasting away.

At first I thought the clear plastic between us had been shifted, like a one-way mirror. I'd seen some interrogation rooms set up that way. When a guard entered Simms' cell, I asked, "What'll your job be if the Crax win? What use to them will you be?"

He flipped me off while making eye contact. Some simple gestures endured. His finger gesture not only survived many decades but had become universal. The guard could've been using an ocular and been connected by radio to my cell, but I didn't think so. Even so, Simms didn't respond, didn't look at me. Didn't even blink.

The guard, like all the others, wore standard penal colony gear. A black bodysuit with an eight centimeter diagonal white stripe across his chest and back. Underneath, a thin layer of body armor protected his chest and abdomen, back, biceps and forearms, thighs and shins. They had close-fitting helmets, shiny black boots and white belts, and were armed only with stun batons. Heavy duty models, probably security locked based upon hand print activation. No nametags or other visual forms of ID.

After several days, estimated by the healing of sores inflicted by my previous cell's flooring, little had changed.

The Intelligence deputy director sat silently. Unmoving. When physically guided by guards, Simms complied so that he could be cleaned, being either incontinent or uncaring. He didn't follow guard movements with head or eyes when one entered our cell. He swallowed when nutritional paste and vitamin-fortified juice was squirted into his mouth, but made a mess as the first attempt always resulted in some dripping down his chin.

He did isometric exercises, but only to music occasionally piped into our rooms. It was intentionally horrendous, fading in and out, skipping seconds at a time, adding random noises. While I ignored it, Simms responded with his exercise. His only response to our environment or external stimulus.

They kept us under constant lighting. Both Simms and I slept, he usually after his exercise. Sometimes immediately, other times after what seemed like several hours. He just curled up against the wall and slept, returning to a sitting position upon awakening. I slept, stretched out, mimicking his cycle.

The main difference between Simms and myself was that both of my arms and legs were shackled to the wall. He only had his left arm secured. The manacles were attached to retractable cables so we could be pulled back and held flat against the wall. Or at least I could be when guards entered, fed me, and cleaned my chamber pot by hosing it down. That, and I didn't think Simms was afflicted with inflamed hemorrhoids. It was impossible to 100%

ignore the burning and need to shift positions constantly. The condition had to be chemically induced. All my years of sitting warehouse duty, they were never a problem. I had no family history. No genetic predisposition.

I spoke to Simms extensively, for hours at a time, relaying to him news about the war. Old news openly broadcast, so that nothing of value was shared with anyone listening or recording. I remembered most of *War of the Worlds* and *Moby Dick*, the two most recent novels I'd read, so I retold them in a summarized fashion, covering major plot events but lacking most of the dialogue. I discussed my thoughts on some of Shakespeare's plays, mainly *Othello* and *Hamlet*.

After that I related to him what I remembered of the *Chronicles of Amber*. It'd been a long time since I'd read them, but it challenged my mind to do so. None of those efforts had any impact on my roommate. I thought of him as that, as opposed to cellmate. My efforts didn't appear to stimulate thought or interest, so I switched to topics and events that would be familiar to him. I spoke of several corporate espionage cases that had been in the news while I was studying to be a security specialist. Being with Intelligence, he certainly had some knowledge of them.

I had to pace myself, my shared stories, leaving hours of silence in between, so that I didn't lose my voice. And run out of things to say. Simms, being an Intel director, certainly had training to endure and survive as a prisoner. Resist interrogation and psychological tricks any captors might employ. I told myself I was a rugged individual, hardened by life and reality. A Relic not dependent on constant computerized stimuli. I'd been trained and used my mind in different ways, had different outlooks and strengths.

But Simms had training, the best training humanity had to offer. Look where it ultimately left him. Catatonic.

Eventually I told Director Simms about Diplomat Silvre's death aboard the *Iron Armadillo*, after he'd been shot, and presumed dead aboard the *Pars Griffin*. Again, all of the information wouldn't be new to Capital Galactic. They had representatives view the *Documentary*'s first showing, and certainly had copies. Simms and the diplomat seemed to hit it off professionally. I thought her name, her death, might twitch his mind into motion. It didn't.

I even told Simms about the battle against the Crax on Tallavaster, something he'd have no knowledge of. Once, when I mentioned Janice Tahgs visiting me, Simms blinked twice. I'd never seen that before, and never saw it again, no matter what I spoke about or tale I told.

I fell back to reciting sections of Scripture and poetry memorized in my youth and a weak attempt at Abbott and Costello's *Who's on First* routine, switching my voice to reflect two speakers. The last one took a lot of practice to get right, but the effort filled what I guessed to be most of a day.

Time passed, days stretching into weeks, into a second month. A small measure of my strength returned. The guards allowed me enough freedom to do basic exercises like pushups, sit-ups, and running in place. Lawyer

Heartwell didn't stop them. The whole time he never showed his face, or spoke through the cell's intercom.

Time's passing concerned me, causing me to weigh the resulting good news and bad news.

The good news was that if Guymin and Vingee eventually found Director Simms, they'd find me. That we hadn't moved, entered condensed space travel—I'd've felt it—provided more opportunity for them to locate us and formulate a rescue plan. The bad news was that if they didn't find him in time, I'd be shipped off to Crax space along with him. What I estimated to be each passing day weighed more and more heavily.

The question was: What use would I be to the Crax?

One day, they changed Simms' gown from tiger lily patterned to one patterned with vines of morning glories. It reminded me of my brief time on the space dock orbiting 70 Virginis, in the market area not far from the Celestial Unicorn Palace's entrance. The moment I'd caught a view of Kent O'Vorley there flashed through my mind, and twists of emptiness formed in my chest. My mind shifted to my encounter with Colossra—Yeong. It seemed ages ago, like my memories of childhood.

I shook it off, deciding that today I would tell Director Simms a few Aesop tales. Maybe *The Tortoise and the Hare* would be a good one to start with. A solid moral to the story for both him and me to remember, locked away in our mind-numbing cell.

A maintenance man in tan coveralls affixed hooks to the wall above Simms. The man carried no weapons, only a couple of plastic hooks and a tube of adhesive. While he worked, stepping around the unmoving deputy director, I asked, "What job will the Crax have for a human maintenance tech if they win the war? What use will they have for you? A liability on their ledgers, food, medicine, oxygen in space, and someone to watch. You turned coat once. With that record of loyalty, why keep you around and risk it?"

It was my standard round of questions for the guards each time one entered to clean my chamber pot set into the floor by using a mild chemical wash hosed out of a pressurized canister. It wasn't technically a chamber pot, but better than calling it a toilet hole. They did the same with Simms, hosing him down when he soiled himself and squeegeeing the contents into the chamber pot. The maintenance tech's response mirrored the guards'. No response. Not even recognition that I'd spoken.

So that my questions didn't become background noise, and no longer noticed, sort of like the stench of our cell had become for me, I changed the contents up a little each time, every repeated opportunity.

They were questions that would bother me. Make me wonder. I knew they dug at them as well, despite any assurances they might get from the higher up CGIG loyalists, or even the Crax themselves.

One angle I hadn't used was the fact that in Crax society, humans would be considered Relics. Something else to add to my repertoire.

Without warning, the cables to my shackles were drawn in. That was normal. As expected, they didn't bother with Simms' single arm shackle. They didn't drop the clear wall between Simms and me before the entry door slide aside.

Lawyer, or Warden Heartwell, strode in wearing an amused grin, as if someone just told him a dirty joke. That didn't match his conservative business suit. Behind him walked a guard that I hadn't seen before. He was thin with gangly arms, and legs that seemed about a half foot shorter than they should've been. That wasn't what made my eyes widen. It was that the guard carried a shotgun—my pump action shotgun—with bayonet affixed.

Was this it? My time had come, Heartwell hoping for some irony? Me being shot or run through with my own weapon? Or would it be Simms? Or both?

It appeared neither. Not at that moment at least. The guard walked to the wall opposite me and rested the shotgun, sling, perforated jacket protecting the barrel, everything apparently oiled and well maintained.

It wasn't a replica, unless they'd perfectly copied scuffs on the stock and scratches on the receiver, all earned in combat against Gar Crax and Stegmar Mantis. That was possible, but not Heartwell's style. Even if loaded, they could've disabled it. Removed the firing pin. But the bayonet, made from a superior Umbelgarri alloy, strong and sharp beyond I-Tech capabilities, including the saw back portion of the blade? It could cut my restraining cables, even pierce and pry the cell's secure door open, if I could get the time, and for the latter, leverage.

But they'd hung it on the opposite wall, far beyond my reach.

"I see, Specialist Keesay, that you're transfixed by the presence of your weapon of choice, archaic yet effective." Heartwell turned and feigned admiration of the shotgun, then pointed at it. "It was this firearm, or your revolver, designed upon even more archaic technology..." He didn't finish the thought.

Having recovered my initial shock of not only seeing a weapon brought into my cell, but *my* weapon, I shrugged, and shifted position.

"Ah," Heartwell said, bringing a thoughtful finger to his chin. "I had forgotten, but those assigned to your care have not." When I didn't reply, he tilted his head and grinned. "When you arrived, my belief that since you'd proven to be such a pain in the ass for me and my associates, we'd return the favor. I see by how you're sitting that your caretakers have continued the...symbolic gesture." He turned and took a step toward Simms, who hadn't moved a muscle from his lotus position. "Or, in my absence, they *may* have discontinued, and the rectal inflammation caused by the chemical added to your food paste has become permanent." He shrugged and glanced back over his shoulder at me. "Either way, I approve."

If he was expecting some sort of response, a request for relief, for some sort of mercy, it wasn't going to happen. He had to know this.

"However, Specialist, what I do disapprove of is the cessation of electrical discharges, to keep you on your toes. Otherwise, life within your cell, your permanent home, might lose some of its allure. Some of its mystery."

I kept a sneer from forming on my face. Refrained from balling my hands into fists.

To emphasize his point, Heartwell pulled his remote from a pocket and thumbed an icon. The shock's length and intensity brought me to the brink of passing out. He sent another brief jolt while I struggled to catch my breath.

"I imagine someone will have to clean that up," he said, referring to my bowel and bladder discharge. "But that reunion will have to wait."

He moved to stand over Simms, then slid to the side so that I could see him take the director's chin in his hand. Turning the director's face up toward him and then to face me, Heartwell said, "Our V'Gun specialists have monitored your cellmate for eighteen months. Brain activity has dropped off, especially within the frontal lobes."

With a look of disgust on his face, Heartwell let go of Simms' chin. The director continued to stare ahead blankly, as always. "It was my hope that your nattering presence might reverse the progression of your associate's spiraling internal psychosis." He sighed. "Place one more failure on your ledger, Specialist Keesay.

"To emphasize how far gone he is," Heartwell continued, "and establish in no uncertain terms what your future holds, I'm placing your archaic firearm here in your cell, within easy reach of your cellmate."

He rocked on his heels, saying, "The Intelligence director is supposedly among the best they have. Highly trained. Mentally the strongest. Truly, Relic, what chance do you have?"

I didn't bother sharing what I knew to be true: Never underestimate a Relic.

The shocks weren't entirely random. Every time I encouraged Simms to reach for my shotgun, I got a good, long jolt.

Heartwell's goal wasn't to break me, at least not quickly, or he would've kept me in the first cell. Besides causing me to suffer, there was some other game he was playing. What he'd said about moving me into a cell with Director Simms. If that was true.

His objective for me? A slow path to mental degeneration. Whatever his goal, I planned to endure.

My primary goal? Survive until Guymin and Vingee found me—us. My secondary goal? Escape my cell, damage the facility, and launch a message rocket. The second part of my second goal was the only one I had confidence I could achieve.

But for anything positive to happen, I had to survive. Await an opportunity. So I went back to my routine, talking to my roommate. Telling him stories. And endured the random electrical shocks.

CHAPTER 39

My flowered gown was a soiled mess, again. Despite the fact that I did my best to use the chamber pot and avoid any buildup in my bladder and bowels, whoever was at the switch caught me in my sleep just before waking to relieve myself. It wasn't difficult to tell how they knew. With V'Gun support, using their advanced medical knowledge, it only made sense. They apparently monitored Simms' brain activity from afar. Why not my bladder and large intestine?

My sense of smell was already deadened to defecation odors. I wasn't humiliated, or ashamed. Constantly disrupted sleep patterns, isolation, and the resulting lack of mental stimulation and boredom were of greater concern. Stinking up the place? I had no control or choice in the matter. But that changed after a gray and wrinkled old woman entered my cell.

The guards hadn't retracted my shackles, allowing me to retain a small range of movement.

She looked to be a centenarian, except for her posture. Too straight, too nimble. Despite my efforts to keep in shape, what I could see of her muscle tone not covered by her hospital gown covered in patterns of violets, she didn't look half as worn down as me.

Her long hair was rolled up in a bun and her sagging cheeks and face held no expression. She carried two ten liter buckets, one in each hand, and two fresh gowns thrown over her shoulder. Morning glories for Simms and daisies for me. From the astringent odor, at least one bucket held the harsh chemical cleanser.

She shuffled over to Simms and began cleaning him and his filth first. She didn't even appear to notice my shotgun. Surveillance would allow the guards to move on the old woman before she could accomplish anything, except maybe to shoot either me or Simms. Maybe she didn't know how to use it, or believed it was a non-functioning replica.

The relative ease with which she toted the filled buckets surprised me.

I didn't say anything to her. No warnings about being useless to the Crax, or even casual conversation. She was a prisoner too, at least her gown said so. Maybe she'd earned this privilege through good behavior? Or maybe through something more nefarious…

The old woman was far gentler than the guards who tore our gowns from us and sprayed us down and used the same hose and squeegee to direct the waste into the chamber pot. She was also adept with the pattern of tie strings around the shoulders and sleeves to accommodate Simms' shackled left arm.

Two buckets. One to cleanse the main waste and grime, and the second, with a separate sponge, to finish the job. Being second, after Simms, I wouldn't end up as clean, but far better than my current condition. From what I could see of the liquid and rinsing, we were first on her list of prisoners to be cleaned.

I wondered at the reason. Heartwell had to have some motivation for our contact with someone other than a rough-handling guard. Were we—or mainly me, considering Simms' catatonic state—being set up for something? I'd just have to roll with whatever metaphorical, or psychological punches, were certain to come.

After placing Simms' soiled gown near the door, the old woman retrieved her buckets and the daisy covered gown, and moved toward me. Why Capital Galactic used flower-adorned gowns, I didn't know. A supposed feminine touch to emasculate, or soften us? To remind us of the outside beauty we'd never see again? Something with more sinister intent? The only thing cheap and available? Asking wouldn't garner a response, and even if a guard did say, he wouldn't provide an honest answer. Of that, I was sure.

Distracted, I didn't immediately notice the old woman had stopped in front of me, so I moved to stand. As I did, she dropped her buckets. One spilled, washing over my bare foot. Her wrinkled and liver-spotted hands shot up to cover her mouth.

It was then that our eyes met, hers purple, with loose folds of skin around and beneath.

Something about her eyes...purple...I knew them.

"Tahgs?" I asked. The administrative specialist was one of a handful that survived the Crax's boarding of the *Kalavar.*

The last time I'd seen Janice was on Tallavaster. I was wounded, dying from Crax acid rounds and being wheeled into surgery under V'Gun surgical scalpels. Heartwell was there, having failed in his attempt to interrogate me. He'd said he'd had better luck with Tahgs, enjoyed the experience, and looked forward to interrogating her again, despite her knowing nothing of value. One of her purple eyes was swollen shut. Her face was bloody and bruised, and wet with tears. Having seen that, I told Heartwell his time would come.

I'd brought down Capital Galactic, but Heartwell had survived, and had been tormenting Janice ever since. She had been so young. What had he done to her?

Less than a second after her name fell from my lips, the jolt of electricity came, coursing through my body, causing me to collapse and convulse. When I recovered, Tahgs was at the cell door, on her knees, pounding feebly. Weak, grief-filled cries filled the otherwise silent cell.

"Janice," I said, struggling to keep my voice steady.

She huddled onto herself and turned away from me.

Through the intercom system, Heartwell said, "I just love organizing reunions."

Sitting up and sneering, I said, "You'll pay for this, Heartwell. Know that it's true, if it's the last thing I do."

Heartwell laughed. "No, Specialist. I've heard that threat from you before. Some day when I neglect to take my finger off the command icon, this is the last thing you'll be doing." With that, he sent another extended jolt of energy through me.

CHAPTER 40

There was little vacillation between who I hated more, Falshire Hawks or Jerden Heartwell. Both were traitorous and evil, but Heartwell was far more malicious and deserving of a slow, painful death.

Janice Tahgs and I became friends on the *Kalavar*. We weren't lovers, and our relationship went in spurts, but friends in my life have always been few and far between. I cared for her. She was softer and more innocent than me. I'd saved her life several times, and McAllister told me that Tahgs saw me as her knight in shining armor. That if I was around, I'd save the day.

That hadn't been true. I brought down most of Capital Galactic, but hadn't helped her. What they'd done to her...

I sat, seething. Heartwell wasn't interested in breaking me, turning me into an unresponsive vegetable like Simms. He wanted payback for what I'd done, and showing me what he'd done to Janice...prematurely aged her, at least superficially. And to break her spirit even more. Demonstrating that he'd captured me, and I was caught in his web, just as she was. And that my life, like hers, lasted as long as he desired. Could be ended on a random sadistic whim.

My focus shifted, from holding on until help arrived, to escaping. Delivering payback to Heartwell no matter the cost. Humanity was losing the war. With diminishing resources, that meant diminishing chances of Guymin and Vingee finding me. McAllister too, if she was still looking. Guymin had some urgency in finding Simms before he was moved out of human-controlled space to Crax-controlled space. Or maybe major swaths of space claimed and colonized by humanity was now under Crax control, including the region where our cell resided.

Doctor Sanchez's medical shuttle wasn't fast and didn't have great distance. I imagined I'd been handed off and shuttled again, presumably while still in hybersleep. But with V'Gun assistance, who could be sure. My guess was that we were stationed somewhere near the border between the inner and outer colonies. Far away from the conflict. Probably aboard a converted freighter orbiting some uninhabited moon or planet. Maybe somewhere in the middle of space, near no sun, planet, or moon. A needle in a colossal haystack. One ten times the size of Jupiter.

I bided my time, observing and seeking patterns to exploit. I continued as before, telling stories to Simms and reminding every guard I saw that their future under Crax rule was destined to be grim. That was, if their future didn't end the moment Humanity's final defenses collapsed.

I no longer said, "If Humanity lost the war." For me, it was over. All that was left was revenge. I'd kill everyone on board the space barge, dock, converted freighter, surface or subsurface colony if I could. Take as many down with me as possible.

Nemo me impune lacessit.

The cell's ceiling held five spotlights. Four shined down from the corners in addition to a central one, powerful and able to rotate. Hidden behind the glare were the intercom and the surveillance system. The walls were metallic, probably steel, with a dura-plastic cover. The chamber pots were nothing more than thirty-centimeter-diameter bowls ten centimeters deep and set into the floor with a small, five-centimeter-diameter drain.

The shackles had magnetic locks secured with a secondary hex key lock. My training indicated that the type on my ankles and wrists received power energizing the magnets through the restraining cable. Even if power was lost, the standard battery reserve was eight hours for four shackles with an additional twelve for one. Usually a wrist. So, even having a hex key wouldn't help, unless it was titanium and the length of a crowbar to give sufficient leverage to overpower the magnetic lock. Which would crush my wrist in the process. Better to hacksaw the wrist off—but if I had a hacksaw, the cable would be the weak link.

If I had an actual crowbar, I might be able to dig at the wall through which the cables emerged. Maybe after ten hours of effort. A hammer and chisel would take several hours of pounding, minimum, for each manacle. That was if I didn't injure myself. Holding the chisel with my feet to work on my wrists would increase the chance of injury.

Those were all fanciful thoughts, and showed my mental sharpness floundering.

The weakness in the system was the cable. An hour with a hacksaw and several fresh blades would take care of them. A pair of heavy-duty bolt cutters would work, more efficiently for the cables running to the legs than the arms, but I'd manage. If I had them. Again, wishful thinking, but it reminded me what I was up against.

Plugs on the other side of the wall stopped me from yanking and unspooling the cable until it could be disconnected with a Herculean yank.

Beyond the cell door, all that could be seen in the poorly lit hallway was the floor with a narrow grate running down the center. A two-meter-wide corridor with maybe a two-foot-wide grating.

Besides my hands and feet, the only weapons I had were the cables and my gown. They could be used to strangle anyone that came within reach. Otherwise I could spit, or throw insults, or fling my crap like a crazed circus monkey. But, except for Tahgs, before a guard approached me, the cables were fully retracted to the wall. A few inches were released, one at a time, to enable my gown to be changed. Even then, the guards' training kept them out of range of my teeth.

The hex locks, I might be able to loosen within the shackles ahead of time, if surveillance wasn't on top of things, and if the manacles' sensors didn't go off. But I had an idea to address that as well. The only weakness in the magnetic lock system might be to break free while power was running through them, shocking me. The magnetic hold would be affected. The problem was I had little to no body control when that happened. Plus, I had four manacles. Maybe if I had only one to deal with...

There was no way to fake catatonia, especially if they monitored my brain activity.

I might just have to wait for someone to mess up. The tool to get out of the cell once I was free hung on the wall above Simms. A weapon to help extract revenge.

So, whenever I got the chance I soaked my manacles in urine to degrade the sensors attached to the hex locks. I chewed and compacted scraps from my gowns, with the intent of stuffing one part into the lock and the other as a bar to twist, giving leverage to unscrew the lock.

Since I had nothing to lose, and to disguise what I was really up to, I sat and scraped the rounded cuff of my manacle against a leg cable. I made efforts to disguise the effort. I'd never cut through the cable, but if they punished me for trying, it'd tell me about their level of surveillance.

While working on that, I periodically reminded Deputy Director Simms that he had my shotgun, with bayonet affixed, resting on hooks attached to the wall behind him. That always earned me a shock.

They sent a long jolt into me, and examined my leg cable while I lay on the floor, recovering. One of the guards actually spoke, warning me to stop or suffer. The backup guard laughed. Then he informed me that urinating on my manacles wouldn't short out the magnetic components. More likely the damage would release an uncontrolled current that they might not be able to shut off in time. They'd responded to me and my actions. A small victory.

They never noticed or at least said anything about my tearing and chewing shredded fibers from my synthetic gown.

All of that effort never found a chance to be used.

CHAPTER 41

I awoke from my standard sleeping position, on my left side with my back leaning against the wall. This time a shadow stood over me.

It was Tahgs, somehow transformed from a woman my age to a centenarian. I'd tried to push that from my thoughts, and not wonder at what had happened to her. If my goal to destroy the ship or dock or colony succeeded, it meant her death too. I wouldn't be Janice's knight in shining armor. I'd be her black-robed grim reaper.

I blinked twice to make sure I wasn't dreaming.

There she was, buckets in hand. I glanced between her bare ankles toward Simms. She'd apparently cleaned him first and I hadn't noticed. My vigilance was slipping.

I braced myself for the anticipated electrical jolt certain to accompany Tahgs' appearance in my cell.

"I have been assigned to clean you, Specialist Keesay." She set the buckets down and tossed my replacement gown to the side, opposite from the chamber pot.

My gaze shot up to the ceiling where the surveillance camera and mic were located. "Are you permitted to converse with me?" I asked. I'd gotten used to speaking with the twist of synthetic threads pressed against the gums above my teeth on the left side of my mouth.

Her purple eyes went wide in worry. I'd seen that look several times before.

Eyes are not wells to the soul. They're vehicles for nonverbal cues.

While Tahgs wasn't a hero, she wasn't a coward either. She stood with a handful of *Kalavar* shipmates against the Stegmar and Crax boarders. She witnessed friends and acquaintances die next to her in the barricade, stopping the advance. Survived the cat and mouse game with the military-trained aliens. One of a small fraction of the crew. But I also witnessed how it had affected her. Enduring the stress of being under a space blockade on Tallavaster, and surrounded on the ground by the enemy. She wasn't a trained, battle-hardened warrior. She was an average civilian, doing the best she could to find her way. To survive. She was doing that now, standing in front of me.

She'd been a prisoner since her capture on Tallavaster. The entire time I'd been under the Cranaltar IV, recovered, joined Intelligence, and participated in the search for Director Simms. The man sitting across from me, unmoving and unaware.

She'd been out of her cell. More than I'd managed, at least while conscious. Did she know who Simms was? Did she know any other prisoners? Where were we being held? Ship or planetside? What star system?

It also occurred to me that she'd somehow earned privileges. Was it her job to get information from other prisoners, from me?

After several seconds of silence, I stood since they hadn't sent a shock into me or retracted my cables. "Complete your assigned duty." While there might be limited information gained, reestablishing a bond, however limited, was something. Something they could take away from her. Away from me.

She removed my gown and tossed it onto Simms' soiled gown near the door. Since I was relatively clean, she wiped me down quickly with a sponge from the cleansing bucket and moved more slowly with the rinse bucket.

We largely maintained eye contact. Less than a year ago I would've been embarrassed to stand naked before her. Situations and experience change things. Her eyes weren't filled with volumes. Rather only with fear and sadness. My gaze was filled with the best expression of courage and defiance I could muster.

When she'd finished slipping my fresh daisy hospital gown over my arms, I stepped forward to give her room to tie it in back. That was one thing that normally I had to do myself after the guard exited. While Tahgs did this task, I felt a narrow pressure against the small of my back where the only set of strings were, just for an instant as she tied my gown closed.

She came back around and our eyes met as she faced me to pick up the buckets.

"Thank you for completing your duty," I said.

"You're welcome," she said, wincing, but nothing happened to her or to me, and she left without another word.

No punishment felt more unnerving than receiving it. That said something about my state of mind. I sat back against the wall and closed my eyes. Yes, I felt something along the edge of the gown, just below the tied strings. Hard and narrow, and hooked...or bent.

Discovering what it was would have to wait. It was time for me to talk to Director Simms. Since we hadn't eaten yet after sleeping, giving me a temporary time anchor, I announced to Simms, "This morning I will tell you about working with automated landscaping equipment, and how a piece of it caused the death of my father, and my brother trying to save him."

Then, I thought better of it. CGIG probably had that basic information on me, but why go into detail? Tahgs' visit reminded me of something from my youth, so I continued after a breath, saying, "Not interested in that, Director Simms? How about a story about post-apocalyptic Earth? Everyone enjoys those. My teacher assigned me to read and research this for a cross curriculum assignment back when I was about nine."

I paused, gathering my thoughts. "*Pail of Air* by Fritz Leiber..."

The question was: Where to hide the hex key Tahgs had given to me?

I couldn't leave it stuck in the lining of my current gown. They changed them infrequently, sure. But without warning, and the cables were always drawn in immediately beforehand. Also without warning. So I wouldn't be able to remove it from the gown before the garment was taken from me.

They used a sonic depilator to cut my hair and shave my beard, again, without warning. So, hiding the key in my hair wasn't an option. Its size, L-shaped with the longer leg over three inches and the shorter leg a little less than one and about 1/8 of an inch cross section, meant hiding it in my mouth wouldn't work. The rectum, a cavity regularly searched among penal colony prisoners, wouldn't work either. In addition to the danger of perforating an intestinal wall, the uncontrollable bowel discharges Heartwell enjoyed inflicting would prove troublesome. Similar concerns if I swallowed it. Plus, if the opportunity to escape presented itself, I wouldn't have immediate access.

Hiding it in the chamber pot drain or in the ankle or wrist cuff of my manacles wouldn't be effective. It'd be washed out of reach in the drain. It'd be visible if stuffed between my wrist or ankle and the manacle, especially if its color contrasted with the metallic shackles.

Until I could find a satisfactory solution, I removed the hex key from my daisy gown while lying against the wall, and later stuck it between the back of my ankle and the shackle. Both were a dull metallic color so it blended well enough—if someone wasn't paying close attention.

In addition, I kept the gathered synthetic fiber hidden in my mouth, and added to it a little, even if it wouldn't be used. Avoid any pattern changes, especially if they were watching. Doing otherwise might bring attention to what Tahgs had given me.

My shotgun was one small step closer. An uncertain step, and not likely an enduring one. The key offered a tenuous route to revenge. Another, better one, might present itself. Unlikely, but I never guessed a hex key would fall into my lap. Keep my eyes and ears open. I didn't pray for opportunities or for any special help. My goal was to kill, revenge killings. And if I succeeded, innocents would go down too. It'd aid the war effort, one we were losing and probably would lose, but that wouldn't wash the blood of intention, blood of guilt from my hands.

My destiny wasn't to end up catatonic like Deputy Director Simms or prematurely aged like Janice Tahgs. Although calibrated for pain and not permanent damage, the frequent jolts were certain to impact my muscles and nervous system.

Beyond the potential physical damage, I noticed my habit of involuntarily tensing up for no apparent reason. Anticipating a jolt. Sometimes I was even right. Or someone was watching and obliged my anticipation. Maybe Heartwell was sending some subtle, subconscious signal. A sound at a frequency on the edge of detection, or a barely perceptible change in the light's intensity. Messing with my mind. Conditioning me.

He planned to have me in his clutches for years. Why would the bastard be   impatient?

CHAPTER 42

I was telling Director Simms about my security training coursework related to crime scene preservation when our cell shuddered. The lighting flickered. For several seconds I felt lighter, not quite floating. We were on a space craft of some sort, one with a gravity plate. One with minimal power reserves. Something, either an internal explosion or an outside impact caused the shudder and a temporary power loss. It was impossible to tell if main power had been knocked out and she was on auxiliary or even battery power. Probably not battery, as the grav plate wouldn't be functioning.

The cables attached to my shackles remained locked in place. The emergency default is to fully retract and lock in place. It might be only seconds before someone entered that verbal command or tapped the icon. Kneeling down, and still talking to Simms, I removed the hex key from behind my ankle and did my best to block surveillance's observation with the bottom of my gown.

The lock on my ankle was still functioning. Even under battery power it would.

Kneeling, I continued talking to Simms. I did a double take. Despite no music being piped in, he'd begun his isometric exercise routine. Maybe the change in gravity affected him.

"You know, Deputy Director Simms," I said, "my shotgun with bayonet is still hanging on hooks above your head."

While I braced for the expected shock, he ignored me and continued his routine.

Nothing happened to me, which was curious. I decided to relieve myself in the chamber pot and sat back against the wall, hex key held tight in my fist. I waited, ears listening, eyes watching for any light fluctuation, feet on the floor and back against the wall feeling for any vibrations. It'd take something of unusual magnitude to be felt or heard within our cell.

Watching Simms complete his routine made me think. I began stretching and loosening up. I'd lost a lot of my strength and stamina, but if something did happen, pulling a muscle might ruin a chance that presented itself. What chance was that? It didn't matter. I'd take anything. What did I have to lose?

Another shuddering with subsequent light flickering and temporary grav plate fluctuation happened, and repeated a few seconds later.

Simms sat in his lotus position, no reaction. Me? Adrenaline was flowing. Other than the hallway, the cell was my whole world. A small one with occasional music, and guards entering to clean and offer food. And Heartwell to taunt, but he hadn't been around in a long time. And the pain of shocks, and Tahgs, twice.

My thoughts were straying. "Director Simms. Karlton Simms, you know my shotgun with bayonet is behind you, within easy reach."

No response.

Then the lights went out, fading over several seconds.

I slid the hex key into the left manacle. It took several tries but it turned! Fifteen seconds later my wrist was free. Within a minute I was free.

The lights hadn't turned back on. Crawling across the floor I found Simms, right where I expected him to be. The magnetic lock to his ankle had failed as well. My first thought was McAllister. She'd have the code to power down and deactivate the locks.

"Help's here," I whispered into Simms' ear before reaching up for my shotgun. It felt good in my hands. I checked. Even in the dark, having it in hand came back to me. Not loaded. But it had my bayonet. I took Simms' forearm and lifted. "Follow me," I said, and led him to the door. When I dropped his hand he stopped.

After forcing my bayonet into the door's edge, I pried. The lug wasn't built for excessive lateral stress, so I moved my hand further down and pried again. The door gave way, until a sliver of light reached the room, as well as a warning claxon. The light was red, and the claxon muted.

I listened, thinking of escape rather than destroying the ship. At least primarily. Simms would follow, but he'd slow me down. There might be other prisoners. They could help. Hijack the ship? Not likely, unless it was a small vessel with minimal crew. Maybe we could reach a shuttle. I didn't even know what kind of ship we were on. Maybe a converted barge. Maybe a space dock. I knew virtually nothing.

Move forward, I told myself. Don't lock up. Bold over timid.

If I died, it'd be on my own terms. Gritting my teeth, I whispered to Simms, "Stick with me, and we'll get you straightened out."

I shouldered the door open and peered out. A long hallway, with the central floor grate and doors, probably to cells on both sides running both ways. To the right, the dim red lighting outlined two men. One with a computer clip and the other with a cart, standing in front of a door.

I ducked back in and leaned close to Director Simms' ear. "Two guards outside. I'll be back for you once I take them out."

The hyper-vigilant men were thirty feet away. Before I took five steps the man with the computer clip pointed to me. "One's out. Get him!"

The voice identified the pointing man as Heartwell. The second man dropped a fist-sized canister back into the cart before pulling and telescoping his stun baton.

Either the guard was a fool and didn't look, or the lighting didn't show him I was armed. He shouted, "Back in your cell," while charging, and discovered his error when I thrust my bayonet into his chest, piercing the diagonal white stripe and body armor. He gasped and slapped the energized baton against my shotgun. The discharge was muted, having to pass along the perforated jacket made from an Umbelgarri alloy and the stock to reach me.

It also coursed through the jacket and barrel, and bayonet to reach him. The zap wasn't enough to deter me from twisting before yanking my blade free. He bent over, clutching his chest, allowing me to slam my shotgun's butt across his temple. He stumbled back and collapsed.

"Warden Heartwell, you're next," I growled.

Rather than run or draw his own weapon, Heartwell laughed and pointed his remote at me.

The next thing I knew, the side of my face was rebounding off the metal floor.

I could move my eyes and jaw. Nothing else. My arms and legs didn't even twitch when I tried to get to my feet; I couldn't lift my head to better see Heartwell stepping closer. My shotgun, lying in front of me, partially blocked my view.

"V'Gun surgeons are very useful," Heartwell said, "installing central nervous system interrupters in potentially troublesome prisoners." He stopped several strides away, presumably so I could see him. His hand went to his mouth, feigning surprise. "Oh, Specialist Keesay, did I neglect to inform you? I apologize. Upon my request they installed one along the vertebra in your neck shortly after your arrival."

While I continued breathing, I only had partial control of my throat and tongue and couldn't reply. It didn't matter. What was there to say?

Heartwell looked up from me. It was hard to tell the expression on his face. "No," he said and he took an initial step back, then decided to bend over and grab the fallen guard's stun baton.

Someone next to me picked up my shotgun. The red lighting made it hard to pick out details. The person was barefoot. Another prisoner. Heartwell turned to run. With a grunt, the prisoner hurled my shotgun at the retreating lawyer.

My bayonet pierced him in the back, right where his left kidney should be.

Heartwell twisted as he fell, causing my shotgun to clatter to the floor against the wall, but the damage was done. He cried out in pain and tried to get to his feet, collapsed and began crawling, alternating between groaning and crying, "No...no!"

The prisoner was tall and bald and thin, his gown covered in a pattern of vine-twisted morning glories. It was Director Simms!

My cellmate ignored my shotgun and picked up Heartwell's remote, examining it. He caught up with the crawling lawyer and kicked him across the face before bending over to grab the lawyer's hand.

Pressing the lawyer's thumb on the small screen, I felt my muscles again, my strength returning.

Then Simms stood up straight and backed away from Heartwell. The lawyer screamed once before an acidic stench began filling the hallway. I'd only gotten to my knees and realized what was happening. I'd witnessed it several times before. Heartwell had a Crax suicide device implanted behind his aortic artery. I didn't know all of the triggering parameters, but severe wounding was one of them.

"Step back," I warned Simms. "It's the result of a Crax implant and will completely devour his body." Wondering why he was up and moving about with mental faculties intact and working wasn't something to worry about now. There'd be time later. Maybe.

Simms glanced over at me and nodded once. The dim light was enough to reveal he was fully alert, glancing up and down the hallway. I walked over and picked up my shotgun and the guard's discarded stun baton. "What's in the cart?"

Simms ignored me and picked up Heartwell's dropped computer clip.

"We've got to get moving," I said, looking over the fallen guard. "I think this ship or barge, or whatever is under attack, maybe being liberated. Maybe not."

Simms looked from the computer clip to the cart.

"What?" I asked pulling off the guard's boots. They were too big for me. "These might fit you. Socks too." The dead guard wasn't wearing his helmet. Odd since the ship was under attack. I'd've had mine. I took off his white belt, which had a small computer clip attached and a hook for his stun baton. No hex key that I could find, which was odd, too. "I get his uniform. You can have the belt."

Simms tried to talk, but his voice was too raspy and weak for me to hear. The claxon, even muted, didn't help. Uniform and belt in hand, I hurried over to the cart and picked up one of the metallic canisters. A small tab with several wires was affixed to the top. On the sides it read: Sarin Aerosol. I immediately placed it back in the cart.

"Sarin gas," I said. "They were going to kill us." I glanced up and down the corridor. "They might've killed some of the prisoners already." Simms shook his head and pointed to the computer screen, being careful to keep his hands from touching even the edges of the screen.

He showed it to me. Of the sixteen cells, four were listed as empty. Of the twelve remaining, nine had been highlighted in red, listed as Sarin prepared.

"Computer controlled release," I said and took a hold of the cart's handle. Inside it, a sectioned plastic crate held three canisters, and nine empty slots. The one I'd read had been sitting atop the others—the one the guard had tossed back when he saw me. Who trusted containment enough to toss a canister holding such a deadly agent? A fool or an idiot, or both.

"I'm taking this into our cell and shut it inside. Watch for trouble."

After I'd wheeled the cart in, Simms helped me slide the door closed. The hallway's circulation system had to run separate from the cells', otherwise the stench of the prisoners and their waste would be present in the hallway.

"We should open the cells with the poison placed in them first," I said.

He nodded. Before we moved, our eyes shot down to the computer clip's screen resting on the floor. It beeped as a red ribbon with bold white text appeared across the top: Lower two decks have been captured. Respond immediately to receive instructions.

My eyes shifted down to the tasks and security bar. Authorized iris and finger print access. I pointed to the task bar, showing Simms my concern. "You knew this?"

He nodded.

Even though it was old technology, it was difficult to fool or override. I didn't have the skills to attempt an override. Simms probably had the skills to at least attempt, but not the necessary equipment. Heartwell's higher ups were trying to contact him. Probably through his implanted ear receiver, and followed up through his computer. Heartwell was gone, his communications implants dissolved along with him. If someone was boarding, they weren't going to be patient.

I said, "We'll have to move fast and now."

He nodded and scooped up the clip. After looking down the hallway, he pointed to a red cell on the diagram and then to the corresponding closed door.

I dropped the dead guard's uniform and boots before pulling the hex key from the seam I'd shoved it into and handed it to Simms. Then I went and jammed my bayonet in the door Simms had pointed to, right along the frame.

Just as I put my weight into prying the door open, Simms grabbed my shoulder and pulled me away. "No," he rasped.

"What?" I asked. "Why?"

He pointed to the screen. All of the red cells, plus ours, still green, had an image of a black skull and crossbones centered in them. The red cells had a yellow barrier appear around them. Our cell didn't.

"Sarin's been released," I said. "Our cell isn't sealed off." I looked up, not seeing any vents above. "Its ventilation must still be open."

"Monitor," I said, moving across the hallway to one of the white cells and began prying the door open. "Rescue!" I shouted when it was open a half inch. A pair of wrinkled hands slid along the door and helped me open it. When it was wide enough, Janice Tahgs squeezed out.

"Spreading," Simms rasped. He pointed to another door. "Next."

Tahgs tried to hug me.

"No time," I told her, pushing her away. "Sarin gas. Poison. Get the hex key from him," I said, pointing to Simms and hurried to the next door.

This room was dark inside. "Rescue," I shouted. Two voices replied at the same time. A man's yelled, "We're here." A woman's cried out, "Yes, help us."

After prying it open wide enough, I signaled Tahgs to go in. Worried about running out of time, I asked her, "Any cells where they aren't shackled?"

She pointed across the hall to one that the computer diagram identified as filled with poison gas. "Okay," I said, not wanting to slow her down. Then I said to Simms, "Make sure whoever comes out with Tahgs pushes the door closed."

He nodded. "Last one," he said, pointing.

"Last one?" I asked for clarification, as I wasn't sure what he'd said because of the claxon combined with the man and woman with Tahgs shouting at her to hurry. After Simms nodded I said, "Send Tahgs with the key," and ran to the door of an occupied cell farthest from ours.

Somehow the door locks had been disabled, like the shackles' power had been cut. My thoughts already suspected McAllister. It made some sense for her to not open the doors, since it required a manual key to remove the shackles. If it was her. It could've been a traitor to CGIG—a humanity loyalist, or a computer expert from Intel or the military, or a Bahklack.

With a concerted effort, the door opened. Slower than the others. I wasn't in very good physical shape. Plus, the exertion caused my hemorrhoids to flare with increased pain. In comparison to what I'd suffered, that was easy to set aside. A reminder of Heartwell and all he'd done, not only to me, but Simms, Tahgs, and everyone else. Including those who'd died because he'd prepped their cells with poison. If anyone deserved to die with Crax acid flowing through his arteries, dissolved alive, it was him.

"Rescue!" I shouted into the darkened room.

There was no reply. I pried the door open a little further, saying, "Rescue. Anyone in here?"

The red light fell in the middle of the room, but illuminated it enough to show one body shackled by a leg to the wall. It was a woman, bloated and covered in welts. The welts were a different color from her pale skin, but the red lighting made it difficult to see exactly what color.

A man with bulging muscles lumbered up behind me. He was Colossra on steroids, so much that it was difficult for him to walk, turn his head, and limited his arms' range of motion. He was dark skinned, and had penetrating dark eyes, probably brown.

"I'm Keesay," I said to the hulking man. "Poison gas is spreading. We may need to close this door quickly."

He replied in a calm, deliberate tone. "I can handle that. Just say when."

"The man with the computer clip is monitoring. He'll tell us. Actually, he'll tell you as I'm going inside. Send Tahgs in with the hex key."

The muscular man tipped his body forward, instead of nodding, before I turned. "Got it," he said. "I'm Gerard, by the way. Thank you for the rescue."

I went over to the woman lying on the floor. "Don't thank me yet," I shouted over the claxon. "There's a fight going on somewhere. Do you know what this is? A dock, a converted freighter?"

"Hunh," he said. "I always figured this was a medical research ship converted to a prison."

That was news to me.

The woman was sprawled out, unconscious. She appeared bloated and the flesh around her wrist felt squishy. She had a pulse, slow, but steady. I looked up and around, wondering if I'd get any warning if the Sarin started flowing into the cell. If any of the poison touched my skin it would do me in. Do everyone in.

I took my bayonet and began sawing at the cable. The serrated sawback edge bit into the twisted reinforced steel, but it'd take longer than we had. I kept at it anyway.

Gerard said to someone behind me, "He needs the key."

A few seconds later Tahgs knelt next to me. She inserted the key and began twisting.

The big man urged Tahgs, saying, "The man says hurry!"

With nowhere else to put it, I affixed my bayonet and slung my shotgun. "She is hurrying, Gerard."

The unconscious woman was like lifting a man-sized rigid water balloon, and I didn't have the strength to hoist her for a fireman's carry. Janice lifted and draped one of the woman's arms over her shoulder. I did the same. "You first, Tahgs."

We squeezed through the doorway, trying to keep the woman from hitting her head on the door or its frame. Gerard slid the door closed.

A woman with long, tangled hair stood next to Simms. We all wore flowered gowns. The woman's face looked deformed, with her forehead and the bridge of her nose bulging out. Her nose was three times the size it should've been. She held a hand over it while her eyes watered. She wasn't crying. The tears appeared to be due to a physical response. The acidic smell lingering from Heartwell's demise came to mind.

"We need to move," I said, thinking that Sarin might make its way into the corridor. "All that Simms and I know is that this ship or dock is being attacked and the lower decks have been captured. Anybody know anything about where we are?"

The big-nosed woman shook her head. Gerard, standing protectively close to the woman, said, "You know more than us."

"Tahgs?" I asked, looking at the guard's uniform. Simms already had on the boots and belt. He picked it up and draped it over a forearm.

"I've never been outside of this corridor," Tahgs said. "At least not while conscious."

I thought Simms might know more than me. When I asked, he shook his head.

"Okay," I said, starting to lead them down the hall away from my cell. The unconscious woman's arms around mine and Tahgs' shoulders. "Unless there're any objections, I say we make our way down toward the fighting.

Toward friendly forces."

I glanced at Simms with a raised eyebrow. He took my meaning and said in his raspy voice, "You lead."

We went down the long corridor without any doors to where it formed a T intersection. I peeked around and didn't see anybody. A standard corridor lit in normal fluorescent light a short way down to the right.

Tahgs asked, "How do you know they're friendly, Kra?"

"They're fighting Capital Galactic."

"I'm strong but can't fight too well," Gerard said. "Drape that unconscious lady over my shoulders. That'll leave you free with your shotgun."

"Good idea," I said, stopping. "No shells, just a bayonet. Simms has a stun baton." Once we laid the waterlogged woman over Gerard's shoulders, I said to Simms, "Give me that uniform. Tahgs the computer clip," and told Tahgs, "Don't touch the screen, if you can avoid it."

The computer reminded me of Heartwell and his remote, and the central nervous system interrupter the V'Gun inserted in my neck. Very few would know or have ready access to activate it, or so I told myself. Slamming against the floor left my face tender, probably bruised. I shrugged it off. I'd been in far worse shape. Plus, there was nothing I could do about it, other than move forward and escape.

I turned to the large-nosed woman while slipping into the guard's uniform. It had a blood stain on the white stripe. "I'm Keesay. What can we call you?"

"Marguerite," she said. I expected a nasal voice. Instead it was a nervous contralto. Her eyes were no longer tearing up from irritation. Instead they were wide with fear. The uniform was a little big so I cuffed the sleeves and ankles. The daisy gown underneath helped keep it filled out in my thin and weakened condition. Simms must've put on the socks with the boots. That was okay. The socks would've been slick on the metallic and tiled floor surfaces.

"Okay, Marguerite," I said, gently gripping her shoulder. She was in a flowered gown too. "Simms and I will lead since we're armed. Gerard, you and your load next. Tahgs and Marguerite, watch behind us and bring up the rear."

CHAPTER 43

Not far down the corridor we came to an elevator. Even if it was the most efficient method of movement—if it worked—it wasn't a great option. Next to the elevator was an information console common to space docks and civil transports. Simms stepped up next to me. With a few taps he gained access to guest information. The screen immediately flashed to an emergency default setting telling visitors to report to their assigned accommodations, Class A and B personnel report to duty stations, all others report to and remain in their assigned quarters for the duration of the emergency.

I turned to ask Gerard if he could handle carrying the woman down a ladder, but took a second to observe the woman draped over his shoulders. Her body was bloated, like it'd been pumped full of fluid to the point of bursting. Welts between one and five inches in diameter covered her skin. They were waxy and bright green, appeared more rigid than her taught skin, and covered almost half her body. Where the welts showed across the woman's scalp, her tangled auburn hair had fallen out, emphasizing her diseased appearance, like an alien mold or fungus afflicted her. But looking at Gerard and Tahgs and the large-nosed Marguerite, disease wasn't what afflicted the unconscious woman.

The floor shifted beneath our feet as a dull *thunk* reverberated through what had to be the hull. That drew my attention away from the woman and back to our situation.

"That didn't feel like a weapon strike," I said. "More like something bumping into this ship—or dock—in the side. Like a breaching pod," I said, recalling my experience aboard the *Kalavar*. "But larger."

Tahgs and Simms nodded in agreement.

"Gerard, can you descend access ladders with her?"

"Her skin feels pretty fragile. Whatever the warden did to her, she's barely alive."

Marguerite said, "Any chance at survival she has depends on escape."

"Elevators may not work," I said. "If they do, we could end up in the middle of something we won't survive."

"We don't even know how many decks there are," Marguerite said. "And which way is down."

"There will be information posted along the access routes maintenance techs use."

Tahgs said, "We could always look inside an elevator, even if we don't use it."

"Are you a soldier?" Gerard asked me.

"I've been a conscript, but I'm a trained Security Specialist."

"Who's killed more Crax and Stegmar than you can count," Tahgs said.

"Some in hand-to-hand with his shotgun and bayonet."

Gerard's eyebrows pinched downward in suspicion. "How'd you get that shotgun, Specialist?"

"Heartwell, the warden, hung it in our cell," I said, nodding to Simms. "To taunt me."

"Keep moving," Simms said, hardly above a ragged whisper.

"Right," I said. "Follow me. If there's gunfire, drop to the floor and crawl the opposite direction. I'd suggest a rally point if we get separated, but the only place I know is the cell block."

"No interest in going back there," Gerard said, slowly shaking his head. "Not for no reason, ever."

I hefted my shotgun and signaled with my head for everyone to follow. "No argument there."

The corridor we traversed was well lit. Conduits ran along the ceiling and intermittent grating along the floor, which was scuffed and not recently cleaned. I hadn't been on many civil transports, but it seemed like we were on one, passing doors with computer entry pads mounted next to them.

Somehow my pace had fallen into cadence with the claxon. I spotted two surveillance cameras. While that was a concern, if there was an armed incursion below, the focus wouldn't be on us, I hoped. Destroying them with my bayonet might draw attention. The deck was barren. No robots, no crew or anyone. If it was a civil transport, the cell block would be away from crew quartering. And the crew would be small in comparison to the number of passengers the interstellar vessel could carry.

Ship decks were listed '1' at the top or along the dorsal part of the hull all the way down to the largest number at the bottom or ventral hull.

Midway down the corridor I spotted a recessed ladder. Looking next to the ladder a stamped plate showed that we were on Deck 4. And the access wasn't sealed off anywhere above or below. It should've been, but maybe this one was open for the same reason that enabled us to escape our cells.

We'd have to climb down, and pass through the gravity plate to reach the lower decks. Then, with the gravity plate right at our feet, we'd have to start climbing away from the plate, toward the ventral sections of the ship, or dock.

"I'll go first, with my uniform. It'll be an advantage," I said, "until we near the attacking forces." Looking down, this access didn't appear to extend through the gravity plate. On ships, most access ladders didn't. "We might have to risk an elevator. If it'll open for us."

Simms's face remained blank. Marguerite and Gerard looked skeptical. Tahgs nodded in agreement.

"At least for a level to get through the gravity plate," I said, "Or seek a maintenance access. Unless someone knows a better option."

Nobody offered one.

I went first, after removing my bayonet and putting it between my teeth like pirates did in old flat-screen videos. Having it affixed to my slung shotgun in the crowded access seemed like a bad idea. And I didn't have a belt or scabbard to hold it, and a pocket wouldn't do. At least when spotted, they'd see a black uniform with a white diagonal stripe along the back. Good if it was someone from CGIG seeing me first. Bad if the attackers, the friendly forces, spotted me first.

Of course, being barefoot might cause those from either camp to wonder.

I stopped at every level to lean out and check for potential enemies. The corridors, looking like civil transport quartering levels, were clear. That was even more eerie than if there were patrols, or maintenance techs hurrying to repair something or shut off some section. There might not be that many people aboard. Or those who were, few or many, were fighting below. Or stationed at critical areas.

We reached Level 12, the end of the ladder access. We needed to find one that passed through the gravity plate, or risk an elevator. If they had sufficient forces to guard strategic locations, both would be defended, or at least closely monitored by surveillance.

Simms watched as I helped Gerard out of the access with the unconscious woman.

"You doing okay with her?"

He was breathing heavy. "Strong," he said, "but no endurance." Before I said anything else, he added with a grin, "I'm nowhere spent yet, fella."

The chance for freedom. It drove me. Tahgs and Simms had been prisoners longer than me. My guess was the same with Gerard and Marguerite. I nodded, grinned back at them, and then made eye contact with Tahgs.

She met my gaze. "I'd hate to be the warden when you find him."

"See the blood on my bayonet?" I nodded over toward Simms. "He took Heartwell in the back. Bastard was running away. Crax acid, like what happened with the traitors on the *Kalavar* finished him off."

"Thank you, man," Gerard said to Simms.

Marguerite wiped a tear from her eye after a sharp intake of breath. "What Gerard said."

I walked past them, picking a direction. Left. "We'll celebrate later."

After a short trek down a narrow corridor with wall panels that appeared newer than anything previously seen, we came to a T intersection. Peeking around, I spotted a maintenance tech standing guard about fifty feet away. He fidgeted with an MP pistol while trying to watch four ways. His manner showed lack of training. But, he was armed.

I gave my bayonet to Tahgs. She handed the computer clip to Marguerite.

"Give me the boots," I whispered to Simms, loud enough that everyone in our group could hear. "There's an untrained maintenance tech guarding an intersection. I'll have to bluff my way up to him."

The boots were at least five sizes too big and *clomped* as I trotted up to the maintenance tech. He immediately turned toward me, half pointing the pistol my way, then at the floor when he spotted my black and white prison guard uniform. The fact that I had my shotgun slung allowed me to get close before he challenged me.

"What are you doing down here?" He was an older man, with gray frizzy hair and a matching mustache.

Reading his name tag, I said, "Tech Debattes," and pointed at the ceiling above him. "What's that?"

"Hunh, what?"

I slowed and shied away and pointed again with urgency, "That! Above you."

When the man ducked and glanced up I closed the gap and drove my fist into his throat. His eyes bulged and he instinctively reached for his throat as he stumbled back. I grabbed the pistol before the old maintenance tech fell against the wall. He slid to the floor, gasping for air. I'd crushed his trachea.

I ignored what he was trying to say and drove my fist into his face, slamming the back of his head against the wall. Blood erupted from his nose as he slumped to the floor. Although his injuries would do him in, I stomped on his neck to make sure. Kent probably wouldn't have approved. But he wasn't there, and that was the point.

Feeling no remorse at killing the man didn't bother me at the time, adrenaline and anger flowing. He was a Capital Galactic loyalist. He made his choice to align with the Crax. Humanity's mortal enemy.

Three directions down the narrow cross hallways were deserted. I signaled and Simms led the others up to me. Pointing, I said, "Elevator that way, about ten yards down."

Marguerite's eyes were wide, staring down at the man I'd killed.

The corridor lights dimmed for a second as the floor shifted under our feet.

"Feels like something just hit her," Tahgs said.

It wasn't a laser strike. Those didn't move ships unless they caused something like a fuel cell to explode. Or breached a large section, causing a catastrophic loss of internal atmosphere. Maybe a near miss by a missile, or a direct hit with a small warhead. If any of those were happening, with the accesses between decks not sealed, the whole ship—or dock—could be lost, and us with it.

I handed Simms the MP pistol.

He offered the stun baton to Tahgs. "Can you use?" his voice rasped, trying to conserve words. "Risk the elevator," he told me. "Haste important."

Tahgs nodded and gave me back my bayonet. "Watch the hallway," I said. "This dead guy's boots look more my size. Simms, you get to play Maintenance Tech."

After Simms and I were dressed, I said, "The elevator may be locked down. It may open up to a set of guards, or worse." Everyone met my gaze, except for Simms. He watched up and down the hallway and listened down the cross hall. "Move fast. Just follow and keep low. Simms and I will be most at risk when we break through to the good guys. It's our only chance to get off this...get off here."

When he wasn't moving, Gerard held the unconscious woman with ease. I wanted to ask if she was still alive...sort of wondered if she wanted to be alive. So many prisoners died from Heartwell's Sarin gas. Was that a mercy? It wasn't my decision, and I'd never know anyway.

We made it to the elevator without incident. Simms pressed the call button. Nothing happened. I put my ear to the doors and listened.

Looking up at the recessed security camera I said, "I'm prying them," and jammed my bayonet between the doors. When they'd been separated an inch, a shrill alarm added its voice to the muted claxon.

"Kra," Tahgs gasped. "Hurry."

"Gerard," I said.

Before I'd stepped aside, Marguerite and Simms were holding the green-splotched woman. Gerard jammed his fingers into the gap. The big man's muscles flexed and the door mechanisms screeched as his strength overpowered the internal gears and motors.

Scattered LED lights lit up the shaft. The bottom of the elevator was two levels below. The neon green line with brown diagonal striping identified where the gravity plate was. It was eighteen inches above the top of the elevator, or technically the bottom, as anyone on the other side of the plate would say.

Off to the right was a recessed ladder. A few feet below was a wider recessed circular area were the ladder could rotate 180 degrees to reorient the person, depending on their direction. Even this section was set up with rods that would emerge from the walls and into fittings in the elevator so that it could rotate as well.

For about eighteen inches there'd be neutral gravity.

"Simms," I said, "you go first. Then me. While we're doing that, Tahgs, watch, and Marguerite, tear up Simms' hospital gown and tie the woman to Gerard's shoulders.

"We've got to move before someone shows up. Same plan, just keep following."

Tahgs held out the flowered garment that Simms had stuffed in a pocket. I sliced it several times with my bayonet. Those gashes would make the garment easier for her to tear into long strips.

"Same plan as before. Just follow. Tahgs, you bring up the rear." She looked far older than anyone but physically she might've been in the best overall shape. "The doors are just on rollers now, so push them closed as best you can."

Tearing cloth, she said, "Okay." Her voice trembled a bit. The stress was getting to her.

I glanced in the elevator shaft. Simms was holding onto the ladder. He'd already pressed the rotation release and hung on while it spun 180 degrees.

"Kra!"

I looked back and followed Tahgs' gaze. Down the hall two men appeared from the cross hall.

"Hey," one of the men shouted. "Halt. Don't move!" Both were armed with MP rifles. Simms' and my uniforms might've fooled them, but the flowered gowns of everyone else sent up a red flag.

Fixing my bayonet I said, "Tahgs, down. Finish up here," and charged the tan-clad maintenance techs.

CHAPTER 44

Both maintenance techs were tall and lanky. The dark-skinned one on the right had straight black hair that stopped just above his shoulders. The light-skinned one had close-cropped brown hair with a thin mustache. The long-haired tech shouldered his rifle, and shouted, "Halt, or I'll shoot." The other didn't bother and inexpertly fired from the hip. Both glanced at their rifles in confusion. They'd forgotten to click off the safeties. That gave me time to close with them.

They were going to get some shots off. I hoped the built-in armor of my prison guard uniform could resist penetration by any rounds that might strike. That they didn't get a lucky head shot was on my list as well.

This was CGIG. How much would they spend on their mundane loyalists?

The long-haired tech stood several paces closer to me than his partner, so I veered right, narrowing the mustached tech's angle of fire.

Above the claxon and my boots pounding on the metal floor, the sharp snaps of MP rifle fire sounded. Both men backpedaled, still triggering off rounds in semiautomatic mode. I slid like a man stealing second base but with my shotgun and bayonet braced to strike the nearest man's gut. Rounds ricocheted off the walls and floor. One hit me in the leg. A second in the gut, knocking the wind out of me.

The long-haired tech tried to dodge, earning him a bayonet thrust that tore into his intestines just above the hip. I held firm, forcing the stabbed man to the left to keep him between me and the other rifleman, struggling to avoid ending up in a tumbled mess with one or both of them on top of me.

The wounded man cried out in pain, dropped his rifle and grabbed my shotgun's muzzle.

The wind was knocked out of me and I wasn't able to draw a breath, but the uniform's body armor held. I managed to twist and shove the wounded man away from me, further blocking the other maintenance tech.

The second man was shouting into his collar mic, "Intruders, Deck Twelve—"

That was all he said because I managed to grab the discarded MP rifle and got in a lucky shot to the side of his forehead. It didn't penetrate, but it knocked him to the floor and shut him up. That gave me a moment to catch a breath.

The bayonetted man began to scurry away like a kid in a crab race relay, with a glob of intestines threating to spill out. I shot him. The first round deflected off the floor into his leg. The second took him in the throat. Favoring my right leg, I climbed to my feet and limped over to the head-shot maintenance tech. Again, my prison guard uniform had resisted MP fire, but my thigh felt like Gerard had slammed it with a ball-peen hammer.

The guy had called for help on Deck 12. That meant someone might be coming, or at least searching through surveillance. I shot out two recessed cameras before finishing off the second man. Then I took the rifles, boots and belts, and limped back toward the elevator shaft. I took my shotgun and bayonet too. It was extra weight. Don't ask me why, but even with a loaded MP rifle in hand, I felt naked without my shotgun.

I should've checked their pockets. Shaking my head at my oversight, I continued forward. There wasn't time to go back.

Everyone but Gerard and the unconscious woman had entered the shaft. He knelt over her, trying to shove a wadded strip of gown against a wound where her neck curved into her shoulder. Already a huge pool of blood had formed. It was red, but with a flecks of green.

"Leave her," I said, offering him the larger pair of boots and a rifle.

A stray shot must've struck the woman. Or her skin and flesh had split along one of the welts. I warned Gerard, "One of the techs called for help."

He balked taking the rifle, saying, "We can't leave her."

I shot out the camera opposite the elevator shaft. "You know how to use a standard MP rifle?"

He nodded. "I do, Specialist." Hints of anger and betrayal hung in his voice.

"She's taken a round to a carotid or vertebral artery." It was a logical guess based on the profuse bleeding. More viscous than normal blood. "She's going to bleed out no matter what we do." I matched his intense gaze. "You did more for her than anyone could ask." It was the truth. We weren't surgeons and didn't have the tools to probe into the wound and attempt to cauterize the severed artery, let alone clamp it off or sew it shut.

Then he nodded, trying not to tear up.

I took one of the gown strips and tied a makeshift sling to his rifle. "Best thing we can do to honor her is to escape and kill a few more Capital Galactic loyalists along the way. Now, hurry down." My voice was stern. I buckled on the remaining belt and I tied another makeshift sling for my MP rifle. "I'll watch for enemies and follow."

Gerard wiped blood from his hands onto his gown and whispered something to the dying woman. I joined him, placing a hand on her forehead. The swollen skin felt spongy.

"Lord, we ask that you watch over this woman, your child, as she returns to you. We pray that her suffering, inflicted by fellow humans, comes swiftly to an end, and that she soon basks in the light of your love."

Gerard nodded at my words, then slid on the boots and the belt, and bundled the other pair of boots inside the remnants of a gown. Since nobody else was visible in the shaft, they must've made it past the elevator. No shouts or screams, so they hadn't run into anybody. Or they were surprised and never got the chance.

No Capital Galactic loyalists appeared while I waited for Gerard to descend through the gravity plate. Feeling guilt at my calloused action, urging Gerard on and abandoning this woman, I again placed a hand on her disease-ridden forehead. The 23rd Psalm crossed my lips. Her breathing faltered as I spoke, and stopped by the time I finished.

Another victim of Capital Galactic.

We all stood atop the elevator except Marguerite. She lay with an ear pressed to the metal, listening. By the size of the elevator and shaft, my guess was that we were gathered atop a small freight elevator.

"We've been quiet as possible and she hasn't heard anything," Tahgs whispered to me and Gerard.

Simms eyed our rifles.

"Forced donation," I whispered.

Tahgs was already slipping on the spare boots. I unslung my shotgun with bayonet. "Give Marguerite the stun baton," I told Tahgs. "Gerard," I whispered, pointing to the emergency hatch, "you open that and I'll go down first."

Simms stepped between me and the hatch with his MP pistol held ready.

"Right," I said. "You're better armed for it." Maybe he saw my limp too. My leg no longer throbbed with pain but it ached.

Simms took Marguerite's stun baton, whispering, "A moment only."

The hatch wasn't locked. Within seconds Gerard had it open. Simms stuck the MP pistol in the elevator, searched and then dropped down. Immediately he reached up and discharged the stun baton against the surveillance camera.

Simms then examined the panel and interior before tossing the stun baton back up to me.

I handed the baton back to Marguerite. "Okay. Simms and me and Gerard are the best armed. We'll drop down, pry the doors open. Move out and then you two follow once it's clear. Cover our backs."

Tahgs glared at me, a look of hardened determination. "We're not staying up here. We're not." She held up a wrinkled hand, before I said anything. "How can we follow up if we're up here? Have your back if we're up here jumping down while you're somewhere out there?"

I tilted my head, assessing her weak argument. "Fair enough," I said loud enough so Simms could hear. Something had switched in Tahgs. Maybe it was being imprisoned here. Maybe it built upon her experience aboard the *Kalavar* and then on Tallavaster. Combat, war. Suffering. "Same plan but with you and her down there with us."

Inspired by Tahgs' new-found fierceness. Marguerite said, "If they get any of you, I'll pick up your gun and shoot any of the bastards that are left."

Once we were all down, Gerard used my bayonet to pry apart the inner doors, just a crack. Then, with deep a breath, he pulled them apart.

Before he began prying the second set of doors, Marguerite stepped forward and rested a hand on the muscled man's shoulder. She still had Heartwell's computer clip, although she or someone had touched the screen as it displayed a locked screen. "Let me listen first," she said.

Gerard stepped aside, allowing her to place an ear against the door. Elevator doors were thick and insulated. Even so, with eyes closed in concentration, she reported, "Shouts. Not right outside the door. I think."

"Good enough," I said. "Thanks."

Gerard cracked open the outer doors. Tahgs took the bayonet from him before he spread the doors open. I rushed out, ducking under his right arm. Simms went under his left.

We were in a large manufacturing sector. Crates, lifts, conveyers, and swivel-mounted robots of all sizes, with precision tools, welding and soldering heads. Yellow, orange, red colors and shining stainless steel dominated the landscape, all with the Capital Galactic Logo: CGIG emblazoned atop a glittering Milky Way. The fabrication and assembly equipment appeared to be constructing some sort of armored turret housings and internal control components, shut down mid job. The double height area was well lit with a combination of halogen and LED bulbs. While a manufacturing area was unexpected, what stood out even more were the scattered Chicher bodies in their combat harnesses, bloodied and broken. I could see six or seven from where I stood. A recent battle. The blood glistened, wet in pools and splatters. The scarred walls, floors, and equipment from laser fire and pockmarks and etched grooves from rifle fire and small grenade blasts attested to the fight's intensity. There weren't any human bodies, but blood aplenty, and boot prints from men passing through. Carried off the dead and wounded?

The stench of battle, blood and burned metal and spilled bowels. It affected everyone, but Marguerite more. She ran into the elevator struggling not to vomit.

The layout appeared organized in rows with only a few feet between floor level conveyer paths, metallic like old-time escalator steps, but moving flat. Circular rotation areas enabled 90 or even 180 degree changes of direction at intersections. Some equipment sat slightly askew, other machines and construction robots appeared undamaged.

Two women, an engineering tech and an information systems specialist based upon their red and sky blue coveralls, stood atop a squat robot, facing opposite the elevator. Their interest was focused in the direction echoing with random shouts accented by sporadic small arms fire. A hydraulic robotic arm half-elevated offered concealment. From their front, not from us.

Simms and I crept up on the two women, followed by Gerard and Tahgs. Simms signaled for me to take the information specialist on the right and for Gerard, along with him, to focus on the red clad engineer on the left. It made sense. Simms had a pistol which was less accurate than a rifle, and Gerard was an unknown. The big man might be competent with a rifle, or it might be his first time firing a gun, let alone at a human being. Simms knew of my gunfight under pressure when an assassin attempted to kill Representative Vorishnov on the Mavinrom Dock.

"On three," Simms whispered while taking aim using a two handed stance.

We were less than twenty yards away. Using a plastic crate to steady my aim, I went for the center of her back rather than risk a head shot. Even though MP rifles had less recoil than a .22 caliber rifle of equivalent size, the selected three shot burst would rise a little. If my aim was true and remained centered, the third round would strike the base of her neck.

Years ago, while training to be a Security Specialist, I'd never have considered shooting anyone in the back, especially a woman. War, treachery, and survival had overridden that naive stance. I've always believed in winning a fight by doing whatever was necessary. Shooting an unsuspecting enemy guard, a human, in the back now constituted what was necessary. Another blemish on my already tainted soul.

Another act that might allow other souls—loyal souls, innocent human souls—to survive. That's what I told myself.

A fraction of a second after Simms counted, "Three," my target fell forward, momentarily draped over the robotic arm before slipping to rest atop the robot's aluminum cover. She twitched twice. The engineering tech tumbled backwards, falling and striking the floor shoulder first. Before any of us could target her for a second burst, Tahgs raced past us and drove my shotgun's bayonet into her chest. It wasn't necessary. Simms had gotten her in the back of the skull. Gerard's single shot took her in the back of the knee.

We all followed Tahgs, taking cover behind the boxy robot and listened. She'd already removed the engineering tech's belt and holstered MP pistol. She drew and checked it before putting the belt around her gown. Then she picked up and slung my shotgun over her left shoulder. "I'll keep this for you," she said.

In the meantime, Simms climbed up to retrieve the info specialist's sidearm and belt. He bent low and offered it to Marguerite. "You know how to use this?" His voice was nearly gone.

She shook her head. I took the firearm. "Put the belt on over your gown," I said. "Better we have a couple of you not in uniform. New boots for you and Tahgs, if they fit better. Then I showed Marguerite the basics of her newly acquired MP pistol. The safety, how to shoot, and reminding her never to point at anyone she didn't intend to kill.

Gerard stood watch next to us while Simms observed from the dead women's perch. From what I could see the area had been policed of weapons and human casualties. The dead rat-like aliens had been left, but someone had picked up their small firearms.

I'd read about Chicher soldiers. They were tenacious and fearless, and had a tendency to selflessly throw themselves upon the enemy in support of fellow pack members. The normal result was that they either emerged victorious or utterly wiped out to the last man, or more accurately, pack member.

After I finished my firearm instruction and examining the nearest two dead Chicher, Simms signaled for me to join him. From the elevated vantage we spotted wounded men lying on the floor between robotic equipment. They were being bandaged and placed on tarps used as makeshift stretchers. They were being moved to a functioning conveyer which carried them to an elevator along a distant sidewall on the right. The conveyer was the only mechanical device working.

A short distance from where the emergency triage was happening, a trio of Chicher, bound at the ankles and wrists, with their prehensile tails duct-taped to their chests, were being interrogated. That consisted mainly of one man shouting at them. Nevertheless, the shouts were one in a choir. Orders given to med techs and the pleading cries of wounded men and women, and the sound of distant combat. Most of the Capital Galactic personnel were armed with MP pistols. That everyone was armed, even the Med Techs treating the wounded, said something about the renegade corporation's expectations and culture.

Several wide archways with doors elevated, opened to what appeared to be a balcony area. Waist-high guard rails overlooked enormous cranes and robotic welding arms and other manufacturing equipment. If the area we stood in put together dual and tri-beam pulse lasers for shuttles, out there must be where Capital Galactic was building warship-sized laser turrets.

Doing so broke more laws than I could count but, since they'd turned on humanity and sided with the Crax, what did that matter?

"Rear area," I said in a low voice to Simms. "We'll approach silently, strike fast, drive through. Free those three Chicher and any others along the way. If they're taking prisoners, the loyalists must be holding, and maybe advancing against the boarders."

Simms nodded in agreement.

"Oh," I said. "Do you recall your .22 caliber pistol, the antique with rosewood grips?"

He smiled. "I do."

I grinned back. "It's still knocking around. Intel Agent Guymin or Vingee have it. It was with my gear on our shuttle, before I got separated from them." I wasn't sure why I wanted to share that. I didn't want to mention it to him while we were in the cell together, not sure how Capital Galactic could use the information. Maybe I wanted him to know that I was a man of my word. He'd lent it to me while we were on the *Pars Griffin*, while I was wounded and dying. Just before he was wounded and subsequently captured. I'd promised to return it to him.

He shook his head, amused. "Appreciate," he rasped.

It was an odd time to bring up something so trivial. Was I subconsciously trying to set the record straight, take care of obligations before I died? Something likely to happen. But it'd been that way for a long time.

We climbed down. I continued giving Simms my assessment. "If they repel the incursion, we're stuck."

I told Tahgs, Gerard and Marguerite what Simms and I saw and my assessment, and the plan. Simms again nodded in agreement.

"Any of us go down," I said, "press on. If we break the line from behind, it'll help the Chicher pour through, capture this ship. It's our best chance to escape, and the best chance for any of us that fall wounded."

"They're aliens," Gerard said. "I've seen vids of them before. Can hardly tell one from another. They don't dress in colors and use insignias like we do. Won't we just be humans to them?"

"They'll know me," I said. "At least if they get the chance to smell me."

Marguerite tilted her head. Her nostrils flared as she breathed in deeply. "If you say so, Specialist."

Tahgs stepped between me and Marguerite. "If he says so, it's true," she said, her lip curled.

Before any bad blood could form, I said, "Stay quiet until we get close. Then do as I direct, what Simms signals, or whatever you feel is best." I checked my rifle, making sure it was set on three-round bursts. "*Nemo me impune lacessit.*"

Gerard asked, "What's that mean?"

"I'll tell you when this is over."

CHAPTER 45

The three Chicher prisoners were in sight. We hunkered down behind a row of yellow crates. We viewed the interrogation framed between a multi-armed riveting robot and a wheeled bin filled with rows of rectangular steel panels.

A pudgy, puffy-eyed Capital Galactic executive spoke into a computer clip, allowing it to translate. "How many Chicher troops make up the second wave of your assault force?" Anger and contempt dripped from his shouted words. "Answer now or your pack member dies." The man's soft hands and features shouted 'arrogant executive.'

Next to him a security specialist, an S2 supervisor according to the patch above her chest pocket, held a medium duty laser rifle. While the executive's words emanated from the computer clip in chattering and squeaks, the Chicher language, the S2 leveled her rifle at the Chicher on the right, smaller and more agitated than the others.

"Now," I ordered, squeezing off a headshot at the S2. Guessing her jacket and smooth coveralls might have built-in body armor, it was the best choice. She should've been wearing her riot helmet instead of allowing the executive's assistant to hold it. The assistant, a diminutive woman with dark hair covering half her face, looked overwhelmed, like she wanted to drop the helmet and run away. She would've lived longer if she had.

Tahgs and I shared the same target. Simms and Marguerite had the executive, and Gerard, the assistant. The S2 staggered for two steps before dropping, the top of her skull shattered in a spray of blood. At least one of Tahgs' rounds took her in the torso, but didn't appear to penetrate.

I didn't focus on that. The executive was on the ground, but Gerard had missed the assistant. Simms and I brought her down before her shock voiced itself as a scream.

Tahgs clambered over the crates, racing for the Chicher. She'd discarded my shotgun but carried my bayonet. I was right behind her with Simms on my heels. I didn't look back to see if the other two followed.

I took up position to the Chicher captives' rear, partially concealed by the wheeled bin. Down the aisle, a number of the loyalists looked our way. I targeted with small bursts, a med tech looking up from patching up wounded guards, then a security specialist, and an information specialist and computer technician carrying the wounded our direction, toward the elevator located a hundred yards behind me. Simms faced the other direction. Sharp snaps sounded as he let loose with his MP pistol.

Tahgs sliced through the plastic ties holding the nearest Chicher. She shoved her MP pistol into the alien's hands and started freeing the next one. Shouts and warnings rang out, causing all those working along the wide conveyer to duck, taking cover between the parts bins, robots, and other machinery. Within five seconds, everyone able to move was out of sight. No more easy targets, except those unconscious or on the floor, unable to move.

Pressing ahead, firing at any signs of movement, I urged everyone, "Go now."

We had to make it to the balcony and beyond before fright and shock wore off the nearby loyalists and they got organized.

The second Chicher was up, grabbing the fallen laser rifle. It was lighter than an MP rifle. Still, the three-foot alien looked like a seven year-old toting his father's gun in a loping bipedal gait.

"Hurry, Tahgs," I urged, firing off a couple short bursts. Fortunately MP rifles carried over a hundred rounds.

"I am, Keesay." She moved from the Chicher's back to the front, working on his legs while the Chicher tore at the duct tape holding his tail against his chest. "Go. We'll catch up in a second."

Simms led Marguerite and Gerard through the equipment, toward the balcony. Someone opened up on us. One round ricocheted off the floor and glanced off my shin. It caused me to lose my balance while returning fire. Fortunately the floor had absorbed most of its momentum. Before the last Chicher was able to get to his feet, he took a round to the back of the head. The brown-furred alien slumped to the floor, blood oozing from the fatal wound.

"Dammit," Tahgs shouted, firing off unaimed MP pistol rounds. She didn't stay put, however, showing once again that her strength and agility didn't match her aged appearance. I struggled to keep up.

I followed her between a dual-beam laser housing under construction and a deactivated eight-wheeled dolly-bot hauling a rusting bin filled with scrap metal. A flash of laser fire struck a metal strut over my head as we ran. MP rounds *cracked* and *clanged* off a large drill press behind us. I didn't bother returning fire. There were dozens more of them than us, each one armed. Putting more machines and metal between us and them meant survival, at least for a few more minutes.

Tahgs and I made it through the main entryway to the balcony. Wheeled and spot-welded into place along the railing, a half-inch steel plate with crude firing slits cut into it offered Simms and Gerard protection. They and one Chicher fired through the slits, down at the enemy below. Simms and Gerard with MP rifles. The Chicher stood upon two dead bodies to gain the necessary angle with his laser rifle.

Marguerite almost shot Janice with her MP pistol, but the second Chicher, squealed and chattered, causing the frazzled woman to pull up instead. From behind the steel barrier, the rat-alien then shoved a third bleeding body under the balcony's bottom rail. It crashed onto debris scattered across the floor below.

I pulled Tahgs down to the floor an instant before laser and MP fire whizzed past, some impacting next to and above the doorway.

The setup reminded me of the *Iron Oxen*'s hold where we overlooked the staged breaching pods. Instead of pods, below stood huge cranes and robotic construction equipment organized in diamond patterns, with scattered forklifts and massive storage bins.

Blood and fallen bodies covered the floor and equipment, like a violent game of capture the flag was underway. It was apparent both sides had surged and retreated more than once. Neither side appeared to have more than small arms. Superior tactics must've supported the Chicher forces, but wasn't enough against Capital Galactic's overwhelming numbers.

That was, until Simms and his group opened up. Where the Chicher had been driven back into a corner covering less than a quarter of the cavernous construction area below, the unexpected fire support from behind broke Capital Galactic's advance. The remaining Chicher surged forward to sunder the line.

Among the rats I spotted a braided red head in orange and a tall woman in a quasi-gray uniform. "Watch where you shoot," I shouted over my shoulder towards Simms. "Agents Guymin and Vingee are down there with the Chicher." At the same time I turned and fired from my prone position, clipping the shoulder of the first pursuer trying to follow us onto the balcony. I didn't see Guymin but Simms would know him. I didn't think he'd know who McAllister was.

"We know that," Gerard shouted, pulling a rearming tube from the barrel of his gun and securing another from one of the fallen men. "You just keep shooting at them your direction."

Gerard didn't know Vingee and Guymin, did he? Humans among the Chicher was probably evidence enough. In any case, we couldn't communicate with them. The Capital Galactic loyalists below would certainly be able to communicate with those above, and in the rest of the ship. Coordinate despite the pitch battle going on down there.

Tahgs was lying next to me, pressed against the wall and ready to shoot her pistol. I told her, "McAllister's down there." I didn't know the extent of the two women's relationship, but they'd served aboard the *Kalavar*, and were in contact on Tallavaster, prior to the invasion.

"Really?"

"What I really hope is that they don't have any grenades." With the shouting and ring of Chicher small arms fire, like .22 caliber gunfire, along with the ever present claxon, I wasn't worried about anyone overhearing our conversation.

Her eyes went wide. "That's for sure."

"Wish they hadn't shoved that body off the balcony," I said. "Could've used it for cover."

"Right," she said, pushing sweaty strands of gray hair from her face.

Around the corner, they were formulating a plan of action. There were two open archways: the near one and the second about twenty-five yards further down. And equipment they could push ahead of them for protection, both from us and gunfire from below. We'd be wide open. Couldn't let that happen.

"Trade weapons," I said, "Quick."

"Bayonet too?"

"Why not," I said, preparing for a charge back into the construction area.

"Thanks, Kra, for coming for me."

"Later," I said, offering her a wink. "If I shout *Kalavar*, slow count to ten. Only then come running."

"Want me to come with you now?"

I shook my head. "I got this." With that, I raced forward, hunched low with pistol and bayonet held ready.

CHAPTER 46

I ran, shooting at anything that didn't resemble a machine. A woman standing with her back to the opening went down with one of my MP rounds in her throat. Two maintenance techs standing with partial cover behind an automated drill press went down next. One struck in the shoulder, the other in the forehead.

I dove between the drill press and a stack of metal plates. Flashes zipped by and snapping MP fire struck near where I crouched. Rounds continued to bounce and ricochet off the plates and drill press. I drove my bayonet in to the chest of the wounded maintenance tech trying to get to his feet. In his stunned condition, he never saw it coming. The other tech on the floor, I slit his throat, to be sure. After slipping my bloody bayonet into my belt, I picked up one of the dead men's MP pistols and crawled forward, under and between machinery.

They must've lost sight of me because the *snap* of MP rounds and the *cracks* and *clangs* as they struck metal ceased.

The dead maintenance techs had been directing a dolly-bot with a steel sheet attached toward the balcony. When their remote was dropped, the bot stopped.

I popped up and fired both pistols in several directions. My shots weren't aimed but they caused the engineering and med techs to duck for cover. That gave me a chance to winnow my way back toward the drill press. Doubling back might temporarily fool those gunning for me. Who'd choose to hunker down between a pair of dead bodies?

There was no way I could take out the two or three dozen loyalists scattered around me. I was playing for time. Enough time for the Chicher commandos and McAllister to break through. I exchanged fire against the semi-circle that closed in on me. None of them were marksmen. Still, a couple of ricochets struck home. None penetrated my body armor. In the meantime, I only wounded two. My luck was bound to run out.

I missed the comforting grip and recoil of my single-action revolver and the scattering blasts of buckshot my shotgun threw. The sounds of combat beyond the balcony continued, giving me a wistful sliver of hope.

One of my pistols *clicked* empty, confirmed by the pale arming light that had shifted to red. I picked up another pistol lying next to one of the dead maintenance techs. His body had taken a few stray rounds deflected off the floor and stack of steel plates. Hunkering down between a pair of dead bodies wasn't the worst idea I'd ever had.

I'd probably feel remorse for that, and the callused way I'd gunned down the med techs and even some of the wounded in the triage area. If remorse were to have a chance of forming, I had to survive.

Crouched low, I prepared to lay down a spray of fire and return to my previous position.

Snaps of MP fire emerged from the balcony.

It was Tahgs lying prone, taking aimed shots. I saw only her MP rifle's muzzle, meaning she was using the wall for cover. It limited her range of targets, but freed me up to concentrate on only two-thirds of the semi-circle, and forced the untrained attackers to consider another threat.

If the Chicher offensive faltered I'd shift to my backup plan. Make a break for the elevator used to carry away the wounded. Do as much damage as possible before they brought me down.

Narrowing my scope of fire to a 120 degree arc helped, plus watching along the entrances to the balcony. Those opposing me weren't interested in unduly risking their lives, and they lacked any form of effective leadership. They appeared content to keep me pinned down and hope for a lucky shot.

Popping up and shooting between equipment, moving again, and placing my back to a CNC lathe, I reviewed the layout and pieced together a route to the elevator.

The battle's tenor beyond the balcony changed, faltering to near silence. Shouts of "I give up" and "We surrender" rose.

"You're all warp-screwed now," I shouted. "If you can't take out one half-starved prisoner, what chance do you have against a company of Chicher commandos?"

While crawling to reposition and avoid becoming a target for accurate gunfire that my prolonged taunt offered, I was surprised how effective my ploy had been. Tahgs confirmed the movement spotted between the machines and equipment, shouting, "They're running, Kra!"

"Stay down," I warned, doubling back. "Might be a few stubborn ones."

I was right. Tahgs and I exchanged gunfire with four committed loyalists until a squad of Chicher entered the upper manufacturing area.

The few remaining loyalists fled and I set my MP pistols down, saying, "Don't shoot. We're on the same side."

One of the commandos came up to me, a tan-furred male with scattered bits of black. After sniffing me while two of his company leveled their automatic rifles, the leader bowed his head once and flicked his prehensile tail affixed with a tri-bladed knife to the left. He chattered something to his fellow commandos and they moved past.

"Isn't hard for one Relic to recognize another, Keesay." It was McAllister, lugging a satchel and one of the Chicher sub machine guns. It looked like a toy in her hands. "A prison guard uniform? Moved up from Security Specialist I see."

Her chiding words didn't match the purpose showing in her face. The trio of Chicher following her appeared agitated beyond measure.

I stood, hunched to keep the stack of steel plates between me and any possible stray rounds, while trying to figure a way to slide the MP pistols into my belt. "Didn't think I'd ever be saying this, McAllister. I'm really happy to see you."

"Don't put your guns away yet, Relic. Soon as your Intel buddies wrap up their reunion, we've got to get off this modular dock."

Modular dock. That answered a few questions. "Where's Tahgs?" I asked.

McAllister came up next to me, hunched down for cover as well. "Who?"

"Janice Tahgs," I said. "She was on the balcony, providing me cover fire."

A look of confusion, followed by surprised recognition crossed McAllister's face. "With the MP rifle?" she asked.

I didn't have to say yes, or even nod.

"Damn," McAllister cursed. "What the hell did those Capital Galactic bastards do to her?"

CHAPTER 47

The use of modular docks established a more rapid system for humanity's expansion into the galaxy. A series of specially designed ships travel to a destination. Upon arrival, each ship's aft thrust engine section and forward cascading engine compartment detach from the vessel's central hull section. Engineers and construction-bots weld center sections together, forming a functioning dock. The forward and aft engine sections then unite for a return trip.

The modular docks require higher degrees of maintenance and the return trips are difficult on crews as ship facilities are limited. It's the price humanity has chosen to endure for the ability to swiftly establish distant footholds. It was also the price Capital Galactic chose to accept when stationing a modular dock for the purpose of manufacturing external ship weapons systems.

Or those were my thoughts when McAllister told me what the imprisoning ship actually was. She was too busy to say much more, like how they'd found me—or located the prison that held Deputy Director Simms, and me, and Tahgs. I think the fact McAllister didn't recognize Janice embarrassed the engineer, and reopened a form of devastation that tore at Janice's heart. The genetic manipulation performed on Janice, Marguerite, and Gerard, and the woman Gerard carried until her death, added another voice to McAllister's choir of anger directed at Capital Galactic and their Crax allies, or overlords.

McAllister was kneeling with her computer on the floor. She'd hardwired it to Heartwell's. Based on her skills, she'd have access to his files within minutes. I stood behind the Senior Engineer with my arm around Janice, trying to comfort her while listening to the Chicher commando outline some sort of plan to his subordinate pack members, and to Agents Guymin, and probably McAllister, if she was listening. The Chicher leader wore a translator affixed to his harness, but it was slow, and was set only to listen and translate anything Guymin might say. My guess was that Intelligence provided their agents, and probably McAllister, with a translation device of some sort, maybe even software incorporated into their receiving ear implants.

Agent Vingee was there, across from us, whispering to Deputy Director Simms, and offering him water from a medical canteen. The salve spread across Vingee's burned bicep glistened under the array of lights. Other than a hurried "Glad you made it" from her and a heartfelt smile and brief handshake from Guymin, I was quickly forgotten, the recovery of Deputy Director Simms being their primary mission. Early in the battle, Capital Galactic had employed heavy lasers and 40mm grenade launchers, but in severely limited numbers and supply. It was sufficient to wipe out one of the two Chicher companies within minutes after boarding.

Vingee was lucky. Another quarter of an inch and her salve-covered arm would've been charbroiled, despite her Intel-supplied body armor. I'd suffered laser burns, and knew the pain she was enduring.

Gerard and Marguerite sat huddled between a dolly-bot and a robotic welder. Both were exhausted, with a Chicher medic providing them water and some sort of energy paste. I held the same in my left hand. It looked and smelled a lot like peanut butter in a collapsible dish.

Janice's body shook as she sobbed. Exactly what caused her to break down, I could only guess. An aftereffect of coming off an adrenaline rush coupled with surviving a hopeless predicament played a part. McAllister's inability to recognize Tahgs reminded the Information Specialist of the cruel damage Heartwell had inflicted upon her once youthful appearance.

Gray hair, wrinkled, liver-spotted skin. Tahgs retained muscle tone beneath what was out of line with the centenarian she resembled. Her internal organs or at least her respiratory and circulatory systems, and her reflexes responded as a woman still in her youthful prime.

My physical condition was nothing to brag about. Genetically damaged as Tahgs was, her stamina outshined mine.

All but five of the Chicher commandos had spread out around us, what was left of them. Fewer than fifty, and ten of those injured to some degree or another. An interesting use for their battle harnesses was the ability to attach a wounded pack member to their back. It slowed the healthy combatant down, but allowed the carrier to move, and fight in a limited fashion.

"Got access," McAllister hissed with enthusiasm and began calling up dock diagrams on one part of the screen, color coding them, and attaching relevant security video in some instances. Modular docks weren't standard construction like many interstellar vessels. Within reasonable parameters, each section could be modified to meet individual requirements. She showed the screen and information to the Chicher and Guymin.

Tahgs wiped her nose on her sleeve and asked, "Want to bet it was McAllister who disabled the prison locks?"

"Special Agent Guymin isn't a slouch when it comes to hacking systems," I replied. Squeezing her shoulder, I added, "You're probably right." I offered her what was left of my Chicher food. "Not bad. Smells like peanut butter but tastes like wheat paste with a touch of sulfur."

She crinkled her nose.

"Not bad as you might think, Janice. Reminds me of the 'field rations' we shared on Tallavaster, minus the sorghum syrup."

She smiled at the memory. A brief, quiet meal shared in my bunker in the trench line.

"It's making me feel like I might have a second wind," I said. "Both the food and the memory."

She took the Chicher rations. "We're not out of this yet."

"No," I said, trying to catch a little of what Guymin and the Chicher leader were planning. "No, we're not."

She saw my distraction and impatience. I wanted to move. She knew as well that time was against us. She also recognized the situation was dire, and we needed a plan, and that our participating in its formation wasn't in the cards.

She turned toward me, capturing my eyes in her fading purple ones, their intensity outshining the sagging eyelids and creasing crow's feet framing them. "I kept telling myself you'd come. Through it all. Then, when I saw you, chained up...at the warden's mercy." She grimaced. "Mercy—something he never had..."

I interrupted her as she took a breath. "Janice, I'm glad I came. Found you. But I'm not a knight in shining armor. I'm just a Relic. A stubborn and angry one."

"Doesn't matter, Kra, what you think I think." She looked at the Chicher commandos around us, and the blood and bodies. "Look at where we are. What's happened. We might be dead ten minutes from now, but I wanted to thank you for saving me...again. You killed those Crax on the *Kalavar*. Fought against that armored one even when Chief Brold ordered you not to. I can only imagine what part you played in forcing their retreat on Tallavaster. And then you came here, where I was, and because I needed you."

What could I say? She wasn't the main reason I came. Being a prisoner for years, she had no idea of my part in bringing Capital Galactic down, and the wrath the loyalists intended for me. All of that didn't matter. I shrugged. "Janice, as long as I'm drawing breath, Capital Galactic, and the Crax, can expect to pay."

She smiled deeply and we embraced. "Maybe not in the same way," she whispered, "but they can expect the same from me."

She wasn't the same person I'd met upon boarding the *Kalavar*. A new-found determination, even in the face of terrible odds had grown, despite Heartwell's bid to break her spirit.

"Hey, knight and damsel," McAllister said. "In ten minutes they'll override my infiltration program. When they manage that, we don't want to be here."

We split up into two groups. The objectives being the modular dock's transport, its two detachable components: aft thrust engine section and forward cascading engine compartment. Both were currently attached to the central of three modular sections. The transport's thrust engines weren't powerful enough to move all three dock modules with any efficiency, and the cascading atomic engine of the forward section wouldn't be able to generate a sufficient antigravity field, let alone initiate condensed space travel for such a large midsection.

I was part of McAllister's cohort, along with, Tahgs, Gerard, Marguerite, and fifteen Chicher commandos, five of them wounded with three attached to bearers, and two of the wounded secured to Gerard's back. Wounded Chicher would fare better if in contact with a pack member, but having unencumbered fighters outweighed this temporary concern.

Our objective was to capture the modular transport's forward section, detach it and move to rendezvous with the rear section. Guymin, Vingee, and Simms, along with the Chicher commando leader and the rest of his pack, were to capture the rear thrust section.

Guymin and Vingee got Chicher escorts as they had to travel farther and faced greater obstacles. Plus, almost any competent pilot could handle the rear thrust section, which was basically a small living area attached to four massive thrust engines along with their accompanying metallic hydrogen fuel tanks.

McAllister was a Senior Engineer and an expert in numerous areas, including cascading atomic engines. One of the Chicher commandos had rudimentary knowledge. A Relic Tech with rudimentary knowledge of what is, in essence, an Intermediate Tech component of space travel? Being a genius, McAllister probably knew as much as the Chicher Engineering Tech trainee upon her graduation from grammar school.

The other advantage McAllister's group had was her computer expertise. She'd mapped a route for Guymin's team, but CGIG units were on the move and situations changed. Vingee was more than competent once McAllister had gotten her into the dock's system. McAllister, however, was better, hands down.

Four Chicher commandos were in the lead. I ran on McAllister's right and Tahgs kept pace on her left. I had my MP rifle and McAllister had picked up a medium duty laser carbine. We each carried two holstered MP pistols scavenged from fallen enemies. Behind us were the three Chicher carrying a wounded pack member each, followed by Gerard and Marguerite. He had an MP rifle and she carried an MP pistol. An unburdened Chicher trio brought up our rear.

McAllister spoke as we jogged, glancing at her computer. "They just sealed off the area we left, Keesay. Decompression initiated."

"Didn't even bother to check for any survivors?"

"I looped some surveillance," she replied with a wicked grin. "Apparently worked and they thought we were still there organizing our breakout."

She checked the screen and spoke into her collar to the lead Chicher. "Left up here, then down the access ladder." The leader's translator did its job and he chattered instructions to his team.

To me and Tahgs, McAllister said, "We're in the Capella system. This particular area was a scrap metal navigational hazard even before we arrived."

"Debris from multiple engagements during the Silicate War," I said. "Where the *Iron Armadillo* carved its way into history."

McAllister rolled her eyes and checked her computer clip's screen.

The *Armadillo* was a first series intragalactic military scout. Twenty-five years ago it was considered a very fast ship. It still would be by current I-Tech standards with a sub-condensed space speed of .38 percent the speed of light. It was the first vessel designed and built with direct Umbelgarri assistance and carried its own cascading atomic engine for initiating condensed space travel.

The *Armadillo* first saw action late in the Silicate War, eight years after the Umbelgarri recruited humans in what was termed the Carbon Cause. She was one of the first human vessels sent into action against the Shards without Umbelgarri or other allied support. Until that time, humanity had been restricted to a very miniscule corner of the Milky Way because humans were incapable of condensing space. Fortunately or unfortunately, depending on who is asked, the Umbelgarri contacted Earth through its Mars Colony and sponsored mankind into Interstellar Society.

Initially mankind was recruited for ground combat with human ships limited to rear echelon support. Humanity's violent history ever honed its combat resourcefulness, and the Umbelgarri directed that against the Shards. Human ships, like the Colonial Marines, bristled with effective weaponry. The Umbelgarri helped humans design the first series scout to add speed and mobility to humanity's arsenal.

After detecting a Silicate fleet exiting a wormhole near the double star Capella, the *Armadillo* outfought two Shard frigates, destroying one, damaging and outrunning the second. The *Armadillo* escaped to warn a mixed Umbelgarri-Felgan fleet. The heroic action stalled a Silicate flanking maneuver. It also earned respect among several alien races.

The combat damage sustained necessitated emergency patching over forty percent of the *Armadillo*'s hull. The result wasn't pretty, with the dockworkers dubbing the hastily repaired ship the *Iron Armadillo*. The name stuck.

That wasn't the only battle fought around the double star Capella. Two others had been fought there. The second engagement sent a combined fleet to disrupt development of a Shard supply depot. The third battle started with a combined fleet surprising and destroying a small Shard patrol. Named Poseidon's Trident, at least by human admirals, each race involved in the action was symbolized by one of the trident's tines. It was also the place the attack fleet waited for less than a day to enact its primary mission. The famed military strategist Maximar Drizdon Sr. had anticipated a Shard created wormhole's formation. That allowed the staged Umbelgarri task force, supported by human and Felgan war and supply ships, to overwhelm the Shards as they exited the wormhole, and then enter the intergalactic conduit before it closed.

Exactly what happened on the other end, where the Umbelgarri-Felgan-Human attack fleet appeared, thought to be the Andromeda Galaxy, remains unknown. It's believed the ships participating in Poseidon's Trident survived the transit and took the fight to an unprepared enemy. What's known for sure? From the date of the combined fleet's departure, moving forward, no created wormholes have been detected and Shard reinforcements ceased. That allowed the carbon-based races to get the upper hand and ultimately defeat the silicon-based invaders.

The key had been Dr. Drizdon's accurate prediction of the wormhole's appearance, the Shards' mode of travel between galaxies. No known races hailing from the Milky Way have either the knowledge to create or the technological prowess to harness the power necessary for a wormhole's formation, both stable and large enough for intergalactic travel.

McAllister tapped a few places on her screen, altering the angle of security cameras apparently observing our movement.

"They already think we're two decks below our current position," McAllister said. "We'll turn left up here. They'll see us turning right." With that, she spoke orders to the lead Chicher commando through her collar mic. "Left ahead, then straight. Almost there."

I was still curious, but also getting winded. With the Chicher leading, I could adequately watch for an ambush while listening to McAllister. Taking a breath I realized I wasn't thinking straight. Insignificant as it was, her voice added to our tromping boots and the rattling equipment attached to the Chicher harnesses as they scampered along on all fours. And adequately watching for an ambush?

I gripped my MP rifle and began closer observation of the narrow corridor we traversed. Ahead we were to turn left, into a wider corridor. With a tap on her screen, ahead of us panels to ladder accesses slid closed, ensuring our safety.

McAllister slowed and worked her screen. "The other team blew through a random patrol. I wasn't able to stop the position report, only truncate it."

"Bad news for them," Gerard said, working hard to keep pace.

"Lethal news for us if they don't make it," McAllister said. "Even with a cascading atomic engine, we won't get anywhere fast with a pair of class three auxiliary thrust engines." She focused on her computer readouts again. "That's if we manage to outrun the remaining corporate fighters, and the armed freighters chasing down what's left of the Chicher battlewagon and surviving Felgan destroyer."

"Get down and behind me," I ordered McAllister while stepping in front of her. "Nobody but you knows how to operate a cascading atomic engine."

The Chicher commandos pressed forward, two of them going down to laser blasts. Tahgs and I added our fire down the wide corridor. It led to the hatch connecting the forward section of the modular transport to the dock.

The corridor was oval shaped, wider than it was tall with a platform floor and wide conduits running beneath it, and in conduit bundles along the concave sidewalls. What wasn't covered by the multicolored and labeled conduits was metallic and polished to a sheen. A thirty-yard run without cover. The two male guards must've expected us. They had partial cover near the hatch.

We had to rush. Dock Security must've figured out McAllister's electronic ruse. She reported thirty armed and angry loyalists closing in, less than two minutes away.

Our fire kept the two guards ducking and flinching, and from taking careful aim. That didn't matter to them. They knew help was on the way.

The Chicher advance faltered as another two went down. The rest of our lead team took up positions beneath two conduit bundles running along the walls and opened fire.

I dropped my MP rifle and picked up one of the fallen Chicher. He'd taken a blast through the eye, cooking his brain. Smoke rose from the singed fur and charred flesh. Holding the rat-alien in front of me like a shield, I charged forward, yelling incoherently. Words didn't matter. Closing the remaining twenty yards did.

Luckily I'd gripped his harness by the bottom. That meant the limp tail didn't drag along the floor as I pounded forward. The body offered me about sixty percent cover. I hoped none of the Chicher commandos took exception to my tactic and shot me in the back, which was one hundred percent vulnerable—except for the built-in body armor. If they wanted to avenge the crude use of their fallen pack member, they'd nail me in the back of the head.

Pretty morbid thoughts as I closed.

One laser blast caught the top of my right shoulder, causing my aim to stray off target. My Chicher shield absorbed three shots, turning into flash-broiled meat in the process. I shoved the alien into the face of one guard while I sent two MP pistol rounds into the panicked face of the other.

A Chicher commando that must've been hot on my heels shot past me and brought down the guard trying to shove back against the singeing hot flesh. That was the difference between a light and medium duty laser. A heavy duty one would've burned through to me by the second shot, if I were lucky. Those were used to take down Gar Crax shields.

A *thunk* sounded above the dying guard's screams, silenced when the commando slit his throat. McAllister had worked her computer magic. The reinforced steel hatch swung open.

Two more Chicher commandos scampered past me, into the ship. The sound of their gunfire and snap of MP rounds said we weren't home free, yet. I followed them in, keeping low.

Tahgs was right on my heels. "I'm behind you."

"Be sure of your target," I warned over my shoulder.

"Right," she agreed, but it didn't matter. The instant everyone still alive was through the hatch, McAllister closed it and overrode the local security network and ordered the dock's clamps to release the forward section of the modular transport. It was a good thing she wasn't on Capital Galactic's side.

The CGIG pilot and engineer, unconscious and bleeding out, were the only two on board. The Chicher ahead of us took them down within ten seconds of the hatch closing. We didn't know that until several minutes of searching. I counted only four healthy Chicher, two of them burdened with a wounded pack member. Gerard and his two didn't make it, but Marguerite had. She stood, her back to everyone, staring at the closed hatch.

McAllister shouted. "Team!"

Everyone looked her way. She pointed to me. "Keesay, I've got to crash start the cascading atomic engine. I want you to man the pulse laser above the cockpit, after you get everyone organized." She took a Chicher with her, probably the Apprentice Engineering Tech.

I'd read about the modular dock project. The transport ship was a modified interstellar tug, stripped down to support a skeleton crew with minimal facilities. Three decks, with the pilot compartment top and up front with fuel and storage behind. The mid deck where we'd entered had three compartments. One for cold sleep, a common room for dining and recreation, and an office area. The bottom deck housed the cascading atomic engine in the bulbous chin, maintenance and machining equipment behind that, and the auxiliary thrust engines aft.

"Tahgs," I said, "help the Chicher unbind from their wounded."

"You," I continued, snapping my finger and pointing at one of the Chichers. Then I pointed to at the silver disk on his harness.

He spun the plastic knob, switching it on. From experience, I knew it'd take a moment to warm up. It reminded me how much it would've helped to have my old com-set.

Marguerite hadn't moved from her spot. I strode up to her. "I'm sorry about Gerard."

She stared down at me, eyes wide and brimming with tears. "His face…" she whispered shakily. "It's gone."

"Piloting," I said, taking her hand and trying to gauge how hard to press her. We were floating away from Capital Galactic's modular dock. We needed to get underway. Join up with Guymin and his team aboard the drive half of the transport. Any moment, the ships chasing the Felgan and Chicher vessels would be receiving a recall order to take care of us.

Gerard had been slated as our primary pilot, experienced with intrasolar mass transit as a ferry pilot. We'd lost the ranking pack member who'd served several seasons as a midget frigate pilot, an oversized twin-boomed fighter. While we were deciding how to divide our forces, Marguerite claimed experience piloting her personal intrasolar yacht.

I pulled Marguerite across the room, toward the ladder leading to the pilot's cockpit. "We're counting on you."

Marguerite's nostrils flared and she resisted, twisting her arm.

Tahgs joined us. She replaced my grip with her gentle hands. "She and I will take care of it, Kra." A reassuring smile spread across her wrinkled face. "Come on, Marguerite, I'll copilot, okay?"

A hum ran through the ship, a steady vibration penetrating the soles of my appropriated boots. The Chicher exchanged looks and chittered. They noticed it, too.

I pointed to the one with the translator. He'd just plugged in the wire and stuck in the earbud. I'd find out if they had a problem with me using one of their fallen pack members as a shield. "You, select a pack member to care for your wounded." I chose my words carefully, knowing complex translations confused the inexperienced. "The other will have to monitor the thrust engines, located aft, bottom of this ship. Engineer McAllister will control them through forward engineering."

I waited for the device to translate. When the alien nodded once, I continued, being direct and concise. "You, with the translation disk, help your pack member assigned to the auxiliary thrust engines establish radio communication with the Engineer. Then act as runner of messages for Engineer McAllister. I will be manning the pulse lasers above the pilot compartment."

The Chicher bowed once, his tail twitching to the left twice. "I hear and track your path, Pollinated Pack Member." Before I could say anything else he turned and scampered over to the other Chicher and began issuing orders.

Rather than wait to see what they did, I made my way to the ladder and climbed up to the pilot station. There, Marguerite and Tahgs were strapped into their seats and working through the startup sequence. They wore headsets plugged into the flight data console. Tahgs was reading from a screen displayed checklist, and Marguerite verified or enacted a system as directed, repeating the directive when finished. Their voices were hurried and stressed.

A narrow aluminum ladder bolted to the compartment's wall behind the copilot's seat led to a circular deck hatch, armored and reinforced. I climbed up and in, noting the modular housing's minimal safety features encompassing the dual-beam pulse laser. The guns appeared to have their own bank of batteries for a backup power source. The close proximity to the pilot's controls enabled the guns' targeting and tracking to tie into the ship's sensors with minimal wiring. The slapped-on afterthought that the pulse laser compartment was, if it took a direct hit, it'd shear away. Cheap and expendable, taking the turret gunner with it.

Buckling into the gunner seat, I then switched on the power. It was a standard setup, designed for minimal retraining from one ship's or shuttle's pulse laser to another, especially as pulse laser gunner was a secondary or even tertiary assigned duty. I had some training and several instances of combat experience with a dual-beam pulse laser.

I adjusted my seating and controls before spotting a compartment that held my own headset. Taking the headset, I closed my bayonet in the compartment. Keeping it without a scabbard was going to be a problem, especially if something happened. Sharp blades and zero gravity, or tumbling about didn't mix. With the headset slipped on and plugged in, I selected Internal 1 as the primary channel.

McAllister was giving Tahgs directions. Searching for CGIG communications could wait. Besides, McAllister or Tahgs would be more efficient plugging in to what the enemy was up to.

"Tahgs, don't fire up the thrust engines yet," McAllister ordered.

I looked back down through the hatch to see if Marguerite was still there. She was.

"They just rearmed and launched twelve fighters ten minutes ago," McAllister continued. "Six of those twelve are patrolling what's left of their outpost. The others are racing off to chase the Chicher battlewagon and Felgan destroyer. Give them a few minutes and they'll be too distant to be an immediate concern. They just started refueling and rearming a squadron on the converted escort carrier. No sense encouraging them to take additional notice of us and launch."

After a pause, the Senior Engineer said, "Keesay, I see you're online. Don't power up targeting sensors, or even rotate the guns. The dock is sending out confused reports. What they're able to sort out is being routed through the carrier to the fighters, slowing their potential response."

"Won't their sensors pick up the cascading atomic engine's buildup?"

"That's why the local six are coming to investigate. It should make you feel important to know you're our only defense, Relic."

"So keeping our tail near to the freighter for as long as possible is important," I confirmed, more to clarify for Tahgs and Marguerite than myself.

"A garbage scow's faster and more maneuverable than us." Mild disgust echoed in McAllister's voice.

"Sooo, we won't be outrunning them?" I said, laying on a little sarcasm.

"Six minutes, Keesay. Just be ready to shoot the bastards when I tell you."

"Understood, Senior Engineer."

Ignoring the chatter between McAllister and Tahgs, I examined the setup. One-hundred-fifty-degree range of targeting movement, vertical and horizontal. McAllister turned on the passive sensors for me. She didn't trust me to do it right. She also preset targeting to manual with computer assist targeting. The combative engineer remembered my preferences.

At one time I was competent as a pulse laser gunner, but that was a long time ago. I was rusty.

Corporate colony fighters were upgraded military trainers. Slower, less maneuverable, and lighter armed than their standard military counterparts, but still lethal to an unarmored transport.

There was a lot of debris floating within sight of my gunner's viewport. There'd been quite a battle. Capital Galactic had apparently affixed military grade tri-beam lasers to their freighters and transports, and slapped-on armor plating. Made sense, as those were the only ships they had available. Their sensors, speed and maneuverability would be inferior to capital ships, and the armor plating would be hit and miss. If they packed nuclear reactors in the cargo spaces, they'd have plenty of energy to power their weapons. Missiles and missile launchers were another story. Fortunately for them, the Chicher armed their ships with fusion beams and balled electricity. Being R-Tech, their range and targeting systems were inferior to Capital Galactic's armed freighters.

I'd never seen a Felgan, let alone one of their ships in combat. The Crax burned through Felgan territory early in the war, leaving them broken and scattered. Video footage from the Silicate War gave me basic knowledge of their interstellar combat vessels. They resembled a metallic jack, like from the childhood game with a bouncing rubber ball. Not exactly, but more than anything else. The different size classes, from frigate up to dreadnought, kept the same basic structure. Carriers and troop transports had boxy sections attached to the spars near the crossbar hub. Thrust engines were mounted along the four spars. Each spar ended in a knob-like sphere which fired an advanced tech particle beam. For self-defense, they mounted turrets similar to pulse lasers, but armed with a quad set of pulse particle beams. The pointed spars without the knobs housed sensors, communications, and their space-condensing atomic engines.

The Felgans were more technologically advanced than humans but not quite in the Umbelgarri or Primus Crax league, and they weren't renowned as accomplished military tacticians.

From my limited angle, I spotted what must've been a Felgan destroyer floating dead in space. One spar had been shot away and the rest of the hull was battle-scarred, with sheared off parts floating nearby. I also spotted battered parts of two of the Chicher twin-boomed midget frigates.

The fight hadn't gone all Capital Galactic's way. Shattered colony fighters, including one where the pilot might've ejected. And six armored freighters, holed and sliced open looking like an angry teenager had attacked aluminum cans with an ice pick and a blow torch.

And that was only from the limited view through my gunner's port. That and the escort carrier, converted to its purpose from the hull of a methane freighter. Simple magnification showed it had limited launch ports and landing bay facilities. But I could see at least three tri-beam laser turrets mounted to its cylindrical hull, one covered in a patchwork of armor plates. More than a few of those plates showed signs of damage. Scars that suggested fusion beams. She was also holed, along her stern side, probably a prolonged particle beam strike.

The fighting must've gotten up close and nasty because Chicher fusion beams were pretty short-ranged compared to lasers.

The com-line was quiet so I asked, "McAllister, how did you, Guymin, Vingee and the Chicher commandos get aboard the modular dock?"

Several seconds of silence followed. I leaned over and looked through the hatch to see if my station was still sending, if Tahgs and Marguerite heard my question. They were working, trying to familiarize themselves with the ship's control systems and their layout. I could've been doing the same, re-familiarizing myself. In a few minutes it'd be life and death again.

"They're all dead, Keesay." McAllister's voice bristled with anger. "The *Nuclear Pitchfork* and *Loki's Lady* landed in one of the shuttle bays. The Capital Galactic bastards tore the bay open with their tri-beam lasers to get at them, and a couple Chicher mini-transports. Hummelson replaced your friend O'Vorley, boarded with me. Took an MP round to the head. He was loyal, but an ass. You two would've gotten along." She paused. "Everyone else died aboard the shuttles. Their bodies are floating debris along with the shuttles, and every other destroyed ship out there."

She continued, saying how Chicher breaching pods, the few that survived, and their midget frigates had to fight through a squadron of Crax fighters. Those pods that attached and breached were sheared away by laser fire. While she spoke, I thought of everyone aboard the *Pitchfork* and *Loki's Lady*. Dvoracek and Axin, Detter and Devatha. All of them, dead. I'd seen enough dead friends and comrades in my time, and pictured their bloody remains drifting, forever frozen in space.

"When you arrived," McAllister said, the anger disappearing from her voice, "we'd been driven back, with no escape, preparing to fight to the last man."

"It was you who unlocked the cell doors," I said. It wasn't a question. "Thanks."

She took a breath. "Two minute warning, Keesay. I'm counting on you to fire them up."

CHAPTER 48

"Now, Keesay."

On McAllister's order I energized my dual-beam pulse laser. I couldn't see Tahgs. She'd closed and sealed the hatch on my order. The odds of my slapped-on auxiliary self-defense turret being blown off was high. One good hit.

The six fighters came on straight, without any evasive maneuvers. Why wouldn't they. We were detached and floating. The cascading atomic engine's cycle had been triggered, but we weren't going anywhere. "Incorrect," I said to no one in particular, swinging and elevating the crosshairs on the lead fighter in the first of two Vic formations.

Resembling late 20th century stealth fighters, only larger and faded cobalt in color, they were fast, but not fast enough. The lead fighter went up with a flash, my dual-beam pulse lasers pasting it with the first blast. No time to jettison. The second fighter took a direct hit to its left wing even as the mounted mini-cannon opened fire. It spun away, causing the following Vic to veer off or risk collision. The pilot managed to jettison, his escape pod vectoring away from the dock.

A little luck for me, a little for him.

Loss of his partners didn't affect the third in the lead formation. His mini-cannon on the left wing and single-pulse laser mounted on the right struck home. The impacting cannon rounds sounded like a snare drum riff. The minimal armor held as the fighter shot past overhead. Ignoring him, I targeted the second scattered formation. I clipped one near the engine and scarred another with light damage near the cockpit. Both emerged at least eighty percent effective.

"Two destroyed," I reported over the com system. "Two light damage. They appear to be reforming beyond my field of view."

"Fire thrusters now," McAllister ordered. I knew she wasn't talking to me.

The underpowered grav-plate struggled to maintain equilibrium as we spun sixty degrees left before accelerating. Out of the corner of my eye I caught sight of light beams lancing our way, flashing behind us, where we'd just been floating.

"That was the escort carrier," Tahgs reported. "She hit the dock."

"Did nothing more than scar her," McAllister said. "Reduced intensity setting intended to cripple us."

"No," I said. "Enough to kill us, but not enough to penetrate the dock's armor. Wager it's the setting they used on the Chicher breaching pods."

"The main engine section just launched and fired her engines," Tahgs announced. "They have a self-defense gun too. One more fighter gone."

"Maneuvering to put the dock between us and the carrier," Marguerite said. "She flies like a truck with four flat tires. Tahgs, coordinate with our other half for a hitching maneuver so we can get out of here."

Marguerite's comparison caught my attention. She'd piloted a yacht…but was she a Relic too?

Before we ducked behind the dock for cover, I targeted the jettisoned escape pod, wrecking it. One less trained Capital Galactic pilot. I fired a pair of bursts at the distant carrier. It was like throwing rocks at an armored personnel carrier, if I even hit.

McAllister said, "That was against the code of combat, Keesay."

"They're traitors," I replied, checking my targeting scanners for the surviving fighters' location. "I never signed any code with them, did you?"

"That'll piss them off even more, Keesay."

"They can only kill us once, McAllister. What would you recommend?"

"Next time don't offer any hope by waiting so long."

"Correct," I said. They were going to strafe the engine section first. Out of my firing arc. I targeted gaps between the armor welded to the dock. "Does the modular dock have laser turrets?"

"The Chicher shot out all of the pulse laser turrets," McAllister said. "Two medium-range dual beam turrets still functioning. Our pilot's keeping out of their arc."

This close that should be easy. On the other hand, how the heck were we going to make a break to enter condensed space travel once we reattached? Wasn't my problem. Targeting those repair bots welding a plate over a damaged section was.

Marguerite said, "Preparing for 180 degree pivot to align for connecting with the engine section."

I entered the data into my assisted targeting program. "Acknowledged, Pilot."

The three fighters in Vic formation swept in. The main engine section sent a series of pulse laser shots at them, missing wide left. She began her spin the same time we did. Our other half's lasers fell out of arc the same time I got to take my shot. The fighters bore in, no longer maneuvering, trading away defense for accuracy. One fighter exploded the instant the trio opened up. My second shot missed as did my third, but my fourth tore into the trailing fighter, already damaged. Spinning, it flamed out.

"Shock damage to the cascading atomic engine's housing," McAllister reported. "No penetration. Recalibrating. That means an additional five minutes to buildup."

"One fighter left," I said.

"Nine have apparently been recalled," Tahgs reported. Eighteen minutes until they're in range."

"It'll be longer than that once we couple with the rear section," our pilot said.

Pretty optimistic. The remaining fighter was circling around, angling to come in beneath my range of fire. My partner gunner probably wouldn't have a shot. "Can we communicate with our sister half?"

"We are," McAllister said. "Capital Galactic com equipment. They're listening in to anything we say. Once attached we can use hardwired com."

"Isn't encryption one of your plethora of expertise areas?" I asked.

"It is, Keesay. Not a current priority. Getting into condensed space travel is."

"Understood," I said. "Pilot, we have a fighter coming up, beyond— beneath my angle of fire. Probably same with my counterpart. Any help you can lend?"

"Not until our two vessels are attached."

My body shifted forward as our vessel decelerated. Sliding back in response, my case of hemorrhoid inflammation announced its continued presence. One of Heartwell's gifts. Enduring it for so long, and all the worse pains I'd suffered, it wouldn't impact my effectiveness. I just leaned to the left and focused on the fighter I couldn't target. Another gap in the dock's armor presented itself. Eight consistent blasts later, bits of debris erupted from the gap, meaning I'd managed to penetrate the hull.

I followed the remaining fighter's trajectory as our forward section closed to dock with the rear section. The fighter pilot sent a few bursts of cannon and laser fire, but nothing sustained. Then his escape pod ejected.

"Tahgs!" I shouted into my mic. "Marguerite, reverse thrust now. Full burn!"

Marguerite asked, "Why?"

Tahgs didn't hesitate. Forward thrust pressed my back against the seat. I braced for impact. The nearby explosion rocked our ship. Marguerite and Tahgs quickly regained control. McAllister sent an intermittently digitized video feed to my secondary screen. The rear section preparing to dock with us had suffered severe damage. The ramming fighter wrecked the coupling area. The rear section spun out of control and all but one of the main thrust engines flamed out.

"Vacate the area as best you can," came over my com-set. It was Agent Guymin. He sounded both rote and distracted, probably piloting, intent on recovery.

A female voice followed. Agent Vingee's. "The director expresses his gratitude. He says to persevere." Her comment confused me for a second, until I considered that Simms' voice failed while we escaped. Beyond that, it didn't matter. Dock surveillance would've seen who boarded each vessel.

Then a Chicher's voice chittered in their language. Already we were angling away from the modular dock, keeping it between us and the carrier.

"Turnabout's fair play," Guymin said. "Godspeed."

Their pulse laser gunner shot the ramming fighter's escape pod as the single engine flared from minimum to full strength, granting the wounded ship mounting speed.

The medium class tri-beam laser turret rotated and fired on the damaged rear section, missing wide by less than twenty yards.

That was the only shot they got before the rear section's escape pod jettisoned. The abandoned engine section raced on until it collided next to the tri-beam laser turret. The resulting impact and explosion destroyed the surrounding structure, knocking the turret out of commission.

"Targeting the fighter's escape pod?" McAllister asked. "Think that will result in turnabout against them?"

"Capital Galactic won't grant them that mercy," Tahgs said.

I agreed. We also collectively knew that swinging around in a desperate bid to recover them from their pod would be a useless gesture. The enemy fighters would be upon us before the maneuver could be completed. It'd be an insult to their sacrifice. They gave us a chance, miniscule as it was. A brave gesture, even if it meant no more than an additional thirty minutes of defiance. Of freedom.

We continued on full thrust. Fighters and one trailing armored freighter on our tail. Gaining fast.

"At the current rate of closing," Marguerite said, "Twelve minutes to fighter intercept."

I didn't bother to correct her statement. Intercept or come within effective firing range. It didn't matter. We continued racing toward the distant double stars, occasionally passing small hunks of debris, remnants from previous battles within the Capella system.

My turret's arc of fire was forward. They'd come up on our six. No way our pilot could turn us about with any reasonable degree of combat effectiveness. Swift hares, lethal ones, closing on a plodding tortoise. In this case, slow and steady was destined to lose the race.

I expressed my sentiment of impending doom. "Twenty minutes until the freighter closes to maximum range for its tri-beam lasers."

As if to one-up me on the Impending Doom Scale, McAllister said, "Thirty-nine minutes until condensed space travel can be initiated."

That was our death sentence. Even if for some reason we survived unmolested for thirty-nine minutes, despite the high condensation factor of our cascading atomic engine, the anemic acceleration provided by our auxiliary thrust engines meant an effective speed of less than six times the speed of light. Far slower than outdated Chicher ships. Almost an eight year journey to reach Earth.

Message rockets. We had one and McAllister ordered Marguerite to enter all relevant data and recordings available, for what it was worth. It was something I expected McAllister to do herself.

We'd launch the rocket in the next few minutes so the fighters couldn't intercept and destroy it. Such rockets carried their own cascading atomic engines, and could easily outdistance and escape what was pursuing us. I'd seen such rockets used as a weapon, but our pursuers were alert to our every move and wouldn't be caught unprepared. Ultimately the data would prove more valuable than the potential destruction of a fighter or two, or even the outside chance of crippling an armed freighter.

I didn't think anyone aboard our ship would elect the escape pod. I wondered if Simms had. Then I thought…I might if it offered me an opportunity to kill just one more Capital Galactic loyalist. One more traitor to Humanity.

"Nothing I can see of value," Tahgs reported. She'd gone to check on what Capital Galactic had stowed on the ship. "Enough food for three to last for one year. Sufficient cold sleep injections for twelve crew members."

I didn't know what she hoped to find that would help us in a running space battle. "McAllister." I adjusted my belt and seated position before asking over my com-set. "Any way to pack the escape pod with metallic hydrogen fuel?"

"Logical train of thought, Keesay. I don't have the equipment to siphon it off or a container to place it in. Then there's the lack of a detonator. I lack adequate time despite the fact that I *could* scrounge the necessary components."

"That was bordering on a complement," McAllister.

She laughed. "Only because I have a superior idea, Relic. And it's infinitely more straightforward, but virtually impossible to accomplish. Unless you factor in someone as brilliant and desperately ruthless as me."

CHAPTER 49

We ran, they gained.

"Tahgs," I asked. "Does this ship have a name?"

"What?" she asked. "Shouldn't you be focused on something important like shooting those Capital Galactic fighters?"

"They're not in range yet, Tahgs. I can't climb out to see if someone painted it on the hull." I checked my targeting scanner. Ninety seconds. "You're an administrative specialist. I figured it'd be easy for you to find, rather than me to muck around the files to find out. *That*, might distract me—and you if I mess something up."

"That might be accurate," she said. "But answer me this. Why?"

"Just want to know where I'm going to die," I said. "The Capella system, but on what ship."

"Oh," she said.

Marguerite cut in, saying, "*Gravel Box A*. The other half I imagine was *Gravel Box B*. Not much of a name, but I can think of worse."

"Thanks, Marguerite."

"Thank you, Specialist Keesay, for your part in effecting my freedom, even if temporary. Janice told me about you."

I started to reply with, "You're welcome," but she cut me off.

"I want to say this while there's time, Specialist Keesay. I am not only thankful, but respect you. If we'd met under other circumstances, before my capture and imprisonment, I would have dismissed you as an individual of minimal importance. Yet, despite what Capital Galactic did to me, and to Gerard...the warden's genetic manipulation, it didn't cause you to hesitate. To discount my value. I'm ashamed to say, I might not have—no, I wouldn't have done the same."

"I'm no saint," I cut in, watching the fighters approach the edge of engagement range. "I've done more wrong, wronged more people than I care to count."

Marguerite laughed. "Janice told me a little about you. No, you're not perfect, maybe not always a gentleman. But as we are soon fated to die, may I claim you among my friends?"

It would've been easy to just say, 'Sure,' and move on, but it wouldn't have been true. "I'm sorry, Marguerite, but no. I don't know you and you really don't know me. I will say that I already name you a comrade-in-arms against Capital Galactic. Against the Crax, the enemy. A defender of humanity. That means more to me—"

Marguerite interrupted me again, speaking over me. I relented, as it was an intense concern for her. More so than for me. I had very few friends, and it'd always be that way. And with thirty seconds until an unwinnable combat…one pulse laser on a sluggish front end of a tug versus a dozen colony fighters and an armored freighter armed with military grade tri-beam lasers.

"Thank you, that means a lot, to me. Should we survive—"

It was McAllister's turn to interrupt. "Message rocket launched. Therapy time is over, boys and girls. Hostilities are about to commence."

She was right. The fighters began long range firing, not at us but at the message rocket accelerating away at a twenty degree angle from us. One Vic formation broke away to pursue it, miniscule chance that they had. The armed freighter opened up with a pair of tri-beams at the rocket. At their current distance, a shot wouldn't do more than flash burn the *Gravel Box*'s hull, unable to inflict any real damage. It'd be enough, however, to damage the message rocket and allow the fighters to catch up and finish it off.

The freighter missed, but came closer than I expected. Maybe luck. More likely they'd installed military grade targeting sensors in conjunction with their lasers. The anticipated rate of our demise just accelerated.

"Fifteen seconds," I warned. Before I got the chance to open up, the remaining fighters that weren't chasing the message rocket formed into two Vic formations. One Vic slowed and paced us, just out of range. One broke right. The message rocket chasing Vic that had broken left gave up their chase. "Keep running straight," I ordered.

Tahgs and Marguerite's sensors would've spotted their maneuver. Instead of closing on our six to take pot shots at our thrust engines, they'd come at us from different directions.

Marguerite sighed. "The end is delayed."

I watched my targeting screen. It wouldn't be long. Actually it'd work out so that the freighter's lasers would be in range about the same time the fighters had position on our two, ten and six o'clock positions. That didn't really matter. They were just there to keep us from escaping. The armed freighter could reach us long before then.

Tahgs called out over the com-system, "They're calling on us to give up and surrender."

It must've been over a different channel. It didn't matter. I laughed while McAllister asked, "Do you need me to provide the words for our reply?"

"Why not let the Chicher speak for everyone?" I interjected. "Having to translate will add an extra layer of annoyance."

"The runner you sent me looks angry enough," McAllister said. "They're conferring on what to say."

"Stand by, *Cheval de Travail*," Tahgs said, presumably to the enemy freighter's captain.

Then the Chicher's chattering punctuated by guttural squeaks went over the system, transmitted to the *Cheval de Travail*, presumably the closing armed freighter.

Tahgs or McAllister sent the translation across our system. "Remove the fecal globs from your corpse molars so that we, the mirrors of the orb that crosses the sky, may comprehend the addled mutterings you create."

It must've taken the armed freighter's crew a little longer to translate, or for the captain to interpret the meaning and respond. After a ten second wait, the arrogant woman replied on all channels, including mine, "Renegades and prison escapees, it is my intention to retrieve Capital Galactic's stolen property. The condition in which you emerge from the inevitable result is upon your heads."

I couldn't help myself, whether my gear was set to transmit or not. "*Nemo me impune lacessit.*"

After a pause, the captain said, "Ah, the infamous Specialist Keesay. It is my understanding that upon recapture, you will be turned over to a certain Gar Crax Elite of the officer class. Utter your drivel of impunity to him."

I knew who she was referring to. The armored Crax warrior who'd dismissed me too soon after shooting me, and lost his foot when I shoved a micro explosive between his armored toes.

"I take it then, Captain, that your allies provide their wounded with prosthetic limbs?" The question came from McAllister. She'd provided me with the micro explosive prior to my emergence from the secret Umbelgarri breeding ground to face two elite Crax and an accompanying squad of Stegmar warriors. From her vantage, she'd seen me kill one Crax before being brought down by the second.

Nothing else was said. During the exchange, we continued to run, the fighters continued racing toward their positions, and the *Cheval de Travail* closed the distance between us.

"Something's happening," McAllister said. She sounded exasperated. "They must be using Crax technology. Something I've never seen."

"What is it," Tahgs asked.

"Gravity distortion…they must've guessed my intent to detonate the cascading atomic engine. I don't know how they can project that much energy. The cascading engine's buildup…it's resetting…locked in perpetual reset. A stabilized antigravity field is out of the question."

A few seconds passed. "Argggh! Shutting both systems down."

"Why?" asked Tahgs.

"Because," I said, having read horror stories of early experiments with cascading atomic engines, "if it goes critical in the wrong configuration, we'll get caught up in what'll be a micro black hole. It won't last long, but to us, with time warped, we'd suffer for what would be decades."

"Centuries," McAllister corrected. "I'm reprogramming thrust engine control. We'll self-destruct that way."

"We've lost the chance to take any of them with us," Marguerite lamented.

"What are you trying to say?" McAllister said. She must've been talking to one of the Chicher. "I believe you're right."

I waited a few breaths before pointing out, "Two minutes until the armed freighter will be in range for her tri-beam lasers." I shifted in my seat, seeing that the fighters were in position. "She'll be accurate. Recommend we turn about to protect our thrust engines, if we intend to use them to avoid capture."

"One-eighty-degree turn!" McAllister shouted, urgency in her voice. "Full burn. Bring us to a stop!"

"Enacting turn," Marguerite said.

I felt fits of centrifugal force with our gravity plate weakening and then strengthening in undulating waves.

"We're losing control of artificial gravity," Marguerite said. "Shutting it down."

"Shut everything down," McAllister ordered. "Safe mode everything now!"

I didn't hesitate to enact McAllister's order. I shut down power to all active gun systems. I released my buckle and climbed up to open the hatch in case *everything* included heat and oxygen piped into my exposed turret. "What's up, McAllister?" I shouted, hoping my voice reached all the way down to forward engineering.

Looking back through my gunner viewport, even unmagnified, I saw the armed freighter continuing to close.

McAllister, trailed by the two Chicher stuck her head in the cockpit area. Her freckled face paler than I'd ever seen. I asked her, "What is it?"

"The *Cheval de Travail* and fighters are the least of our worries, Keesay. We want to look like one of the pieces of combat debris out there."

"Just tell me, McAllister," I said, floating through the open hatchway. "Tell us. Spit it out."

"A wormhole is forming," she said. "The Shards. They're returning."

CHAPTER 50

A few seconds later the Capital Galactic forces recognized their peril. They turned and fled, but sent a few pot shots at us using rear arc turrets. We took a glancing hit, which raised the surface temperature along our ventral section and sent us tumbling.

Marguerite activated maneuvering thrusters to stabilize our ship, facing the area where McAllister predicted the wormhole would open.

"Only forty kilometers away," McAllister said. "Our only hope is that the Shards are interested in the fleeing freighter and fighters and the distant outpost. More than our little boat floating on the doorstep of their intergalactic conduit."

McAllister shut down all lighting systems. Tahgs asked her, "They might not take the time to scan us—do they even scan for heat emissions and trails left by expended metallic hydrogen?"

That seemed a pretty astute question.

"We never discovered much about them," McAllister replied. "This will be only the third wormhole emergence observed directly by human eyes."

"How long until it appears?" I asked.

"Without active sensors?" McAllister shrugged and pointed out the pilot's viewport, a 'windshield' that suddenly seemed fragile. "See the distortion?"

It reminded me of heat rising from a desert road. The stars flickered and wavered in an undulating dance. Pulses like a donut, but with a pinwheel where the donut hole would be.

"Might want to look away," McAllister warned, she reached past Tahgs and energized the anti-radiation screen.

"What're you doing?" Tahgs asked.

"You should be doing like me and looking the other way," McAllister said.

"The screens are used to intercept radiation when approaching a stellar mass," Marguerite said.

I signaled for the Chicher to face the other way and cover their eyes. "Tahgs, we have to survive the radiation in order to be killed by the Shards."

The instant I finished speaking, a flash erupted, like someone shined a spotlight on my eyes, despite being closed and shielded by my hands. It lasted only a fraction of a second. Spots filled my vision, but began to fade within a few breaths.

The Chichers' eyes must've recovered more quickly as they began chittering. They sounded more excited than fearful.

My eyes cleared, revealing the Chicher bowing their heads and pointing with one clawed hand while gripping their pack member's fur with the other.

The wormhole's exit reminded me of a black hole, no light emerging, while sparks shimmered along its circular rim. While that was memorable, the enormous planarian-shaped ship that emerged imposed a greater emotional impact. An Umbelgarri heavy cruiser, flanked by a far smaller and boxier human destroyer and a jack-shaped Felgan light cruiser.

"Tahgs," I said. "Hail them, quick. Now."

"What channel?" she asked, stunned by the sight.

"Any channel," I said. "All of them."

McAllister was already on it. "Umbelgarri Heavy Cruiser," she called. "Mayday. Mayday. We are in need of assistance."

With racing fingers and voice commands, Marguerite brought the *Gravel Box*'s systems to life. From my vantage I saw McAllister had selected a directional, narrow beam radio communication.

"Send to the destroyer," I said, coming to stand behind Tahgs as the gravity plate powered up.

"Who do you think is the senior partner out there?" McAllister replied.

The three vessels, Umbelgarri, Human, and Felgan held station as the wormhole behind them collapsed. All appeared as if the galaxy traversing conduit never existed.

"We need to tell them what's happening," I said. "Before the Capital Galactic loyalists initiate with a raft of lies. They departed as a combined taskforce to take the fight to the Shards almost two decades ago. They have no idea what's happening, to humanity—to the Umbelgarri."

"They're sending," Tahgs said. "I'm calling up Umbelgarri translation files." After a series of agitated screen taps, she added, "Our ship isn't equipped with military codes."

"Let me see," I said. While under the Cranaltar, the Umbelgarri directed their thralls to implant the ability to comprehend their splotchy and swirling, mosaic of colors form of communication. I didn't have the ability to hear the low-frequency pachyderm-like sounds that accompanied the primary color component, the sound adding emotion to the words.

They asked, 'What is the source of your distress, unrecognized partial interstellar vessel?'

"Give me your headset," I told Tahgs. "Let me speak to them."

Janice removed her headset and held it back over her head. McAllister reached for it, but I blocked her with my forearm. "Back off, McAllister."

"Relic, this is beyond you."

She knew about the Umbelgarri. Had probably interacted with them more, but her first call was a Mayday.

The Chicher pair must've guessed the source of our disagreement. With ears laid back and hands on their holstered machine pistols, they released a guttural trill.

Seething with annoyance, McAllister said, "Some sort of Relic coalition." She pointed at me, inches from my face. "Don't warp-screw this up, Relic."

I turned my back on McAllister, slipped on Tahgs's headset and adjusted the microphone. "Umbelgarri Heavy Cruiser, we are no longer in immediate danger. The retreating armed freighter and colony fighters serve a renegade corporation, Capital Galactic Investment Group. They have sided with the Crax alliance who have gone to war with the Umbelgarri. The Chicher and Humanity have joined the Umbelgarri-Felgan alliance. We are losing. After you departed our galaxy using the wormhole predicted by Dr. Maximar Drizdon Senior, no more Shards appeared. The Carbon Cause prevailed. However, using their advanced knowledge and ability to manipulate gravity, the remaining Shards knocked your home world, the moon, out of its orbit. Sent it careening into the planet it orbited."

I took a breath, Tahgs and Marguerite watching wide-eyed in anticipation. "Three Earth standard years ago, the Crax launched their invasion. Sometime after, an influential corporation, Capital Galactic Investment Group, covertly sided with the enemy. I and two others aboard this damaged ship played a major role in revealing Capital Galactic's treacherous support of the Crax."

After waiting several breaths for some reply, and none coming, I continued. "I and two other humans have just escaped from a hidden Capital Galactic outpost prison, because of a raid mounted by human Intelligence, mainly with Chicher and Felgan forces. Three surviving Chicher are among those on our vessel. It's believed the Chicher battlewagon, Chicher midget-frigate flotilla and their tender, and two Felgan combat vessels were destroyed in the engagement. Or were being chased last we observed."

I put my hand over the mic. "Are they receiving, Tahgs?"

"We're sending on three standard Umbelgarri frequencies, and two human frequencies, one military and one civilian, consistent with those from the height of the Silicate War." She paused. "I think Capital Galactic is transmitting to the destroyer. They're now overriding our ship from receiving, using an ID exclusion code." She continued tapping, bringing up screens and icons. "Attempting to go around and access the transmissions."

I nodded and continued. "It's imperative that you move to intercept and destroy any ships before they depart, and destroy any message rockets they might send which would inform the enemy of your arrival."

I looked over my shoulder to McAllister before finishing my message. "Go take care of the enemy. We aren't going anywhere."

Twenty seconds passed without reply.

McAllister looked like she'd sucked on a dozen bitter limes. "Way to go, Relic."

"There. Circumvented their block," Tahgs said, and spun in her seat to face McAllister. "What would you have said different?"

The receiving screen spun with colors. I translated. "Unrecognized partial interstellar vessel, the dominant human financial pod reports data that forms obtuse thought angles as opposed to parallel."

"Tahgs," I said, "call up our communication exchange with the *Cheval de Travail*'s captain. Send it after I finish." I took a deep breath. "Umbelgarri Heavy Cruiser, review the communication exchange that occurred between this ship and the armed and armored freighter that has since halted its retreat. Analyze not only the content but verify the voice patterns for authenticity."

I nodded to Tahgs and she tapped an icon, sending the audio file.

Marguerite asked, "How long will it take a message rocket, once deployed to depart under condensed space travel?"

McAllister told our pilot, "Give me your seat and your headset."

While taking the pilot's seat, she slipped on the headset. "Pay attention, Keesay." She then tapped a few controls and screen icons. I couldn't see exactly what she was doing. It appeared she was sending number sequences and formulas.

"I just sent a narrow beam communication. From my experience working with the Umbelgarri, the content should be identified as proprietary knowledge."

Seconds passed. "A bit of a gambit?" I asked.

"What I sent should give our words more weight." McAllister squinted at the screen readouts. "With this substandard sensor suite, from this distance it is impossible to determine if they've launched message rockets."

"They're responding," Tahgs said.

Four letters appeared on her com-screen: ARTC.

McAllister stared, uncomprehending. She glanced up at me. "Keesay?"

Searching my brain for any connection, I shrugged. It was some sort of code. "McAllister, can you convert it into Umbelgarri?"

"I cannot. This ship's computers lack the files and I don't have any of my equipment."

"Tahgs, request them to resend in Umbelgarri, not human text."

She complied, and a brief colorful reply appeared on her screen. As I watched, something deep in my brain clicked on. A phrase. A key that matched a lock. "Dolphins yearn for speech." "What?" Tahgs asked me.

"An implanted response," McAllister suggested. All three women stared at me.

I keyed my mic active and repeated, "Dolphins yearn for speech."

The Umbelgarri responded: AD 1985

I replied, "Rory Rammer."

Within seconds, the Umbelgarri replied one word that I translated: "Received."

Before the word had finished crossing my lips the Umbelgarri heavy cruiser surged to life, racing past us, opening fire. Five silver beams lanced out. Two appeared to miss wide of any target. One tore into the nearest armed freighter, the *Cheval de Travail*, like a white-hot shaft of iron piercing paper-mâché. The other two Umbelgarri beams struck more distant freighters.

Almost immediately the Felgan light cruiser moved to keep pace with the larger Umbelgarri cruiser, loosing their own weapon. The particle beam tore into a modular dock, one more distant and twice the size of the one where we'd been held prisoner.

The human destroyer sent a communication, but what they said was lost to me. The *Cheval de Travail* returned fire. One tri-beam blast struck the smooth planarian shaped heavy cruiser in the nose. The other struck us in the rear, tearing deep into our vulnerable aft section. We were holed. Outer hull breached and internal walls and compartments compromised. Hatches slammed shut in an effort to preserve life and precious air in the few undamaged sections.

I leapt out of the co-pilot seat, allowing Tahgs to sit. Red warning lights signaled power and systems failing. Belatedly, the human destroyer launched two missiles and opened fire with her pair of forward tri-beam lasers. Who or what she targeted could only be guessed as the pilot view portal was our only connection with what was going on.

The two Chicher commandos stood, facing the dropped hatch, their heads twitching, their eyes darting around. They must've realized they were the only two remaining of their pack. I tapped the nearest to get his attention, then pointed toward the hatch leading into the pulse gunner turret. Getting them in there would make room in the cramped area, and double the chances of someone surviving, should the pilot compartment lose integrity.

The gravity plate failed, as did lighting. Emergency batteries kicked in, restoring light while McAllister used what little control she had over the two surviving docking thrusters, trying to halt our tumble caused by the laser strike and decompression of damaged sections.

Life support was gone. Warmth and fresh air was in short supply. All that we had in the two adjoining compartments. We'd never make it to the emergency life pod, if it was still intact.

"Spiteful bastards," McAllister spat.

In their position, it's what I would've done—if I were a traitor. But I would've fired both laser batteries on us, instead of just one. The best they could do against the Umbelgarri heavy cruiser was to bloody its nose. I didn't express that sentiment. Instead, after the Chicher commandoes floated up, into the pulse laser turret, I gently gripped Tahgs' shoulders with both hands. "We'll make it," I said.

"So close," she said, her voice wavering. "Just my luck."

"Luck?" I asked. "What are the odds that a wormhole would appear, and three friendly ships emerge?"

"Of all the potential locations," McAllister said, "the probability for their return into this star system is quite high."

"Want to calculate the odds on the timing?"

"Shut up, Relic. You're wasting oxygen." While her words were harsh, the tone through which she delivered them wasn't.

CHAPTER 51

I was lying on a hospital bed with an IV dripping into my arm. White light reflecting off shiny metal assaulted my eyes and hospital antiseptic smells entertained my nose. I was in my own room, an examination room. Tahgs and Marguerite had been whisked away for a more intense medical examination. The Chicher commandos and McAllister were being debriefed. At least that's what I was told.

Med Tech Leach, a curly gray haired man with a friendly smile, reviewed the readouts. "We removed the micro neural interrupter device from your neck," he said.

That was a relief. "Thank you."

He nodded once. "I'll relay to the ship's surgeon." Then he frowned. "You have a severe hemorrhoid inflammation," he said. "Tests indicate the condition is chemically induced, and should clear up within days." He paused, checking a computer monitor readout. "The doctor isn't sure what was used to cause the inflammation. If it doesn't clear up, we can try treating it directly." He met my gaze with raised eyebrows. "Would you be more comfortable lying on your side or stomach, Specialist Keesay?"

Despite everything that had happened and my utter exhaustion, I sensed the burning pain, wasn't going to be an everlasting gift from Lawyer Heartwell.

While the human destroyer deployed an emergency rescue shuttle, McAllister had used the *Gravel Box*'s docking thrusters to alter our facing. A minimal expenditure of battery power provided optical magnification so we could witness the Umbelgarri and Felgan cruisers slice through what remained of the loyalist ships and resistance. They targeted thrust engines and weapon mounts, calling for the enemy's surrender, which they did in droves, except for two ships. One armed freighter's captain and crew chose self-destruction rather than capture. A second attempted to ram the Umbelgarri heavy cruiser. It was like an arthritic dairy cow trying to out maneuver a wild pinto in his prime. With that one the Phibs appeared to lose their patience, or decided to prove a point. She opened up with all guns. Two minutes later she'd rendered the freighter a hunk of scrap metal, floating holed and on fire.

My guess was the Umbelgarri, realizing they were at war—and losing—intended to preserve as many usable assets as possible. The Felgan light cruiser recovered the escape pod containing Simms, Vingee and Guymin, along with a handful of Chicher commandos. The second Felgan destroyer had been destroyed, but the Chicher battlewagon survived. Apparently the loyalists disabled the ship and intended to force a surrender. To what end, I wasn't sure, and wasn't told.

"Specialist Keesay," Med Tech Leach said. "Would you like assistance rolling onto your side?"

They'd removed my appropriated prison guard uniform for a plain white hospital gown. No flowers. Ensign Ciriegio was in the room, waiting for her turn to question me. This was to be her second session. I stayed on my back. A little modesty over comfort seemed in order, even if it wasn't her first session.

Ensign Ciriegio was an older woman, thin with a welcoming, toothy smile. Everyone serving aboard the *Reef Shark* appeared to be, on average, older than those holding similar positions in the fleet. It made sense, since they'd departed through a wormhole nearly twenty years ago to take the fight to the Shards, and were only now returning. How had the fight gone? Did they establish a foothold for Human-Felgan-Umbelgarri society? They'd figured out how to create and harness a wormhole as evidenced by their return to the Orion Arm of the Milky Way. I was sure there were many stories to be told, but my time for hearing any wasn't at hand.

Med Tech Leach observed me, waiting for an answer and standing ready to assist.

"No, thank you," I said to the med tech. "I don't know how long I was imprisoned, but I've grown accustomed to discomfort."

Ensign Ciriegio tapped a note onto her computer clip and said, "We must corroborate dates with the Intelligence agents currently aboard the Felgan light cruiser, however I am authorized to share that we believe no fewer than four months yet no greater than seven."

Her voice carried a joyful lilt, even when explaining an estimate based on gathered facts. I didn't know her well enough to accurately assess if she was just a cheerful person, or someone who could project happiness despite her mood.

"That's a wide timespan," I commented, then shrugged. "If you'd've said two years, I wouldn't've disputed your estimate."

She nodded to me and then dismissed the med tech. She pulled up a stool. "You have already chronicled how you came to be imprisoned and who was involved The Senior Engineer's recollection fits with what you've shared."

I knew what they were after, and were trying to fit the pieces together, which they'd report to Fleet and Intelligence at the first opportunity. They knew I worked for Intel, serving in the guise of a Security Specialist, and a little about why Capital Galactic had offered a bounty on me. I had nothing to hide, at least until her next line of questioning began.

After a few taps at her computer clip's screen, Ensign Ciriegio asked, "My captain would like to know why the Umbelgarri acted so decisively when the scenario playing out upon our arrival was anything but clear cut."

"They accurately assessed the situation."

"Are you indicating that you played no part in that assessment?"

"No, Ensign, I am not."

"What did you say to them and why did you communicate with them instead of this vessel and our captain?"

"Senior Engineer McAllister selected the party to be communicated with." She also must have purged *Gravel Box*'s system of the communication exchanged with the Umbelgarri.

The ensign nodded and smiled. I glanced up at the surveillance camera. Both it and the ensign were recording my debriefing.

"Is there a reason you're being less than forthcoming in your answers, Specialist Keesay?"

I shrugged. "I am tired. It happened so fast."

"You appeared to spare few details in our previous session."

"I had a lot of alone time to think on that and the treachery involved. Many months it would seem. That makes a difference."

"The forward section of the *Gravel Box* has been retrieved and examined. Standard files for such vessels would not include the ability to translate Umbelgarri into a format humans can normally understand. How were you able to communicate? We detected scrambled signals. Bursts consistent with Umbelgarri rather than human communication."

McAllister *had* wiped the communication files, probably made it look like damage sustained in the *Cheval de Travail*'s final spiteful gesture. Corrupted the communications data. She owed some amount of loyalty to the Umbelgarri as well. I think Tahgs recognized what she was doing, and maybe Marguerite did as well but, as a Relic Tech, I could reasonably get away feigning ignorance. Still, telling a lie would eventually catch up with me.

"The Umbelgarri implanted the ability for me to comprehend their color-coded language. My hearing is unable to detect the auditory portion, so I must interpret what I see without the benefit of emotional emphasis."

"When did the Umbelgarri do this?"

"Actually, I believe it was their thralls that assisted in the process while I was under the Cranaltar IV, which is information both Intelligence and the Umbelgarri probably want to remain unknown to the general population.

"I mentioned it briefly during your first interview, Ensign. Why Capital Galactic placed a bounty on my head?"

McAllister, to my understanding, was providing an update of what was happening in the war. Guymin, Vingee, and any of the Chicher commandos and the battlewagon's surviving crew could do that as well. And probably were.

The losing war scenario wasn't one the crews emerging from the wormhole were prepared for, and a portion of that war revealing itself immediately upon their emergence. That they experienced it was to their benefit. Otherwise, if the three ships had split off, the Umbelgarri heavy cruiser and the Felgan light cruiser might've stumbled into their home territory, enemy occupied territory. The Felgans having been overrun with only remnants remaining free, and most of the Umbelgarri colonies and outposts having been destroyed.

The ensign asked, "Why did the Bahklack thralls, under the direction of their Umbelgarri masters, implant the ability in your brain?"

"That'd be something to ask the Umbelgarri."

She smiled. "The ones we are associated with would have no knowledge of this."

Still lying on my back, I frowned and shrugged. "You could ask Special Agent Guymin."

"Please speculate, Specialist." The ensign's voice was calm and patient. "Why would the Umbelgarri implant the ability for you to comprehend their language?"

"They had the opportunity," I said. "The Cranaltar IV was an experimental device of Umbelgarri origin."

"How were you able to convince them which side to believe so quickly without evidence?"

It was easy to see and hear in her voice that Ensign Ciriegio was following a line of questioning that wasn't her own. She was under orders. "Those Umbelgarri are here. Ask them."

"True, but you're here in front of me now."

"You travelled between galaxies with them?"

"We did. We fought alongside them. Died alongside them. Did what we could to establish a secure outpost before returning." She paused to tap at her screen. "How did you convince our Umbelgarri allies?"

McAllister was right. The Phibs remained the senior partner in our alliance. "Your captain wants to know? Can't your captain ask them?"

Ensign Ciriegio's eyebrows pinched together as she tapped at her screen.

They'd already asked, and the Umbelgarri didn't give them an answer. Refused to answer, or give one that was satisfactory. "Consider this," I said. "How many of your crew have family that's tied to Capital Galactic? How many even now are wondering which side their family—their husbands, wives, parents and grandparents, children, nieces, nephews are on? That doesn't count lovers, friends. And acquaintances. Wondering which side should they be on?"

The ensign's head snapped up and she looked at me sharply. What I'd said hadn't occurred to her. Had it occurred to the captain? I stared into the surveillance camera. "Something that maybe oughta be looked into, Captain?"

Ensign Ciriegio escorted me to the wardroom. She politely refused to answer my questions. Her lack of eye contact and mannerisms suggested she wasn't fully onboard with refusing, and maybe even with my being isolated from everyone. Everyone being Tahgs and McAllister, even the *Reef Shark*'s crew. Meeting the captain in her wardroom as opposed to the captain's office didn't fit. Destroyer layouts from the Silicate War showed the wardroom as being little more than an antechamber off the captain's quarters. Whatever the reason for tight lips and isolation, I'd find out soon enough.

The limited scope of reading material to which I'd been granted access consisted of twenty year-old journals and predictable romance novels filled with smut. Many historical articles were listed, but my account didn't have access. Needless to say I found absolutely nothing about what happened to the task force after it reached the Andromeda Galaxy. At least Heartwell and the CGIG loyalists had a reason to imprison me. I wasn't in shackles, but restricted to quarters and not seeing or being allowed to communicate with McAllister or Tahgs, or even Guymin, who was my direct supervisor.

The old destroyer's corridors were well maintained. Many hatches clearly had replaced bolts and there were spots where the grays and light blue repainted over the years didn't match. Faded in places like the fleet uniform I wore, drab blue and gray, and without any identification or insignias. Pulled out of some disposal bin to replace my acquired prison guard attire, with a hole and blood stains where I'd stabbed the previous owner.

One thing they managed was to eliminate any vermin. Not unheard of in a destroyer, but it said positive things. No signs of cockroaches or rodents, normally brought aboard with foodstuffs and supplies. If there was a trick or secret, maybe they could patent it.

When we reached the wardroom, the ensign signaled for me to wait. Through a com system she asked for permission to enter, saluted while standing in the doorway and then announced she'd brought me as ordered.

"Thank you, Ensign," the captain replied. Her confident voice held a hint of weariness. "Show him in, close the door, and wait outside."

Ensign Ciriegio stepped back out, her smile gone and no emotion on her face. "The captain will see you," she said and gestured for me to enter the wardroom. After I had, she pulled the hatch closed behind me.

Not surprisingly, the wardroom was cramped. Its centerpiece was a table inset with four computer screens that could be combined into one. Probably for individual and group games, as well as reading and research. It didn't appear to have holographic capability. The room was painted in light blues and dark grays, with padded chairs set around the table. Along one wall was a food and drink dispenser. Next to it a cupboard, probably for dishes, and below that a door that slid up, probably a conveyer belt that carried away dirty dishes and other waste.

The captain sat on one of the padded chairs, facing the door instead of the game table. Her forearm rested against the edge of the table, allowing her to casually hold a steaming cup of coffee.

She set the cup on the table and stood, offering her right hand. "I'm Captain Jaiden Fitzgerald. Good to finally meet you, Specialist Keesay."

The captain's grip was firm but her hand's skin was rough and dry, and her face looked haggard. Her blue uniform was neatly pressed and precisely fitted. I'd studied a little about the Silicate War. Humanity had sent sixteen ships as part of the combined task force, including supply and support vessels. I didn't recall a Captain Fitzgerald being mentioned. Twenty years was a long time. A lot of things could've happened. The *Reef Shark*'s original captain may have died. May have gotten promoted, to a larger ship in the task force. Maybe he—or she—governed a colony established in the Andromeda Galaxy.

"Special Agent Keesay," I corrected her. "Thank you for meeting with me."

"I stand corrected," she said. With a gesture she continued, saying, "Please, have a seat. Would you like anything to drink?"

We were the only ones in the room. Asking the captain to serve me a drink, probably not a good idea. "No, thank you for the offer." I waited for her to sit and then took a seat, angling it to face hers. While I did this, she pushed her cup of coffee away, toward the center of the table.

"Your time is valuable, Captain, so I'll get straight to it." I leaned forward, my fist resting on the table. "While I fought hard for liberation from Capital Galactic imprisonment, many people—human, Chicher, and Felgan—sacrificed." My voice's intensity had risen, so I took a breath. "Sacrificed, for many, of which only a few survived. And in truth, my liberation was ancillary to the main effort. Yet, after all that, I sit, locked away in one of the vessels that played a part securing my ultimate escape."

The captain nodded. "You have been confined, for your own protection. Word of the bounty offered on your head had already spread. You're assertion that there may be Capital Galactic sympathizers played a part in my decision, Specialist "

I raised an eyebrow for several reasons, including her insistence in naming me a specialist. "Did it, Commander?"

It was her turn to raise a graying eyebrow, then a narrowing of her eyes. "I'd been informed you were a combative individual. A Security Specialist by training."

Too bad if she was insulted. "Weren't you trained to be a commander before being promoted to captain? So referring to you as Commander is in order."

"Your cover, from my understanding is as a Security Specialist. A personal guard."

I glanced around, spotting at least one of the recesses that likely held a fiber optic camera and miniaturized microphones. Gear from when I was a youth. "Is your ship so insecure that untrustworthy individuals would be able to listen in on our conversation?"

She shifted in her seat, then reached for her cup of coffee. "What exactly is it you desire?"

That she left off my title wasn't lost on me. "I want to know what's happening. I want freedom of movement and freedom to communicate."

She took a long sip of synthesized coffee, or that's what I guessed it to be. "There are roughly nine thousand what you would call Loyalists on the surviving freighters and docks. Your associates are assisting elements of my crew with interviews and interrogations, segregating and separating, determining who should be placed in cold sleep, who can be locked up, and who might be docile enough to be kept under light guard during our return trip to Earth."

"They're traitors," I said. "Execution. Mass execution is a viable option. It's what they have envisioned, what they support for their fellow man."

"We've sent message rockets and await a response," she said, "In the meantime, the main dock is being stripped of all communication gear, and ways to construct it. All machinery not necessary for survival is being removed to another dock, jettisoned, or destroyed in place. My prediction is that Earth Gov will send appropriately trained personnel, equipment, and tugs to uncouple the docks and transport them elsewhere. The surviving armed freighters, they'll send pilots and engineers to fly them wherever they're needed. Freighter drives and systems aren't very complex or specialized, so the personnel should be available."

I shook my head. "You may be overestimating the resources Fleet has available."

"We may be waiting here a while." She might've suppressed a smile. "During that time we'll keep busy."

"One destroyer," I said. "Crew scattered. What if some Crax appear?"

She held up a finger to forestall more questioning. "Our Umbelgarri allies deployed two mines. Radio signal detonation."

"Destroying the docks," I finished.

She nodded. "Freedom of movement," she said. After taking another sip she continued. "Once we depart, you'll be granted freedom of movement equal to any other civilian. It's been a conscious decision to keep you out of sight, for your own safety."

I leaned forward ready to tell her what I thought about that, but she held up a hand to forestall my objection. "Not necessarily immediate," she said. "But the fewer that can verify that you indeed survived imprisonment and the...prison break, the better your chances to avoid being sought by bounty hunters."

"Only takes one," I said and shrugged. "And there is more than one you've left alive. Awake and alive. Far more than one."

She looked up as if in momentary thought, and changed the subject. "As for communication, unless you attempted to communicate something deemed inappropriate for the general network, you have had, and continue to enjoy, access to the general network. If you attempted to send via electronic message or voice message, something deemed inappropriate, Ensign Ciriegio would have notified me."

"I have received no messages," I said. "No replies to my messages." I'd only sent one to McAllister, two to Tahgs, one to Vingee and three to

Guymin. Not a lot, but in each I'd requested return communication.

The captain finished her cup of coffee before curling both hands around it. "Your Intelligence associates are quite busy as you might imagine. They may not have had ample opportunity. The Senior Engineer is assisting my crew in retrieving data from the docks' systems and advising my crew in preparing the docks for our departure. The Administrative Specialist is organizing files and also undergoing medical tests to determine the extent of genetic manipulation and damage inflicted upon her. The CEO has just undergone reconstructive surgery to return her nose and face to their former proportions."

Marguerite was a CEO? I wondered from what corporation. Being imprisoned, probably a serious Capital Galactic competitor, or maybe wealthy and held for ransom.

"I can't believe that at minimum one of them couldn't find a spare moment to reply to at least one of my electronic messages," I said, knowing I merited at least thirty seconds between the lot of them. Maybe we weren't friends, but colleague fit. McAllister would enjoy making some snide remark.

The captain stood and I followed suit. "I have much to attend to," she said. "Ensign Ciriegio will escort you back to your quarters."

"May I petition Ensign Ciriegio to look into the routing of my communications and possible return messages?"

"You may, as long as it's performed on her personal time."

Personal time? Under the circumstances, what would the ensign get? Six hours a day, counting sleep? The captain wasn't doing me any favors. Comforting to know that some things in the universe remain constant.

I'd ask the ensign anyway. What else did I have to lose?

I considered thanking Captain Fitzgerald for the action her ship took on our behalf but, in truth, it was the Umbelgarri that took immediate, decisive action. Sure, we contacted them first, but McAllister had been right. The Phibs were the senior partner. The only ones with the firepower to emerge both victorious *and* unscathed.

I offered my hand. "Thank you for your time, Captain."

She stiffly shook my hand and said, "You're welcome." Her voice was as equally reserved as her handshake, and that she hadn't named me with any title again said volumes.

I asked Ensign Ciriegio to look into my communications and access complaint, telling her of the captain's restrictions, and that if it might cause her grief, not to worry. I'd get by. Two days later, she entered my isolation room with a look of consternation on her face. The first words out of her mouth were: "I've heard it said, Special Agent Keesay, that you have to pay closer attention to your friends than your enemies, because it's easier to defend against an enemy than to defend against someone on your own side." Her voice lacked its usual upbeat tone, and continued so through our conversation. "This appears to be a prime example."

A chief petty officer had been rerouting my electronic messages directly to the computer system's trash, leaving me to believe they'd been sent and received. The messages directed to me had been blocked, with the sender receiving notification that each had been opened and deleted.

I was pretty sure McAllister and Guymin could've uncovered the chief petty officer's intervention without assistance or unusual system access, but they were extremely busy, and not looking to uncover 'friendly' deception. It disturbed me that they hadn't tried harder to contact me...or maybe they had.

The chief petty officer had invested all of his stocks in Capital Galactic prior to departure and eventual rendezvous with the wormhole during the Silicate War. Over the years he eagerly anticipated his accumulating wealth, planning to live lavishly upon returning from Andromeda to the Milky Way. The Ensign Ciriegio determined the petty officer's motivation: He blamed me for destroying his wealth.

He added new meaning to 'petty' in chief petty officer. He was up for disciplinary action and the ensign's immediate superior encouraged me to send new messages, which I did, explaining what had happened. I also petitioned for assignment to one of the captured armed freighters, as a gunner.

Captain Fitzgerald initially rejected the notion, until I pointed out my experience and, with the lack of crew able to support such a function, it would benefit the mission should any Capital Galactic vessels or those of their Crax allies appear while we waited for Fleet to relieve us. Plus, I wouldn't have any potential interaction with captured Capital Galactic loyalists, and would be functioning essentially alone, except for whatever small number of crewmen was serving aboard the armed freighter. All that said, Guymin's support for the move made it happen.

With Guymin's support and little reason to deny my request, the captain assigned me to the *Ashkelon*. Not as a pulse laser gunner, but a tri-beam laser gunner. She provided me access to training files and simulations. The controls were like a pulse laser system's on steroids, slower with more computing long-range tracking power and a vastly slower rate of fire. Extensive computer interface was necessary. After two weeks of practice, and numerous simulated scenarios, the computer rated my competence as 'substandard,' but at least I was on the scale and above 'ineffective.' If anyone gave me grief, I'd argue that I was acting alone, whereas most tri-beam laser turrets were manned by two individuals. Normally a warrant officer for sensors and communication, and a lieutenant JG for targeting and firing.

In my down time, when I wasn't working out to recover my strength, I watched interview videos Agent Guymin sent me. He wanted me to form an opinion of various Capital Galactic loyalists. I wrote reports based upon my observations of their nonverbal cues, assessing the reliability of their answers, and divulged information. Guymin admitted that I was jaded, but my experience as a Security Specialist and someone outside normal agency training might offer alternative insight.

What else did I have to do? Every armed freighter was manned by less than a crew of six and running almost entirely on automated systems.

Agent Vingee was assisting Guymin, as was Deputy Director Simms, who was still recovering. Janice Tahgs had undergone testing, and what Capital Galactic's genetic experimentation had done to her appeared permanent. She'd live a normal life span, but would forever appear decades beyond her actual age. It was a particularly sadistic thing they did. The induced mutation even overrode attempted cosmetic surgery. Janice put on a happy face during our brief video communications, talking about how busy she was assisting in medical aboard the dock we'd escaped from. I commended Janice for her willingness to go back aboard the dock where she'd been imprisoned.

She also shared that none of the prison guards had survived the fight.

Querying Guymin, I learned that some of the genetic manipulation research had originated in the 70 Virginis system, stolen from the Celestial Unicorn Palace. Colossra, or Yeong, and Gerard likely had a shared root in their manipulated DNA.

Marguerite had undergone reconstructive and cosmetic surgery with success, as opposed to Tahgs. She even retained a measure of her enhanced olfactory senses. Of all our group, she appeared the happiest, despite being assigned to resource management, overseeing energy needs and predicted output and consumption of the docks and freighters. Something she said she had little knowledge or aptitude for. In one of our video chats, I told her that she probably rated better than 'substandard' in her assigned duty, outdoing me. That bit of truth earned a long laugh.

So, between laser gunnery training, video observation, workouts, sporadic communication exchanges, and sleep, the twenty-seven days I served aboard the *Ashkelon* passed quickly, with a measure of tranquility.

When the small relief flotilla arrived, that was all upended.

CHAPTER 52

"Warrant Officer Tron," I called into my com-set's mic, "my turret's sensors just picked up six ships exiting condensed space travel."

The commander of the vessel was a warrant officer. That said a lot about our situation, especially should it come to combat. In addition, my call came during his off time, interrupting his earned five hours of shuteye after serving nineteen on duty.

I watched the sensors' data. They were designed and calibrated for basic identification and tracking. They reported two destroyers, a medium class civil transport, a patrol gunboat, a military tug, all human, and a sleek ship with a boxy midsection. Sensors couldn't pin it down. Based upon the optical files, I tried to identify a match while waiting for the warrant officer's reply.

"Acknowledged, Keesay," he said in his calm, bass voice. "The *Reef Shark* notified me seconds after you did. Good work. Stand by."

The targeting system identified the comparatively sleek ship as Umbelgarri, with an eighty-three percent probability it was a utility transport. After examining the system's profiles, I agreed. When they closed the distance, it'd be verified.

A sense of relief washed over me. I hadn't realized how tense I'd been. A combination of two destroyers and an Umbelgarri vessel ruled out Capital Galactic ships.

What followed was a long wait. I tracked shuttles being exchanged. I could only guess at the communications. Turrets didn't receive many, and I didn't have the skills to intercept anything not directed to my station.

My assigned duty time passed. I notified the warrant officer that I was going to get a meal, a couple energy bars and a vitamin-enriched drink, and a shower, and would return to my turret. The seat there wasn't as comfortable as a bed, but it'd do. After months of captivity, I was anxious to be away from the double-star Capella system.

Agent Vingee's voice startled me to wakefulness after only ninety minute's sleep. "Agent Keesay," came over my com-set, relayed through the *Ashkelon*'s bridge. Her voice held a ring of urgency. "Report."

"Agent Vingee," I replied, "I'm off duty but remain on station in Tri-Beam Turret One."

"Notify Warrant Officer Tron to expect company. Two shuttles will arrive within thirty minutes. You, and *only* you, are to meet them in the *Ashkelon*'s main shuttle bay.

"Acknowledged," I said. "Any special arrangements?"

"Negative, Keesay. Out."

An old model military shuttle was the first to land in the main bay. Probably from the *Reef Shark*, since its patched hull showed signs of having been warped and scarred. Evidence it'd seen combat against the Shards. That wasn't surprising.

Agent Guymin was on board, if not piloting. It was his voice that requested permission from Warrant Officer Tron to land, including permission for the follow-on shuttle. That one happened to be teardrop-shaped, sleek and silvery. Twice as large as the military shuttle, it looked fast...and dangerous with its two side-mounted energy beam cannons. Umbelgarri. What did they want on the *Ashkelon*? With no one else invited, what did they want with me?

Standing next to the bank of computer screens in the observation room, adjacent to the control room, I ran my hands over my ill-fitting Fleet uniform. I checked the holstered MP pistol on my right hip and my bayonet hanging in a makeshift scabbard on my left. I didn't have a comb, so I ran my fingers through my short hair.

What was making me so nervous?

Agent Guymin was the first to disembark from the military shuttle. He strode down the ramp, flanked by Agent Vingee on his right and a Chicher commando scampering behind on his left. Vingee was taller than Guymin, and towered over the furry alien as they stopped and stood to face the Umbelgarri shuttle.

A circular section in the Phib shuttle's nose depressed and then rolled upward. A ramp, black to the point of absorbing color, rolled out like a lizard's tongue.

My com-set was on, with normal frequencies open to receive. My headset was connected and functioning. Maybe they wanted me here for security. If so, Guymin would've let me know. But, with the secretive Umbelgarri, humans were always on the outside, looking in...that was, when the Phibs allowed.

A crab-like Umbelgarri thrall with a black synthetic harness holding various electronic gadgets in its loops and pouches skittered sideways down the black ramp and up to Agent Guymin. Its eyestalks swiveled about as it moved, its lesser claw hovering near a dangling energy beam baton. Everyone looked at ease except the Chicher. He stood on his hind legs, bobbing his head from side to side, his nose twitching as he sniffed.

Guymin said something to the Bahklack, and then they must've exchanged words. With a nod of agreement, Guymin spoke into his collar mic. "Keesay, the Umbelgarri have recently contacted me with a proposal that involves you." He glanced behind him to the Chicher commando and then back to the Bahklack. "Thus, they have invited you to join us here in the shuttle bay."

"Understood," I replied into my mic and tapped the controls to unlock the shuttle bay entrance. The way Guymin said 'invited' suggested something other than that, but I wasn't sure what.

The Bahklack spun, its chitinous feet clicking on the metal floor. The alien raised its large claw, angling its genetically manipulated surface and began to speak through the colors that swirled and formed, and reformed across its surface.

My ability to comprehend the alien form of communication certainly was a factor in the upcoming proposal.

"The Masters transmitted a request for your superior to bind you to the Masters' desires. The superior receiving the request before me has deferred the request to his subordinate's verdict, which is you, Subclass Warrior Human of Lowly Relic Aspiration."

Again, the way this Bahklack spoke was different from others I'd communicated with. A dialect? Maybe they spoke different languages. Although humanity had mainly a single language, pockets of nationalistic languages yet remained, mainly among Relics. I wasn't knowledgeable enough to blame it on non-standardization of translation software.

I glanced over at Agent Guymin. "He means the Umbelgarri desire to pick up my contract?"

Guymin nodded. "They want you to provide security for their diplomatic representative to the Chicher."

That was unexpected. Umbelgarri rarely intermingled with humans. Their immune systems weren't effective against many of the microbes humans carried. My only experience with an 'Umbelgarri diplomat' had been Diplomat Silvre, a brilliant woman—which is the only type of human they deign to accept. Of course, many races avoided the Chicher for much the same concern, leaving both of our races as intragalactic pariahs.

They'd worked directly with McAllister, at least temporarily, in their secret subterranean breeding ground on Tallavaster. They'd masked me and kept their distance while I was in their underground warren. They managed with her, and I never asked why. Not like she would've told me. But the McAllister situation took place under desperate circumstances. At the time Crax forces were in the process of overrunning the third of Tallavaster's three human colony cities. And similar to Diplomat Silvre, Senior Engineer McAllister is a genius. *Unlike* me.

"Do I have an option?"

Guymin tilted his head with a raised eyebrow. "An option? To modify the contract?"

"The option to say, no," I said. The Umbelgarri thrall was right in front of me and the Umbelgarri diplomat might be observing from the shuttle not ten yards away. "My reading and experience suggest they're not used to us humans saying no."

Agent Guymin glanced at the Bahklack and then beyond it to the alien shuttle. "The Umbelgarri made assumptions with respect to Intelligence's command structure. Their normal points of contact are diplomats, followed by military representatives, and government officials. Often using intermediaries." With an expressionless look he added, "I chose to defer to you rather than exert my authority."

I grinned. "In other words, you said, 'No.'"

Vingee's eyebrows pinched together, and she tilted forward a little, like she wanted to say something.

Guymin probably didn't notice. The Bahklack wouldn't have missed it. But it probably wasn't good at reading human body language. The question was, what did she want to say?

Guymin shook his head. "Not exactly, Agent Keesay."

"Do I get to read and review the contract?"

"The Umbelgarri prefer you get it from the thrall." He pointed at the Bahklack. "You are aware, they prefer verbal contracts."

I'd read historic treaties and a few corporate-Umbelgarri contracts released to news sources, and pointed it out to Guymin. He responded, "Litigious as we humans are, we write them out for our reference and benefit. Theirs is a more conceptual framework for an agreement."

It made a sort of sense. Alien brains functioned differently from humans. How they perceived and interpreted the world around them was often radically different. I was basing that not only on what I'd read, but my interactions with a few Chicher and Bahklack. The Chicher were a pack animal and formed communities not all that different from humans. The Bahklack were servants, rigid in their service to their Umbelgarri masters that created them, but seemingly flexible in rare instances, and too aloof to care, when interacting with humans.

The Umbelgarri? Just from what I knew of their language, the colors and patterns, and physiology…low slung quadruped amphibian creatures, like a cross between a giant salamander and an alligator, eighty percent salamander…

They had manipulative appendages, spindly arms and hands, able to jut out from beneath their broad chins. I'd never seen one up close, except several young ones in an underground pool. Those resembled mudpuppies in both shape and size. I hadn't been close enough to spot anything more than basic size and shape, including if they had the arms under their chins. In truth, I didn't recognize what they were and the purpose of the pool—a breeding nursery—until after I'd left the underground area. Left to face the Crax, setting off detonations to appear like I was trying to kill them and their Stegmar warrior allies. The real objective, beyond killing a few more Crax before they brought me down, had been to collapse the hidden entry. While trying to evade the pursuing Crax after splitting up with O'Vorley, I discovered the entrance within a fenced off area of a gravel quarry. I'd entered the dilapidated tool shed screened by rusted parts and broken-down equipment. The Fhibs logically figured the Crax would eventually stumble across the entrance too.

I looked over at the Bahklack, then stepped directly in front of him. "So you want me to negotiate a possible contract agreement, right here and right now?"

The thrall stood as straight as its crab-like legs allowed. "The Masters require your service. Accompany. Protect. Consult, when requested." Although he wore a translation device strapped to his dominant claw, the thrall spoke through the patterns formed on his claw. The device was also a transmitter, and had the ability to receive and direct a communication light beam into one of its stalk eyes.

It was odd discussing this in a shuttle bay. It might've even been more odd for those standing and listening only to my end of the conversation. It'd be even harder for the Chicher commando, whose translation device surely lacked the ability to transform optical language into its native auditory form.

I thought a moment before saying, "Should a contract be agreed upon, the Umbelgarri diplomat I'd work for understands the difference between a contracted employee and a thrall? That would include all Umbelgarri, not just those in the diplomatic corps. I would require that I retain a similar measure of autonomy that any standard bodyguard would while serving within human society."

"The Masters recognize humans were not created and are not spawned to serve their needs and desires." The crab-like alien's stalk eyes angled a fraction toward me. "Negative. Human among the Masters, access to habitation and destinations are set by the Masters. Not for humans to decide."

"The situation sounds like, other than when I am performing a specified task, I would be confined to quarters. I understand the disease vector concerns, but humans have moved among the Umbelgarri before."

"Subclass Warrior Human of Lowly Relic Aspiration, confined harboring was caused by humans who desire retribution against you. The Masters believe it will occur again, or your span of existence will be truncated. That is not preferred compared to what serving the Masters will provide?"

For a moment the Bahklack's phrasing had been more smooth and conversational in content. That it changed, or reverted, meant something. Maybe reflexive when its masters are challenged. Or the previous words had been part of a prepared statement? What Ensign Ciriegio had said about the difficulty of guarding against friends came back to me. I'd been captured because Colonial Marines turned on me. Delivered me to the enemy in exchange for credits. An exorbitant amount. Nevertheless, I owed them some payback. Them and Capital Galactic loyalists, along with the Crax.

I crossed my arms. "The Umbelgarri don't desire my service as a protector because of any training or extensive expertise in that field. The Umbelgarri want to contract for my service because, among the Chicher, I am a Pollinated Pack Member. Not only that, but I am a Relic Tech, like the Chicher. Because of the Cranaltar IV, I can understand Umbelgarri language, and through my experience under the device, they are confident in my loyalty to them and their secrets. That is of value."

The thrall's eye stalks returned to a more vertical positioning. "The Masters will grant credit remuneration three fold accumulation superior to what your current masters grant."

It was my turn to lean forward. "I have no masters. And if I work for the Umbelgarri, they will be employers, not masters." I held up a finger to forestall the Bahklack's reply. "In confinement, what will I be able to spend my earned credits on? What value are they to me in Umbelgarri society?"

The thrall's eyestalks spun at the top, like a straw in a stirred drink. Was that a sign of annoyance, or of frustration?

"The Masters will provide for all physical needs. Nourishment, health, body coverings, tools."

"What's in it for me?" I asked, gesturing with my hands, palms up. "I'd rather fight the Crax, or Capital Galactic, until they take me down rather than follow an Umbelgarri diplomat around." I glanced over my shoulder at the commando standing on his hind legs. "Diplomats aren't known for front line duty and the odds of the Chicher trying to assassinate one of their A-Tech allies is as close to nil as you can get."

The alien thrall paused. "After Superior Class Warriors exchanged you, Subclass Warrior Human of Lowly Relic Aspiration, and the exertion and death of fellow humans and Relic Rodent Segregated by Hordes, and the Advanced Thinking Terrestrial Avians whom the Masters have allied with for centuries to secure your unexchangement, the Masters do not believe your masters will permit you to mingle among humans."

The thrall had a point, but I wasn't going to concede that. What I decided to say might ruffle some feathers if Vingee or Guymin reported it. There might even be truth to the words. I never fully trusted Intelligence. Like the government and the military and the various corporations, Intelligence had its own methods and hidden agenda.

"What makes the Umbelgarri think that my superiors in Intelligence didn't allow my capture to aid in their locating of this outpost? The rescue attempt wasn't mounted for me. Your Umbelgarri leaders know that."

Even as I said it, the remote possibility of its truth struck me as being less than remote.

McAllister and I had played many games of chess. She routinely beat me, although on rare occasion I managed a stalemate. She said I didn't think or plan enough moves ahead. Maybe that was true, but I knew enough about the game to know no matter how many moves ahead I planned, pawns were always on the line to be sacrificed. That Intelligence okayed my contract to be taken up by the Umbelgarri indicated they saw benefit to my working for the Phibs. I didn't think Guymin would have the authority. Deputy Director Simms might have onsite authority, but hadn't been in the loop for a long time. The Umbelgarri probably initiated this once they got word from the *Reef Shark* or their returning heavy cruiser.

While I'd been talking and thinking, one of the thrall's eyestalks tipped toward the communication device on his claw. He was receiving information from an Umbelgarri.

I wasn't familiar with Bahklack body language, but the way his legs flexed and then became rigid, and his smaller claw and two manipulative appendages dipped, something positive wasn't being relayed to him.

His problems weren't my problems. Mine was my future. The Bahklack had a point. Intelligence might shovel me off somewhere dark and isolated—for my own safety. After my involvement in the Colonization Riots, I ended up doing warehouse security on Pluto. Out of the way. I was lucky to escape that fate, one which Intel shipped me off to. No need to think ahead, like McAllister recommended. I had one move. One available that might offer more future opportunities and not a dead end. It wasn't a reliable one, more like a wild card. I smiled, thinking of McAllister fuming at me for mixing chess and cards, games that allowed room for luck in the strategy.

But just because there wasn't much in the cards for me, that didn't mean I wouldn't play to benefit others.

Guymin raised his eyebrows when I turned and he saw my smile. I gave him a wink. His eyes shifted to focus beyond my shoulder. Vingee's did too. Looking back, I saw what caught their attention. An actual Umbelgarri was lumbering its way down the ramp.

I'd seen one from a distance before, after it exited one of their battle tanks, surrounded by Bahklacks. It died, killed by the Crax bearing down on our defensive line on Tallavaster.

This one wasn't burdened with a back-mounted beam cannon or a bunch of other gear. Narrow harness straps, one that ran along the spine, and three along its sides, and anchored at its legs. The straps were clear, like plastic, and allowed the shifting colors of its smooth skin, much like a squid's. The Umbelgarri was about twelve-feet long, including its tail. It looked like a salamander but walked like an alligator. Its snout was caught somewhere between rounded and blunt like a salamander's and long and narrow, like an alligator's. It didn't have any teeth that I could see, or claws, and its eyes were red, like an albino rabbit's. Its head was marginally oversized compared to its body, but not abnormally so. The arms under its chin were tucked back and held close. They appeared to have three fingers and an opposable thumb. Rather than an alien with a highly functional brain and creators of advanced technology, the Umbelgarri appeared more like a prehistoric throwback. Something hailing from Earth's Paleozoic Era.

If I agreed with my contract's transfer, this was probably the Umbelgarri I'd be protecting. Its glistening skin flowed from a coral pink to pastels of blue and purple, with streaks of sharp green. It was telling the Bahklack in front of me to move aside.

What caught my attention, more than the Phib, rare as it was to meet one face-to-face, was the occasional pinprick flashes, like ethereal sparks, whose appearance offered a rough outline of an oval shield or barrier surrounding it. That, and the object floating and keeping pace about eight feet above the A-Tech alien. No larger than a watermelon, I sensed it was there, not really seeing it. Whatever it was caused a distortion when I looked through it to the Umbelgarri shuttle and the dull metallic shuttle bay wall as the quadrupedal alien advanced. Either light waves bent around the object, or a holographic image formed to mimic what I, and others, would normally see if it weren't there. My credits would be wagered on the latter. I also guessed that the Phib wanted us to see the screen and notice the hovering object, probably a weapon.

As it got closer, taking the spot where its thrall had stood, tiny electronic devices, faceted and intermingled with fiber optics adorned the harness, seemed to be functioning full speed. Being nearly crystal clear, they'd blended with the Umbelgarri's glistening skin, now gray with waves of yellows and blues rippling from snout to tail. Irregular splotches of browns and pinks appeared and faded, temporarily mimicking the random patterns of a Dalmatian's coat.

A low frequency hum undulated from its throat. It could be felt more than heard. The physical sensation reminded me of the massive pipe organ in the church of my youth, but this subsonic emanation burrowed more deeply beneath the skin, but not quite to the bone.

The Umbelgarri swayed its head from side-to-side, like it was changing the focus of its red eyes. Sizing me up. Rather than requiring me to watch and interpret its visual language, it decided that auditory was more appropriate. That choice allowed everyone else to follow along as well.

"Security Specialist, Fourth Class, Krakista Keesay," it said. The words were slow and measured while its deep voice sounded tinny, like emanating from a bucket at the bottom of a well. "Special Agent Krakista Keesay, now serving Humanity's Intelligence Service in a parallel capacity." Its tail, no longer dragged like a crocodile's or a salamander's, but remained parallel with the floor, swaying left and right, while the appendage's last foot flicked faster, as if two puppeteers controlled it.

"You've properly identified me," I said after the Phib didn't continue. "With whom am I speaking, if I may ask?"

"We require your service. As a protector. As an advisor. As a companion."

Although I was sort of sure, I asked, "Who is 'we?'"

"The one that stands before you and all my kind. Known as Umbelgarri." Its tail began flicking up and down at the tip. You prefer the term 'Phibs.'"

Phibs was said to be a derogatory term, one I occasionally used. Maybe it had some device aboard its shuttle that read my mind? Probably not, as it'd have anticipated my words and provided its thrall with answers to circumvent them. Still, that bit of information shared indicated he'd seen at least part of the *Documentary*, or at least some old recordings, as I tended not to utter the word after they'd assisted in my recovery. When annoyed, however, I did tend to both speak and think 'Phib.'

"To say that I prefer the term Phibs is inaccurate," I said. The only reaction that earned was Vingee taking in a sharp breath. Thinking further, how the Umbelgarri standing before me had answered said something about Umbelgarri society. "Do you, the one standing before me, have a name?"

Its tail continued swaying, but stopped flicking up and down at the tip, until it answered, "This one does."

"Would you share it?"

"If you transfer your contract."

I replied, "The assigned duties, protector, advisor, companion are vague."

"We do not know the parameters, other than in the broadest terms."

The increasing accuracy in which the Umbelgarri communicated, its fluency and mimicry of human conversation and speech patterns…the translation device was doing it. If the one before me was a diplomat, it made sense he'd have the most effective model available.

"I'm a Relic," I said. "My gear is technologically inferior to what you and your Bahklack thralls have access to. I've gotten along well with the Chichers I've encountered, but have limited knowledge of their culture, politics, military tactics. As a human, more than a few would say I'm far from the mainstream, an outsider, an agitator, a loner, and not a reliable source on humanity's norms. As a companion, I don't have a lot of friends, and of those I have had, most are dead. Killed by the Crax or their allies."

I crossed my arms. "I wonder at your motivation. I question your choice."

"What's he doing?" Vingee whispered, presumably into Guymin's ear.

He didn't reply. The Umbelgarri did.

"We believe in you, Krakista Keesay. We believe in your tenacity. In your daring. In your reliability."

Without realizing it my arms uncrossed. That response wasn't what I expected.

"You will not serve only beside the Umbelgarri before you. We will expect you to serve us as an emissary and as a soldier."

"Would I have autonomy, serve as a contracted employee and not as a thrall?" I couldn't think of a proper term, so added, "Not along the lines of an indentured servant until my contract expires, and that when it does, I will be transported to a human settlement or colony of my choice?"

"That is understood and will be done," the Umbelgarri said, his tail no longer swaying or flicking, "if you choose to sever your service to us." His head tipped slightly from side to side. "The Chicher have agreed to receive you serving with me in my capacity as diplomat to the Chicher. Their representative has insisted that you be allowed a human companion during your service."

That was what I was waiting for. An opening to make my play. "In lieu of a companion, and as part of my agreeing to contract with the Umbelgarri, I ask that you use your influence to ensure that Marguerite Corvelzchik lands on her feet, with a contract suitable to her talents with a stable corporation or government organization."

Other than her full name and former position as a CEO, I'd never been able to research anything about her background, skills or why she'd been taken captive, other than for Heartwell's torturous experimentation. The thought of him caused me to grit my teeth. I motioned with my hand, signaling additional requirements. "I ask that the Umbelgarri use their influence to have Fleet name a warship after my deceased friend, Kent O'Vorley."

I looked over my shoulder, making eye contact with Guymin and Vingee. He nodded once. She continued to stand straight, but her eyes widened.

"Finally," I said, once again facing the Umbelgarri diplomat, "I ask that the Umbelgarri employ your advanced technology to undo the genetic damage inflicted upon Administrative Specialist Janice Tahgs."

From behind, a distressed cry, "No!" caught everyone's attention. I recognized the voice and turned to see Janice running down the military shuttle's ramp. She dropped my shotgun and shrugged a belt holster from her shoulder. It held my single-action revolver. "Agent Guymin promised. He promised I could go with you!"

CHAPTER 53

"**Leave it to** you, Keesay." McAllister shook her head in amusement. The video link was detailed enough to count her freckles, if I wanted to. "You broke her heart. At the same time, you offered her hope."

I packed my few belongings and supplemented that with gear scrounged from what the *Ashkelon*'s crew abandoned after surrendering. I even found two decks of cards. Useful for, if nothing else, many games of solitaire.

Through the communication screen, I observed McAllister leaning back. "I'd ask you to pick up any programming tips from the Umbelgarri, but..." She grinned broadly.

"Maybe I'll have the Umbelgarri diplomat show me a few nifty chess strategies."

"Good luck with that," she said, and leaned close, her face filling the screen. "Guymin told me they're planning to rename one of the captured armed freighters after O'Vorley."

"He deserves better than that."

"Rare as it may be, I agree with you." She shrugged. "Your first two requests, they didn't cost the Umbelgarri anything. The last...shrewd, Keesay."

It was my turn to shrug. "Thanks, I know. Only way she wouldn't be shoved aside."

"Remember that old revolver you gave me, to give to Tahgs if I ever got the chance?"

I nodded. I gave it to McAllister just before leaving the subterranean Umbelgarri breeding ground on Tallavaster. Before I went out, figuring on dying. "My backup .38 I used to keep in an ankle holster."

"It's in storage," McAllister said. "I'll have it sent to Tahgs once she reaches Io."

That the Senior Engineer bothered to keep it suggested a measure of respect for me. "You think that'll be a good idea?"

McAllister nodded. "If you ask me, she'll get over you not long after she arrives. But my opinion of you isn't exactly high and may be skewing my analysis."

"You kept the .38," I said, teasing.

She changed the subject. "I know you won't pass up any opportunities to kill a few Crax, Keesay. But when you do, make it painful. For me...and for Anatol."

The name brought up mixed feelings. Her lover had been my shipboard enemy. He died defending her from Crax boarding the *Kalavar*. I arrived too late to save him but in time to help her bring down the Crax and Stegmars around them. McAllister and I weren't exactly friends. I'd killed her fiancé during the Colonization Riots and, despite all we'd been through, a friendship between us wasn't in the cards. But we'd come a long way. If it weren't for the war, maybe Anatol Gudkov and I would've buried the hatchet, at least up to a point, too.

"I'll be sure to, McAllister, if you promise to do the same on your end."

"That you can be sure of," she said, leaning closer, preparing to end the signal. "Out."

With that, I deactivated the communication screen.

I'd already said my goodbyes to Simms by communication relay, and Guymin and Vingee in person. I asked Vingee to relay my thoughts and well-wishes to Marguerite, since I couldn't find and connect with her.

I was wearing a collared, loose-fitting set of gray-green coveralls. They were military quality, able to resist blades, bullets and lasers. Only moderate protection against Stegmar needles and Crax acid, but maybe the A-Tech Phibs could come up with something to cover that. I had my shotgun and bayonet, revolver, and MP pistol, one that McAllister sent over and said O'Vorley had carried and used. Of everyone, he'd've been my choice to join me during my service with the Umbelgarri. He'd been a true friend.

Pulling my cart filled with gear, after double checking to see if the two decks of cards were safely stowed, I made my way toward the *Ashkelon*'s primary bay where the Umbelgarri shuttle waited.

Down the corridor, near the elevator, stood Janice Tahgs. Her eyes were red and swollen. She used a handkerchief to wipe the tears from her wrinkled cheeks.

A few steps before I made it to her, she held up the white handkerchief. "Remember the one you gave me, the one you used to plug the wound in my back? When you rescued me on the Mavinrom Dock?"

I nodded.

She half laughed, half sobbed. "Well, this isn't it. It was lost on Tallavaster, after I was taken prisoner by Capital Galactic, and Heartwell. But I didn't forget it. You saved me then, and you saved me on the *Kalavar*, even when I doubted you—when I...turned away from you. And you came for me out here anyway. I won't forget it."

I opened my arms and we hugged, despite my gear and slung shotgun.

"I'll wait for you, Kra. Because of you, I'll look young again."

It wasn't a guarantee that the Umbelgarri would be able to undo what Capital Galactic had done. No need to mention that. They had Heartwell's files on genetic manipulations, many of them stolen from the Celestial Unicorn Palace, so the odds of success were high.

"Ten years is a long time, Janice." I held her at arm's length. "Don't romanticize me. I'm not very likable. Hard to get along with. Ask McAllister."

That brought forth a laugh, although Janice tried to hold it back. Then she let it out and we hugged again. "Why would anyone ask her, Kra? She's even harder to get along with than you."

Whatever Janice said, ten years was a long time, an eternity in time of war. I wasn't going to hold my breath, believing she'd wait. Odds were I wouldn't survive anyway.

I held her at arm's length again. "Seriously, a decade is an eternity. Don't wait for me." My face turned serious. "There's a good chance I won't survive the war. A war that we're losing. Don't wait."

Janice sighed. "Agent Guymin said I could send messages to him and he could get them to you. You could reply back to me through him." She shrugged. "I think it'll work." She looked away, staring at the floor, pursing her lips and pulling them to the right. "Oh, and Agent Guymin said there'd be a surprise on the Phib—" She winked when she said it. "—Umbelgarri shuttle."

A sparkle of mischief flashed in her purple eyes. "Close your eyes," she said.

I tipped my head and looked at her with suspicion.

"Do it."

I complied, and felt her move close.

"Imagine me as I was," she said, and kissed me.

I pulled off my com-set's mic and head gear, and returned the kiss. After a moment, we separated.

"Did you imagine," she asked?

I nodded with a smile, saying, "I did, Janice."

"Keep that memory, Kra. When you return, I'll be that way again."

The End

ABOUT THE AUTHOR

Terry W. Ervin II is an English teacher who enjoys writing Fantasy and Science Fiction. He is the author of the Crax War Chronicles, the First Civilization's Legacy Series, and Genre Shotgun, a collection of his previously published short stories.

When Terry isn't writing or enjoying time with his wife and daughters, he can be found in his basement raising turtles. To contact Terry, or to learn more about his writing endeavors, visit his website at www.ervin-author.com or his blog, *Up Around the Corner.*

www.ingramcontent.com/pod-product-compliance
Lightning Source LLC
Chambersburg PA
CBHW030557180626
46816CB00005B/1574